DIVISIBLE MAN™
EIGHT BALL

by

Howard Seaborne

DIVISIBLE MAN:
EIGHT BALL

By

Howard Seaborne

ALSO BY HOWARD SEABORNE

DIVISIBLE MAN
A Novel – September 2017
DIVISIBLE MAN: THE SIXTH PAWN
A Novel – June 2018
DIVISIBLE MAN: THE SECOND GHOST
A Novel – September 2018
ANGEL FLIGHT
A Story – September 2018
DIVISIBLE MAN: THE SEVENTH STAR
A Novel – June 2019
ENGINE OUT
A Story – September 2019
WHEN IT MATTERS
A Story – October 2019
A SNOWBALL'S CHANCE
A Story – November 2019
DIVISIBLE MAN: TEN MAN CREW
A Novel – November 2019
DIVISIBLE MAN: THE THIRD LIE
A Novel – May 2020
DIVISIBLE MAN: THREE NINES FINE
A Novel – November 2020
DIVISIBLE MAN: EIGHT BALL
A Novel – September 2021
SHORT FLIGHTS
A Story Collection – Coming 2022
DIVISIBLE MAN: NINE LIVES LOST
A Novel – Coming 2022

PRAISE FOR HOWARD SEABORNE

"This book is a strong start to a series...Well-written and engaging, with memorable characters and an intriguing hero."
  —*Kirkus Reviews*
  DIVISIBLE MAN [DM1]

"Seaborne's crisp prose, playful dialogue, and mastery of technical details of flight distinguish the story...this is a striking and original start to a series, buoyed by fresh and vivid depictions of extra-human powers and a clutch of memorably drawn characters..."
  —*BookLife*
  DIVISIBLE MAN [DM1]

"Even more than flight, (Will's relationship with Andy)—and that crack prose—powers this thriller to a satisfying climax that sets up more to come."
  —*BookLife*
  DIVISIBLE MAN [DM1]

"Seaborne, a former flight instructor and charter pilot, once again gives readers a crisply written thriller. Self-powered flight is a potent fantasy, and Seaborne explores its joys and difficulties engagingly. Will's narrative voice is amusing, intelligent and humane; he draws readers in with his wit, appreciation for his wife, and his flight-drunk joy...Even more entertaining than its predecessor—a great read."
  —*Kirkus Reviews*
  DIVISIBLE MAN: THE SIXTH PAWN [DM2]

"Seaborne, a former flight instructor and pilot, delivers a solid, well-written tale that taps into the near-universal dream of personal flight. Will's narrative voice is engaging and crisp, clearly explaining technical matters while never losing sight of humane, emotional concerns. The

environments he describes…feel absolutely real. Another intelligent and exciting superpowered thriller."
—*Kirkus Reviews*
DIVISIBLE MAN: THE SECOND GHOST [DM3]

"As in this series' three previous books, Seaborne…proves he's a natural born storyteller, serving up an exciting, well-written thriller. He makes even minor moments in the story memorable with his sharp, evocative prose…Will's smart, humane and humorous narrative voice is appealing, as is his sincere appreciation for Andy—not just for her considerable beauty, but also for her dedication and intelligence…Seaborne does a fine job making side characters and locales believable. It's deeply gratifying to see Will deliver righteous justice to some very bad people. An intensely satisfying thriller—another winner from Seaborne."
—*Kirkus Reviews*
DIVISIBLE MAN: THE SECOND GHOST [DM4]

"Seaborne…continues his winning streak in this series, offering another page-turner. By having Will's knowledge of and control over his powers continue to expand while the questions over how he should best deploy his abilities grow, Seaborne keeps the concept fresh and readers guessing…Will's enemies are becoming aware of him and perhaps developing techniques to detect him, which makes the question of how he can protect himself while doing the most good a thorny one. The conspiracy is highly dramatic yet not implausible given today's political events, and the action sequences are excitingly cinematic…Another compelling and hugely fun adventure that delivers a thrill ride."
—*Kirkus Reviews*
DIVISIBLE MAN: TEN MAN CREW [DM5]

"Seaborne shows himself to be a reliably splendid storyteller in this latest outing. The plot is intricate and could have been confusing in lesser hands, but the author manages it well, keeping readers oriented amid unexpected developments…His crisp writing about complex scenes and concepts is another strong suit…The fantasy of self-powered flight remains absolutely compelling…As a former charter pilot, Seaborne conveys Will's delight not only in 'the other thing,' but also in airplanes and the world of flight—an engaging subculture that he ably brings to life for the reader. Will is heroic and daring, as one would expect, but he's also funny, compassionate, and affectionate... A gripping, timely, and twisty thriller."

—*Kirkus Reviews*
DIVISIBLE MAN: THE THIRD LIE [DM6]

"Seaborne is never less than a spellbinding storyteller, keeping his complicated but clearly explicated plot moving smoothly from one nail-biting scenario to another. As the tale goes along, seemingly disparate plot lines begin to satisfyingly connect in ways that will keep readers guessing until the explosive (in more ways than one) action-movie denouement. The author's grasp of global politics gives depth to the book's thriller elements, which are nicely balanced by thoughtful characterizations. Even minor characters come across in three dimensions, and Will himself is an endearing narrator. He's lovestruck by his gorgeous, intelligent, and strong-willed wife; has his heart and social conscience in the right place; and is boyishly thrilled by the other thing. A solid series entry that is, as usual, exciting, intricately plotted, and thoroughly entertaining."

—*Kirkus Reviews*
DIVISIBLE MAN: THREE NINES FINE [DM7]

Any reader of this series knows that they're in good hands with Seaborne, who's a natural storyteller. His descriptions and dialogue are crisp, and his characters deftly sketched...The book keeps readers tied into its complex and exciting thriller plot with lucid and graceful exposition, laying out clues with cleverness and subtlety...Also, although Will's abilities are powerful, they have reasonable limitations, and the protagonist is always a relatable character with plenty of humanity and humor...Another riveting, taut, and timely adventure with engaging characters and a great premise."

— *Kirkus Reviews*
DIVISIBLE MAN: EIGHT BALL [DM8]

THE SERIES

While each DIVISIBLE MAN ^{TM} novel tells its own tale, many elements carry forward and the novels are best enjoyed in sequence. The short story "Angel Flight" is a bridge between the third and fourth novels and is included with the third novel, DIVISIBLE MAN - THE SECOND GHOST.

DIVISIBLE MAN ^{TM} is available in print, digital and audio.

For a Cast of Characters, visit **HowardSeaborne.com**

For advance notice of new releases and exclusive material available only to Email Members, join the DIVISIBLE MAN ^{TM} Email List at

HowardSeaborne.com.

Sign up today and get a FREE DOWNLOAD.

ACKNOWLEDGMENTS

Enough has been written about the solitary nature of writing that it gets just one sentence here. That was it. All else about this endeavor is collaborative and deserves recognition. The "read and write" evenings spent in connected silence with my wife. The massive effort and endless patience of dear friends at big events like the EAA Airventure (thank you, Robin, Rich, Ariana and Chryste!) And of course, the usual suspects on the DM's Ten Most Wanted List: Stephen Parolini the editor; David, Carol, April, Claire, Kristie, Rebecca and Steve at Trans World Data; Maddog my dear friend, cheerleader, challenger and beta reader; and the indispensable Roberta Ann, my incredible beta reader, Copy Editor and muse for so much. This is the Divisible Man's eighth mission. Like all before it, and the many more to come, it would never have left the ground without such willing and supportive hands. Thank you.

*For all who see through the lies
and shine a light.*

She walks in beauty, like the night
Of cloudless climes and starry skies;
And all that's best of dark and bright
Meet in her aspect and her eyes;
Thus mellowed to that tender light
Which heaven to gaudy day denies.

—

George Gordon
(Lord Byron)

PART I

1

Oh crap.

The hospital corridor lights burst from dim to blazing. People in scrubs materialized from all directions.

"That's my doctor," the girl hugging my neck whispered a little too loudly. "My nighttime doctor." I felt her move and point with an arm neither of us could see. We floated five feet above the carpet at the intersection of three wide hallways. The woman she pointed at hustled toward the room where I'd found this child.

Where did all these people come from?

I did not hear a PA announcement. No piercing digital alarm or squawking siren broke the semi-silence of the night shift. Yet a growing number of people in an assortment of medical attire converged on the recently empty hallway and this child's hospital room.

This is not good.

The child in my arms was number seven. Lucky seven. I started just after eleven p.m. and the first six went smoothly. Easy in and out. All of them asleep—all of them except this one. I've grown adept at simply closing a grip on an arm or ankle and pushing *the other thing* over their small bodies. A gentle touch, then—

Fwooomp!

The sound in my head jars me but the silence in the room remains

3

unbroken. The child vanishes, creating an empty child-shaped cavern beneath fuzzy blankets. I give it a minute or two. I have no idea if duration matters. Sometimes the sensation of going weightless seeps into the child's dreams and they stir or wiggle. None have ever fought it.

When it feels right, I release my grip.

Fwooomp! They settle back on the mattress, often stirring, perhaps reacting to the sensation of falling.

In. Out. Unseen. Easy.

Until number seven.

"Hey!" This girl spoke the moment she flashed out of sight. My gentle grip on her wrist shifted, telling me she sat up in bed. "Who's there?"

"It's okay."

The light blanket covering empty space squirmed and shifted.

"Are you invi—?"

"Shhhhhh!" I cut off her full-voiced question. "Yes," I whispered back. "And I'm not going to hurt you."

I expected her to pull her arm free. Instead, her free hand found mine. She probed up my arm.

"Are you a ghost?"

"No."

"Are you an angel?"

"Nope."

"Superhero?"

"You ask a lot of questions."

"Well, duh." She reached higher, found my neck, then touched my face. I felt her hand jerk away. "I can't see myself! I can't see my hand! How did you do that?"

A stream of answers, ranging from sweet to smartass, flashed through my mind.

"The truth? I have no idea."

There had been no time to gauge the child's age. Propelled by a blend of overconfidence and what had become a bit of an assembly line routine, I had moved into the room quickly, assessed that no adults slept on a spare bed or sofa, found her arm above the covers, and went to work without looking too closely. In the dark, she was just another sadly bald head indenting a pillow. In my haste, I failed to see that she was awake.

She occupied an adult-sized bed. From her voice I estimated her age between seven and twelve, although like many her age, her attitude suggested twenty-something.

She moved. The blanket wiggled on the bed. I guessed that she waved her other hand in front of her own face.

"Am I invisi—?"

"Yes."

"Cool! Is this a dream?"

I have used that gimmick, but only with groggy kids half in and out of sleep. This girl was fully awake.

"Nope. Keep your voice down, please."

She still had not pulled free of my light grip on her wrist. She moved on the mattress. From the way the sheets flipped off, I surmised that she swung her legs off the bed. An IV line followed her movement, then popped loose and dangled, dripping on the floor.

"It feels cool—I don't mean *cool* cool, but you know, like—"

"Water?"

"Yeah! Like going swimming!" She tried to stand. The act of pushing off the mattress sent us floating. *"What's happening?"*

I shushed her again and grabbed the bedrail with my free hand. She wiggled against the sensation of weightlessness.

"I'm floating!"

"That's part of the deal. We're weightless. Like astronauts. You. Me, too." I maintained a light grip. She seemed to be enjoying this, at least enough not to shriek.

"Why are you holding my wrist?"

"It only works if we stay in contact with each other. May I hold your hand?"

She thought it over.

"I guess."

I slid my grip away from her wrist and found her hand.

"Am I dead?"

I squeezed her hand. "Does that feel dead?"

She squeezed back. I lifted my arm and abetted her launch from the mattress. She giggled. To my surprise, she probed my arm again, found my neck and threw her free arm around it.

"This is the coolest thing ever!" she whispered loudly in my ear.

"It kinda is," I conceded. *In for a penny...* "You want to see something really cool?"

"Uh-huh!"

Off we went.

"WHAT, EXACTLY, DO YOU DO?"

Pidge asked the question less than twenty-four hours earlier. We flopped in a pair of ratty old lawn chairs and tipped end-of-the-duty-day beers at the Education Foundation hangar at Essex County Airport. A September sunset painted shades of orange in the western sky, hinting of fall. Warm light fell on us through the open hangar door. The Foundation's twin-engine Piper Navajo crouched at my shoulder. Pidge ranks among a handful of people who know about my ability to vanish.

"Sneak in. Zap sleeping children in their beds."

Pidge whistled over the lip of her beer. "Yeah...I wouldn't let that get around. This is that crazy Marshfield shit, right? I mean—you told me that you fixed that kid. What? Now you're taking that show on the road?"

"I didn't fix that kid. *The other thing* fixed the kid."

"Right. Any idea how?"

"No clue."

"FM."

"FM?"

"Fucking magic. Have you told Arun yet?"

Pidge, a little under five feet of coiled cobra with short blonde hair and a disarming pixie smile, is a hotshot pilot who can fly circles around every throttle jockey I ever met. I rank her as the best pilot on the roster at Essex County Air Service and it has nothing to do with the fact that I taught her to fly. She's also a dervish with a dockworker's foul mouth, but she transforms into the image of cotillion charm around Arun Dewar who is, nominally, my boss at the Foundation. Arun joined the Christine and Paulette Paulesky Education Foundation as a gofer and office organizer after Sandy Stone, Director of the Foundation, all but drowned in grant applications. When Sandy, a kindergarten teacher both by trade and in the depths of her soul, returned to her flock for the new school year, Arun took over the day-to-day Foundation work. Pidge, who I had always assumed would die alone in a bar fight at the age of ninety, fell hard for Arun. I credited the young man's English accent.

"No, I haven't, and don't you go spilling it during pillow talk either." Pidge carries an Airline Transport Pilot rating in her wallet, but she will always be my former flight student. I shot her a warning glance. She shot back a sly grin. "I mean it."

"Relax. I pinky swore about your disappearing act and when I fucking pinky swear, Fort Knox takes notice."

We drank our beer and watched the Essex County Air Service hangar and office across the ramp turn to black silhouettes. Only Earl Jackson's office remained illuminated. I rarely see it extinguished before I leave.

"So, like what—you do this routine in hospitals when you're on Foundation trips?"

"Try to. On overnights. Plays havoc with my sleep time."

"Sleep is overrated. You ever think about going public? I mean—if it really works, there are a lot of sick kids out there..."

"Don't."

"Don't what?"

"Don't guilt me about this. Look," I said, "I have no idea how it works, but worse, I don't know why it works most of the time, but not all the time." The ache of a recent failure involving a young woman named Angeline Landry lingered, always within reach. "What happens when it works for nine kids and not for number ten? How do you think the parents will feel? How do you think the kid would feel? People expect perfection, or else you'll hear from their lawyer."

"Fuckin' assholes. Lawyers, I mean. So, like tomorrow you guys have an overnight in St. Louis. You sneak out so Arun doesn't know?"

"Pretty much. I can hit ten, maybe fifteen rooms. Get in. Make the kid disappear for a minute or so. Then get out."

"Doesn't this scare the shit outta the kid?"

"They never know I'm there. Mostly. A few wake up, but these kids are accustomed to strangers coming and going at all hours, sticking them with needles, checking vitals, plugging in new medicine drips. Even the little ones are kinda worldly."

"How do you know when the kid is...cooked?"

"I don't. I don't know. I don't want to know."

Because that would mean knowing when it doesn't work.

7

"Not very scientific."

She said nothing for a long minute, prompting me to fill the silence.

"Sometimes…sometimes, I kinda feel it. Maybe it's just wishful thinking. But you're right. It's far from scientific."

"How do you know it works at all?"

"I have someone who loosely tracks the results."

Pidge lifted her eyebrows. "Someone else *knows*? Who?"

I held up a stop-sign hand. "Compartmental. He doesn't know about you. You don't know about him."

"It's that fucking head doctor! The one in Madison."

"Jesus Christ, what does a guy have to do to keep a secret?"

"Yeah, you just keep tryin' there, partner. Your wife told me all about him. The one who got your ticket back. It's gotta be him. Steve-something."

"Dr. Stephenson."

"That's the one!"

"He's a neurologist."

"What does that have to do with kids who have cancer?"

"His reputation opens doors. I let him know where I've been. He looks into case results, don't ask me how. Remind me to tell you a story about him and Earl back in the day in Thailand."

"No shit?"

"Crazy story. Anyway, like I said, he's been quietly tracking the whole thing. Places I've been. Remission statistics. Doc says we're running about eighty percent."

She looked sideways at me.

"What?"

"Somebody's going to notice. You get that, right? Somebody's going to start asking how it is that kids are mysteriously getting cured at random hospitals. You watch."

"I THINK they know you're missing," I said to the girl in my arms. We hovered near the ceiling of the broad hallway.

"Really? What was your first clue?"

I liked this kid. A fellow smartass.

"How old are you?" She felt small, which was no reliable indicator.

The disease killing her likes to shrink its victims first. I recalled that her scalp was hairless but could not picture her face.

"Eleven."

"Got a name?"

"Sure. Do you?"

"Divisible Man."

"That's stupid."

"I didn't come up with it. I know it's a little late for this, but would you promise not to tell anyone about...all this? If you promise, I'll tell you my name."

"I guess. Who would believe me anyway?"

"I know. It's crazy. I'm Will."

"I'm Amber."

"Cut it out. Really? You've got to be kidding me."

"What?"

"Amber?"

"What's wrong with Amber?"

"As in 'Amber Alert?'" As I said it, a deputy sheriff in full uniform hurried down the hall beneath us. His leather holster and belt creaked and squeaked. Keys on his belt jangled.

"Oh. I get it. Ha. Ha. Very funny."

Staff clustered around Amber's hospital room door now fanned out, checking adjoining rooms, opening closet doors, searching the unisex bathroom. Returning the girl to her own bed was not an option. A worried-looking woman in scrubs blocked the door. She held a phone to her ear and gestured at the empty room as she spoke. When she saw the deputy, she waved him to hurry to her. They traded words. The deputy lifted his radio mic to his lips.

"This is not good," I said, as much to myself as the girl.

Totally my fault.

The weightless aspect of *the other thing* had been problematic for me at first, and occasionally downright frightening. Drifting untethered, or worse, the risk of floating unabated to the airless edge of Earth's atmosphere, inspired me to engineer a means of propulsion. The solution came naturally to a pilot. I needed an engine and propeller. A few harrowing experiments with what looked like a small flashlight with an electric motor and a six-inch two-bladed hobby-shop propeller helped me

9

hone the means to lift off and fly under control. Indoors or out. What had been frightening became exhilarating.

Along the way, I found what I can only describe as a core muscle that runs down my center when I vanish. It allows me to rotate and lever my body without the need for an anchor point. The discovery ended a disturbing tendency to knock over lamps and tumble out of control.

Between the power units, the ability to rotate in space, and a genetic love of flying, I had no one to blame except me for the fact that I invited Amber to go for a joy ride. We slipped out of her room and cruised down what had been the dim, nighttime hallway. We made a few turns, descended a staircase, and found the hospital's main entrance and lobby where I bumped the Handicap Entrance button and opened the front door.

We zoomed into the cool night, soared across the street fronting the hospital and explored a broad park at treetop level.

Amber's gasps and giggles paid her airfare. I flew her over forty-foot maple trees and initiated a series of dives and climbs over a placid pond. We skimmed the glass surface of the water. We followed the winding path of a running trail. We wove a low racecourse around empty picnic tables beneath a bloated moon. I made her shriek by colliding harmlessly with a row of tall arborvitae.

We had a blast.

We lost track of time.

Eventually I navigated back to the hospital, and back to her room.

Too late. All hell had slipped its leash.

The deputy taking up station at Amber's room door carried on an urgent radio conversation, no doubt calling in reinforcements or initiating a lockdown of the hospital.

"You ever wander off in the night before?" I asked.

"Me? No!" She sounded offended. "Am I going to be in trouble?"

Well, it sure as hell won't be me, I thought, instantly regretting that this child would take the heat for my impulsiveness.

"Just…give me a minute to think…"

I rotated and applied power to the hand-held propeller. Thrust pulled us away from the expanding search party. We cruised over a burnt-orange carpet embedded with a dizzying geometric pattern. Two more hospital staffers jogged toward us, bent on joining the search. Amber twisted against me as they passed. Her grip on my neck tightened, laden with tension and worry.

"What did you think of the flying?" I whispered, looking to lighten the moment.

"I love it!"

"You should become a pilot. When you grow up. You can take flying lessons and solo when you're sixteen. Get your private license when you're seventeen. Commercial license at eighteen."

She said nothing.

"Lots of women fly. The best pilot I know is a woman."

We retraced our path to the atrium where hospital signage sparked a plan.

"I'm not going to," she said faintly.

"What? Fly? Why not? You didn't like it?"

I felt her shake her head. "I'm not going to grow up."

Her matter-of-fact tone tied a knot in my throat.

"Don't be silly."

"This is my third time here. I had two remissions, but it keeps coming back. My mom and dad think I don't know what the doctors talk about, but I do. I know what's going to happen. I'm okay. But Mom cries a lot."

We soared over a staircase railing. This time there were no giggles and gasps. I aimed the power unit downward. We settled toward the first floor.

"Bullshit," I said.

"Daddy says that's a quarter for the swear jar."

"Bullshit, bullshit, bullshit. I owe you a buck. You ever been to Wisconsin?"

"My grandparents live in Wausau."

"Do you know where Essex is?"

"No."

"Well, your grandparents will know. Here's the deal. On the day of your sixteenth birthday, get your parents or your grandparents to drive you to the city of Essex. Get them to take you to the airport, east of town. You walk right in the office door and tell a lady named Rosemary II that Will said you get a free flying lesson. Got it?"

"Okay, but—"

"No buts. Promise me."

I halted our descent just above the lobby floor. I found the sign I was looking for.

"You mean flying like this?"

"No. Real flying. In an airplane."

"I like this better."

She had a point. "Okay. Well, then I'll give you both. Airplane, and this. Sweet sixteen. You'll be there. Trust me." I'd never made a promise like that before. It barely squeezed past my lips and left a sting in its wake.

"If you say so."

"I say so. Are you hungry?"

2

E xcept for a few operating coffee machines meant for third-shift workers, the stainless-steel shelves and tray slides of the slumbering cafeteria lay bare. The stoves were cold; the salad bars lay empty under sparkling glass.

Amber confessed that she wasn't hungry. She said it hurts to eat and makes her throw up.

I settled her in place on a plastic cafeteria chair and released her hand. She reappeared. Gravity embraced her. She gripped the seat of the chair as if it might launch her. Along with her naked scalp she wore the gaunt look and carried the thin appendages too often found in late-night TV ads meant to Save The Children. *Just a few pennies a day...*

All the pennies in the world weren't going to save Amber.

I maneuvered to the glass face of a snack vending machine, the kind that uses corkscrews to release treats. A small padlock secured the transparent front panel. I wrapped my hand around the padlock body and made it vanish. The border between the vanished body and visible shackle quivered. I tugged. The shackle snapped on the borderline. I dropped the pieces and heaved the door open.

"Here you go," I said. "My treat."

I feared she would reject the offer.

To my surprise, her eyes widened. She stood and took half a dozen steps to the unbound junk food riches. Her strides had a forced steadiness. Like a drunk trying hard to look sober. The idea of her wandering all the way from her room to the cafeteria in the middle of the night might test credibility. Her thin legs didn't look capable of the trip.

Something about the beckoning sugar and salty carbs awakened her. She held the open glass door and contemplated rows of gaudy choices.

"I have to go now," I said. She pulled her gaze free of the candy riches and searched for me in the empty air.

"Are you coming back?"

I pushed off and slowly floated toward the cafeteria exit.

"I might be back someday, but you won't be here."

A flash of resignation on her small face put a spotlight on my stupid choice of words.

"Hey! I don't mean it that way. You and I have a date for a flying lesson. Sweet sixteen. Promise?"

"Sure," she said. "Promise."

"Don't bullshit me."

"That's a buck and a quarter now. And I promise."

"For real?"

"For real."

She waved in the direction of my voice.

I didn't leave immediately. I watched her carefully pick out a Ritz cracker and cheese snack. Then a bag of Doritos. Then a Mars bar. By the time she retraced her steps to the chair and table, she clutched a load of goodies to her chest. She sat down and gingerly ate the Ritz crackers. She waited a moment, hesitant. Then she eagerly tore into the Doritos. I watched her munch and savor the chips, devouring the bag quickly and moving on to the next snack.

I never know for sure.

Except this time.

On the way out, feeling better about the night's work, I reappeared in a corridor long enough to flag down an orderly and report seeing a kid in the empty cafeteria who seemed to be eating the place clean.

3

I reached the TownePlace Suites hotel across from Spirit of St. Louis Airport just before four a.m. Zipping around behind a handheld power unit can be delightful, but it's dangerous at night when transmission and telephone lines become impossible to see and avoid. I traveled by Nissan rental car from the hotel to the hospital and back again. I parked in the hotel lot feeling tired but satisfied.

I feeped the car's door locks and hiked the full length of the silent parking lot, the penalty for being the last guest arriving at a hotel. The lobby was empty. The check-in desk stood deserted. I counted both as a blessing and hurried to the elevators happy to avoid a judgmental hello from a curious night clerk.

A few hours of sleep—that's all I wanted.

Arun's schedule lined up a full day of meetings and school tours. He had asked me to go along, or at the very least, meet him for breakfast to bolster his courage—being new to handling Education Foundation business trips on his own. I told him I wanted to sleep in. It felt selfish at the time, but it wasn't a lie. I told him I would check out at eleven and wait for him at the airport.

I planned to sleep up to the moment of checkout.

I slotted the plastic key card in my room door. The pessimist in me anticipated the card not working, necessitating a hike back down to the front desk for a new card.

The tiny green light flashed. The lock clicked.

I slipped into the room and had just long enough to wonder if I had left all the lights on before a woman's voice nearly stopped my heart.

"*Where the shit have you been?*"

Fwooomp! I threw forward the levers in my head and disappeared.

A tug on the core muscle jerked me off the carpet. An instant later I hung prone just below the ceiling, eyeballing a fire suppression sprinkler. The move startled me as much as the intruder's jarring inquiry.

She sat in the room's single occasional chair near the curtained window. Boyish dark hair, thin, dressed in a black blazer over a black t-shirt. Her dark eyes searched as the room door slammed shut behind me. Despite her angry tone and grim demeanor, her face gave the impression of suppressing a smile sprung from an inside joke. She carried a Glock semi-automatic handgun in a shoulder rig under her left arm.

"Christ," I said, "you scared the shit outta me."

Her eyes lifted toward the sound of my voice. FBI Special Agent Leslie Carson-Pelham rose from the chair.

"What are you doing here?" I asked.

"Do you always do that when you're startled?"

"Do you always break into people's hotel rooms?" I pushed off the ceiling and rotated to an upright position. The instant my feet touched the carpet—

Fwooomp!

—I reappeared. She blinked at me.

"Where the hell were you? I've been here for hours."

I glanced up at the ceiling. In an instant, I had not only vanished but, propelled by an instinct to move out of harm's way, had shot to the top of the room and swung to a prone position.

Without pushing off.

Without deploying the power unit in my pocket.

Without thinking.

Not for the first time, a strange emergency autopilot launched me at a moment of threat. Andy and I experienced a nearly identical move in a motel room in Montana seconds before gunfire tore apart the bed we occupied. The same thing happened over a frozen lake, where I hung helpless holding the drowned body of Andy's pregnant sister in my arms.

The first time it happened, it launched me and Lane Franklin out the window of a burning room. For months since, I've tried to replicate it, without success.

During the flashcard review of these events in my head, Leslie continued speaking to me.

"...to make this work." She fixed an angry expression on me. "Is your phone dead? I tried calling."

"I...uh..."

"Never mind. Let's go."

"Go where?"

She spotted my flight bag on the desktop. She hooked it and thrust it at me as she marched past me on her way to the door.

"I'll tell you on the way."

"On the way where?"

"A picnic."

4

———

Andy drives like a demon. Her driving is the reason I always grab the car keys when we leave the house. FBI Special Agent Carson-Pelham could have been Andy's driving instructor. We covered the short distance between the hotel and the airport at just below the speed of sound. She treated a pair of red traffic lights like quaint mood lighting.

I cinched my seatbelt tighter and didn't speak. Ten minutes ago, I could have flopped on a memory foam mattress and winked out within a few breaths. By the time Leslie stood on the chattering anti-lock brakes in front of the Tac-Air portico I had enough adrenalin pumping through my veins to file a flight plan and fly home to Essex County.

"Special Agent—"

"Leslie." She stabbed the start/stop button on the dash and killed the car engine. "Let's go."

I grabbed my bag and hopped out. She breezed through sliding glass doors. I hustled after her. She walked through the FBO lobby at a pace that made me trot to catch up.

"If you want me to fly us somewhere, I need to—"

"No. You don't." She tossed the car keys to a desk clerk who buzzed open the door to the ramp. I hurried out behind her. She made a bee line for a parked Cessna Citation jet. The pilot sat in his command seat under red cockpit lights. The copilot waited for us at the open hatch.

"Hey!" I stopped cold. "What the hell?"

She turned. She glanced at her watch, then glanced at the plane, which had begun to spool up one engine. She weighed whatever she planned to say next, then retreated until she faced me, drilling me with a judgmental stare.

"I don't know how things are with you and your wife, who I like a lot, by the way. But if you feel a need to dip your wick outside your marriage, that's going to be a big problem. Not because I'm a prude, but because shit like that really, *really* messes things up—evidenced by the fact that I couldn't reach you or find you for the last five hours, which means we're about to miss a rare window of opportunity."

"You've got it wrong."

She grabbed the sleeve of my flight jacket and jerked me forward. "Fine. Get on the goddamned plane and explain it to me. We don't have time for this here!"

Five minutes later we rolled for takeoff.

"I WASN'T CHEATING on my wife," I said.

Leslie faced me in a matching, plush leather seat. Dim cabin lights shaded a stony expression riddled with doubt. I heard it, too. My denial sounded less than credible. On top of that, I felt my face redden. Auto-blush. Not helping.

Leslie and I occupied the cabin alone. The crew closed the cockpit door as soon as we began taxiing. The flight carried no cabin steward. Contrary to the Hollywood image, the interior of most business jets isn't much bigger than a family minivan—with about as much headroom. Nevertheless, I struggled not to be impressed. I have nearly zero flight time in executive jets as pilot or passenger.

"Come on. You've met Andy. It would take me fifty lifetimes to be so lucky again. I'd have to be nuts to want anyone else."

"Men don't want anyone else. They want more."

"Getting a little personal here, aren't you?"

Her eyebrows shot up. "There's no such thing as too personal, Will. I need to know everything about you if we're going to make *this* happen." She leaned forward. "Director Lindsay was high enough up in the Bureau to work without a net. I'm not. I'm hiding shit from my bosses and they're hiding shit from their bosses."

"Speaking of hiding things—this hasn't exactly been a two-way street." The question of Leslie's chain of command after Deputy Director Mitchell Lindsay lost his life remained unanswered. My relationship with the FBI had barely taken its first breath when Lindsay had been killed. When Leslie stepped in, Andy and I nearly pulled out. We relented only after Leslie swore that she would sustain Lindsay's decision to restrict knowledge of me and *the other thing*.

"I told you. It's—"

"Don't you dare say 'complicated.' I hate that."

"It's unsettled."

"Bullshit."

"You're not that politically naïve, Will. You know where the FBI stands with this administration. For Heaven's sake, there's a Special Counsel from Homeland—that little fascist asshole from the White House—sniffing around everything Lindsay did, said or had. Trying to make him look bad because that makes the FBI look bad. I told you up front, I'm being careful. Everyone's paranoid, and with good reason. Director Lindsay had the right idea about protecting you, but there are people crawling through his files right now. People I do not trust. People you do not want laying their hands on…this *thing*."

"*The other thing.*"

"You seriously need a better name for it."

I didn't argue. I also wasn't convinced that Leslie had been entirely honest in implying that she had full autonomy to take up where Lindsay left off. She lived in a professional food chain, which meant someone ranked above her.

Whoever it is, I thought, *they have the power to pull a jet out of their hat in the middle of the night.*

"Look, Will, I'm out on a limb with you—more than you can possibly imagine. So, you can see how it would not go down well to have some psycho side piece blasting social media with descriptions of hot sex while floating under the St. Louis arch." She leaned back, then shot forward again. "And trust me, the side piece is always psycho."

"Wow. Is that the voice of experience?"

"This isn't about me, Stewart." She folded her arms, a gesture that reminded me of my wife. "Fine. Explain."

I folded my arms, too.

"No. You first." She said nothing. "Look, you're the one that jacked me out of a hotel in the middle of the night. All this…the jet…the rush… something's up. What is it?"

"Nothing's up, or ever will be with you, unless I can be confident that you won't compromise everything we do."

"I won't."

She frowned.

I dug for my phone. I keep a candid photo of Andy in its own gallery folder. When I snapped the photo, Andy had been sitting beside me on our porch steps. Evening sun lent a glow to her light caramel skin. She wore an old Metallica t-shirt, her hair still kinked after release from the workday's French braid. Her head angled toward me, not the camera. I shot the picture as a selfie with the lens on zoom. Only Andy filled the frame.

I had been talking—about God knows what. Andy's face said she wasn't hearing a word I said, yet her gaze said she had never heard anything so wondrous. In that photo—in that instant—her relaxed expression of unconditional love guaranteed—at least to me—that we would share our last breaths together.

I held up the phone.

"You really think I'd cheat on her?"

Leslie studied the image. She shrugged.

"We just met. I don't know how crazy or stupid you are."

I closed the screen and tucked away my phone. Point made.

"A little of both," I said. I glanced out the window. "We're headed west northwest. Where?"

She said nothing.

"Talk to me," I said, "or I'm out that door. Which I can do, by the way." She didn't need to know that jumping out of a light jet would be damned near impossible at this speed.

Leslie used a moment of silence and a penetrating stare to make a final point: *This conversation isn't over.*

After a resct breath, she asked, "What's the greatest domestic threat in America?"

"Kale?"

Leslie reached into a backpack that had been in the seat across the aisle when we boarded. She pulled out a folder. She extracted the tray table from the fuselage wall and laid the folder between us.

"Domestic terrorism. Not ISIS. Not Islamic fundamentalists. Not commies or aliens or cable news. Domestic terrorists." She pulled a sheaf of papers from the folder and held it up. "This is a classified report from the office of the DNI. And no, you can't read it."

"Is that the report that was all over the news?"

"The media got the redacted public version of this report. You and Andy had a hand in stirring things up by exposing General Winslow Pemmick when he tried to build his hate group coalition. The Pemmick case prompted the Director of National Intelligence to release portions of the classified report spotlighting what we've known for some time. Domestic terror groups have been oozing out of the muck for years. They got a shot in the arm from the current political climate. And thanks to politicians giving cover to these groups, every time we bring it up, we get pushback. The Bureau has to swim upstream."

"Waco? Ruby Ridge?"

She frowned. "Please. That's like saying the Titanic represents the cruise industry, Will. I don't have time to educate you, but the origins of today's crop of domestic terror groups—more precisely, white power groups—go back to Vietnam. There's a good book on it by Professor Kathleen Belew of the University of Chicago. I'll get you a copy. Point is, DHS has identified lone wolf extremists and Domestic Violence Extremist groups as the top terrorist threat. DVE groups are merging under a militia-style umbrella. A proliferation of over-the-counter weapons is arming people who used to steal military hardware. Now they buy it retail. Training camps have popped up again—they were a thing in the 90's until creative court actions shut them down. But it's like Whack-A-Mole. And these groups are restless. We're hearing chatter about soft targets. Public events. Mass casualty events."

She pulled a sheaf of photos from the folder and handed them to me. I leafed through them.

"Those were taken at rallies in Michigan, Missouri and Texas. If you look closely, you'll see participants common across multiple states and multiple events."

Venom-infused faces filled the photos. They reminded me of a line of chanting neo-Nazis I'd seen at the state capitol in Nebraska not long ago —moments before I lit all their flags on fire.

"A lot of these groups just play guns and warriors on the weekends. But there's a serious core with a dangerous agenda."

"Government takeover?"

She laughed. "They don't want to be the government. They just want to burn it down. There's never a plan or enough initiative to actually take over and run the government, no matter how much they talk up The Revolution. No matter how many rallies they organize, or pickup truck parades they launch. I mean—think about it. You join one of these groups and then one day you finally get the call to arms. You load up your guns and hop in your pickup truck and race off to the rally point. Then what? Occupy the state capitol? The local post office? Where are your reinforcements? Supplies? Logistics? These goofballs talk all this shit, but they never ask the most important question."

"Which is?"

"*And then what?*"

"They're idiots."

"No argument. But they're idiots who can do a lot of harm to innocent people. It was one thing when their enemies were all fantasy-based. Cabals of deep state politicians. World banking conspiracies. But things change when they target a bunch of college kids marching for racial justice. Or a voting rights rally. Suddenly these goons have enemies they can sink their teeth into. The old skinhead gangs used to go looking for fights with two-by-fours and baseball bats. These guys want to start a firefight with their AR-15s."

I flipped through the photos. Men marching. Men fighting. Nazi and Confederate flags waving. Jacked-up pickups with men hanging onto roll bars and waving long rifles. Beards and bellies. A lot of pale faces full of white power poison.

Leslie pointed at one individual. Even without her fingertip tapping the photo, he stood out. Tall. Wavy long hair that belonged on the cover of a romance novel. A chiseled face with stark, alert eyes. He carried wide shoulders and intimidatingly muscled arms branded with tattoos.

"This guy gets around."

"Who is he?"

"Darryl Spellman. Ex-marine. Iraq war veteran. Demoted while he

23

was in the service for racist aggression against fellow marines. He finished with an OTH discharge."

My expression asked the question.

"Other Than Honorable," she replied. "Not that it matters. If you read bios posted on white supremacist websites, he's Audie Murphy and Dwight Eisenhower rolled into John Wayne's resurrected body. One site claims he's a Medal of Honor winner. He's not."

"I take it he's a leader?"

"He's been bouncing around from group to group since he got out of the service in '07. We have intel that a couple of groups kicked him out for being too aggressive, even for their tastes. Worse, he has one quality that most of these moron's lack."

"Which is?"

"He's articulate and photogenic. He's capable of transiting the thin line between nut job conspiracy websites and right-wing conservative media. He was a favored guest of your old pal Josiah James. He's a stone's throw away from showing up on Carlson or Hannity on Fox News."

I handed the photos back to Leslie. She tucked them in the folder.

"On the upside, most of our intel comes from inside these groups. You'd be surprised how many of these guys sell out their buddies. They assuage their turncoat guilt by feeding us misinformation so they can fantasize about being double agents, but the truth is for a few hundred bucks in beer money, they'll sell out their own mothers. Sometimes we insert undercover agents. That's harder, and it takes longer. It's a high-risk proposition that pressures our own agents to violate the law. The hard-core groups force newbies to commit acts that cross a line they think an undercover agent would not cross. We've had some close calls and a couple of tragic outcomes."

"Is this where I come in?"

Leslie pushed the photos and documents to one side of the tray table. A little of the ice in her earlier demeanor melted. "Do you want some coffee?"

"God, please! Yes!" She slipped out of her seat and went to a cabinet in the back of the cabin. The crew had stocked it with coffee mugs and a thermos. She returned to her seat and poured for us both. My expectations were low, but the brew was not bad.

She sipped and fingered through the photos again, pulling out two.

"Spellman...and this guy..." She pointed at a heavy-set older man with a prospector's beard, hippy hair, and a fat-handed grip on a semi-automatic rifle. "They currently head up two of the more vocal, more active cells we're tracking in the western white power movement. Spellman runs an outfit they call Company W and Louis Blaze here runs the American Bloodline Coalition, an off-shoot of Aryan Nation."

"Cute names."

"Company W is quasi-military with a white supremacy agenda. You can guess what the W stands for. They recruit by dredging up the post-Vietnam line about betrayal of the American soldier, updated for Iraq and Afghanistan vets. Strongly anti-government. American Bloodline is, as you would expect, all about purity. It's their religion. They peddle a radically edited version of the Bible, which they claim is the true text before the International Jewish Banking Conspiracy rewrote it in the 1930s. They claim that Hitler's European war was a righteous war against the corruption of the Christian faith by godless communists. They publish fantasy novels about how the western allies join Germany to crush the Soviets."

"Nazis. I hate those guys." I paused, but Leslie didn't acknowledge the reference. "You want me to spy on them?"

"Yes."

"Time out. This kind of surveillance could take weeks. You pulled me out of the middle of a Foundation trip. Arun's going to show up at the airport this afternoon expecting me to fly him home. I can't just drop everything and—"

"This isn't a long-term op. This is a one-off opportunity. Granted, you may have to call your friend Arun and tell him to make other arrangements to get home today, but I should be able to get you back to St. Louis tomorrow."

I was not pleased and showed it.

"Will," she lifted her mug for a sip, "the white power movement dreams of a race war, a chance to cleanse America once and for all, and implement their fantasy social order—a military, survivalist culture where men rule, and women are property. Contextual to that vision, women play the role of reproductive slaves. Chattel. It's one of the ways these groups form alliances. They exchange daughters in political marriages. I told you we're going to a picnic. We are. It's also a wedding. Blaze is giving his daughter to Spellman as a symbol of their two groups forming a union. We don't care about the wedding, but we have grave concerns about the merging of these two groups. We have solid intel that Blaze and Spellman will do a sit-down before or after the ceremony to seal the real deal. I want you there."

"Why? For a copy of their new bylaws?"

Leslie reached into her folder and pulled a fresh photo. I recognized the torn concrete façade of the Alfred P. Murrah Federal Building in Oklahoma City. It might have been a hive of bureaucratic offices, the target of some insane anti-government manifesto, but all I ever saw in that monument to mass murder was a daycare center full of innocent children.

"No," Leslie said. "This union, we think, is the lynchpin in a plan to hit the U.S. Government in a way that, they say, will make Murrah look like a pinprick. A way to light the fuse on their civil slash race war. We want to know what that plan is."

5

I had never been to Coeur d'Alene, Idaho, but first impressions verified everything I'd ever heard about it. Stunning blue waters kissed evergreen-covered mountains. Distant snowcapped peaks intruded on a sky that drew a monstrous breath and expanded. Even the high, sailing wisps of mare's tail cirrus seemed sharper, more sculpted. I spent the final fifteen minutes of the flight leaning against the fuselage looking out the window like a kid on a Disney ride.

Leslie's initial description of the mission prompted me to envision a militia mountain stronghold, a remote barbed wire-protected encampment full of camo-clad men toting and shooting automatic weapons.

I did not expect suburbia.

After disembarking the private jet at Coeur d'Alene International Airport, we checked into a rented mini Jeep full of plastic cupholders. Despite the manufacturer's badge, I pictured the vehicle less on a muddy mountain road and more in the parking lot of a Starbucks.

"Where's the tactical team? The task force?" I asked.

"Are you kidding?" She chuckled. "What? You were expecting a secret nerve center lair full of computer screens? An HRT squad?"

"Kinda…"

She navigated the little red Jeep out of the airport parking lot.

"And just how would I explain you?"

"Ride along?"

Twenty minutes later we cruised the winding streets of a middle-class suburban subdivision. Leslie steadfastly obeyed the speed limit signs. Lawns and landscaping—probably governed by strict homeowner association standards—gave the parade of gray-, pale blue-, and cream-stained cedar-siding homes a striking uniformity. A yellow school bus lumbered past us, either dropping off or picking up half-day kindergarten children.

"On your right." Leslie pointed. "Look between the houses. Look at the backyards on the next street over. See it?"

"Are you serious? A bounce house? The neo-Nazis and the white supremacists have a bounce house?"

"Told you it was a picnic. We're not going to drive on that street, but I assume you can mark the location."

"A bounce house makes a pretty good landmark."

The street hosting the domestic terrorist picnic defined the outer border of the housing development. Beyond it, raw land expanded into rising terrain. The undeveloped land showed the scars of new roads cutting a new subdivision out of the landscape. Scattered half-finished homes rose over new basements.

The entire setting lent an absurdly pedestrian tint to domestic terrorism. I imagined armed militiamen gathered over a breakfast omelet bar sharing veggie smoothies before hiking up into the hills to practice killing people with extra pigment in their skin. I pictured their wives and mothers packing power bars to snack on between lessons on garroting racial justice protesters.

"Let's find a spot and get you wired up," Leslie said.

She backtracked to a small park at the center of the subdivision. The communal park featured playground equipment and tennis courts, an effort to add value and cohesion to the development. Leslie killed the engine in the corner of an empty asphalt lot. A few minutes later she tucked a recording device in my shirt pocket and clipped the microphone to my collar. "It's nice not having to hide this."

"Is this the same toy you used in D.C.?" I asked.

"It's an upgrade."

"Can't fault the recording quality." The dust had not yet settled on the attack on the U.S. Supreme Court justices. News channels still aired bits and pieces of a recording I made of a U.S. Senator and a cartel leader discussing what they believed at the time to be the successful murder of all nine justices. Said U.S. Senator—my very own from Wisconsin—has since resigned and disappeared into the protective arms of the FBI, anxious to spill his corrupt guts and save his own skin from execution for treason.

"You have the advantage of getting close."

"Unless they lock themselves in the basement rec room. I make no guarantees."

"From what I just saw, the wedding will be in the back yard. More than likely, Spellman and Blaze will parley at a picnic table."

"Doesn't mean they'll openly discuss bombing a statehouse or launching a gas attack on a protest march."

"Just try to get in tight."

"Roger that."

"Leave your cell phone. I know you and Andy like that as a means of communication, but these guys routinely use cell disrupters, so it won't work."

"That must drive the neighbors crazy."

"It's not like anyone will complain."

I dropped my phone into her outstretched hand.

"How do you want to do this?" She gestured at the windshield. Fifty yards away, a woman walked her dog on a winding cinder path.

"Why don't you hop out and take a walk. Just another book club mom, taking a breather from the kids and the housework. Hold your door open long enough for me to slide out. I don't want to disappear with somebody watching."

"Obviously."

I twisted in the seat and pulled a pair of power units and companion propellers from my flight bag. One set fit neatly into a zippered pocket on my thigh. The other, I snapped together and tested. The prop issued a satisfying whine.

"Take as much time as you need," she said. "If you can get anything, *anything* indicating their plans or a target, obviously that would be golden. I can't stay here all day. I'll make a pass on this lot every hour on the..." she checked her watch "...quarter hour."

"I can't see my watch. Don't worry," I said. "I'll find you. I'll bang on the roof."

I tucked the power unit into my armpit and—

Fwooomp!

—I vanished. A cool sensation washed over me.

"Okay. That's freaky." She reached out and gingerly found my arm. "I don't know why…I keep thinking you're not solid when you do that."

"Sorry. Can't go through walls."

She opened her door and stepped out. The woman with the dog casually watched Leslie stretch and lift her face to the afternoon sun. I reached across the seat and grasped the top of the door frame. A smooth pull lifted me free of the vehicle.

"Clear," I said, rising.

She could not help herself. She glanced toward the sound of my voice.

I could not help myself, either. The high blue sky felt welcoming. Perspective shifted. The grass and parking lot fell away. The electric sensation of pure flight hastened my pulse.

I slid the controller on the power unit forward. The prop buzzed. I pulled away.

THE SUBDIVISION HAD BEEN DESIGNED as a series of concentric oval roads. The little park formed a center hub. To the west, the residential suburb eventually merged with urban sprawl. To the east, undeveloped land surrendered to new roads and vacant lots. Spellman's little piece of heaven occupied the border between new and old. The front of his house looked across the street at fresh new streets and staked, empty lots.

The bounce house excelled as a beacon. A bright yellow roof covered fat red walls on the back corner of a one-acre lot.

I leveled off at two hundred feet and cruised a quarter-mile arc using the bounce house beacon as an anchor point. A light westerly breeze pushed my path and I adjusted for it. Young trees among the existing homes suggested that the development was less than twenty years old. Adjacent wilderness sloped toward distant mountains. I wondered how Spellman and his neighbors felt about the trucks and builder's vans lifting dust from the new construction. Workmen labored on several of the properties. A loaded gravel truck idled on the next concentric road near a lot where a backhoe dug the foundation of a home that would soon intrude on Spellman's view.

I tightened my reconnaissance arc and studied the target.

Rows of picnic tables covered in checkered plastic lined one side of a watered and fertilized lawn. Colorful figures circulated among the tables. Children darted. Women in bright summer dresses laid out picnic paraphernalia.

A cluster of men occupied a patio bordering one side of the house. At the edge, a plank bar had been laid out beneath a pop-up canopy. Stacked aluminum kegs promised abundant free-flowing beer.

The men on the patio modeled a loose uniformity. Most had already drunk their share of beer in life, if the bellies pouting over belts served as any indication. Beards were common, a few of them salt and pepper and descending to the diaphragm. Younger men sported the modern badge of ruggedness—the three- to five-day shadow. Almost all wore cargo pants and boots. A few wore camo t-shirts. Some wore black. Others wore flannel. None of the attire hinted that a wedding anchored this event. None of the guests appeared to carry weapons.

I inspected the vehicles. Not one sedan. A mix of SUVs, pickup trucks and a stand-out black Hummer filled the driveway and spread along the road in both directions. From my height I could not read the license plates, but multiple color schemes indicated multi-state vehicles.

I mapped an approach across the new construction. The path offered a straight shot at the makeshift bar. A grunting backhoe covered the sound of my power unit. I swept in low over a new basement being carved out of heavy brown clay. I crossed ground that had been scraped free of topsoil, passed the loaded gravel truck idling on the new street, and sailed over the vehicles parked in front of Spellman's house.

Decelerating over Spellman's lawn, I approached the patio bar. Voices rose to meet me. Men laughed. Someone called someone else an asshole and laughed. A boom box played Creedence below the hubbub of conversation.

I pulsed the power unit. My forward movement diminished to a crawl. A shallow descent took me lower until I trotted lightly across the grass. I gripped a pole securing one corner of the canopy and came to a halt at the edge of the party.

Close enough now to be served a cold beer, I watched two women shuttling red Solo cups from keg to customer. Men in their late teens or early twenties leaned on the two-by-ten plank bar, competing for attention. The two barmaids wore matching shirts tied just below the bosom over tight, short cutoffs. The women toyed with a leering crowd. Men joked and stared at their chests. The drinkers almost uniformly displayed tattoos of swastikas, numbers, and incoherent lettering. Skin exhibited glyphs and symbols, some of which had faded with time. One or two of the marked displayed huge swaths of black on their skin, ink applied to blot out previous affiliations.

Separated from this cloud of testosterone, women at the back of the house attended to tables crowded with covered dishes. Younger women wore tight jeans and midriff-exposing tops. Others wore modest summer dresses. Children tagged in and out of the cluster of women but avoided the male-dominated bar area. More children tested the resilience of the bounce house at the back of the yard, adding shrieks and laughter to the Creedence soundtrack.

Seated at a card table in the bar area, a hefty Louis Blaze challenged the durability of a folding aluminum lawn chair. A shock of steel-colored hair hung from the sweatband of a weathered ball cap. His beard, jutting from the perimeter of a fleshy, pale face, carried only random dark strands among the silver and gray. He had fat lips beneath small, wide-set eyes that looked down on everyone around him, despite being seated while everyone else stood.

A young woman bearing an unflattering family resemblance sat beside him. She wore a simple white dress with lace at the ends of short sleeves and at a hem that fell below her bare knees. A knot of tiny flowers accented her drab brown hair.

The bride. This was her day. Her earnest investment in the dress and flowers revealed harbored dreams, yet her demeanor confessed that she knew she was neither pretty nor the center of attention—a point underscored by the two flirting beer servers just yards away. She folded her hands in her lap and fixed her eyes on her knees. Her father beside her gave no sign that he detected her discomfort. He sipped from his red plastic cup and patted dewdrops of beer from his thick moustache.

I tuned out the chatter except for the broad strokes. Sports. Movies. Goddamned liberals. That bitch in Congress. Cars. Nothing floating in the boisterous conversations suggested sinister plans. Leslie worried that we were late to the party and may have missed the main event. I read this as a social hour preceding the ceremony. If the men intended to adjourn for deeper discussions, I expected it to be after the bridal transaction.

"Spellman! Darryl! Get your ass over here!" someone shouted.

Heads turned to where a man emerged from the back of the house.

Darryl Spellman moved with casual grace among the women, drawing smiles and coy glances, more than a few of which landed on the back of his jeans. His broad shoulders, thick hair and cultivated tan tugged a glance from nearly every one of the women. Some let their eyes linger. One boldly drew close, lifted herself on tiptoe and whispered in his ear. He laughed and let his eyes stroke the exposed cleavage she offered him. He said something in her ear. She giggled and touched his arm. His hand wandered to her backside, but she pushed him away with a laugh.

I glanced at the would-be bride in time to see her drop her eyes. Louis Blaze cast a limpid glance at his future son-in-law. The father of the bride expressed no offense at the overt flirting.

Spellman broke away from the women and sauntered toward the group of men.

"Somebody get me a beer!" he called out.

One of the bar girls about to hand a customer a cup filled to spilling diverted her delivery. She leaned over the plank bar and extended the beer and her own deep cleavage toward Spellman, who took in both.

"To the groom!" someone shouted. The crowd repeated the outcry in rough unison. Cups lifted. Men drank. Spellman turned a smirk on his admirers. His satisfied grin signaled not just comfort with the charisma others saw in him, but a taste for it.

A buzzing sound thrummed past my head as two things happened in the same instant.

Something disturbed the air beside my ear.

And Darryl Spellman's head exploded.

6

S hocked silence followed a wet cracking sound and the splash of gore. Most of Darryl Spellman's brains landed on the bride and her father. The bride froze, eyes ringed by white, her mouth open for a scream that could not escape her throat.

Spellman's body collapsed in an awkward heap where he stood. Nothing remained above his lower jaw and earlobes.

A few who had been drinking lowered their cups, unaware. Someone laughed and loudly said, "And may he find th—" The toast died on parted lips and a slack jaw.

Louis Blaze flicked blood and gore off himself as if someone had spilled a beer. The golden liquid in his cup had turned red. He dropped the plastic cup to the patio bricks.

"Fuck!" someone uttered.

No one moved.

A scream tugged my attention from Spellman to the women among the food tables. A woman in a flower-patterned dress sat on the grass with her legs splayed. She had dropped where she stood. A blue bowl rested inverted between her thighs. She clutched both hands across her abdomen. The flowers on her dress were yellow and orange with green leaf accents. Beneath her fingers, red roses bloomed on the fabric. Her face flashed starkly white as if the blood running from her belly drained directly from her cheeks. In seconds, her startled expression went slack. She toppled over backward.

Several women rushed to help. The one who had whispered in Spellman's ear stood with her hands to her lips, screaming. The sound broke the spell among the men.

"Sniper! Sniper!"

Men broke in every direction. Some ducked and scrambled for cover. One young man tried to dive over the bar, but flopped onto it instead, knocking the planks loose and crashing the entire works to the ground. The barmaids screamed.

"Get down! Get down!"

Men collided, tangled and fell.

"Fuck! Get offa me!"

"Goddammit!"

"Sniper!"

Louis Blaze struggled to his feet, tangled in the lightweight lawn chair. He staggered, fell forward, and crawled toward the corner of the house with the tenacious chair clamped on his substantial ass.

The bride sat frozen.

I kicked the earth and shot skyward. As I rose, I rotated and searched for a rifle barrel sticking out of a window or a sniper prone in the meadow grass. A search up and down the line of vehicles and of the half-constructed homes across the street yielded nothing. I looked for a vehicle racing to escape the scene, but the streets lay quiet.

I thought the buzzing was a wasp!

The insect sound was no wasp. The tickle at my ear had been air disturbed by a bullet. A big bullet. Big enough to remove a man's head at the upper lip and above. Powerful enough to do the job and move on to the belly of a woman holding a dish of potato salad fifty feet away.

There had been no gunshot. No supersonic crack from the bullet.

I searched the line of the bullet's path for a speeding car or racing motorcycle. Nothing moved on the streets. The hydraulic arm of the distant backhoe clawed the earth. Carpenters applied nail gun shots to the rising wooden frames on two new homes. No one I could see carried a rifle. None of the workmen broke their casual stride or steady application of nails.

On Spellman's lawn, a few men staggered to their feet and ran. Two of them crossed the mowed grass and ducked beside their trucks and SUVs. After stealing glances across the street, they clawed open vehicle doors. One by one, they extracted rifles, jerked rounds into chambers, and lifted the weapons to their shoulders. A man in green camo threw himself prone under the front corner of his truck and aimed across the street. I followed his aim, thinking he might have seen the shooter.

Empty, barren lots offered no hint of an enemy. Nothing moved. In Spellman's yard, screaming and shouting marked mounting chaos. Voices swore. Men yelled for everyone to get down. Women shouted at the children. Near the bounce house, kids stood bewildered by the shift in atmosphere.

"Over there! Over there!"

The man beneath his pickup crawled forward and swung his rifle back and forth. "Where? Where goddammit?"

A hundred feet above the scene, I lifted the power unit to arrest my ascent. I searched. Except for the mayhem in the picnic yard, quiet ruled the surrounding neighborhood. Darryl Spellman's headless body lay in a heap at the feet of his bride-to-be. She might have been a vandalized statue. She sat covered in red, staring down at her headless groom.

I rotated and examined the two homes under construction. I calculated the path of the bullet based on the wasp-wing tickle at my ear, the explosive hit on Spellman and the subsequent strike on the woman with the potato salad. The shot clearly came from the construction zone across the street, yet I could see no sign of an assassin.

Gunfire erupted, sharp and rapid. I looked down and saw the prone gunman and his companion firing. They aimed at a dirt mound sixty yards from the road. Clods of dirt snapped into the air.

The fusillade was pointless. No one crouched behind the dirt mound.

The firing continued relentlessly until both men had emptied their clips.

"Didja geddim?"

"I don't know!"

Neither ventured into the open to assess the battle damage. I searched the landscape and found nothing.

Dammit.

I gripped the power unit tighter. Sweat broke from my palm. Every muscle in my body felt jittery.

Right past my head! Inches from my head!
I flew a tight circle above the construction but saw nothing.

TEN MINUTES LATER, I located Leslie's compact red Jeep cruising several streets over. A sharp dive took me to the roof rack. I grabbed it and banged on the sheet metal. The Jeep stopped. I dropped beside the passenger door and reappeared without so much as a glance at the homes on either side of the street. I didn't care. I jerked open the door and slid onto the passenger seat.

"What the hell is happening?" she demanded. "I heard shots."

"Drive. Quickly. Get as far from the Spellman house as possible."

"What the—"

"Somebody killed him. Go!"

She stared.

"Go!"

"I'm not sure you understand that I'm a law enforcement officer, Will."

"And I'm not sure that you want to wander into a live fire zone waving your FBI badge in front of a bunch of rabid anti-government militia types who just saw their beloved leader assassinated."

LESLIE WHEELED into a parking space near the air pump at the back of a gas station quick mart. I finished explaining what I'd seen as she killed the engine.

She reached across the console and pulled the recording device from my shirt pocket. She unclipped the microphone and wound the lead around two fingers, then dropped the coil into a cupholder. Taking the device in hand, she pulled out her phone. She produced a loop of thin black wire from her pocket and pushed a connector into the bottom of the recording device. The other end she connected to her phone. Using her thumbs, she worked the screen, opening an app and touching command buttons. A bar appeared. A green line crept across the bar.

Sirens sounded nearby. The volume rose and fell.

I wiped my palms on my pants, then closed a grip on my thighs to keep my hands from shaking. The wasp sound played in my head like a pop tune earworm.

Inches.

On Leslie's screen, the green bar reached its destination and disappeared. Leslie thumbed commands into the phone. A video screen appeared. On it, the interior of the Jeep wiggled incoherently, then the driver-side door, the parking lot, then the landscape seen from a bird's eye.

"That thing has a camera?"

"Uh-huh." She watched the aerial view captured by my circuit around the Spellman house. She watched me approach the patio bar. The fisheye lens reduced and separated the figures in the wide-angle view.

She watched Spellman's head explode without flinching.

She watched the aftermath to the point where I rose and rotated. When the camera view faced the construction area, she froze the frame. She examined it for a moment, then closed the frame and the app and pocketed her phone.

"Huh." She sat and stared at nothing. "I guess you weren't the shooter."

"What?"

She said nothing.

"You thought I did that?"

"I wouldn't put it that way."

"How would you put it?"

"You have an independent streak. Lee Donaldson warned Director Lindsay. The Director, putting it bluntly, wasn't sure you could be trusted. Lee thought you were impulsive."

"Jesus Christ! That bullet missed my head by—I don't know—this much!" I raised a thumb and finger measurement. "I felt the damned thing go past my ear!"

"Good."

"Good? What do you mean *good*? You saw what it did! That could have been me!" My voice climbed an octave.

"Good that you weren't five inches to your right. Good that you can pinpoint your location at the time of the shooting and help us determine the precise path of the bullet. Good that we should be able to figure out where the shooter set up. See? All good."

I swallowed, momentarily speechless.

She started the engine, checked her mirrors and the backup camera display, then put the Jeep in reverse and backed up, spinning the steering wheel.

"Where are we going?"

"Back to the airport."

"You're not going to—I don't know—check in with the local office? Turn over what we know? Help with the investigation?"

"And how would I do that? This is the point you and your wife have made from the beginning." She checked both ways and pulled onto the street. "You can't exactly tell anyone your story."

"What if the shooter is still up there?"

She shook her head. "The shooter is long gone. From what happened to Spellman's head, I'd say that was a heavy round. Maybe fifty-caliber. Most weapons firing that kind of round are accurate a thousand yards out. The shooter was never anywhere near Spellman."

"You're just going to drop this?"

"Not by a long shot." She cracked a smile at the pun. "But your part in this is done."

"Just put your toy back in the box," I said sourly.

"One way of stating it." She glanced over to catch me pouting, which is not my strong suit. "Look, Will, you—and more specifically, Andy—spelled out the limitations when you met with Director Lindsay. There's the world in which you can do what you do and don't get me wrong, it's invaluable. And then there's the world of warrants and Miranda and probable cause. I have to walk the line between the two."

"You're doing nothing?"

"I didn't say that. When we get back, you and I will pull up a satellite image of that subdivision and get into the finer points of trajectory. Your report and the video will provide data. I'll find a way to mainstream that data into the investigation. But we were never going to drive back up there, join the local LEOs and point to where the shot came from."

7

The miracle that is general aviation returned us to Spirit of St. Louis Airport before my absence created a problem for Arun. A few minutes after four p.m. the FBI chartered jet deposited Leslie and me on the ramp where our day began. A text from Arun said he was running late as usual, and that he anticipated arriving for our departure by six.

I double checked with Leslie to make sure she didn't plan to whisk me off to Key West or Alaska, then text-replied Arun that I'd be waiting.

"Food," I said when we entered the fixed base operation office and lounge.

"We don't have time."

I veered left and caught the eye of the desk manager. "Can you order a pizza for us?"

"Certainly," he replied cheerfully producing a pen and memo pad.

"Pepperoni, sausage, onions and mushrooms."

"On half!" Leslie called out as she marched toward the restroom. "Veggie on the other half."

I watched her disappear, then said, "That figures. Make it a large. And see if you can get some garlic bread with that. We'll be in the pilot's lounge. Thanks!"

"No problem!"

. . .

"Here," I pointed at the Google Earth image. I sat beside Leslie on a leather sofa. We huddled over her laptop. "This is the patio. This is where they put the bar tent at the edge. I landed and anchored to a tent pole...here."

Leslie squeezed her fingers on the touchscreen and zoomed closer.

"The round parted my hair right about...here."

She said nothing. Her dark eyes narrowed.

I pointed.

"This is Spellman. And this would be the second victim, the woman."

Leslie pulled her phone and the recording device, still connected, from the pocket of her black blazer. She tapped the phone screen to life, found the video app, and replayed what I had recorded. I turned away. With pizza coming I didn't need to see Spellman's brains splatter his never-to-be-bride again. After a moment Leslie put away the phone and returned to the laptop. She expanded the view and moved the Spellman property to the upper left corner of the screen. Then she lifted a copy of *AOPA Pilot* from the coffee table and ripped out a page.

"That's rude," I said.

She ignored me. She folded the page lengthwise twice, then laid the makeshift ruler on her laptop screen, aligning it with the points we had identified.

The line extended across Spellman's yard, across his street, and into empty land which, in the Google image, had new roads but did not show the new construction or freshly dug basements.

"The shooter was on this line," she said. She picked up the phone and video recorder again. She cued it to a wide shot captured when I rotated to search for the source of the shot.

"There's nothing there," I said. "This is where they're putting in a new house, which might have been a place to hide, but it's off the line. Your trajectory path is empty."

"It just looks empty."

Twenty minutes later the pizza arrived. The front desk manager hustled it into the lounge along with a tray containing plates and utensils. He spread the meal on a table. A cloud of pizza scent filled the room and stirred my stomach. The desk manager asked, "Can I get you anything to drink?"

"Coffee, please?" I asked.

"Just water," Leslie added. The desk manager spared a glance at the device in her hands, then hurried out.

Leslie stowed the pocket camera and closed the laptop. We moved to a table where I began eating my first meal of a long day. I needed the food. And more coffee. A flight from St. Louis to Essex County remained on my agenda, and fatigue born of a sleepless night lurked in ambush.

"So?" I asked.

Leslie fixed her attention a thousand yards beyond the wall of the lounge. I wasn't sure she heard me until she finally spoke.

"Sniper rifle. High caliber. Military grade. A long-range shot. Someone with skill and experience. Military training."

"Lots of that in these groups."

She shook her head. "Not as much as you think. Most of these cosplay militia guys have never been in the military. Of the few who have, not many are serious combatants."

"What do you mean?"

She made a face. "They're wannabes. Wannabe soldiers. Wannabe special forces. We call them 'special farces.' Guys who did unremarkable tours as wheeled vehicle mechanics or warehouse clerks, but who beef up their service records on the militia websites with a lot of bullshit. Very few of them are genuine special forces vets, or vets who saw combat. These fools want a race war or a war to overthrow the government. People who have seen actual combat want nothing to do with either."

"That's reassuring."

"Mostly. But this shot—I gotta say. This was something different." She picked up a piece of disturbingly topped pizza and plucked off an errant slice of pepperoni. She bit the end and chewed, deep in thought.

"How do you plan to 'mainstream' what I've given you?"

"I don't know yet. There's a task force on this. They knew about the wedding. The intel was channeled to me. My job is to channel it back. You complicate things, Will. You really do."

I didn't answer. Not for the first time, I wondered about the decision Andy and I made in New York, driven largely by Lee Donaldson—the decision to introduce me and *the other thing* to the FBI. Like most candidates for regret, it seemed like a good idea at the time.

"Speaking of complicated," she said, chewing enthusiastically, "do you see the service weapon I carry?"

I wasn't sure I understood the question. I glanced at her shoulder holster.

"Yes…?"

"Good. Now you're going to tell me what you were doing in the middle of the night last night or I'm going to take that weapon out of the holster, remove the safety, and put a round through one of your blue eyes."

She smiled. I think.

I MARVEL at the tectonic shift my life took the day a beautiful woman in a light summer dress strolled into the offices of Essex County Air Service. She arrived on the arm of a man I disliked intensely, more so after he gave her an airplane ride and made her airsick. My world flipped while I held Andy's hair as she vomited into a wastebasket. That moment, unannounced, marked the point at which much of what I do began to flow through the filter of *what would Andrea Katherine Taylor Stewart do?*

The question popped into my mind as Leslie looked at me with a glitter in her eye and a smile on her lips and a loaded Glock under her left armpit. I didn't contemplate how my next words might affect my interaction with the FBI. I imagined instead the conversation that would take place when I explained to my wife of four plus years how I revealed to Leslie the last sacred layer of secrecy about *the other thing.* I vividly pictured the look on her face. The words out of her mouth. The way she would stab her fingers into the waves of her hair as if to massage the next thought from her mind.

Irony flooded the moment—that Leslie thought I could be unfaithful to Andy when the secret I kept reflected my devotion to my wife.

"Well?"

Given that I'd not seen Andy in person for eighteen days (and a precise number of hours easily calculated) since she left for FBI training in Virginia, I decided that any objections she might voice could be rationalized by the fact that we both served the Federal Bureau of Investigation.

"Do you know what an Angel Flight is?"

8

"Hi, gorgeous."

The number on my phone screen wasn't the same as the last time Andy called, but I recognized the Virginia area code. Trainees were not allowed personal mobile devices during the 20-week course at Quantico. Limited access to landline phones during personal time on weekends provided our only connection. Demand for a few landline phones ran high and call time was limited, so on Friday night, when the window for personal phone time opened for Andy and her fellow trainees, I waited for the call on the screened porch of our rented farmhouse with my phone charged and a cold Corona in hand.

"Hello, handsome." Andy's voice warmed me as much as the slanted fall sunshine penetrating the screens.

Questions and demands raced through my head.

I miss you.

When can I visit?

When will they release you for time off base?

I suppressed them one by one, knowing my needs and impulses only put needless pressure on Andy.

"Are you kicking academic ass?"

"It's exhausting. We're in class nine hours a day and it feels like the homework is another sixteen."

"That's twenty-five hours."

"Feels like it."

"Leaving the competition in the dust, I'm sure."

"Will, you have no idea. The people in my class are—I don't know how to put it—*daunting*. Lawyers. Engineers. I haven't met a cadet who doesn't have a master's degree. One woman has a doctorate in counterintelligence. Where do you even get something like that?"

I smiled. This was an old song with Andy, who hides her county technical college associate degree in police sciences the way a middle school girl hides new orthodontics. Nothing about law enforcement scared her more than the idea of competing against peers she could not imagine as her equal. I knew better. My handshake bet with her Essex PD boss, Tom Ceeves, placed a hundred dollars on Andy finishing in the top three, and double that if she finished number one in her graduating class. I think Tom took the bet in her presence just to give her permission to finish fourth or lower.

"Been out to Hogan's Alley yet?" I asked.

"Heaven's no. We all walk around with inert weapons. We don't go to the range until—I think—week six or seven. They call us 'children' and don't trust us with anything sharper than a pencil. It's all classroom right now. You would not believe the lecturers, Will! Incredible people. Counter-terrorism experts. Agents who have worked foreign posts and international investigations. Law professors who have clerked for the Supreme Court. Top investigators who worked 9/11, Lebanon, Bin Ladin, and cases I can't mention. Legal experts. Firearms experts. Explosives experts. We had a ballistics and weapons expert who worked the Las Vegas shooting. The things they've seen and done!"

I sat back and listened to schoolgirl enthusiasm bubble up in Andy. She talked about her classes, her schedule, the reading list, and the long hours of study. She spoke in awe of her classmates, the best of the best out of tens of thousands of applicants. I recognized her insecurity and embarrassment for having been given a slot without having traversed the unforgiving application process. Director Lindsay had arranged the opening.

After Lindsay's death, the door would have closed if not for Leslie. What she did or who she did it to, Leslie refused to say. One week after Andy and I met Agent Carson-Pelham, Andy received a call to report to a class assembling in a matter of days. The call set off a whirlwind. It seemed like only minutes later when I dropped her off at Shannon Field in Fredericksburg, Virginia. Andy asked that we part on the airport ramp rather than at the gates of the FBI training center. I hid my disappointment and agreed. This was her journey, not mine. She viewed her backdoor entrance to the academy as less than legitimate, a deficit she needed to overcome on her own terms, starting with an arrival sans ceremony.

Andy talked. I savored the sound of her voice.

"…thought I was in shape, but I have aches in muscles I didn't know I had. We do morning and afternoon PT. And next week we start combat and self-defense training. And…"

The line went quiet for a moment.

"And?"

"And…it's magical, Will! I—I don't know how to put it, but this is the most incredible experience. I never imagined!"

"I'm glad," I said sincerely.

"I miss you." Her shift to intimacy caught me by surprise. "I do. I miss you every day. I know I go on and on about all this, but I *do* miss you."

"I miss you, too. But it's okay. I couldn't be happier for you."

"We still need to talk about '*the* other *other thing.*'"

I laughed. She had previously dismissed my suggestion of a name for our as-yet unconceived child.

After several years of postponing the topic of a family, Andy, propelled by impulses I could not fathom, rather suddenly announced her desire to have a baby. Just as suddenly, the call to join the FBI Academy derailed our plans. I quickly shifted from assuring Andy that I wanted a family to assuring her that we could wait.

"I still want it."

"Dee, I do, too. There's time. Let's climb one hill at a time, okay?"

"I just…I feel selfish…after what happened. After we decided."

"No. Crazy, maybe. But there's nothing selfish about jumping all over this opening to train for the FBI. Dee, this is something you never even dared to dream was possible. To have it happen and pass it up…?"

"I guess."

"You know I'm right."

"Okay." She closed the topic, having prompted me to say the words she needed to hear. "Any news from Leslie?"

"Funny," I chuckled. "More than news. Usual disclaimer?"

"What, now you're asking me?" She laughed.

"Hey, I'm now an asset of the Eff-Bee-Eye!"

"Right. So, what's the news?"

"You're not going to belie—"

"Wait! Maybe this isn't such a good topic for the phone."

"Really? You're at a secure facility on a Marine base, sweetheart. Surrounded by the federal officers." The instant I said it, I realized that was the point.

She didn't speak for a moment—a message in itself. Then she said, "I just mean there are other people waiting to use this phone. We can talk about it when you come out."

"Come out?" My heart accelerated.

"We get a 24-hour leave next weekend. Noon Saturday to noon Sunday. Wanna go on a date?"

The feline purr in her voice stirred the answer before I could say it aloud. I leaned back on my ratty old lounge chair.

"I don't know. I usually wash my hair on Saturday night."

9

P olice Chief Tom Ceeves looks at me differently since I vanished before his startled eyes at the kitchen table where Andy and I eat breakfast. He tries to be cool about it, the way I imagine myself attempting to not notice if I ever wind up sitting on a commercial airliner next to Tom Hanks or Charlize Theron. He fails exactly the way I imagine myself failing in that first-class seat I doubt I will ever occupy.

He can't peel away his initial glance. His gaze hangs longer than it should. He leaves me with the sense that he has something to say. Tom is a man of few words, but lately his already slender word count has dropped.

I worry that the chief's knowledge of *the other thing* will have consequences for Andy. I fear that he will second-guess her sterling police work, that he will wonder if she cheats by using me. Discrediting her would be absurd and unfair. I can cite ample examples of cases Andy resolved with no influence or input from me. Andy recently spent scores of hours—many of them on her own time—crawling through social media posts to ferret out a suspect who thought it would be funny to give hallucinogenic mushrooms to half a dozen grade school kids on the Indian Line Running Trail that courses through Essex County. The investigation and subsequent arrest belonged entirely to Detective Andrea Stewart. I spent many of her investigative hours reading a Craig Johnson novel on the front porch.

The question hangs in the air when I see the Chief. I suppose it also hangs in the air with Pidge, Lillian, Spiro Lewko, and Earl Jackson—with everyone who knows what I can do.

And what do you plan to do with it today?

Ordinarily, it's a question unasked.

The morning after Andy's call, on the last Saturday of September, Chief Tom Ceeves asked the question outright.

10

"There was the lady that died from eating a garden slug on a dare," Fire Chief Joe Boettcher offered between bites of pancake.

"Guy got his head caught in an electric footrest in a movie theater. I think it was in England," Armin Kirk proposed. "They said he was looking for his cell phone, got stuck, and then had a cardiac arrest."

"Turning off a cell phone in a theater is serious business," I pointed out.

"How 'bout this one?" James Rankin proposed. "Guy shoots himself at a gun range in Oklahoma."

"Not exactly unusual," Joe Boettcher responded. "There's something like four hundred accidental gun deaths every year."

Rankin shook his head. "Wasn't that kind of accidental. A couple weeks ago this guy was in a line with a bunch of his buddies at a private outdoor range. Best anybody can guess is that when he fired, the bullet somehow ricocheted back and hit him between the eyes."

Weird topics often air out at the Saturday morning breakfasts at the Silver Spoon café in Essex. Strange deaths barely crack the top ten.

"I read that three people suffocated when they dumped dry ice into a swimming pool to make spooky fog," Armin Kirk tried again.

"Saw that one."

"Yah."

"The CO_2 displaced the oxygen," Joe Boettcher said.

"I got one," Earl Jackson announced. Heads turned. "Not the death itself, but the last wish, on account it almost killed me, too."

Earl had, without ceremony, won the conversation competition.

"Old Captain Dobbs. One of my first captains. When I was a rookie copilot at the old Honeymoon Express…" Earl paused as the high school-aged Silver Spoon server poured him a coffee refill. She darted off, and Earl resumed his tale. "He was a big fan of John Wayne."

Name dropping at a Silver Spoon breakfast is frowned upon, making it doubly effective when performed deftly.

"You ever meet The Duke?" Rankin asked.

"Couple times. Flew him and Ford out to Catalina once or twice."

"Didja talk to him?"

"Did he talk like he does in the movies?"

"Was he really that tall?"

Earl chuckled. "Shit, I was too scared to pass a word with those guys. I was a green kid holding down the right seat, fetching bags and picking up the empties in the cabin. Cap'n Dobbs was the Lord God Himself. I don't think I touched the controls the first six months I was there."

"Well, then, what happened?"

Earl sipped the fresh refill. We had come to the part of the Saturday morning meal where plates were clean, bellies were full, and stories were doled out in droll monosyllables.

"This was in the eighties—"

"When you flew with him?"

"Nah. Flew with him in the late fifties and early sixties. When Dobbs died, it was the eighties. I forget what year. It was right after Ronald Ray-Guns told Gorby to tear down the wall—"

"Eighty-seven," Boettcher informed us. Like his fellow Republicans at the table, he let Earl's abuse of Reagan's holy name slide. The Regulars acknowledge that Earl is a Democrat and forgive him his disability.

"I guess," Earl allowed. "Cap'n Dobbs wasn't all that old. Seventy-six when the cancer got him. Even at the end, pulling oxygen from nose cannulas, he smoked a pack a day. Surprised he didn't blow himself up. After he passed, his daughter tracked me down. She remembered me flying with her dad. She asked if I could help fulfill his last wish. At the time, I was hauling freight for an oil exploration outfit down in Belize.

This was back before Belize was 'discovered' by rich folks who don't want to mingle with crowds from the cruise ships. Sweet duty, that. I had a couple of…well, let's just say my nights were not lonely down that way."

Earl allowed a mildly pornographic pause before he continued. I sat back and sipped my coffee and tried not to let my mind wander to Andy's phone call and the prospect of seeing her in seven days.

"They shot a bunch of Ford's westerns up in Monument Valley. You see all those rock formations in the movies—in them cavalry movies he shot with Wayne. Those were in Monument Valley."

"*Stagecoach*," Armin Kirk offered.

"*The Searchers*," Joe Boettcher added.

"Dobbs liked the cavalry movies the best. His daughter said her dad was specific. She showed us pictures of the exact formations where he wanted his ashes spread. Me and a guy named Prout—we were the only two that showed up. That was in San Diego, where Dobbs died. She handed him over to us—I kid you not—in what I swear was a shoe box. Dobbs was a cheap bastard."

The girl came around and asked if there would be anything else. The answer is always no, and she is always ready. She circled the table dropping check slips beside each plate, parting with a pretty smile that always finishes in my direction. I chalk it up to being the only one present that isn't her grandfather's age. Wallets appeared. Singles fluttered into a cluster at the center of the table, rewarding our server with a substantial tip.

"I flew commercial up from Belize City through Mexico City, so I didn't have no car. Prout didn't want to drive all the way up to Utah. He had an old Cessna 170, so we piled into that thing. I took left seat and turned over command of the shoe box to Prout. My mistake."

"What happened?"

"Aside from it being a thousand-mile round trip, with four gas stops and desert turbulence all the way? Aside from Prout pulling out a flask before we reached the California border claiming it was his airsick medicine? And him being drunk as a skunk by the time we got to the Navajo Reservation?"

"You sure you didn't violate some regulations or treaties by dumping human remains on tribal land?" Joe Boettcher inquired.

"Can't say I am." Earl sipped and savored his coffee. "The trouble started when we got ourselves to the big valley where those movies were shot, and we ended up flying in giant circles arguing about which was the right rock formation. From the air, those damned things look nothing like their photos. We finally settled on what we thought Dobbs wanted. I lined up to make a run with Prout holding that box of ashes on his lap when—"

"Will?"

Tom Ceeves, whose chair at the table had been empty for this morning's meeting of The Regulars, landed his big hand on my shoulder. The Regulars took notice of his tardiness.

"Well look what the cat dragged in."

"You're just in time. We had 'em put everything on your tab."

"Mornin' fellas," Tom paid the assemblage a brief glance before focusing on me. "Will, I need you."

"Andy okay?" I asked automatically.

"Andy's fine, I imagine. But yeah, it's business. Sorry, fellas. Can't stay."

I slid my check and eight bucks under the corner of my plate.

"Don't you wanna hear the end of this?" Joe Boettcher asked.

I stood and carefully moved clear of Earl's reach.

"You mean how Prout, instead of opening the side window and lowering the box into the slipstream, he shoves open the door with his knee and tries to pour Dobbs out, but the door creates a backdraft, which fills up the cabin with Dobbs' ashes, covers every instrument and paints the windshield opaque, and how Earl nearly took the top off one of those famous rocks while he's coughing and spitting out the remains of his old captain? Nah. Heard this one."

I figured if Tom needed my help, he'd see that I got out of the Silver Spoon alive.

"I ASKED Sandy Stone for use of the Foundation's airplane." I rode with Tom, having hitched a ride to breakfast with Earl. Tom wheeled us onto Highway 34. He pointed the nose of his big SUV in the direction of the airport. "She said it was up to you."

I gave it a moment's thought. Parting with Leslie in St. Louis, the FBI agent said she would be in touch. Since then, I heard nothing, not that I saw any role for me in the Spellman investigation. I decided she couldn't expect me to hang by the phone.

"Fine by me. Where to?"

"Bear County."

"Okay." It seemed a simple request, if a little odd. I've known the Chief to drive five hours to a thirty-minute meeting after declining Andy's offers to have me fly him and save four and a half of those hours. "Something urgent?"

Tom hesitated. He aimed a pointed look in my direction.

"You mean...?"

"Yeah, uh...you know...if that's okay with you."

This was about *the other thing*. The chief had transitioned from looking at my ability as freakish to finding it useful.

"Goes without saying, Chief. Happy to help. Where in hell is Bear County?"

"'Tween Ashland and Iron. Occupies a chunk of Lake Superior shoreline to the north and parts of the Turtle Flambeau Flowage on the south end. Some good hunting up that way."

I didn't hunt and had never heard of the Turtle thing, but a second realization hit me. Tom was burying the lead.

"Wait! Is this that thing? That woman that disappeared?"

"Yup." We slipped out of town headed for the airport. Tom didn't apply the lights and siren, but he generously applied his foot to the accelerator.

"It's been all over the news. Jesus, Tom—she's in Congress or something."

"Married to a Congressman."

"Right. I don't know what you think I can do about it. I heard they were combing the woods. I mean—that's a lotta woods." I tried to imagine flying a search grid at treetop level. With a power unit only good for around forty minutes, I wondered how many batteries I would need.

"Not what I had in mind." He didn't elaborate.

We arrived at the airport. He parked at the Foundation hangar. It came as no surprise to me that Arun Dewar's Toyota Corolla occupied his usual spot beside the hangar despite it being a Saturday morning. As near as I can tell, Arun is on a seven-day work week.

"Okay, first things first. Where am I flight planning to?"

"Ironwood. We'll get a car there and drive over the county line to Linden."

I climbed out of the SUV and used my key on the hangar's office door. Tom followed me inside.

The lights were out. The coffee maker was off. Arun's office was dark. I put two and two together and arrived at the conclusion that Pidge had more than likely devoured the young man at her place last night.

"Gimme five minutes to pull up weather and file a flight plan."

Tom read his watch. The gesture told me to hurry. "I'm going to hit the head."

WITH HIS PREFLIGHT BUSINESS CONCLUDED, Tom joined me in the hangar as the big door rose to a stop.

"I take it this isn't a garden variety missing person case—her being a politician's wife."

"She's married to Congressman Martin Gregg."

I grabbed the command handle on the battery-powered tow bar and steered it to the nose of the Navajo where I bent to attach it to the strut. I looked up at Tom.

"The conspiracy theory nut?"

He nodded.

"One of these days they're going to ask Wisconsin to stop sending people to Congress," I muttered.

With the nose gear secured by the tow bar, I grabbed the power handles. I checked the wings and tail for clearance.

"What exactly are you expecting me to do?"

"For starters, get me up there."

I pulled the airplane out of the hangar, stowed the electric tow bar, and closed the hangar door. Flight bag in hand, I stopped at the aircraft airstair.

"I gotta ask, Chief. What's the real deal here? It's not like you to step out of your jurisdiction."

Tom paused. He hunted for words. "The Bear County Sheriff is an old friend. I called her last night."

Her?

He glanced at his watch again.

"Okay." I took the hint. "We'll talk on the way."

TOM DIDN'T JOIN me in the cockpit. I pushed the right-side club seats as far apart as possible for maximum legroom. He squeezed in, facing forward. I handed him a headset. Twelve minutes after takeoff we leveled off at ten thousand feet. I completed the cruise flight checklist, then waved at him to put on the headset.

"Can you hear me?" I glanced back.

"Loud and clear." He mouthed the words but failed to transmit.

"Push the mic closer to your lips. Almost touching. Then talk. Pause if you hear anyone else on the line. That'll be air traffic control. They can't hear you."

"Got it."

"See that controller about midway down the headset line? Press the button at the center." I glanced back to see his face change appreciatively. "That's the noise cancelling."

He found the button and pressed. "Nice."

I checked the panel. The primary flight display revealed a twenty-two-knot headwind. This would have been a short flight if not for the giant hand pushing against us.

"What's going on?" I asked without looking back.

Tom spoke in a matter-of-fact monotone. "You know the headline. Missing woman. Wife of Congressman Martin Gregg. Republican from the Seventh District."

"It was on the box at The Silver Spoon this morning. The banner said something about kidnapping."

"Huh."

"You think it's something else? What does your sheriff friend say?"

"She said the Congressman and his wife have a colorful history. The most recent chapter involves a paternity suit filed by a twenty-something campaign volunteer. Rumor has it the Congressman got involved with the girl before she could vote."

"That'll put a dent in a marriage."

"Did The Spoon have on the Fox News this morning?"

"Like always."

"Gregg is a regular on the Fox News. A lot of face time, but they never seem to mention the paternity suit."

"I heard he's eyeballing a run for Gianni's Senate seat when they call the special."

"Yup."

"That won't make the Democrats happy."

"Actually, it will. The Dems want him to take the plunge. Gianni's Senate seat will go GOP no matter how hard they huff and puff, but Gregg running for Senate clears the Seventh Congressional. Gives the Dems a shot."

"I should think the GOP would pass him over because he's a looney tune."

Tom snorted. "That never stopped 'em before."

"And now his wife is missing? Did he do it?"

"Sure as shit."

This made me turn in my seat. Tom wasn't given to bold accusations. He met my glance with a steely squint.

"Your sheriff friend up there suggest that?"

"Her name is Kresky." Tom paused long enough for me to wonder how well he knew the woman. "Not out loud."

"Is this where I come in?"

"Maybe. Sue and I had a long talk. I didn't say anything about the kind of help I might—you might—be able to offer, but from what she told me I figure just about the only way this situation had a prayer of coming out right was if you got involved."

Sue?

I said nothing, a tactic that fails with Tom. He said even more nothing. After a moment I glanced back. Tom stared out the window.

"Involved how?" I asked.

"Let's let Sue lay out the situation when we get there. Then you and I will talk. If you decide you don't like the lay of the land, we'll go home."

"Does she know about me?"

"Course not."

"Does she know we're coming?"

"Figured I'd tell her when we get there."

I waited for more, but Tom's few words had run out.

. . .

I RADIOED AHEAD to the fixed base operator at Ironwood and arranged a rental car. After landing, I attended to aircraft parking and tiedown details while Tom hiked from the FBO shack to the commercial terminal. Fifteen minutes later he drove onto the FBO's gravel parking lot. I grabbed my flight bag and slipped through the gate. He climbed out and tossed me the keys to a blue Honda Fit.

"I can't drive this thing with my knees up around my ears."

I suppressed a grin and wondered how he got the car this far. He marched to the passenger side and shoved the passenger seat all the way back before wedging himself inside.

"This was all they had," he muttered.

The little car had no GPS navigation. I pulled my iPad from my flight bag. Driving directions to the Bear County Courthouse in the county seat of Linden tallied a forty-eight-minute drive.

"Gregg has been screaming to bring the feds in," Tom said as we hit the highway. "He's charging hard on conspiracy and kidnapping and terrorism."

"Terrorism. Huh," I grunted. "That's rich. He's the one with *Al Qaeda.*"

Tom's glance told me he didn't get it.

"What? Gregg's not with *Al Qaeda.*"

"Figure of speech. He's the one with The Base."

Tom's blank look told me I'd stretched word play a little too far. I tried to salvage it. "Gregg taps into the party's extremist *base*—I imagine it's how he plans to go after Gianni's seat. *Al Qaeda* translates to The Base."

"No, it doesn't. It means The Leaders. The Arabic for The Base is *Alqaeida.* Subtle distinction."

I threw Tom a sideways glance. He shrugged.

"Ten years as an embassy Marine in the Middle East."

"No shit. You learn something new every day."

11

"I understand you're married to Tom's star detective."

"Every day," I replied over a brisk handshake.

Sheriff Sue Kresky made no effort to camouflage a thorough assessment of me during and after Tom's introduction.

We met in an antique office under a high, pressed-tin ceiling in a courthouse that claimed to have welcomed William Jennings Bryant during one of his oratory tours. Tall doors, old wood paneling and creaking floors felt out of phase with high tech touchscreens and laptops. The Sheriff's personal office housed a desk the size of a small armored vehicle and enjoyed a high bank of muntin barred windows overlooking a town square. I checked out the view. The row of news vans parked bumper to bumper on the park perimeter looked familiar. Not long ago, Essex hosted a similar media horde.

The Sheriff, a tall woman with steel gray hair bound in a ponytail and a long, narrow face, mustered a piercing gaze through eyes the color of gunmetal. Her intensity and irises were amplified by strong lenses in a heavy black frame. I guessed her to be Tom's age, an estimate aided by his disclosure that she had served overseas with him in the same Marine unit. Unlike Tom, whose sheriff's uniform was rumpled flannel at best, Sheriff Kresky wore a neatly pressed polyester uniform shirt over creased uniform pants.

"Word gets around. She's impressive." Kresky turned her attention to Tom. "I appreciated you lending an ear last night, Tom, but not so much you dropping in. I don't need to tell you how busy I am herding cats here. I'm not sure what you think you can do."

"Five minutes." He gestured at one of the two chairs facing her desk.

"What about him?"

"Tell him what you told me last night."

"Why?"

"Coffee at oh dark thirty."

I didn't know what Tom meant, but she did. Tom seated himself. The code prompted her to gesture for me to sit.

"Can he be counted on to keep what he hears in this office to himself?"

"Yup."

"The usual disclaimer," I said. I held up my wedding ring. She nodded.

"Start at the beginning," Tom suggested.

"Okay. Tuesday morning, the wife, Casey Gregg, told her sister she was driving out to the Gregg property to pick up her things. She's been staying with the sister ever since the news got out about Gregg and his intern. You know that part?"

"I heard."

"The sister said she—the wife—planned to collect a suitcase and head down to their parents' place in Phillips. And then line up a lawyer."

"A busted marriage isn't good for a Senate race. Especially when there's a paternity scandal," I said. "Is that rumor, slander or fact?"

"I guess it depends on what cable news you like. Anyway, the sister told me that Casey Gregg drove her car up to where the Congressman has one of those horse farms that tops the new money wish list. The sister said she tried to talk Mrs. Gregg out of it. There's no love lost between the sister and the Congressman."

"Must be a Democrat," Tom muttered.

"When Casey didn't show up in Phillips or answer her calls, the sister raised the alarm."

"Doesn't someone have to be missing for—?"

"Bear County doesn't require a 24-hour period to file a missing person report."

Tom added, "We don't either."

"Makes no sense. We encourage people to act quickly. Details are fresh and more accurate. If true harm is imminent, time and speed of response matter. I'd rather have a dozen false alarms than fail to act in time when it counts. The sister called me the minute Casey Gregg didn't show up when she said she would. I got the feeling the sister paced all morning with a watch in her hand."

I tried to imagine what Andy would ask. "Any signs of violence? Ransom note?"

"Nope, although we did notify the FBI. Him being in Congress and whatnot."

"Any violence before? Between the Congressman and his wife?"

"The sister says wife has been 'accident prone' like some women can be around certain kinds of men. She points a finger at Gregg, but the wife never admitted it or reported it."

"Making the Congressman suspect number one."

Sheriff Kresky flexed her eyebrows. "I drove out to the Gregg place and found the wife's car there. Gregg acknowledged that his wife had been there. He admits to marital 'issues.' He told me they got into a row on the phone the night before, and he lost his temper and pitched her clothes out. Said if she wanted to pack a suitcase, she could collect them."

"Out? Like on the lawn?"

"All over the property. And that's no lie. When I got there, the woman's clothes were everywhere. But he swears that when she showed up, they worked it all through. Had a breakthrough. Tears and all."

"Even after he threw her clothes into the weeds? Jesus," I said, "a jury would convict on that alone. So…where is she?"

"Congressman Gregg claims after they kissed and made up and he promised to pay for the dry cleaning, his wife told him she needed to spend a few days with some girlfriends—to get her head straight. To catch her breath. He says they agreed to go to counseling after she got back. No, he didn't know who the friends were. He claims they came by and picked her up. He said he was in one of the outbuildings and he didn't see them come and go. No, he didn't know where they were going. He thought maybe a B&B over in Ashland or on Madeline Island."

"So, he didn't file the report," Tom noted.

"The sister did. When I told him, he called the sister a vindictive b-word and said she's lying. He said the sister is the one pushing for a separation. He says the sister has been brainwashed by the left-wing media elite. His words. I asked, but he denies the paternity story."

"And how did all that smell to you?"

I caught a glint in the sheriff's eyes.

"Tangy." She sipped from a water bottle on her desk and glanced at Tom, who sat stone faced. I think she wanted him to explain why she was laying all this out for a civilian.

I pressed on. "Did he seem worried?"

"He worked hard to put out the loving-husband-worried vibe. He tried calling Mrs. Gregg. No answer, of course. At that point, I invited the Congressman to return with me to my office."

"Lemme guess," I said. "He got testy. Demanded to know if he's a suspect. Told you he'd have your badge. That you'd never work in law enforcement again."

"You watch too many movies, Mr. Stewart."

"Will, please. And I've seen how politicians treated my wife."

Kresky smirked. "I did think it was funny when the governor kept calling her a 'deputy.' Anyway, he followed me back here and spent the better part of the day in my office. Mr. Helpful. I couldn't get rid of him."

"Helpful how?" I sincerely wished the Great Stone Face sitting next to me would throw in a question or two.

"The man was nonstop chatty. First it was all about these mysterious girlfriends of the wife. Who they might be. Where they went. He rattled off names of people to call. We made calls. Nobody knew anything about a weekend getaway."

"How did he react to that?"

"He went through a transition. The picture changed."

"He changed his story?"

"No. He's a little too smart for that. But he put on show of concern when none of the wife's friends knew about the weekend getaway."

"Put on?" Tom asked. *Finally.*

"The man's an actor. Everything is an act. Anyway, the girlfriends became nefarious operators, and the weekend getaway became a kidnapping. And that opened a floodgate. He said people have been making threats. Deep State operatives have been watching him. He shifted gears and declared his wife had been abducted. He laid out all the dire things that must have happened to his wife. He made all manner of investigative suggestions and demanded we follow up with him on each one."

I let silence prompt the Sheriff to go on.

"You see what he did, of course. He didn't change his story."

"He let the facts change it for him."

"By the time he left my office he had cooked up a conspiracy bigger than JFK. Then he got in front of a camera as fast as he could. You probably know the rest. It's all about kidnapping and forces out to destroy him. He claims to have evidence that Deep State operatives have him on a target list and abducted his wife to cripple his run for the Senate seat. He claims to have evidence that Satan-worshiping Democrats are behind the abduction."

"Democrats aren't that organized or religious," Tom muttered.

"Did he produce any evidence?"

"Not to me. He says it's classified. Locked up in a secure vault in D.C. because it's the key to a major Congressional investigation he's launching." Kresky rolled her eyes. "Gregg's a big believer in the Deep State and that Q crap. He says Antifa has him on a death list."

"Ah. The go-to villain ever since Bond put SPECTRE out of business," I said.

"I don't know how that conspiracy shit gets in the blood, but Gregg's all in. A devotee. He's a regular talking head on some of the Fox shows, and he's the darling of the right-wing streaming sites. Even the ones talking about lizard people. I looked at some of his blog posts. He wants to impeach three of the Supreme Court Justices—the same three that internet sources claim are aliens. He advocates for arming every American to prepare for the coming civil war. He wants a death penalty for Wisconsin. He's all in on most of the anti-immigration stuff that fronts for white supremacy. And anyone or anything that voices an opinion to the contrary is—according to Gregg—controlled by the Deep State or the Jewish international banking conspiracy—"

"Ah, yes," I said. "The people seeking world domination through overdraft fees."

"Gregg blames everyone in sight. Even one of our county commissioners. She happens to be the one who presided over his last OUI. He's had four, you know."

"Convictions?"

"Arrests. Three of the four got converted. The fourth went before said commissioner, who is not a fan and wouldn't play ball and is now an enemy of the state, according to Gregg. And don't get me started on how he rings the chime for the backwoods militia up here. You know, we have a robust minority community. Gregg and his close ties to the local militia types makes many of our citizens of color deeply uncomfortable."

"Does he have a theory about his wife?"

Kresky made a sour face. "Gregg's theory is that the Deep State operatives took her into the woods and are holding her in a cabin or a cave – the story fluctuates. He says they're going to put her on trial and execute her like those dimwits in Michigan said they wanted to do to the governor there. But then he also says they're going to make it look like she got lost. Died of exposure. He claims that's how these operators do things. Make things look accidental."

"Jesus."

Tom twisted in his seat to face me. "I don't know if Andy ever told you, but some suspects we interrogate tell us what happened by making it sound like they're spit-balling ideas, pretending to be helpful, thinking we won't suspect them when it turns out to be true."

"Is that what Gregg did?" I asked the sheriff.

"Gregg is all over the board. But he said something that stuck out. He insists that the clock is ticking—that we do something fast to find his beloved wife, because people can go without food for a couple weeks but can only go without water for three days. A hundred hours, he said, like he looked it up."

"Why would he assume she has no water?"

"Exactly."

"Even in the woods up here, if she's just lost, there's water around."

"It rained last night." Kresky sat back in her chair. She picked up a pen and rolled it between her fingers. "A comment like that—a bit of extra unsolicited insight—it might as well be fluorescent."

Kresky stopped speaking. I left the silence alone. A moment passed.

"Did he let you search his place?" Tom asked.

"Mister Cooperation, like I said. Didn't find anything, except for the wife's clothes tossed all over."

"All over the house?"

"All over the property. I mean everywhere. Admitting he dumped her clothes all over the place proves he's innocent, of course."

"*If I'm guilty, I would have covered it up,*" Tom said. "Heard that one before.

Kresky looked me over again. She sighed.

"What do you think, Sheriff?" I asked.

"I will deny I said it if you repeat this, Will, but I think he has her. Maybe he's denying her water so that when she perishes, he thinks there will be no sign of foul play. That water comment…I don't know, it just stood out."

I began to see the light.

"When did you say she went missing?" I asked.

"Tuesday morning."

I checked my watch and did the math.

12

"Oh, what fresh recipe for shit is this?" Sheriff Kresky turned to the windows behind her desk. Tom and I stood to see what she was seeing.

Figures scrambled from the parked press vans on the street below. Camera operators mounted cameras on their shoulders and hustled across the pavement chasing their on-air talent. The minor invasion angled toward the courthouse steps.

A silver crew cab pickup truck docked at the curb below the steps. The front passenger door opened and a man in a blue suit with a bright red tie stepped into the collected camera focus. There was no mistaking the high, pale forehead of Congressman Gregg. The too-narrow set of his eyes conflicted with his square forehead and square jaw. He struck me as a man who saw himself as handsome in a mirror or on television, more so than his features warranted. He gauged the gathering crowd and hurried up the steps, touching perfectly coiffed hair on the way. Halfway to the top, he turned and established the pillared courthouse façade as a backdrop. A row of reporters formed a semicircle. They held out microphones and mobile devices. He struck a pose.

"I told that man to go home and stay there," the Bear County Sheriff muttered.

"And who are these dipshits?" I asked.

A motley parade of pickup trucks and SUVs rolled up the street. The lead vehicle swung to a stop angled across the nose of Gregg's truck. Half of the trucks mounted flag poles. A mix of American flags, MIA flags and bastardizations of the American standard with imprinted slogans fluttered as the trucks pulled up.

The roadhouse train stopped in the traffic lane.

Sheriff Kresky huffed a clipped sigh. "The Bunker Hill Victory Brigade. Our version of northwoods militia. Buncha Rambo wannabes."

Men piled out of the vehicles. Most looked older than me if the gray- and silver-streaked beards and unruly hair told the tale. They paused long enough to pull military-style weapons from the pickup and SUV cabs and sling the straps over their shoulders or hold the guns at port arms. In a half-hearted attempt at order, they formed a single file. A few reached out to grasp the shoulder of the man ahead. The group trotted up the court-house steps and assembled in a line behind the Congressman, who nodded at them.

"Dummies," I said. "Don't they know the battle was fought on Breed's hill? And that we lost?"

"Don't confuse them with the facts." Sheriff Kresky turned and retrieved her holstered handgun from a desk drawer. She clipped the weapon to her belt. "Tom, I appreciate you coming, and you're welcome to assist if you stay out of my way and away from cameras. Mr. Stewart, I'm sorry, but you have to go."

"No worries," I quickly raised both hands. "I know the drill. Chief, a word?"

"I'll be along, Sue," Tom said.

Her expression formed a question. He shook his head. Whatever code or secret language these two shared, his gesture signaled the end of the conversation.

She escorted us out, then hurried to join a pair of deputies looking in her direction for instructions. The three of them quickly left the Sheriff's Office.

Tom and I followed at a distance. We descended a wide marble stair-case and crossed the broad public entrance to the courthouse. We watched the impromptu press conference from behind ornate glass and brass doors. Kresky and her deputies took up positions outside, carefully avoiding the camera lenses. News crews and reporters clustered in front of Gregg and his paunchy color guard.

"Sue told me that they did a second search of Gregg's property. No objection. No resistance. No wife. I think you should go up there."

"And what?"

"Watch him. Be there with him when he thinks no one is looking." He looked me over. "Did you bring some of those little motor things?"

I patted the thigh pocket of my cargo pants. He nodded.

"Gregg may think because his place has been searched twice, he can let his guard down. Sue wanted to hit the place again. With dogs. With the K-9 unit from Rhinelander. But she knows that won't help."

"Why not?"

Tom stared at the back of Gregg's head. "Because he knew. He knew they'd bring in dogs."

"Ah! The clothes."

Tom nodded. "Can you find your way?"

"I think I can hitch a ride."

13

Tom and I split up. He exited the building's main entrance. I hiked
back through the marble lobby to the first floor's arterial hallway. A
red Exit sign at the end of the hall caught my eye. I followed the beacon
to a side-door entrance. I anticipated alarm warnings, but the heavy twin
doors made no such threat. I pushed the safety bar and the door opened.

The Bear County Courthouse dominated a block across from a park at
the center of Linden. Storefronts and shops surrounded the courthouse and
park. Saturday foot traffic took advantage of summer's last sunshine and
the warm September air. The sudden traffic jam and media assembly
below Sheriff Kresky's office windows drew pedestrians from the
surrounding sidewalks.

I chose the opposite direction. I followed a sidewalk to the back of the
courthouse. There, I found a set of concrete steps that descended below
ground level to a door accessing the basement of the old building. I
checked for a camera and found none. Perfect.

Trying to look like someone who belonged, I dropped down the steps
until my head sank out of sight.

Fwooomp!

I vanished. Without breaking stride, I kicked off and ascended. I rose
quickly and grabbed the railing that surrounded the cellar entrance.
Hanging weightless, I pulled a small flashlight body from my pocket

along with an accompanying carbon-fiber propeller—both of which had vanished with me. I snapped the prop onto the shaft of a small electric motor mounted on the end of the tube, then used my thumb on a slide control to test the power unit. The fan hummed—first forward, then in reverse.

"Aerodynamic Navigation and Drive Inertia—Electric," I announced to myself. "Behold. The ANDIE."

I couldn't wait to tell my wife that I had finally come up with a name for the power units that she would appreciate. Serious effort went into the project—at least one six-pack of Corona and several long evenings on the front porch while the sun set. The prospect of unveiling it during my visit doubled my anticipation.

I heaved myself off the steel rail. The power unit whined. I surged forward, retracing my route ten feet above the sidewalk.

A short flight around the building took me to the impromptu press conference on the courthouse steps. A small crowd of onlookers gathered, wildly outnumbered by the reporters, on-camera talent, and camera operators. The line of armed civilian militia actors had grown. Some wore helmets—motorcycle, sports and what looked like military surplus. A few wore obvious body armor. Others had bloated torsos suggesting armor under their shirts. A wild range of belts and equipment draped nearly every militiaman. The belts carried extra ammunition for rifles slung in the current military fashion of American combat soldiers. Canteens, pouches, and batons added weight to the web belts. One militiaman mounted a selection of Tasers on a pair of crossed bandoliers. The men (there were no women in the ranks) represented the full spectrum of size and age. I spotted a teen who looked a lot like a kid who made the news after killing two protesters in Kenosha, Wisconsin—fresh faced, barely shaving and armed to the teeth. The man beside him in line looked flushed and breathless for having climbed the steps. He had to be eighty. Unlike a legitimate military assembly, the brigade lacked uniformity of anything except the grim game faces they aimed at the media.

This group could have been recruited from Spellman's marriage picnic.

Congressman Martin Gregg posed, silent. Tom joined Kresky on the perimeter. She spoke to her phone. Whatever she had to say, she didn't want it said over open radio waves.

I looked for federal authorities. Tom's comment that Gregg demanded a U.S. Government investigation made me wonder if the FBI had sent a team. No one present suggested federal credentials, but then I thought of Leslie, who could easily look like anything but a federal officer if she wanted to.

Reporters shouted questions for Gregg. He held a defiant pose and ignored them. I took the delay for vanity until I saw two Bunker Hill Patriots trot from the pickup trucks with American flags in hand. They climbed the steps and after a bit of stage direction from Gregg, they posed in bracket formation behind him, tilting the flags to center so that The Stars and Stripes hung broadly behind the Congressman.

With this final touch in place, Gregg turned to face the cameras.

I thumbed the power unit control slide and brought myself to a halt at center stage, roughly ten feet above the reporters on the steps. I got a little aggressive and the unit whined briefly, causing several faces to turn upward. As always, fear of discovery fluttered in my gut, but seeing nothing overhead to explain the noise, the curious faces turned back to Gregg.

Gregg lifted his arms, gesturing for silence. He sustained the righteous pose a moment longer than necessary, then spoke.

"They came for my wife!" he cried out. "My family!" Long pause. "The woman I love!" Another long pause. I wondered how his pregnant intern would feel about that pronouncement. "How long have I warned you about this? How long have you ignored the signs? I hear it every day! I see it every day in the festering halls of Congress! Left-wing socialist radicals plotting against America. Fascist Antifa organizers who send mobs of protesters to burn our cities and beat and murder our brave men and women in blue. I have shouted the warnings and the lamestream media has laughed at me or denigrated me or outright lied. Now I've been targeted. Why? To silence me. To make me cower."

"Never happen!" one of the men backing Gregg shouted. "Got your back!"

"Not leaving your sight!"

"We've got you! Twenty-four seven!"

A few others grunted approval.

Gregg paused. He pulled a cloth handkerchief from his suit pocket and dramatically dabbed his eyes. "They took my wife...and they think they will win. But my beloved Casey would never want me to surrender. *I will not surrender!* Not going to happen. No way. Never." More eye dabbing. I squinted but detected no sign of moisture.

The backup singers grunted support and approval. Gregg paid them an appreciative nod. He turned to the cameras and stuck out his arm, one finger extended, pointing.

"You're next. And you. And you. They're coming for your freedom. For your rights. For your family. *For your guns!*" I glanced down the line of his arm, aimed over the heads of the reporters and cameras. For the most part his finger landed on empty lawn and sidewalk.

Gregg dropped his arm. "In a moment, I will go inside to confer with state and federal law enforcement officials. I have here…" he extracted a folded document from his coat pocket and held it up "…key evidence that proves the conspiracy against me. It will be up to law enforcement to root out these traitors to America and, I pray to my Lord and Savior above, return my beloved Casey to me!"

He turned his back. Reporters below the steps shouted over each other for his attention. He ignored them. The ranks of his militia bodyguards split for him to pass. His flag bearers shuffled for a moment, confused, before falling in beside Gregg. They escorted him up the remaining steps to the courthouse doors.

Sheriff Kresky hustled inside, using the door farthest from the center.

Tom stayed back and watched the procession, then shoved his hands in his pockets and strolled down the steps. He walked across the lawn to the corner of the building. Without a glance back, he turned the corner and disappeared from my view.

"THAT WAS QUITE A SHOW," I said when I caught up to him. "Didn't know the feds were here."

"They're not," he growled. "FBI was notified. State DCI did a conference call with Sue, but they haven't sent investigators either."

Tom stopped and looked around. "Are you going to show yourself or are you going to make me look like I'm talking to myself?"

"That's not weird anymore, you know," I said. "People talk to phone earpieces all the time."

"Still looks stupid."

"Meet me in back."

I waited for him by the cellar entrance after using the stairwell to reappear. Tom sauntered to the railing, hands still in his pockets, deep in thought. He didn't speak immediately, so I ventured to ask, "What's coffee at oh dark thirty?"

He shuffled his feet and huffed a breath. I saw a trace of smile, the mark of a distant but still warm memory.

"I told you. Sue and I served in the same unit. We pulled some long night duty shifts. You slog through the small hours and you're ready to staple your eyelids. Drank gallons of coffee. A cup with a brother in arms at those hours, it's just you and the coffee and the night. And truth. No bullshit. No rank."

"Got it."

Tom shoved his hands in his hip pockets.

"He's got her."

"Okay, then."

14

After Gregg made a show of his new "evidence" for the press, I guessed correctly that Kresky was in for another long session of theorizing and grievance-filled prompting. It gave me time to consider the impact of Gregg's round-the-clock security guards on my options.

The media cluster on the courthouse steps broke up. A few reporters stationed themselves with the appropriate backdrop to perform Breaking News remotes for their respective networks. I wondered how much of Gregg's rant would make the cut.

The Bunker Hill Victory Brigade retreated to their trucks. A deputy asked them to move their vehicles out of the traffic lane. Plenty of parking around the corner, I heard him advise the group as I strolled past. He seemed friendly and acquainted with a few of the armed militiamen. The presence of their weaponry did not appear to cause concern.

I crossed the street and cut across the town square on an angle that took me past a gazebo large enough to showcase a high school band. At the far side of the square, I crossed the next street. Two businesses attracted the bulk of the Saturday traffic. A corner café that shared DNA with the Silver Spoon in Essex pumped the scent of breakfast sausage and fried onions into the street. At mid-block, an Ace Hardware store lured customers with sidewalk exhibits of pre-season snowblowers, tools and bagged bird seed.

A bell on a heavy hardwood door jingled my arrival at the hardware store. A woman in her sixties or seventies attended to the single cash register at the front counter, deftly scanning purchases for a line of customers. A teenaged boy stood beside her, bagging the goods, ready to carry heavy items out to cars.

Creaky wooden floors and claustrophobic aisles greeted me. The scent of paint and steel and wood sweetened the air. I love a good hardware store. The older the better. I slipped into a narrow aisle lined with paint cans. The depth of the storefront business surprised me. The long aisle took me to the back of the store, which opened to a maze of new aisles, each stacked to the ceiling. An entire wall harbored endless rows of drawers filled with screws, fasteners, and nails.

A man roughly the age of the cashier leaned on a countertop below a sign that advertised Customer Service. He asked if he could help me find something.

"Glue?"

He pointed. "Aisle six, halfway down on your left side."

"Thanks."

I found a robust section of bottled, tubed and syringe-packed glues. It took a few minutes to locate cyanoacrylate. Superglue. The cardboard backer into which a small plastic bottle was sealed promised instant adhesion and strength measured in hundreds of pounds. I plucked two from the display hooks.

At the checkout, I waited for two customers in line to pay and clear before placing the purchase on the scarred countertop.

"Find everything?" the woman asked, waving one of the two cards under a scanner twice.

"I did." I counted out bills to cover the purchase. She rang it up and handed back change.

"Need a bag for those?"

"No, but may I borrow a scissors?"

She produced a pair from a drawer. I took them from her and stepped aside to make room for the next customer. The teenaged boy had disappeared on some errand. I noted a wastebasket near where he had been stationed. I stripped the cardboard and plastic from the two small bottles and dropped the debris in the wastebasket, then removed the bottle caps. I carefully snipped the tips off the pointed dispensers, then tightly resealed each cap. I returned the scissors to the counter.

"Thanks!"

"Don't go gluing your fingers together," she advised me with a smile.

"I'll try not to."

"CEEVES." Tom answers on the second ring.

"It's Will. I've got my phone with me. When I'm outta sight I can't call out, but I use a Bluetooth earpiece, so I can hear an incoming call. Maybe you should check in with me every couple hours. If I can answer, I will."

"Okay."

"Alright, then…uh…over and out."

Tom said nothing so I ended the call feeling like an idiot.

I absorbed late afternoon sun on a bench near the town square gazebo. The convoy of pickup trucks remained parked in traffic in front of the courthouse. Apparently, the Bunker Hill Brigade did not feel inclined to obey the deputy's alternate parking request. Likewise, the deputy did not feel inclined to force the issue. The Brigade milled about on the pavement beside their trucks. The deputy was nowhere to be seen. A few reporters remained in position, but the bulk of the media had retreated to their vehicles.

I wondered how long Gregg would bend the sheriff's ear. The scent coming from the corner café tortured me. I knew the drill, however. The moment I dashed to the café and placed an order Gregg would emerge from the courthouse, his cavalry would mount up, and I'd miss my connection.

I considered texting Tom. Perhaps he could learn Gregg's home address and text it to me. Or I could dig it up myself using my phone. I had time on my hands. With his address and the map on my phone, I wouldn't have to catch a ride with Gregg.

What I didn't have, however, was extra batteries, or room to carry them. Three power units strained the hip pockets of my pants. Each unit offered roughly forty minutes of continuous power. More than enough most of the time, but if I had to travel to Gregg's horse farm under my own power, it would potentially drain a significant portion of my battery fuel. And what if Gregg didn't return home? My plan to hook a ride with Gregg in the back of his pickup truck offered the added benefit of staying with him if he diverted.

Which meant sitting and watching and waiting.

Which meant no sandwich. Or extra batteries from the hardware store, something I should have thought of on my first shopping trip.

The scent from the café harassed me for another hour before Gregg emerged. I cursed my decision not to run to the café.

When Gregg broke through the doors of the courthouse and descended the steps, a few of the reporters hurried to meet him. He paused midway down the steps and fielded questions. The distance between the interview and my park bench perch prohibited me from hearing the exchange. That same distance, however, meant that few people present in the town square were looking in my direction when I stood up and walked toward a narrow gap between a substantial oak tree and one corner of the hexagonal gazebo. Transiting the gap, blocked from view—

Fwooomp!

—I vanished. Released from gravity, my inner organs shifted slightly, a feeling astronauts struggle to describe.

Rising and gliding, I fished a power unit and prop from my pants pocket, snapped them together, and held it forward in my right hand. My thumb found the slide control and the prop whizzed obediently. I accelerated and stabilized my height. I gained enough speed to set up a silent glide to Gregg's pickup, still parked at the curb in front of the courthouse. The truck loitered beside a fire hydrant, yet no ticket had been tucked under his windshield. Was that Congressional privilege or a lack of desire for confrontation on the part of the Sheriff's Department?

The ticketless windshield approached. I rotated lengthwise above the pavement and stuffed my inert power unit in my back pocket. I extended both hands and closed a grip on a light bar above the crew cab. I used my hold on the light bar to stop, rotate, and drop my legs into the empty pickup bed. Provided none of the militiamen jumped in, I had my ride.

Gregg's second press conference of the day continued. A young woman holding a recording device called out.

"Can you tell us what proof you offer the law enforcement authorities of your allegations?"

the line of vehicles, which had thinned out. I counted five. Several had peeled off during the drive from town.

Gregg climbed back in the cab and his truck shot forward. His driver found parking in front of an eight-car garage adjoining the back of the house. One of four broad doors lifted but the driver killed the motor without pulling in.

Splashes of color randomly dotted the property as far as I could see. Women's clothing. A matched set of four-wheel drive Gators parked near the main stable explained how Gregg had executed his tantrum across so much territory.

I didn't think my wife would reconcile with me if I emptied her closet across ten acres.

The pickup cab doors opened.

The man who emerged from behind the wheel of the truck cab had the physique of an NFL linebacker, skin the color of a well-tanned lifeguard, and a head shorn of every hair. His polished scalp caught and reflected glints of the late afternoon sun. He wore a gray silk shirt and matching pants. Gold glinted on his wrist. He turned briefly to watch Gregg climb out of the truck before joining the Congressman and entering the single open garage bay door. In that instant I saw two of the lightest colored eyes I've ever seen. Set in a handsome face, the eyes seemed to be a source of their own illumination. The effect was both startling and piercing.

Walking beside Gregg the driver topped the Congressman by half a head. His shoulder span cast a shadow that looked capable of swallowing any man.

I saw no reason to get anywhere near a physical conflict with this man but renewed a vow of cowardice just the same.

Gregg and the driver disappeared into the house. I stopped to consider; men with guns on the outside; a muscled bodyguard on the inside.

My next move revealed itself when my stomach rumbled.

MY ASSIGNMENT SEEMED SIMPLE ENOUGH. Get close to Gregg and stay close. Watch and listen for him to let his guard down and reveal his involvement in his wife's disappearance. Call in the cavalry the instant he makes a mistake. I doubted that he would let slip what he had done with his wife—or that she would be found alive, if found. The countdown clock launched by Gregg's pointed comment about dying without water diminished hope with every passing minute.

I tried to acknowledge the slim chance that Gregg knew nothing about his wife's disappearance. He might be telling the truth. Crazed political extremists may have abducted the woman and spirited her away just as he said.

Bullshit.

Imaginary extremists or not, Casey Gregg might be imprisoned at a remote site in the vast empty tracts of northern Wisconsin woods. In a cabin. Or a hole in the ground. Or a cave. She might be bound. Or immobilized. Drugged. Or buried alive. She might be clawing at the inside of a rusted Buick trunk miles from anyone who would hear her cries.

Or she might be dead.

But not at the hands of wild-eyed socialists.

I marched in full agreement with Tom that the Congressman had a dirty hand in Casey Gregg's disappearance. Where I differed with Tom was in the idea that Gregg would reveal his guilt if I hovered around and spied on him. The man thrived as a showman, an actor. He savored the spotlight. I believed he could effortlessly sustain a charade of grief and concern well past the end of his countdown clock.

Unless I found a way to make him break character.

A few minutes behind Gregg and his aide/driver/protector, I slipped through the garage and into the house via the same unlocked door they used. A mudroom the size of my living room separated the main house from the garage. Racks on the walls stored a variety of outdoor wear, coats, hoodies, and fleeces. A woman's boots and riding gear littered the floor and several shelves. Saddles rested on purpose-build racks. The glossy leather smelled good and appeared well-tended.

From the mudroom, I floated into a massive kitchen.

The kitchen featured several huge refrigerator/freezer units, a cooking island with built in griddles, a sink large enough to bathe in, and cabinet space the staff of a small restaurant would envy. A high ceiling dangled tiny halogen lamps that embedded every shiny surface with a sheen of spilled diamonds. Despite the size and the abundance of stainless steel and granite, dark wood trim lent the room an inexplicable comfort and warmth. I imagined living a vibrant life with Andy and nine noisy children in a place like this.

I pocketed my power unit and used a door frame to propel myself to the handle on the nearest refrigerator. I pulled the door open. Though well stocked, nothing looked portable or ready-to-eat. A second refrigerator contained multiple fruit drawers. I scored an apple and then found a package of smoked turkey. I rolled both in the front of my t-shirt. They vanished.

Checking cabinets, I found a cache of imported English biscuits—cookies, to my American taste. I added a tube of the treats to my booty, then retreated from the house, closing the door to the garage quietly in my wake.

I deployed a power unit and launched through the garage. Clear of the open door, I made note of several power lines running between buildings, then initiated a slow flight across the asphalt pad between the house and main stable. I angled to the right and passed the open end of the building. A glance inside revealed a broad central aisle lined with individual horse stalls. Horse scent suggested occupancy, but the stalls were dark. Without a closer look, I could not be sure. Curiosity tugged at me, but lunch remained a priority. Exploring the stable interior could wait until my shirt wasn't bulging with food. I cleared the corral fences and swung around to the back of the stable. A round riding arena spread itself under an open-sided metal roof. At the center, ranks of bleachers nudged the back of the stable.

The bleachers might have been a good place to reappear and eat, but they felt a little exposed. Except for Gregg's pickup truck, I hadn't seen any other vehicles, but a property this size surely had hired hands. I planned to unvanish for my late lunch and didn't need some stable boy spotting me. I widened my circuit. Orderly fenced pastures backed up the stable complex. Beyond the last fence, a mix of farm fields and uncut woodland stretched into the distance.

Two birds with one stone; lunch and a little reconnaissance.

I aimed for a lane that connected to the woodland. The notion of stumbling on Gregg's hiding place for his wife crossed my mind and was just as quickly ejected as an impossible long shot. Kresky said her deputies had already searched the property. What little I knew of the sheriff suggested any search she conducted would have been thorough.

I followed a narrow lane between fenced pastures. Splashes of color lined the path. Gregg had been determined when he threw his wife's clothing all over creation. Colorful blouses, pale undergarments, and items I couldn't readily identify hung on fence posts, lay in tall grass, and dangled from bushes. The trail continued beyond the tidy white board fencing.

Where tilled fields began, I spotted something familiar. A weedy, overgrown rock pile formed an island in the center of a harvested wheat field. As a kid, I had been paid fifty cents an hour to pick stones in such fields and deposit them on similar rock piles or in fence rows. Like some of the stone collections I had seen in my youth, this rock pile also served as the farm's junk heap. Rusted equipment, old appliances, and sundry obsolete hardware nested and decayed among the weeds and rocks. An obsolete hay rake. A discarded water heater. The block of a dead engine. A woman's brassiere hung from the top of a rusting band saw. Gator tracks testified that Gregg had gone out of his way to spread his wife's clothes on the property. A second set of tracks suggested that deputies followed Gregg's tracks.

Tom believed Gregg's clothing tantrum had been a calculated ploy to defeat a K-9 search. Dogs hunting for scent would have alerted to every article of the missing woman's clothing.

If true, by extension—as Andy liked to say and did so in my head—that implied that Casey Gregg was here. Somewhere.

I followed the farm lane to the end of the tilled fields. There, I joined a weedy path into wooded land. Wheel tracks in the grass betrayed passage by Gregg's Gators—again two sets. Gregg flinging clothing. A four-wheeler commandeered by Kresky and her deputies following.

I wondered...was I following the trail Gregg used when he disposed of his wife? The grim notion intensified my examination of the tire indentations. If he stopped and manhandled a woman or her body, there would be signs. I searched for grass crushed by foot traffic where the Gator driver might have dismounted. I looked for but did not find disturbed soil. No shallow graves.

Low branches forced me to descend until my feet swept the top of the grass. Tall thistles brushed my legs.

The trail emerged into a meadow. The wheel tracks made a lollipop loop where the drivers had turned around. Fine meadow grasses would have been crushed if the driver of either Gator had exited the four-wheeler.

No sign of someone leaving their vehicle. Not Gregg. Not the deputies. This has been a simple turnaround. At the center of the loop, a woman's white blouse lay in the grass, arms spread as if sunning itself.

I backtracked to the edge of the meadow. A blown-down dead ash tree with a fan of dirt-coated roots offered a perfect bench seat.

I maneuvered into position and pulled back the levers in my head.

Fwooomp!

Gravity took hold. My butt settled onto the tree's bark, which had not yet begun to rot. The meadow lay before me. Crickets sang. Birds called. A fat bee buzzed past my ear, flashing an unpleasant memory of my trip to Idaho.

I listened intently for unnatural sounds beneath the white noise of nature.

The pounding or scratching of a human hand on the wall of a buried box.

Muted screams.

Nothing.

In any case, such a dungeon or cell would have been betrayed by fresh digging. Except for the tire marks, the meadow remained pristine.

I unrolled my stolen lunch. Halfway through the pack of turkey, my Bluetooth earpiece chirped. I touched the button to connect the call.

Chief Tom Ceeves asked for a report.

"It's just Gregg and a guy who looks like his bodyguard in the house."

"Big fella?"

"And then some."

"That's Heddon."

"Who?"

"His lawyer."

"No shit? Huh. I took him for a bodyguard."

"Sue said the same thing."

"Why wouldn't his lawyer have gone in the Sheriff's Office with Gregg?"

"Confidence."

"In what?" I asked.

"His client either being innocent or getting away with it."

It didn't seem right to me.

"Where are you now?" Tom wanted to know.

"I borrowed some lunch and found a spot at the back of the property. Gave me a chance to search."

"Find anything?"

"No. I'm headed back in shortly."

"Before you go in," Tom said, "I got something for you."

"Permission to beat the truth out of him?"

"Sue put me in touch with the sister-in-law."

I wasn't sure how that helped me.

Tom explained.

16

Before returning to the house, I flew a wide spiral pattern over the property. The search yielded nothing. No shallow graves. No camouflaged Buicks with someone drumming on the inside of the trunk lid. I don't know what I expected to find that the deputies would have missed.

I returned to the house and slipped inside.

I found Gregg and Heddon camped in a weirdly empty room on the first floor. Gregg sat in a plush leather office chair facing a table that supported nothing but a laptop. Photographer's lights on stands bracketed both ends of the table. Screens clamped in front of the lights softened the glow aimed at Gregg. Three of the four walls in the room stood bare. The fourth, behind Gregg, supported floor-to-ceiling bookshelves packed with important-looking hardcover volumes. Several books featuring the face of the President were turned to be fully visible. Another set of American flags bracketed Gregg.

Heddon sat in a second office chair, alternating between watching Gregg, who looked across the top of the open laptop at a small black camera mounted on a tripod, and watching a small monitor resting on an empty crate. He wore a pair of headphones. An open toolbox lay on the floor near a full length mirror off to one side. Brushes and vials of makeup filled the box.

A studio.

Gregg was engaged in animated conversation with someone I could not hear. The Congressman's half of the exchange fervently rehashed the speech he'd given on the courthouse steps. On Heddon's monitor, Gregg shared the screen with an attractive woman. A red banner with white lettering spanned the screen bottom proclaiming the exchange to be Breaking News. Beneath that, the caption read, *"Politically motivated kidnapping threatens Rep. Gregg's bold Senate run."*

The setting had all the trappings of a cable news program, but the logo in the lower right corner was unfamiliar to me. The caption told me this wasn't one of the major news networks, or one particularly concerned with standards of journalism.

Gregg's media campaign held no interest for me except that it tied both men down, giving me free run of the house. I pushed away from the open door and set off to explore the building.

I've been in the homes of wealthy people. Sometimes in the flesh as an invited guest. Other times unseen and unhindered by gravity, wrapped in *the other thing*. Such homes are often like garments; worn rather than lived in. Some are worn with natural grace and others are gaudy costumes adopted by pretenders.

Gregg's horse farm ranch house oozed the latter impression. Heavy wood and leather furniture hammered the rustic vibe. Art, both framed and sculpted, celebrated the horse culture beyond the point of being interesting. A massive great room featured a stone fireplace that could have cooked a bison. Rifles and antique handguns shared space on the walls with several animal heads.

I wished for Andy's company. To my eye, the untouched guest rooms, the mildly rumpled master bedroom, and the pristine oversized bathrooms had all the trappings of wealth and little more. Andy's keen observational skills might have unearthed meaning where I saw none. I left each room feeling as if I missed something.

Touring the second floor, I found a back bedroom with a set of doors that opened onto a small balcony. I checked for alarm wires and found none, although I have no home security expertise. I unlocked the door and opened it just far enough to free the latch bolt from the strike plate.

I waited. No alarm.

Resuming my search, I made a note to ask Tom about Gregg's finances. Whether the horse thing was an affectation or genuine, this property—inside and outside—carried a big price tag. Though I had yet to see any expensive live animals, there was no underestimating the pile of cash this property represented, both in acquisition and maintenance. Kresky said the property was a recent purchase. I wondered if Gregg came from money or if the farm represented the new wealth gained by certain kinds of politicians. If the latter, Gregg did not hesitate to display his good fortune.

I descended from the second floor to a basement that was both vast and empty. The cellar housed nothing but the essential HVAC and plumbing equipment. No secret rooms. No work bench full of nefarious tools. No cages or chains or dungeon. No unpacked boxes from a recent move.

When I returned to the first floor, I found Gregg and Heddon eating microwaved dinners in the great room. They fixed their attention on a huge wall-mounted flatscreen. Gregg used a technology I had at home but had never mastered to divide the screen and watch several cable news channels at the same time. Every few seconds Gregg obsessively changed emphasis, alternating between Fox, Newsmax and something called One America Network. It was easy to see why. Gregg's make-up coated and soft-lit face appeared on each, calmly stating his case, making emphatic accusations, and identifying the many enemies responsible for his tragedy. The appearances featured Gregg's bookish home studio backdrop. Occasionally, tape of his courthouse appearances interrupted, some from the performance I'd seen, some from days earlier. He wore the same suit in all of them, but my aviator's eye caught differences in the weather.

Casey Gregg's image popped up in rotating collages that featured her in social settings, on the arm of the Congressman, meeting the President. She looked pretty and confident, the perfect accessory for a media-hungry politician.

Gregg ate and watched and commented.

"This is good!"

"I should have hit that harder."

"Look at her hair. Jesus."

I saw nothing resembling grief or stress. Heddon made comments about trending and the play of certain phrases.

More and more, I agreed with Tom's uncharacteristic prejudice of guilt. However, nothing in the pleasure Gregg took from looking good on camera advanced my mission.

I floated high in the room near a panel of floor-to-ceiling windows overlooking the empty front yard when the Sheriff and K-9 unit arrived. I saw them first, but in close succession Gregg's phone rang. He grunted a response, then said to Heddon, "The dogs are here."

"I'll get the camera." Heddon set aside his dinner tray and hustled off toward the studio room. He moved with remarkable ease and grace for a large man.

Gregg remained seated. He watched the big screen and scooped up his dinner.

THE K-9 SEARCH unfolded as Tom predicted.

Sheriff Kresky and a deputy dismounted from their SUV. An officer in blue emerged from an SUV with a Rhinelander Police Department decal. He opened the rear hatch and hooked a leash on an anxious dog.

Gregg met the officers on the parking lot behind the house. Heddon tagged along holding the same small black camera that had been used for Gregg's television appearances. I played catch-up after being forced to wait until Heddon and Gregg left the house before making my own exit. I drifted behind and above them.

The K-9 officer immediately asked about the articles of clothing strewn about the yard. Gregg abruptly covered his eyes with one hand and held up the other to signal for a pause. He tried to speak, stopped, tried again. In halting words, he confessed to a moment of anger that he and his wife had since resolved, yet was seared in his memory, something he would regret to his last breath if anything bad has happened to his beloved Casey. Heddon stood to one side documenting the performance.

"Don't you think you should pick all this up?" Kresky asked, gesturing at the garments.

Gregg fought back a forced sob. "I have more important things to think about, Sheriff! You don't seem to grasp that my wife's life is at stake here!" He turned on the K-9 handler. "You're wasting your time here. You should be searching where it matters."

The K-9 officer looked at Kresky and shrugged. "I can't..."

"At all?" Kresky asked.

The officer shook his head.

Gregg abruptly recovered his composure. "I told you. Searching here is a waste of valuable time and resources." He produced a folded map. "This is where you should search." He expanded the map and held it up. "Here. These tracts of land are rumored to belong to Antifa Extremists. There have been reports. Training camps, weapons." He stabbed the map with his finger.

"And you know this...how?" Kresky asked.

"Sources I cannot disclose. Part of an official Congressional investigation. Just sharing this with you, I might be violating Congressional rules. But I'm willing to do anything, *anything,* if my Casey is out there. Leave any stone unturned, Sheriff. We're running out of time! This is where you should set loose the dogs to search."

"You mean leave *no* stone unturned," Kresky said. Gregg pushed the map into the hands of the K-9 officer, who looked helplessly at Kresky.

"You sure the dog won't hunt?"

"The dog takes scent from an article of clothing. Look around." The K-9 officer shook his head. "They'll alert to every blouse and pair of slacks on the property."

Gregg ignored the clothing issue. He renewed his pitch, insisting that the source of his information came from the very top of the conspirator ranks. Inside information, he repeated several times.

The Sheriff asked Gregg to please step back.

As I watched the scene from above, a loose ring of militiamen assembled around the meeting. They kept their distance and stood with rifles at the ready, which Kresky and her deputies ignored.

Kresky took the map from the K-9 officer.

"These tracts are miles away. Some of it as far south as the flowage. We came here to search *this* property."

"For the third time? How does that help? I repeat. You're wasting valuable time."

Heddon joined the conversation. He spoke quietly, clearly and with authority.

"Sheriff, two searches have already been conducted. What is your foundation for requesting a new search? Do you have new information? If not, then the resources deployed, with the deep gratitude of the Congressman, would be better applied to this new information that the Congressman provided."

The K-9 officer asked for a word with the sheriff. They stepped out of earshot, but the way he pointed at the clothing markers said enough. Kresky listened, stood still for a moment, then gestured at her colleagues to go. She strolled back to where Gregg watched her.

"Congressman," she said quietly, "we will know what happened."

"I pray to the Lord in Heaven that we will."

I don't think you should, I thought, noting the cold steel in Kresky's gaze.

The trio of police vehicles U-turned and departed. The gathered militiamen received a fresh word of thanks from Gregg, then watched him retreat with Heddon to the house.

I stayed to make note of where the weekend warriors stationed themselves. Only seven remained of the force that had deployed on the courthouse steps. Two boarded a pickup and drove back to the end of the long driveway. Three went to the full-span porch on the front of the house. The remaining two wandered to the back yard where they had commandeered lawn furniture for their vigil.

I noted the sun, deep orange and half sunk behind black tree silhouettes. It would be dark soon. Even without being able to read my watch, I calculated that Casey Gregg didn't have much time.

I pulled a power unit and initiated a glide across the stable yard. I climbed through a gap in the wires between buildings and skimmed over the roof of the main stable. Far enough from the outside sentries to avoid detection, I added power and aimed for the woods where I'd eaten lunch.

A quick trip out and back.

17

The end of evening civil twilight defines the point at which I can log flight time as night flight time. I asked my first flight instructor when evening civil twilight ends. His answer: When it gets dark. I found out much later that the end of evening civil twilight is calculated as the moment at which the center of the sun is six degrees below the horizon. My old CFI's answer made more sense, since it's impossible to see the sun below the horizon.

My trip out to the meadow and back took just long enough to reach the end of evening civil twilight. A faint blue-black glow remained in the western sky, but I noted that the wires between buildings had become impossible to distinguish when I returned. The darkness became apparent when I glided back into the yard and found the Bunker Hill Victory Brigade guardians huddled around a roaring fire in Gregg's back yard fire pit. The contrasting light from the fire painted the yard black in all directions.

Gregg had closed the garage, and I presume the house as well. I anticipated finding the doors locked. Only after realizing that all of the back bedrooms opened onto identical small balconies overlooking the pastures did it occur to me that I hadn't figured out which door I left ajar. First things first. I cruised along the edge of the roof until it terminated. I swung left, followed the gutter to the front of the house, then hooked left again to where the Bunker Hill Brigade camped on a vast front porch. Like good soldiers, they had stacked their rifles as a ready-for-war tripod not far from where they performed their guard duties in Gregg's plush wicker furniture. A cooler sat on the floor at the center of their small circle. Each man cradled a cold beer.

I grabbed the roof gutter and pocketed my power unit. Keeping a light touch on the gutter, I coasted until I hung directly above the stacked rifles.

From another pocket, I extracted a bottle of cyanoacrylate glue. I pulled the top off and pocketed it, then held the unseen bottle up against a warm porch light set in a classic lantern fixture. I slowly tipped the bottle and squeezed. After a moment, a glistening drop broke from the bottle, appeared, and fell away.

Perfect.

I pushed myself down from the gutter until my toes touched the front porch boards. There, with a grip on the front porch railing, I leaned over the tripod of rifles.

It only took a minute.

Finished, I lightly pushed off and floated back to the gutter. I carefully pulled the plastic cap from my pocket and snapped it on the pointed tip of the glue bottle.

The boys in the back yard did not follow the rifle stacking protocol, probably because they only had two weapons. Instead, they tipped their rifles against the arms of the lawn furniture they had set up around the fire pit. I decided not to use the furniture for hand holds, since my touch might transmit through the frames. I set up a glide from the roof to a small tree, then repositioned and pushed slowly off the tree. I skimmed across the grass on a line that took me to the backs of their chairs. Within reach, I pinched the short-shaved grass to come to a stop.

Stationary, I carefully extracted the glue bottle and went to work. I didn't mind overweight special forces wannabes hanging around. I just didn't like fat fingers on live triggers.

A few minutes later, I let myself in the second-floor balcony door and slipped through the empty guest bedroom. I checked the darkened hallway and listened. Faint, distant television voices rose from the first floor. Gregg and Heddon had returned to monitor media coverage.

Just to be certain, I checked each bedroom on the second floor. All were dark. In the master bedroom, I spotted a framed photo of Casey

Gregg on a dresser top. The woman had a girlish smile that lit up her eyes. She had Pidge's pixie-short hair, but in black. She looked happily at whoever aimed the camera lens in her direction. I wondered if it had been Gregg.

I slipped the frame under my shirt. It disappeared.

GREGG LOUNGED in an overstuffed recliner facing his wall-mounted television. He remained in his business suit, but without jacket or tie. Both were close at hand. It made me wonder if he expected to appear in front of more cameras soon. The end table beside his chair held a tray, and on the tray a tumbler and half-consumed bottle of Wild Turkey. Not my drink of choice, but under the circumstances, I liked that he'd had a few.

Except for the bright dominance of the television, the room relied on shaded lamps for low-level light.

Gregg struck a casual pose in the chair. One leg extended on the recliner pad. One knee raised. He sipped from his drink and fixed a pleased expression on his own television image. Once more, Congressman Martin Gregg hurled allegations of deep threats and complex conspiracies that were so efficiently executed they left no evidence of their existence.

Heddon was nowhere to be seen.

I pushed off the door frame and retreated to the kitchen, thinking that Gregg's associate might be snacking. The kitchen lights were off. The room empty.

When I returned from the meadow, I noted that the garage door had been closed. I assumed the crew cab pickup truck had been pulled inside. A trip through the mudroom and a quick survey of the garage showed me half a dozen vehicles, none of them the crew cab pickup.

Heddon had departed.

Was that good or bad? If he ran out to get pizza and planned to return shortly, it was bad. If he was done for the night and had gone home, it was good.

I had no way of knowing.

I carefully re-closed the garage door and navigated back in the direction of Congressman Martin Gregg.

Showtime.

18

"Y'all missed something, honeybunch."

I used a breathy whisper, a toneless approximation of what I hoped would sound female. I delivered the line in the brief silence that hangs when the cable television talk show host asked his audience to stay tuned, there's more to come.

Gregg's hand hovered over the remote. He froze.

The screen switched to a commercial for erectile disfunction medication, and a rock and roll music track launched loudly. Gregg grabbed the remote, aimed it at the screen for emphasis and punched the mute button.

Silence filled the room. He tipped his head.

I moved behind his chair to the opposite side.

"Y'all slipped up, sweetcakes. They're on to you."

He shot up out of his chair. It startled me. I reflexively grabbed the back of the chair, prepared to shove myself to the tall ceiling.

Gregg spun around.

"What the fuck!" He searched the room. "Who's there?"

I let silence twist his nerves tighter.

Gregg searched the room. He jerked his head from side to side, then stood rigid, head cocked, listening. He did not move for a full minute.

When he huffed and inhaled loudly, I realized he'd been holding his breath. He gulped in air.

"Fuck." He reached for his tumbler. I reached faster. Just before his fingertips touched the glass, I knocked it from the table.

Gregg jumped as if encountering a venomous snake. The tumbler didn't shatter. It rattled and spun across the wooden floor, spraying golden liquid before coming to rest against a sofa.

"That won't help you, hon."

"Nellis! Is that you? Don't screw with me, bitch!"

I had no idea who Nellis was, but Gregg's strained face begged that the disembodied voice came from a prankster and not his imagination...or worse.

"It's me, babe." I delivered the line barely above the silence.

He jerked his head in the direction of my voice. I thought for a moment he might lunge at me. People who accidentally look right at me always give me a jolt. Gregg coiled but did not move.

A good moment for a new trick.

I untucked my t-shirt and pulled out the picture frame. Feeling for the easel back, I determined which end was up. I held it out in Gregg's direction by pinching a grip on the top and placing the palm of my other hand under the bottom. I released the grip on the top. The picture fell from my touch, leaving an electric snap in my fingertips.

The photo of Casey Gregg popped into view.

The frame landed in my palm. I stabilized it.

Gregg shrieked. His beady eyes expanded dramatically. He jittered and stepped back, then waved his arms between himself and the photo which had appeared out of nowhere and hung in the empty air.

Noises escaped his open mouth. Whimpering. Desperate.

"You fucked up, sugarcakes."

"Gaah!" Gregg stumbled backward.

The weight of the picture frame planted my feet on the floor. I squeezed my hands together, then whipped the frame to one side. It sailed through the air and smashed into the wall just below a mounted deer head. Glass shattered. The frame dropped and snapped apart. Casey Gregg's photo slid to the floor. She smiled at her husband through shards of glass.

The act of hurling the photo had the equal and opposite effect of sending me away from Gregg's recliner in the direction of an end table bearing a lamp. For an instant, I considered rotating and grabbing the edge of the table. Instead, I let myself sail into the lamp. The collision tipped and tumbled the lamp to the floor. Shadows leaped up the wall. I kicked the table and shot to the ceiling.

Gregg shrieked again. He backed across the room, away from the twin threats of the photo and the fallen lamp.

I pressed my palms on the ceiling and gained a vector in Gregg's direction. I sailed slowly over his head.

"You left something, sugar pie. They're gonna find it. They're gonna find me."

Jesus, I hope I got the Georgia accent right.

Tom's phone call described his conversation with Casey Gregg's sister. The sisters were raised in the south. Tom shared with me how the sister always felt a little disgusted when Casey would adopt the sticky-sweet caricature of a southern bimbo around her husband.

From the bloodless look on Gregg's face, my imitation worked.

I glided over his head and met the wall next to his giant television. It gave me an idea. Sometimes these wall mounts are rock solid. Sometimes not.

I fixed a grip on the end of the big screen, rotated, and planted my feet on the wall. I kicked. Hard.

The screen jerked free and dropped. One end crashed to the floor. The other end dangled from the power cord. Spider web cracks exploded across the image of a vintage convertible carrying a middle-aged couple anticipating sex. The would-be lovers paid no attention to the shattered screen.

Gregg staggered backward until his legs bumped against the sofa.

"*Casey—!?*"

The television screen maneuver left me hanging below the high ceiling, out of touch with the walls and without a grip. Once or twice, similarly beached, I've flapped my arms to create movement. It works, but it's noisy. The same applies to using a power unit.

I rotated and extended my legs horizontally.

"Y'all missed something, hon. You missed something...you missed something..." I repeated the phrase until it became little more than the sound of my own breath.

"I didn't miss anything!" He shoved his hand through his hair and shook his head. "I didn't miss...anything."

He momentarily slipped into a catatonic state, staring into empty distance. Was he retracing his steps? Reviewing his scheme? Was he back checking every move he made, every measure he took to cover his tracks?

Gregg looked like a man teetering on a razor's edge. He needed a jolt to tip him over.

I reached under my shirt again and extracted the white blouse I'd seen sunning itself—the blouse I retrieved from the meadow. I shook it out as best I could, not sure if I had it upside down or inside out. Then I flicked it forward.

An electric snap signaled the object's release from *the other thing.* The blouse appeared and performed a beautiful, satisfying glide to the floor, arms out.

Gregg shrieked. He turned and ran from the room.

Shit.

I rotated to align my feet under my body. Still five feet above the floor, I had no choice.

Fwooomp!

I dropped and hit hard. I bent my knees and landed my palms on the floor to stabilize. After a quick check to confirm that I hadn't cracked an ankle or foot bone, I lifted myself and darted after Gregg.

He bolted for the kitchen. Lights flashed on. I saw the back of his white shirt disappear. I drew up to the door and glanced in carefully. Gregg dashed past the big center island, toward the mudroom connected to the garage.

I fumbled with my pants pocket, pulled out what I hoped was a fresh power unit, and snapped a prop in place.

Gregg entered the mudroom.

The garage?

I turned and gripped the doorway. I braced myself for a fast shot.

Fwooomp!

The instant I vanished I heaved myself forward on a line that took me all the way through the big kitchen to the mudroom door. I caught both sides of the door frame with both hands.

Gregg was gone, but the door to the garage had not been opened. A chain on the door dangled in place, secured from the inside.

I looked left. The cellar door hung open. Gregg's feet pounded the wooden basement steps.

Christ, he buried her in the basement.

The moment I thought it, I could not imagine how. I'd already toured the basement. Smooth, unbroken concrete spanned the entire floor. The cinderblock walls matched the footprint of the whole house. Nothing new. Nothing fresh. No area of exposed dirt. No hidden rooms. Gregg owned a ridiculously clean basement.

I shoved off and coasted across the room to the open basement door. Without diminishing momentum, I hooked the doorframe and heaved myself downward. I sailed down the stairwell. My feet tapped the concrete floor. I adjusted my flight path and coasted across the floor after Gregg, who had reached the far end near the furnace and water heater.

Gregg paced back and forth in front of the HVAC units, frantically searching. Head down, he examined the floor. He crouched and scanned the concrete like someone looking for a contact lens.

"Ha!" He laughed. "There's nothing. Nothing, you worthless bitch! Nothing!"

He pumped his fist in the air. He spun away and circled the furnace.

"Fuck you!" he shouted. "Nothing!" He stopped. He giggled. "You know what? If I'm hearing your voice, you're fucking dead! Do you get that? You're fucking dead!" He laughed. "And you're wrong. There's nothing here, you miserable piece of sad Georgia ass!"

I continued my glide until the basement wall stopped me. I turned around. Ten feet away, Gregg surveyed the floor one more time, then retreated. He walked the full length of the basement. He stopped at the foot of the stairs and turned for a final look. He crouched and studied the floor from a low angle.

"Bitch," he muttered at last. He rose and climbed the stairs. The lights went out. The door slammed.

"Well," I said aloud in the dark. "That could have gone better."

19

"I thought you couldn't call me," Tom answered his phone without a greeting.

"I'm in the basement. Alone."

"Any luck?"

I had reappeared and pulled out my phone to make the call. Using the Bluetooth earpiece to speak and hear, I held out the phone and let the screen glow illuminate my surroundings.

"Yes, and no. Your intel was spot on. I make a pretty good southern belle. I managed to get him wound up. He led me down to the basement. He did something to her down here. I don't know what. If he killed her, I don't see any sign of it. I had him convinced that he missed something. He searched one particular area."

"Sue said they searched the house. They wouldn't have overlooked the basement. Did he?"

"What?"

"Miss something?"

I heaved a sigh and looked at the spotless floor. "He doesn't think so. But from the way he reacted, I struck a nerve. Something happened down here. He's your guy and it has something to do with this basement."

"Any false walls? Trap doors? Fresh concrete?"

"Nothing. According to Sue's timeline, he wouldn't have had time for any renovations. I dunno...maybe a forensic team can find something, but otherwise it's insanely clean. I'd kill to have a basement like this. But then I'd just fill it up with junk. There's nothing down here."

"Huh."

"Hang on..." I said, thinking. "I made him believe he was hearing her voice. He ended up saying that now that he can hear her, she must be dead."

"Which means he didn't think she was. Huh. Three days...a hundred hours..."

"Yeah. I think you were right. But shit—I'm no closer to finding her.

Tom didn't speak.

We remained connected by silence. I waved my phone back and forth, searching for seams in the floor, wondering why Gregg would drop down to scan if not to look for a piece of evidence he had missed. A fiber? A piece of cloth? A shred of tape used to restrain his wife? A locket's broken chain? He had done something here, but what?

The oversized furnace fed warmth through sheet metal ducts and tubes. Being a gas furnace, it had no burning chamber where the ghoulish murderer incinerates his dismembered victim. An Aprilaire humidifier hung on the side of the furnace, weirdly pedestrian under the circumstances.

Plumbing pipes ran overhead. I followed the lines to a pristine water heater. Everything about this basement seemed new.

I held the phone up to a plastic sleeve taped to the side of the water heater. The sleeve contained an owner's manual and warranty paperwork, along with a sticker giving the contractor's name and number. I had one just like it in my cluttered basement.

Handwritten notes in Sharpie marked the date of installation.

Son of a bitch.

"Tom, I gotta go. I'll call you back."

I RAN.

I pounded across the floor and stomped up the stairs, taking the steps in threes. I hit the door hard. It slammed open. The sound broke like thunder. I didn't care. Let him think a damned poltergeist is on the prowl.

I crossed the mudroom and threw back the latch and deadbolt on the garage door. Pushing the door open, I patted the wall, hunting for and finding the row of buttons. I hit the first button my fingers touched. Light blazed and the nearest of four double doors began a ponderous, rattling rise. I let the mudroom door slam behind me, another clap of thunder to haunt Gregg's house. I crossed the empty garage bay on the run and ducked to clear the slowly rising door.

Jamming my phone in my pocket, I traded it for a power unit.

Fwooomp!

I vanished and leaped, forgetting entirely about the wires running from the house to the stable. In darkness over the asphalt driveway pad, I shot skyward. Something brushed my leg as I rose. The wire startled me but failed to snag or electrocute me. In my head, Andy's voice scolded my impulsiveness.

I fired up the power unit. Full throttle. The prop shrieked and I hurtled forward and upward. The stable roof swept beneath me. My eyes adjusted to the darkness. For safety I aimed higher. White corral and pasture fences took shape. Shadows grew from the glow of the moon rising over my shoulder.

I passed over the arena, then over the individual pastures. I found the lane leading to the back of the property and navigated above the wheel tracks in the grass. My night vision grew stronger. Where the last white wooden fence ended, I veered right over wheat stubble drained of color by the moonlight.

A hump of black lay ahead. My nerves tightened and my heart pounded against my chest wall. I adjusted my aim and dove. Dark pieces of discarded junk took on sinister shapes against slabs of limestone and field stone orbs.

The rock pile sprawled larger than I expected—roughly the footprint of a house. Occupying a convenient place in the center of the wheat field, it floated in a plane of harvested grain like a small island.

I heaved myself to the right and began a tight left orbit, searching.

It had been there earlier. I knew that I had seen it.

There!

I slammed the power unit into reverse. Harsh breeze blew across my wrist and up my arm. I stopped abruptly and just as abruptly cut the power.

Sharp pulses of the power unit took me to a point directly above the discarded water heater. It takes a large water heater to handle a house like Gregg's. The new unit in the basement was nearly as tall as me and at least eighteen inches in diameter.

The unit discarded on this rock pile measured close to the same. The cylinder lay half buried under stones and loose brush.

Farmers pick stones from their fields in the spring, after winter frost heaves rocks up through the soil.

But only in the spring.

The rocks propped against and over this water heater made it look like one or two spring's worth of collected stones had been dumped on it.

Yet this appliance had just been replaced.

I pulsed the power unit until my feet touched the stones.

Fwooomp!

I reappeared. Gravity sank her merciless teeth into me. I dropped against the stones and immediately tumbled when the rocks beneath my feet shifted. I went down hard, skinning my palm on the edge of a stone.

The fall landed me face to face with the steel cylinder.

I slapped it. The sound was flat, not hollow.

I ran my hands over the top, feeling for a seam but finding smoothly welded steel. Not good.

I slapped the steel cylinder again. And again.

I listened for a sound. A raging chorus of crickets interfered. I put my ear against the cylinder, hoping I might hear movement, breathing, screams. Anything.

Nothing. The cricket noise flooded my hearing.

I sat up, looked around, and found a fist-sized granite fieldstone. I put the stone in one hand and my power unit in the other. I held up the power unit and gave it full throttle. The prop whined like a runaway drone. I administered three good whacks to the steel cylinder with the stone.

I cut the power.

The crickets momentarily shut up.

I pressed my ear to the metal.

Was that…?

It might have been a sound. Or my imagination. If it was a sound, it was little more than a rustle, a scrape.

Or my imagination.

Crickets took up their relentless mating calls.

I heaved stones off the lower end of the cylinder. The stones were nothing I couldn't handle. Nothing that Gregg couldn't handle when he repositioned them to partially bury the water heater.

Eventually, I exposed the bottom of the cylinder. Instead of a welded seam, bolts attached the base of the appliance to the steel case. Something I could work with.

I crouched and fixed a grip on the base, then heaved it up out of the shallow depression Gregg had created. The sonofabitch was heavy.

I shoved the cylinder up and over stones until it lay fully exposed. After catching my breath, I pulled out my phone, lit up the screen, and studied the base. Evenly spaced bolts ran the full circumference of the steel case. This I could deal with. I switched on the flashlight feature of my phone and placed the device on a rock. Surprisingly bright light flooded the cylinder and the rock pile. If anyone at the house bothered to look, they'd easily see the glow in a distant field.

Fwooomp!

I vanished and grabbed the lip of the cylinder base. I folded my hand over the first bolt, then pushed the imaginary levers in my head. *The other thing* flowed from my hand, a sensation confirmed by an expanding puddle of nothing that consumed the bolt and the steel lip around it. The edge of the steel appeared fuzzy.

I jerked. The lip of the cylinder containing the bolt came off in my hand.

One down.

One by one I sent *the other thing* flooding over each bolt and the metal lip. Where the border between the seen and unseen quivered and frayed, the metal snapped. As each came free, I tossed it aside. The severed metal pieces clinked and bounced on the stone pile surrounding me.

When the last bolt came free, I anticipated a fight to free the base from the rest of the cylinder. I expected internal plumbing to hold it in place. Instead, it flopped at my feet.

What I saw inside—for a moment I simply didn't comprehend.

A wad of plastic bubbles greeted me where the burner and internal plumbing should have been.

"Bubble wrap?"

Bubble wrap! Of course!

I clawed the plastic out, pulling more and more free. It snapped and popped in my grip. A moment later I saw her.

Bare feet. The bottoms of her legs. Blue jeans.

She smelled bad. A jolt of disappointment stabbed me.

Too damned late!

One of her feet shifted.

Or was it my imagination?

I bent down and closed a grip on her ankles and pulled. More bubble wrap popped. I gently eased her feet, then her legs, out of the cylinder. Bubble wrap and sour smell came with her. I peeled the plastic free and pushed it aside.

Her bare midriff slid free. Her chest. She came faster now, tumbling out in a heap. I reached to cradle her head but found most of her skull encased in a helmet of bubble wrap, generously taped with packing tape.

Gregg left her mouth and nose open. He let her breathe. He made sure she couldn't damage herself. He made sure death wouldn't leave a mark.

I found her arms bound in bubble wrap behind her back. I tore at the packing material. Plastic tape fought me. I pulled my escape knife from my pocket. Careful not to slice her flesh with the razor-sharp knife, I cut away the tape and pulled free the binding wrap.

I heard a voice under all of this, muttering, over and over.

My voice.

"Miserable sonofabitch!"

Casey Gregg lay motionless, a limp mess, but when I touched her neck beneath her chin, I felt life throbbing through her arteries. Looking closer, I saw her chest rise and fall. I pulled my phone off the rock and shined it in her face. Gaunt sunken eyes failed to open on their own. When I lifted one lid, the iris constricted. Good so far.

Her gray cheeks were shallow. Her mouth hung slightly open. Her tongue appeared swollen. Her jeans wore dark urine stains.

Three days like this.

"Miserable sonofabitch!"

Her freed arms flopped at her side, useless. Being bound that long had given her the mother of all paresthesia. The least of her worries.

She needed water.

I killed the light on my phone and tucked it away. I leaned over and lifted her just far enough off the stones to pull her against my chest.

FWOOOMP!

I pushed hard. She vanished with me. We immediately lost contact with gravity. Already a small, light woman, she weighed nothing in my arms. I swung us both upright and adjusted her against me. Sweat and the scent of utter terror stung my nostrils.

I pulled the power unit from my back pocket and nearly dropped it.

I adjusted my grip and held on.

We soared toward the stables.

20

F *wooomp!*
    I timed our reappearance to the instant my feet touched the grass. Even with good timing, I nearly took a header. Casey Gregg went from zero to whatever she weighs and sank against the grip I held around her waist with my left arm, throwing me off balance. I jammed the inert power unit in my back pocket with the prop still attached. With both hands free, I swept the woman into my arms and pulled her head against my shoulder. I jogged toward the fire pit and the startled gaze of two Bunker Hill patriots.

"Water!" I called out. "I need water!"

Entering the circle of firelight, I dropped to my knees and laid the woman on the grass. The flickering light distorted shadows around us. I cradled her head and pushed matted hair out of her eyes.

The two idiots in the lawn chairs stared at me. At her.

"Now!"

"I better get the boss." The younger of the two scrambled out of his chair and disappeared into the darkness beyond the firelight.

The older of the two jumped to his feet and yanked a backpack off the grass. He pulled a zipper and flipped the pack open. After rummaging, he found a plastic water bottle and handed it to me.

I twisted the cap free and leaned the bottle over Casey Gregg's cracked lips, gently dripping crystal-clear liquid and pushing it across her skin with my fingers. She stirred. I dribbled more. Rivulets of wet streamed down her cheeks, down her neck.

She tried to swallow. She coughed and gagged instead.

"Easy," I said. "Take it slow."

I tipped a cap-worth of liquid onto her tongue. She did nothing with it. I pushed my finger in her mouth and moved it around, then added more.

Her tongue moved. Her mouth closed, catching my finger, sucking the liquid. This time when she swallowed, it went down.

"SHOOT HIM! HE HAS MY WIFE!"

The fire pit blocked my view of the house. Someone—I took the frantic figure in a white shirt for Gregg—waved and pointed and shouted.

"SHOOT HIM, FOR GOD'S SAKE! HE'S ONE OF THEM!"

I glanced up to see the man who had remained with me splitting his attention between the woman on the ground and her husband screaming in the dark. I watched the militiaman closely. He glanced at his weapon, still leaning against summer lawn furniture. His eyes met mine. His hand remained at his side.

Casey Gregg moaned.

"Easy there," I said. I pried her mouth open, poured water on my fingers and pushed them onto her tongue. She drew the liquid in. "Slow. Easy."

"Mr. Gregg, I don't think—" The man who fetched his boss tried to speak.

"SHOOT THE FUCKER! HE'S HURTING HER!"

Someone raced across the grass on heavy footsteps. I glanced up in time to see the kid, the one barely old enough to shave.

"I got this sir!" The kid jerked his ugly rifle to his shoulder.

I looked up the line of the weapon's black barrel and cringed.

The kid jerked the trigger. Nothing happened.

He jerked the frozen trigger again.

"Jesus Christ," I muttered, feeling my heart start up in my chest again.

The kid with the rifle looked down at his weapon, bewildered. He would have killed me. Without hesitation. The realization washed over me, a mix of white-hot rage and paralyzing relief. The older of the two men, the one who gave me the water bottle, walked over to the kid and jerked the rifle barrel skyward.

"Gimme that, you fucking idiot." A tussle followed until the man untangled the rifle strap from the bewildered kid and pulled the rifle free.

"YOU! SHOOT HIM!" Gregg shouted from the edge of the firelight. Even the flickering flames could not account for the way his face rippled with fury. Like someone let snakes loose under his skin. His eyes blazed. Spittle flew from his mouth. "HE'S ANTIFA! HE ABDUCTED MY WIFE!"

More of the Bunker Hill Brigade trotted into the circle of light. I turned my attention back to dribbling water on the woman's lips. She reacted now. Thirsting. Desperate. Moaning. I rubbed the water onto her swollen tongue with my fingers.

"Dude," the man now holding the kid's rifle said to Gregg, "I'm not shooting anybody. Christ, I'm just a school bus driver. I think we need to call an ambulance."

21

"They're calling you the Mystery Samaritan." Tom Ceeves leaned against the handrail on the courthouse steps. "Those numbnuts are saying you just walked off."

A light breeze grew out of the morning civil twilight glowing in the east. I held the steel railing to avoid drifting away.

"Any word?"

Tom shook his head. I wondered if he had been a smoker during his life. His ease with solitude outside a public building suggested he had practice.

"The paramedics called for air evac even before they got there. They said whoever called dispatch described symptoms of severe dehydration. Final stages severe. They flew her to Marshfield."

The Bunker Hill patriot and parttime school bus driver who snagged the kid's rifle proved remarkably helpful. After he connected with 9-1-1, I fed him information which he passed on to the dispatcher.

"What about Gregg?"

"Sue called the fire department and told them not to let him go with her. It got a little ugly, but the deputies from the roadblock went in with the ambulance and held him back. He's here."

"Inside? Arrested?"

"He's inside with his lawyer explaining how Deep State Antifa operatives put his wife in the water heater he just replaced last month. An elaborate plot to frame him."

I chuckled.

"What's funny?" Tom asked.

"General Dwight D. Eisenhower was 'antifa.' Winston Churchill was 'antifa.' Every brave kid that stormed Normandy beach was 'antifa.' Anti-fascist. These goddamned idiots have no idea what being 'anti-fascist' means. Gregg rants about 'left wing fascist radicals' which is like saying 'the Green Bay Bears.' These guys are idiots."

"Politics."

"Is politics going to save his worthless ass?"

"Maybe."

The degree of anger I felt surprised me. My decisions, my actions may have prevented Casey Gregg from crossing a thin line from life to death, but each of my choices—including slipping away before the deputies arrived—complicated the chances of bringing Gregg to justice. I did not underestimate the man's ability to lie, twist facts and apply political grease to the system and slide through the fingers of the law.

I used a deep sigh to push aside the anger. In its place I found weariness. And hunger. And an ache for Andy.

"What say we head over to that diner, grab a deeply unhealthy breakfast, then get the hell out of Dodge?"

Tom shrugged. The gesture saved him wasting a word.

Before either of us could move, we heard media van doors slide open. We heard voices. We saw people hustle into the street from the parked vans, a repeat of the show we'd seen less than twenty-four hours ago.

"Uh-oh," Tom said. I followed his eyes when he turned and looked up at high windows set in the courthouse façade. Sheriff Sue Kresky stood behind the glass, looking down at us. She raised upturned palms in a gesture of helplessness. "I think Suspect Number One is about to get his face on camera in time for the morning talk shows. See you at breakfast."

Tom pushed off the rail and threaded his way through the gathering media tribe. I pushed off, too, but on a vertical line. Part of me wanted nothing to do with the spin and lies about to be broadcast for America. Part of me couldn't look away.

I deployed a power unit and used it to hold a position roughly twenty feet above the steps.

Congressman Martin Gregg and his muscle-bound attorney burst through the courthouse doors. Gregg wore a fresh shirt under a neatly pressed blue suit sporting his signature bright red tie. Not a single hair hung out of place. A normally pale man, which doesn't play well on video, he had obviously taken time to apply a light coating of sheen-suppressing makeup. I wondered if his compatriot Heddon brought the kit.

This time the Bunker Hill Victory Brigade did not appear. No one rushed up the steps to plant American flags in Gregg's video frame. Heddon veered off while Gregg marched forward and stopped at the top of the landing, thus forcing everyone with a camera to position themselves below him, angling their lenses upward. He adjusted his tie, then held out his hands, palms down, to suppress the questions shouted at him. He waited for quiet.

This time, no insect buzz announced the bullet's arrival.

This time, I floated well above the line of fire.

Gregg's red silk tie blossomed in the center of his chest. A soft thump preceded a wet slap, the sound of fragments of the Congressman's diaphragm and spine departing the gaping exit wound in the center of his back.

He dropped on his butt, like the woman I'd seen in Idaho. He flopped over backward. His head bounced once on the blood-sprayed concrete, but it did not matter.

He died before he landed.

PART II

22

I have nightmares.

This isn't to say that I wake up each morning wrung out by post-traumatic head cinema or night terrors strumming my nerves like a harp. Or that the still-unanswered cause of the accident that wired my head and body for vanishing haunts me. I sleep like a granite boulder, according to my wife. However, since the accident that left one of Earl Jackson's Piper Navajos in pieces and me with a hole in my memory, I have a recurring dream about flying the RNAV 31 instrument approach into Essex County Airport. Early versions of the dream ended abruptly when an empty nothingness tore away the left side of the cockpit. Later versions morphed into seeing my wife jerked out a smashed window on the thirty-second floor of a Chicago high-rise. In that version I dive after her and variously our fingertips touch, or she refuses to take my hand, or a District of Columbia Police detective named Fanko intercedes and invites her for a drink while I'm still falling. That one bothers me the most. I wake up in a sweat every time Fanko shows up.

Sunday night, I returned alone from Bear County. I put the Foundation Navajo to bed, grabbed a take and bake pizza from the Papa Murphy's in the shopping center at the edge of Essex and I finished half a six pack of Corona on my porch—all of which primed me for deep uninterrupted sleep. Twice in the past week I'd pulled all-nighters, and it registered in

my bones. Pizza and beer perform better than Ambien for me. I anticipated a smooth ten hours, at least.

Until Darryl Spellman's head on Martin Gregg's body exploded.

I launched off the sheets like a Minuteman missile.

I said something more commonly heard from Pidge and tumbled off
the bed onto the cold wooden floor, immediately reminded that I had left
the bedroom window open to add fresh, chilled late September air to my
beer and pizza sleep potion.

"Dammit!" I whispered, automatically trying not to wake my wife
who slept a thousand miles away. "Dammit! Dammit! Dammit!" Another
buck and a quarter for Amber's swear jar, if you counted the f-bomb that
opened my tirade.

I searched my hands for blood and my bed for the spattered remains of
Spellman/Gregg's skull.

A breeze rose and fell. I realized it was me, hyperventilating.

Back at Spirit of St. Louis Airport, Leslie Carson-Pelham had asked if
I was okay. If I would be okay. She'd seen me avert my eyes during her
replay of the Spellman shooting. She asked the question with genuine
concern. After offering to blow out one of my eyes with her Glock, her
tender inquiry made me suspicious.

"Fine," I told her. "Why wouldn't I be?"

"Because you just saw a man get his head blown off."

I mustered bravado and shrugged away her concern. Not something
you see every day, but I'm a big, tough guy who can make a cabin class
twin-engine airplane dance. I have the leather jacket and the Ray Ban
Aviators to prove it.

No big deal until brains spatter the sheets like tapioca pudding. I could
have sworn when I flew off the mattress that my legs were coated in goo.

How long I stood there attempting to bring my breathing under control
and get my heart rate back down to double digits, I do not know. Eventually I looked for the red glow of Andy's clock radio.

1:07.

"Christ," I muttered. Disappointment mingled with comfort. The
disappointment came from the few short hours of sleep I had just logged.
Comfort came from the familiar red clock radio numbers, always in the
same spot, always angled just enough to be seen in the night. Andy's
clock warmly connected me to my absent wife.

1:12.

My weary bones were not amused by the interruption. The pillow called, but an electric charge in my veins threatened to power a sleepless hour of thrashing on the sheets.

I pulled on my pants, fumbled in the dark for yesterday's socks and shirt, and tiptoed into the hall before remembering I was alone in the house.

Dammit, Dee...

I buried the rest of that thought, even from myself.

After a stop to recycle the last of the beer, I mustered the presence of mind to flip on the upstairs hall light and journey to the farmhouse kitchen without tripping in the dark. I wanted to eat but couldn't think of what. I wanted to drink but didn't want a beer or anything else with alcohol. I settled for one bite of cold pizza and a cup of orange juice.

I stood for a long time over the kitchen sink, inspecting the face staring back at me from the window above the faucets. He didn't look like a wimp. So, what was he doing out there when he should have been sleeping? Why was he acting like a wuss just because he'd seen a man's head explode? Who did he expect to play a sad violin for him because he could not take his wife in his arms and inhale the intoxicating scent of her hair?

God, I wanted Andy. Six more days until I see her might as well have been six centuries.

"You're pathetic, you know that?" I told the sad sack staring at me. "I know what you need. But since you ain't gettin' any, I know what you can substitute."

I pulled my boots on and grabbed my flight jacket. From the mudroom, I pocketed three ANDIE units and companion props.

I stopped.

Courtesy of the small, dark hours—*coffee at oh dark thirty*—I faced a truth.

"I like BLASTER better," I said aloud.

Basic Linear Aerial System for Transport, Electric Rechargeable.

A moment later, I stood outside the back door on the concrete stoop. Chilled air whispered warnings of fall and reminded me to close the bedroom window when I got back. I checked the sky above. Shredded patches of cloud illuminated by distant light from Essex hurried against the black, looking like filmy women's night clothing snatched up by devilish breezes. The clouds slid silently from northeast to southwest. In black gaps between the clouds, uncountable stars called to me.

No matter how many times I've done this, a shiver of wonder and anticipation awoke in my veins. It felt good. It washed away lingering bits of the dream.

I crouched and—

Fwooomp!

—vanished, simultaneously springing vertically off the concrete.

The yard, illuminated by security lights whose original purpose had come and gone, fell away. Black trees full of leaves on the verge of turning dropped below my sight level. The house and barn plunged beneath me. As if a carpet had been rolled out in every direction simultaneously, the road in front of the house and the fields surrounding the buildings stretched away to a horizon defined by random lights.

Ordinarily I don't go for height. High altitude serves no real purpose when I'm using *the other thing*. Tonight, kicking myself into a moon shot thrilled me. I watch the earth fall away every time I lift an airplane from an airport runway, but the magic is diminished by power settings that need to be adjusted, turns to an on-course heading that must be made, and contact with air traffic control that must be established.

This was different. This was me alone, silent, shooting skyward untethered. I hadn't gone straight up at night before and suddenly I wondered why. The rush stole my breath.

Essex slid into view. The late hour did nothing to extinguish the island of lights floating on the dark landscape several miles away. I rotated. On the northeast horizon, glitter embedded in black showed me the three fingers of water that make up the Lakes Region. Leander Lake, the largest of the three, reflected the most stars. Few if any of the homeowners on the big lake operated more than minimal lights at night. Andy's sister Lydia lived at the centerpoint of Leander Lake on its eastern flank. I fixated on a spot where Lydia and her daughters Harriet and Elise and their new baby sister Grace slept at this hour, although Grace had a reputation for being nocturnal, much to Lydia's distress. I discovered an unexpected and overwhelming love for my two nieces when I met them. I expected that feeling to spread to their new infant sister. The surprising depth of feeling I found for my sister-in-law's children offered evidence that I could feel the same for a stranger invading my life with Andy. Fingers crossed.

I continued to rise, washing away the gory dream with altitude. Cloud height can be deceiving. What looked like a layer skimming the barn roof ran thousands of feet above the landscape. I reached five hundred feet and my perspective on the cloud layer changed little. When I launched from my back steps, I imagined skimming the tops of the moonlit layer.

Closing in on a thousand feet up, with the layer still high above me, I decided to halt the elevator ride.

I pulled a power unit from my pocket.

"BLASTER," I said to the silent sky. "Oh, yeah. That's way better."

I extracted a prop. Each time I do this, I think of the times I've fumbled the damned things. Just thinking about it made me tense, which increased the likelihood of a screw up.

More than once I've tried to come up with a way of tethering the units to my arms with a strap or loop or Velcro. The concept made sense, until I contemplated the idea of a razor-sharp six-inch propeller spinning at hundreds of RPM while dangling from my wrist—or worse, whipping around out of control. I've since decided it's better to lose the occasional unit than have one slicing the flesh off my arms.

I snapped the unit and prop together and applied power against my ascent. The breeze on my face diminished, then stopped. I cut the power. Moon shot terminated.

I hung in the air and absorbed the silence, wondering for the hundredth time why I could feel my gut clench when standing at the railing of a tall building or bridge, yet feel no fear or concern about the empty air beneath my weightless feet.

The world—my Essex County world—sprawled around me, amazingly silent in the night, amazingly illuminated both by man and the stars.

I drifted for a long time before firing up the prop for home.

23

The motorcycle woke me. Birds should have. Our yard is full of them, thanks to Andy's religious filling of feeders, which has been delegated to me in her absence. But I crashed hard and slept through their morning concert. After landing, I grabbed one of Andy's fuzzy blankets and wrapped myself up like a burrito. I crawled onto my lounge chair on the porch, telling myself that sleeping on the porch had nothing to do with Spellman's splattered brains in my bed upstairs. I winked out seconds after adjusting my head on a throw pillow stolen from the living room sofa.

The distinctive Harley exhaust note downshifted as it approached. Bikers cruise our little two-lane road at a constant speed. The downshift told me I had a visitor. We're the only house on the road.

A few of Andy's cop friends ride. Most of the men and women on the fire department ride, to the point where they have a club and tour on weekends. I wondered if Andy had asked one of her first-responder colleagues to drop in on me. It seemed a little early on Monday morning for—

"Whoa! Crap!" I read my watch. Eleven-fifteen.

I sat up, entangled in my burrito wrap.

The Harley throttled down. I blinked goo out of my eyes and watched the biker turn into the driveway. I don't know my Harleys. I couldn't tell a

Softail from a Road King, which are the only two model names I recall from occasional chats with Andy's friends. All Harleys look good to me; they all shine and call out to the boy in me. The bike wheeling into my driveway threw glitter off polished black and chrome.

The rider rolled to a stop, killed the puttering engine, and kicked the center stand down onto the gravel. He swung a leg over and pulled off a pair of gloves. I know from experience that it's hard to see into our screened porch, yet I scrambled to untangle the blanket and shove it into a chair. I double-checked to ensure I wore pants.

I waited, using my fingertips to comb my hair.

The rider removed his gloves, then unstrapped the dull black ball of a helmet he wore. Using both hands, he lifted the helmet free. Long, light brown hair fell over the collar of his leather jacket.

Son of a bitch.

I recognized him the instant his helmet and eye shield revealed bushy eyebrows and a wide face. Recognition induced a jolt of embarrassment. For weeks, I'd been ignoring his calls, deleting his messages and generally pretending he hadn't done Andy and me a favor with a cool hundred million dollars.

Spiro Lewko, one of the world's richest men, possibly *the* richest, depending on market fluctuations, planted his bike helmet on the gas tank and strolled across my yard. He took in the sights like a tourist. The trees. The house. The cornfields spanning all directions. Checking out the habitat of *homo regularus* I assumed.

"This your place?" he asked.

"Rented." I pushed open the screen door. He caught it and climbed the worn limestone steps.

"It's nice. Why the hell have you been avoiding me? We had a deal."

"Straight to the point. You know, if I wanted to avoid you, I could have just disappeared."

"I figured that out on DeSantorini's rooftop. We have a lot to discuss."

"I don't suppose you'd reschedule if I told you I have to pick up my wife in fifteen minutes."

"That would be a neat trick, but for all I know, when you do your vanishing act you might be able to get to Quantico, Virginia in fifteen minutes. A matter of physics I'd like to discuss with you. Can I get a water?"

I almost asked *sparking or still* but decided not to introduce sarcasm this early.

"Be right back."

The back door and a fistful of power units offered tempting escape, but I returned a moment later with a bottled water for Lewko and a bottled Corona for me. He eyed the beer with naked judgment.

"Day drinker?"

"Only to balance the night drinking." I threw the blanket off the chair and took it, gesturing for him to take the other.

He sat down and stared at me. Then he said, "Want to show me?"

"Not really."

The man wears a permanent smirk, a look that suggests he just caught you ending a sentence in a preposition or pronouncing the "t" in "often." It rode across his wide mouth and masked whether my reluctance annoyed or amused him.

"When I saw you on the roof that night, I realized what had happened at the lab. It was you. You controlled the matter state of the object. I was a bit of a fool. I take that back. Your friend, Dr. Farris. She took me for a bit of a fool. She didn't tell me what you could do. Only that you had more information for me than you let on."

Spiro Lewko got wind of a new stealth technology after a kid in an aircraft salvage company found a piece of whatever I hit jammed inside the remains of the Piper Navajo I crashed. Lewko beat me to the kid and thwarted my chance of recovering the debris. It was only a matter of time before the billionaire connected the debris to me, so Lillian and I tried our hand at stealing it. We not only failed but ended up exposing me to Lewko.

Lillian never filled me in on the tactics she used to persuade Lewko to flash one hundred million of his dollars to reveal the role Emilio DeSantorini's daughter played in a string of murders. In the aftermath, Lillian vanished almost as efficiently as I do, leaving me holding the bag. I didn't think it mattered because the next morning Lee Donaldson and Andy took me and *the other thing* to the office of Deputy Director Mitchell Lindsay of the Federal Bureau of Investigation. I figured a new trajectory within the painted lines of law enforcement superseded Lewko's claims on me.

Yet here we are.

Lewko, looking the perpetual nerd somewhere in his forties, stared, expectant. For the hundredth time since last hearing her voice, I wished Andy stood at my side.

"I have to admit, Mr. Lewko," I said, avoiding the first name I knew he hated, "I expected something more extravagant. More aggressive."

"Like?"

"Ninja teams rappelling from helicopters. Operatives invading in gas masks, knocking me out and transporting me to your secret lab under the Rock of Gibraltar."

"There's a lot under Gibraltar. The Brits built a fortress there. It's on my list of destinations for the zombie apocalypse."

I pointed at the Harley.

"This everyman approach is nice. I almost bought it."

"Really? Did I slip up?"

I shrugged. "I didn't want to rub it in, but you never use the center stand on gravel. It's likely to slide on you. And there's still a tag hanging from the collar of that biker jacket."

He shot a hand to the jacket collar and probed. I laughed.

"Kidding. Sorry," I said. "But I'll guess anyway. You flew in. Bought the bike and the duds and rolled out here like Easy Rider pretending to put us on an equal footing. I bet there's less than ten miles on that bike."

"Wrong. The bike is mine. But the jacket is new. We flew me and the bike into Green Bay and trailered the bike here. My people are freaking out about a mile down the road. They hate it when I ride."

"You don't even have insurance, do you?"

"Why would I?" Lewko propped his elbows on his knees. "Will, I watched you appear out of thin air. Then I watched you disappear. For weeks I had an object that displayed similar characteristics and the best minds in the world made no progress in finding out why. I can't leave it at that. I helped you, remember?"

"I do."

"You owe me."

"Do I? You might not have wanted him dead, but I'm quite sure half the reason you played along with us was to see DeSantorini get his due."

"You're wrong. I did want him dead."

"You used heavy-handed tactics to get that piece of debris from that kid in Wichita. Maybe I was a little insincere, but you don't exactly play on a level field."

"Granted," he said. "What is it you're expecting me to say? I'll crush you? I'll destroy your wife's career? I'll own whatever tech you're using no matter what happens? Sorry. I don't play the Marvel villain, Will."

My teeth locked together on the words *your wife's career.*

"Do you understand where my interest lies?"

I didn't speak.

"We talked about it at the lab, Will. The stars. The limits." He searched my face for understanding the way an adult looks at a toddler to see if the words are too big. "Do you know what that piece of debris is made of?"

I shook my head.

"Nothing special." He shrugged. "Seriously. Nothing out of the ordinary. We thought, maybe this is it. Maybe this establishes proof of an advanced civilization. We thought we might find an element that could not be sourced here on Earth. But no. It's nothing special. A variation on the same stuff that made the tiles for the space shuttle. Any half-assed lab with a dozen MIT grads could create it."

"So, I had an accident with a space shuttle?"

"Don't be ridiculous. It's not a question of the piece inside the tech, *it's the tech!* And that tech is in you, isn't it. You can't tell me that you found a magic amulet, or that some wizard gave you a cloak."

"I say an incantation every time I disappear."

The smirk widened into a smile.

"I like that you have a sense of humor. I think it improves the chances that we can work together."

"I already have a job."

"And bills to pay," he said. The smile faded back to a smirk. "You and your wife are still paying off the medical bills from your accident. How about I leave you with the keys and title to that bike? Keep it. Or sell it and pay off your hospital bill."

"My wife is a cop. She used to scrape bikers off the road as a patrol sergeant. I can't accept it. And the money from selling it would never pay for the divorce."

"Let's not go off the rails, Will. You don't know me, but I can be singularly focused. Let's talk about the tech. Do you even know what it is?"

"What do you think it is?"

"Okay. I'll give you my take. I think that despite the pedestrian nature of the material within, the stealth tech affected that piece of debris—and is the reason you collided with it. I think the tech not only removes the object from the visible spectrum, and several other spectrums I might add, but it also renders it impervious to physical forces we once considered to be unbreakable laws of physics, of nature. I think, Will—and you may have already proven this to yourself—that what you can do might make interstellar travel possible."

"Wow. You and Lillian have a lot in common."

He shrugged. "We might. Dr. Farris has a brilliant mind, but she is a woman with an overly paranoid imagination. I'd be intrigued to know how you two connected."

"She didn't like the idea of me becoming a lab rat."

"I don't have any interest in making you one. I prefer working with a partner. Does this number mean anything to you? 4-2-5-3-5-2-2-0-0-8?"

I shook my head.

Lewko sat back in the chair. "That's your joint checking account number at the Farmer's Union Bank of Essex. Would you like to know the routing number?"

"Not especially."

"Let me ask you this: If you were to wake up tomorrow morning and check your balance and discover it matched today's balance plus one billion dollars, would that be sufficient to get you to drop everything else in your life and become my partner in mastering the technology you possess?"

"Billion? With a B?"

"Yes. Goggle it. You'll find all manner of creative descriptions. What do you say?"

I held his gaze for a moment, trying to read the encrypted message in his light blue eyes, in the smirk, in the confusing dichotomy of an ungraspable dollar figure like one billion and the fact that this man had hundreds of those billions. Trying to estimate what a partnership would be worth to him if it only cost him one of those hundreds. And what it would be worth to me if it cost me everything.

I stood up.

"My wife keeps me on a short leash, Mr. Lewko. Why don't you let me help you get that bike off the center stand?"

I gestured at the door.

"This is about you and your wife and Lindsay, isn't it. Maybe that was a good idea, in a boy scout sort of way, but Lindsay's gone, you know. He was one of a kind."

I said nothing.

"You may want to rethink your partnership with the government. Agent Carson-Pelham is no Lindsay. She doesn't have anywhere near the political capital he had. And with Lindsay out of the picture—well, nature abhors a vacuum."

"Thanks for stopping by." I opened the door. He took the hint.

He followed me down the stone steps. He mounted the bike and pulled on the helmet. I shoved until the Harley dismounted the center stand, then I stepped aside.

"I won't wait as long this time, Will," he said. "I won't wait for someone else to make a move."

"See...now I would have bet that you knew better than to threaten me."

He said nothing. He turned the key, fired the engine, and rolled forward into the farmyard. He performed a reasonably proficient half-circle turn, then accelerated past me without a glance.

24

I rolled the Beechcraft Baron to a new heading and settled in for a
teardrop entry to the published holding pattern.

"Oops! There goes primary nav!" Pidge announced through the
intercom from the co-pilot's seat. The Garmin navigation screen flipped
from the moving map to a useless utility page. She made no effort to mask
the glee in her voice.

I twisted the number two VOR Omni Bearing Selector to the inbound
course for the holding pattern. My heading lined us up to pass over the
fix. The needle would flip regardless. I was ready for her.

"Approach, Baron Six One Niner, we just lost primary navigation," I
reported to Pidge through the intercom, simulating the call I would have
made to air traffic control had this been a real failure. "We'll proceed with
secondary navigation. Request the VOR 24 Approach."

Pidge, in her role as both check pilot and controller, responded.
"Roger, Six One Niner, continue the hold. Expect the VOR 24 approach
clearance at..." Out of the corner of my eye I saw Pidge check her wrist-
watch. "...twenty-three."

I read back the clearance and scanned the instruments beneath a visor-
like plastic hood that simulated instrument flying conditions by obscuring
my view of the sky outside. I'd been flying this way for nearly an hour.
She hadn't tripped me up yet.

"Oh, damn," Pidge said.

"What?"

She reached up and pulled the mixture control for the right engine. "Your right engine just went tits up."

She didn't have to announce it. The airplane pulled hard right and began a roll. I stomped the left rudder and reacted. Everything forward. Everything up. Dead foot, dead engine. Confirm with the throttle. With airspeed well above the blue line on the indicator and altitude steady, I dropped my hand to the floor between the seats.

"Switch tanks. Fuel pump on," I recited aloud without switching tanks or turning on the pump. "Mag check." This, I actually did, clicking the right engine's ignition from Both to Left to Right and back again. Better to do it for real; it builds muscle memory.

"Sorry, didn't restore power," she told me.

"Right engine identified. Feathering." I pulled the prop lever into the detent. I felt the shudder as the right engine stopped windmilling and the blades aligned with the relative wind. The rudder pressure on my left foot eased.

"There goes the PFD!" She hit the switch. The primary flight display went black.

"Merciless harpy."

She laughed. I checked the airspeed and saw that the feathered engine and our relatively light condition meant I didn't need the left engine screaming at full power. I throttled back and lightened more load on my left foot, keeping the speed a comfortable fifteen knots above the blue line on the airspeed indicator. She had me sweating, but I refused to show it.

"Approach, we just shut down the right fan. Thought we'd save the gas. Also just lost our PFD."

"Say intentions, Six One Niner," she mimicked the calm voice of an air traffic controller whose greatest risk in this situation amounted to spilling coffee.

"Six One Niner, declaring an emergency. One and a half souls on board. We're turning outbound on the approach. We'll call you after we remove and stow all external apparel, place our heads between our knees and kiss our asses good-bye."

"Roger that, Six One Niner. Pucker up."

She at least let me fly the outbound leg and do the procedure turn to align with the inbound approach course before she slapped a Post-It note on my attitude indicator and called out a vacuum system failure.

I greased the landing just to spite her.

PIDGE SIGNED my logbook with a flourish. "You're good for another two years, old man." She slid the logbook across the desk. I read her endorsement for a Biennial Flight Review and noted that she gave me an Instrument Proficiency Check endorsement as well. It wasn't necessary, but it was nice. There was more. She pointed at the additional entry that certified me as a Part 135 charter pilot in good standing with Essex County Air Service. "I wrote you up for your six-month, so you don't have to have that conversation until spring. What are you going to tell Earl about flying for him?"

"I don't know. I hear the new hire is working out. You know you're his chief pilot now."

"News to me."

I laughed. "He'd tell you but he's afraid of choking on the words. I don't think there will be as much call for me to fill in. And we're busy here. Arun's taken over the Foundation with a vengeance. He's doubled the number of grant applications we're processing."

"He's making more money than he can give away. Did he tell you?"

"Tell me what?"

"*He didn't tell you?* About Spiro Lewko?"

I felt a jolt.

"What?"

"When the Foundation got the Bitcoin back from that she demon DeSantorini, Lewko personally called Arun. God, I can't believe he didn't tell you. He was quite gah-gah over it. Lewko told Arun to leave the money, or the bulk of it, in Bitcoin. That it was going to jump in value."

"Oh, that. Arun said we were up something like thirty percent."

"More like sixty. Why? What did you think I was going to say?"

I felt a sudden need for a change of subject.

"Did Arun get his car fixed?"

"What are you talking about?"

"I noticed his car here on Saturday morning, but he wasn't in the office. I figure he had car trouble and had to walk all the way home to his empty apartment Friday night." I fixed a leer on Pidge.

"Shut up."

I grinned. "He should have called me. It must have been a long walk home, all alone on a Friday night..."

"Asshole."

"...probably took him all...night...long..."

"Fuck you. You're a real di—"

"Knock! Knock!" A woman's voice interrupted Pidge, who in about ten seconds would have sprung from her chair to slap me around. Pidge and I looked in the direction of the voice.

Leslie Carson-Pelham stepped into the hangar. "Sorry, I didn't see anybody in the office."

The FBI agent caught me off guard. We talked several times since Idaho, mostly filling in details and answering the same questions from different angles. She didn't share anything new with me. I had no idea whether her investigation into Spellman's death had progressed. I had heard nothing from her since the similar shooting of Congressman Martin Gregg.

"Uh...come in." I waved for her to join us.

She walked past the high tail of the parked Piper Navajo, paying it an admiring glance. "That's bigger than I thought. And you must be Miss Page."

"Everybody calls her—"

"Cassidy." Pidge unfolded her legs from her chair and stood. She extended a hand and shook with Leslie. "And you must be Will's fed."

"Badge and all. Nice to meet you." Leslie sent me a look laden with a question.

"Yeah, she knows," I said flatly.

Pidge jerked a thumb in my direction. "About him? Hell, yes. Buy me a drink sometime and I'll tell you how this asshole threw me out a window thirty floors up."

"I'm a little surprised to see you," I said. *You could have called.* I had followed the media frenzy sparked by the Gregg shooting and even chatted with Tom about Sheriff Kresky's immediate and inconclusive investigation. When Leslie didn't call, I assumed, a little grudgingly, it was her way of drawing the line between me as a tool and her as the FBI.

"Is this a bad time?"

"Nope!" Pidge scooped up her headset and offered her chair to Leslie. "I was just teaching Will how to fly. He's a slow learner, but he managed to get it back on the ground shiny side up. I gotta go. Nice to meetcha!"

Leslie watched Pidge prance out of the hangar via the big door.

"Teaching you to fly?"

"Biennial Flight Review," I explained.

"That's her? The one from Montana? Foyle?"

"All ten feet tall of her."

"How old is she?"

I had to think about it for a moment. "Twenty-three?"

Leslie took Pidge's chair at the desk.

"I read the report. Amazing."

"I doubt any report can do it justice. Best flying I've ever seen."

Leslie seemed interested. "It was an airplane like this one, wasn't it?"

"Almost exactly."

"She hit Foyle on that road? Killed him?"

"It wasn't just that," I said. "I mean, yes. She hit him. Took him off at the waist with the right prop." I didn't have to close my eyes to replay the image of Foyle's legs falling over. "But you also must realize, she made a conscious decision to take out an engine at zero altitude. No ejection seat. No parachute. The maneuver—dropping a thousand feet without power, leveling off just high enough to keep the props from striking the road, lining up on Foyle and hitting him without wrecking the leading edge of the wing—that's a feat all by itself, but she did all that knowing she'd wind up single engine at zero feet with pieces coming off." I could still see the Piper Mojave clawing for height, smoking badly, throwing off chunks of engine cowling, and then disappearing behind a low hillside.

That I was alive because Pidge risked everything never wandered far from my mind.

"Quite impressive."

"Yup." I inventoried Leslie's appearance. Jeans. Black t-shirt. Black blazer. Like a uniform with this woman. Her service weapon hung beneath her left armpit. Instead of a purse, she carried a satchel like the one Andy favored. "Not that you're not welcome, but what the hell are you doing here? I thought you were back in New York trying to figure out who gave Spellman a lobotomy."

"I was."

"Something break? The case, I mean."

"Spellman specifically? No..."

"Then you're here because of Gregg."

She lowered her eyes to the desk.

"I'm not officially assigned to the investigation, but I have an interest in the case. Especially when I learned that your airplane—*that airplane*—arrived in Ironwood the day before Gregg was shot and departed the next day." She gave me a look I've seen on Andy's face. The *what aren't you telling me* look that causes my cheeks to turn red and the earth to shift beneath my feet.

"Will, I have to ask."

"Ask what?"

Her dark eyes probed for an answer before the question slipped her lips. I cursed the warmth I felt in my face.

"Was that you?"

Yes, it was me. I pulled Casey Gregg out of her tomb. I carried her into the firelight and nearly got myself shot. Yes.

But that's not what she was asking.

"You mean—did I shoot Gregg?"

Saying it aloud and seeing her anticipation made me see how real the absurd question was to her. Real enough to bring her from New York to the Foundation hangar. I noted that her right hand lay on her lap, not far from where her Glock nested in its leather holster under her arm.

I couldn't help it. I cracked a smile.

"You know that maneuver we just discussed? Pidge—er, Cassidy? Out on that highway in Montana?"

She nodded.

"You know where I was at that moment?"

"The report said you were on the road with Foyle."

"I was on my ass on the road. Flat on my ass. Helpless. With Foyle less than ten yards from me, pointing a rifle at me."

"The report didn't specify."

"Foyle closed in on me, my wife and Sandy Stone. Shooting at us. All we had was Andy's Glock. I think you can do the math. A Glock at fifty yards versus an AR-15. We had nowhere to go. No cover. So, what the report also doesn't specify is that I took Andy's Glock and did my thing.

Went right up to Foyle and set up to shoot him. And when I did—BAM!"
I clapped my hands together. She flinched. "Next thing I knew, I was on
my ass with every nerve in my body on fire. Practically paralyzed. Nearly
deaf and blind. Fully visible. I popped out right in front of the
sonofabitch."

"What happened?"

"You tell me. I have no idea. When I tried to fire Andy's gun from
inside *the other thing* something blew back on me. Like stepping on a live
transmission wire. Like taking a Taser hit—maybe, I dunno, I've never
been tased. The gun discharged. I don't know where the bullet went. It
sure as hell didn't hit Foyle. Next thing I knew, he was standing over me.
I reappeared right in front of his eyes. Fell to the ground jittering like
someone taking a bath with an electric hair dryer. I couldn't talk. I
couldn't move. And by the way, that wasn't the only time it happened. I
got the same jolt in New York when Luciana DeSantorini fired her gun
after I wrapped her up in *the other thing*. Damn near killed me both times.
So...no. It wasn't me."

"But you were there."

"I was."

"Why?"

I explained about Chief Ceeves and Sheriff Kresky, and how the
Chief's gut feeling that Casey Gregg remained alive prompted him to seek
my help.

She weighed the information for a long moment. I thought she might
pay me a compliment for finding the Congressman's wife. Instead she
said, "I didn't know. I had to ask."

"You came all this way to ask me that? You could have called."

"Not if the answer went the other way." Her hand fell away from
her lap.

"You were going to arrest me?"

She laughed. "I'm not sure. That's probably not as easy as it sounds."

"It might prove to be a challenge," I said. "The good news is that I'm
not your shooter. The bad news is, I won't make a good assassin. A gun is
no good to me when I disappear. Plus, how could you think it was me in
Idaho? You're the one who told me the shots came from a distance. And
you have the video."

"I have a hard time with coincidence."

"So does my wife. Now it's my turn to ask. Are you thinking the same shooter killed Gregg and Spellman?"

She drew a long breath, then let it slip away in a contemplative sigh. She looked at me and her eyebrows went up.

"Crap," I said. "Asking if I shot him wasn't the only reason you came."

She shook her head.

"Oh, no. No, no, no, no, no!" I stood up, hands out. "Whatever it is, I'm out. In less than forty-eight hours me and that airplane are on our way to Virginia where I have a date with my wife and nothing—*nothing*—is going to derail those plans. I mean it!"

"Will, sit down."

Dammit!

25

"Do you remember the D.C. Sniper?"

"Vaguely. I was...I think...in high school."

"Well, you're about ten years younger than me. I remember it vividly. The world came to a screaming halt. The case seemed unsolvable. Random people with no connection to one another were shot doing ordinary things like putting gas in their cars. The nightmare lasted weeks."

"They caught the guy—the guys. There were two, right?"

"Yes." Leslie reached for her satchel. She extracted an iPad in a bright pink case. She flipped it open and poked at the screen for a moment. Satisfied with the result, she put the device on the desk between us and rotated the image for me to view.

"Spellman," I said.

She swiped the screen.

"Gregg."

She swiped again. This time I didn't recognize the man in the picture. He sat at an audio console with a fat microphone hanging in front of his face.

"That's Dan Boulton. He ran a fringe talk radio show in Missouri. Anti-abortion. White power. Right wing disinformation—some of it straight from the Russian GRU. He was shot in his driveway one morning after an all-night show."

She swiped. A new image appeared—a woman holding a sign and shouting at someone off camera.

"Sheila Lynn Anders. Houston Texas. One of the most prolific proponents of the Qanon conspiracy theory. Also, a Texas state legislator. Shot and killed in a Walmart parking lot in a Houston suburb."

Another swipe. Another face. This one looked like a member of the Bunker Hill Victory Brigade. In his sixties, bearded. He posed for the camera dressed in drab camo while holding a semi-automatic rifle at port arms.

"Michael Aaron Bennett. Commander of a group that split off from the White Aryan Resistance. They called themselves the *Skorzeny Armee von Kriegern* which is—"

"Named after Hitler's favorite special forces commander."

"Right. This one almost slipped under the radar. He was at a militia training camp with his fellow Blitzkriegers shooting off his AR when he took a round in the center of his forehead. The local coroner wrote it off as a ricochet, a freak accident, because the round was nearly spent, but our office dug a little deeper—literally. The round was a .223, but it didn't come from his own gun."

"Somebody downrange shot him? While he was shooting?"

"In a very crafty way." She stroked the screen. "There are more. Another neo-nazi. A white supremacist newsletter publisher. Are you seeing the pattern?"

"I don't want to say out loud what anybody with a brain and a moral compass is thinking, but…"

"Someone is doing humanity a favor? Uh-huh. Here's one." She swiped the screen forward several images. "A crusading evangelical who specialized in conversion therapy camps. He's been sued half a dozen times and arrested for aggravated assault and kidnapping. The charges are pending, but not slowing him down. He launched a web network devoted to battling what he called Satan's gay war against holy Christian marriage. He recently launched a streaming platform full of anti-gay techniques and instructions. Now you can abuse and torture your demonically possessed sexually confused teen in the comfort of your own home. Shot and killed while driving his car on a freeway in Orlando. Another one that might have been missed because it was first identified as a road rage incident."

"Jesus. How many are there?"

"Eleven that we know of, counting Spellman and Gregg."

I whistled. "How is it that this hasn't been in the news?"

"They have been," she said. "Individually. Gregg is all over the news right now for a lot of reasons. The rest, a story here and there. But so far, the media hasn't tipped to the pattern. To be honest, up until Gregg, the mainstream media hasn't been overly interested—and in his case, it's all about a Member of Congress who had sex with an underaged intern and tried to bury his wife alive. Regarding the others, the fringe media is full of theories and accusations, but they've cried wolf so many times nobody notices any more. For them, anybody who dies is the victim of a Deep State plot."

"Are you sure there's a connection?"

"Frankly, no. Except to say that these are all True Believers. People so deeply programmed that no reasoning, facts or deprogramming penetrates their fantasy world. They're high profile in their own spheres. A militia leader. A right-wing broadcaster. A state legislator. A Member of Congress. Josiah James could easily have made this list if he were still alive. These people are problematic because it's not enough that they have the worms in their own heads, they feel a need to spread their disease."

"And this has been going on…?"

"All summer."

I catch a few headlines on Saturday mornings at the Silver Spoon but tune out conversation dipped in politics. None of the stories Leslie described blipped on my radar.

"You said you weren't part of the investigation. But you hauled me all the way to Idaho for Spellman."

"Spellman wasn't part of all this—not at the time, not for me. That was about domestic terrorism. And to be honest, it was about testing."

"Testing?"

"You. And…you know…" The trip to Idaho wasn't the first time I'd seen Leslie since meeting her in the aftermath of the attempted assassination of the Supreme Court, but it was our first operational outing.

"Did I pass?"

"Jury's still out." She said it through her lopsided smile.

I pointed at her laptop. "So, is there an investigation? Or are you just spit-balling a theory?"

"There is. An SAC has been running an investigation out of the

Chicago office and it's about as quiet as anything I've ever seen. Bin Laden Raid quiet."

"Why?"

"Think about it. The D.C. sniper almost paralyzed the east coast. Can you imagine a story like that across multiple states? And if it got out that someone is offing bright and shining figures in the world of right-wing conspiracy theories and white supremacy there's a good chance for blow-back. Violent blowback. Spellman's group already wants blood and they won't think too hard about who they target. At the very least, this story would be a rallying cry for every anti-government fringe group on the internet."

"Any leads? Evidence?"

"I have no idea. I'm on the outside. I'm only dipping my toe in this because of you. What little I *can* tell you is that whoever is doing this is smart, clean, and may have a law enforcement or military background—or both. You saw it first-hand, Will. In Idaho."

"You didn't get anything from that video?"

"Zilch. And it was damned hard to mainstream it."

"Okay," I said cautiously. "Then can I assume you're not here to ask for my help on this? Because I have no idea what or how I can contribute."

"Neither do I."

I wanted to feel relieved, but she gave me a blank stare. A heavily loaded blank stare.

"Then why do I feel like you're threatening weekend plans that are the only reason I draw my next breath?"

"Will," she said, "the link between these cases is that there are no links. Gregg had no connection to Spellman. Who had no connection to crazy homo-hater. Who had no connections to the Texas Qanon queen. These people are getting methodically picked off and the sole connection is what we assume to be the shooter's feelings toward them."

"Earl's three rules," I mused.

"What?"

"Earl Jackson. My former boss. He has three rules. You can't fix stupid. You can't talk to crazy. And never negotiate with terrorists."

"Pretty good rules."

"Someone is adhering to the first two. You can't fix 'em, and you can't talk to 'em. So…the only solution is a bullet."

"That's dark. And please don't use the word 'solution.'"

"Sorry."

"This goes back to the D.C. Sniper case. The shooter has every advantage. He picks the target. He picks the time. Without knowing when or where he will strike again, we have virtually no chance of finding him. We're perpetually behind the eight ball."

"Didn't you tell me how specialized the shooter had to be to hit Spellman? How the round was heavy? The gun and the ammunition can't be something you can pick up at Dick's Sporting Goods. And the training—you said it had to be military."

"That's certainly where I would look. Those are all parameters that narrow the suspect pool, but it's still a big pool. And the only witness to more than one of the shootings is someone who can't be interviewed."

"Who?"

She gave me a long-suffering look I've seen on my wife's face, usually pertaining to laundry.

"Oh," I said. "Right."

"Compounded by the fact that I don't have access to the investigation."

"I thought you were an 'agent at large.' Your own letter of marque. Go anywhere, do anything you want. Answer to no one."

"Yes. And no. Some of that is true. And don't ask for specifics because part of the deal is that I can't answer you. But the public face of my assignment with Lindsay complicates matters. A lot of people in the Bureau think the way that ended reflects badly on me, or they look at me as Lindsay's prima donna. I have certain authority, but using it means showing my hand. Which is the same thing as not having authority. I can't just waltz in and ask to look at the files, the data, the reports."

"Why not?"

"You're asking the wrong question. The question I'd be asked is 'Why?' What does an agent with no clear portfolio want inside one of the tightest, most locked-down investigations running today? One that's just been supercharged thanks to the assassination of a Member of Congress. And don't get me started on bringing you along. To get you back and forth to Idaho, I had to list you as an IT specialist. Basically, a hacker cooperating with the Bureau. Don't ask."

"Why would you want me along anyway, if you're just accessing reports and files?"

I got the look again. This time I failed to follow.

"Because I'm not the one I want looking at those materials."

"So have them make a copy."

She aimed her near-black eyes at me to make her point. Her pupils reminded me of the rifle aimed at me by the Bunker Hill Victory Brigade kid.

"Crap," I said, catching on. "You don't want to ask permission."

26

Arun's trip to the Pacific Northwest cleared the Navajo's schedule for the week. I booked it for my date with Andy, planning my departure for Friday to assure myself of abundant time to arrive in Virginia, rent a car, book a good hotel, and be at the gates of the FBI training academy at the Quantico Marine base comfortably before noon on Saturday. By staying in Virginia Friday night, I all but eliminated the possibility of bad weather causing me to miss the moment my wife emerged through the gates.

I was damned if I would let Leslie disrupt any part of my plans.

I checked my watch—closing in on four p.m. on Wednesday afternoon.

"Chicago?" I asked. "Where?"

"The FBI Field Office is on Roosevelt." I lifted my palms, clueless. She added, "About thirty blocks due west of the Shedd Aquarium."

"Which is by the late and lamented Meigs Field," I said.

"Baseball field?"

"Airport. On the waterfront. Destroyed one night by the mayor of Chicago, curse him and his progeny for all time. A beautiful airport that would have been ridiculously convenient. Now we're forced to go in via Midway or Palwaukee—er, Chicago Executive—neither of which is as convenient."

"Okay."

"Look," I said. "I'll do this. I'll get you there, although I think the part about poking around inside an FBI headquarters is madness. But at the stroke of three in the afternoon on Friday I'm wheels-up for Virginia. I mean it."

"Good. Let's go."

"What? Now?"

"No time like the present." For a forty-something seasoned FBI agent, she had no trouble looking like an eager schoolgirl. "We can visit the office tonight. Maybe catch a break when no one is around."

I pushed back my chair and stood. She followed suit and hooked her satchel strap over her shoulder, then glanced at the Navajo like we were simply going to hop in, fire it up and fly out of the hangar. I shook my head and stepped around the desk.

"Give me your hands."

"What?"

"Your hands. Both hands." I held mine out for her. She mustered a suspicious glance, then placed her hands, palm to palm, in mine.

I closed a grip and shoved the levers in my head hard against the stops.

FWOOOMP!

We both vanished. I pushed the balls of my feet against the concrete floor.

She shrieked. We shot straight up. I felt her tug to free her hands.

"Don't!" I snapped. "If you break the connection, you'll fall."

She stopped tugging and now attempted to squeeze the blood out of my fingers. She chanted—a desperate whisper.

"Hail Mary, full of grace, the Lord is with thee!"

We rose quickly toward the steel trusses that crossed the hangar ceiling.

"Let go of your left hand. Your left." I raised my voice to break through her steady prayer. I peeled my right hand from her left just in time to reach over my head and grab the steel truss before we cracked our skulls. She used her free hand to double her grip on my left arm.

"Oh lord oh lord oh lord!"

"Cool, huh?" I tried not to laugh. I could feel her twisting back and forth, looking around.

"PUT ME DOWN!"

"If you try to shoot me, it's going to hurt like hell, and we'll both fall about twenty-five feet. Just relax." I gave the beam a shove and we began our descent. "Bend your knees."

We touched down.

Fwooomp!

She staggered. I held on until I felt certain she wouldn't fall and hurt herself. The look on her face—I couldn't help myself. I broke out laughing.

"NOT FUNNY!" she cried, jerking her hands away.

"I'm sorry. But you should see—oh my god—the look—!"

Wide-eyed, furious, frightened, the image of murder searching for a victim, she stepped away. She glanced at the ceiling, then back at me.

"Oh—my—dear—LORD! Stop laughing at me!"

"Sorry!" I held up both hands, figuring if she pulled her gun the universal sign for surrender might save me. "Sorry! Really, I am." I wasn't. Not one bit.

"*What—! Why—?*"

"Easy. Relax. Shake it off." I wiggled my fingers to show her how.

She steadied herself.

"*Why did you do that?*"

"Because I'm not going into an FBI field office by myself. You need to know what it feels like. And you can't be screaming like a little girl the whole time." I chuckled.

She froze. The anger lingered, but the slightly off-center set of her mouth slowly widened into a grin.

"Wow. All I can say is—WOW!"

"You gonna be okay?"

Her head bobbed.

"There's Coke in Arun's fridge. And something stronger in the cabinet under the coffee maker. If we're leaving, I need to run home and pack. I'm not going to go on a date with my wife in jeans, a t-shirt and three-day-old underwear."

I left her staring at her hands and looking up at the hangar ceiling.

27

September and May are my two favorite months. September puts a flourish on summer, retaining summer's warmth and bright skies while cleaning the air and closing more days than not with golden sunsets that make me want to fly west forever. Such a brilliant sun touched the horizon at almost the exact moment the Navajo's wheels touched the pavement of Runway 16 at Chicago Executive Airport. I spared the brakes and rolled past the intersections of both other runways, making the second to last turn onto taxiway Lima for the trip back to Atlantic Aviation.

After parking, Leslie and I disembarked under a glowing orange and blue sky. I took care of the aircraft arrangements while Leslie secured a rental car. Twenty minutes after landing, she navigated out of the lot and onto suburban Chicago streets.

The FBI Field Office nestled within the Chicago Medical District, an expanse of hospitals, medical centers, and parking lots stretching across whole blocks. Leslie drove us past the FBI building on Roosevelt, then looped back to the Hyatt House Center on West Harrison. We released the car to a valet, entered the insanely ornate building, registered, and dropped our bags in our rooms. She asked for half an hour. That gave me twenty minutes on my own to grab a beverage in the bar before she joined me.

"Should you be drinking—you know, if we're going to be doing—uh

—this thing?" she slid onto the seat beside me. The bartender lifted his eyebrows at her. "I'll have what he's having."

"Should you?"

She shrugged. The bartender served up an iced tea.

"I try not to drink and fly," I told Leslie. I asked for menus. The bartender said a server would bring them if we took a table. We seated ourselves and ordered dinner.

"What, exactly, are we looking for?" I asked.

"Depends. Some SACs like to run a war room. They feel it enhances the free flow of information and ideas. Others let everyone work on their own, in their own cubicles, then gather the team for updates. I'm not sure which way Saunders—he's the SAC—will go. If there's a war room, there's a big board. Old school guys like marker boards. New techies like smart boards and monitors, which could be problematic if we don't have password access. We'll just have to nose around."

"Again...I don't get why you can't just stroll in and flash your badge."

"I can. You can't. And I don't want to go in there and explain who I am and what I'm doing poking around in someone else's investigation— or have to mutter to you out of the side of my mouth. Trust me. This is better. When we get up on the floor, if there's no one there, you can let go of me. It'll be easier for me to move."

"What about cameras?"

"On the first floor and in the public areas. In the investigative spaces, no."

"Really? I would have thought they'd be big on security."

"Security isn't an issue. Access is tightly controlled. But cameras mean video. Video means a record. A record can be subpoenaed by crafty lawyers who want to insinuate that a case was not properly investigated, or that there was bias, or that evidence was mishandled. Or that agents were playing solitaire instead of finding their clients not guilty. No video. No subpoenas."

"Makes sense, I guess. Have you thought about how we're getting in?"

"I was planning on using the front door. Unless you have a better idea?"

The server brought our sandwiches while I thought it over. After asking if we wanted ketchup and producing a squeeze bottle, the server moved away.

"Depends. Do you want to leave evidence of visiting the building?"

"Not really. I figured…you know…"

I bit into an overly expensive and equally over-cooked burger and kept my doubts to myself.

WE MET in the lobby at two a.m. After dinner, I returned to my room, set the alarm on my phone, and grabbed a nap on top of the bedsheets. The sleep ended up being deep and difficult to climb out of when my phone chirped at 1:30. I needed cold water on my face to get up to speed.

Leslie looked alert and determined when I found her in the lobby. She wore a leather jacket and dark blue baseball cap with no markings. I wore my flight jacket. The night air had cooled, dipping into the mid-fifties. We strolled out past a parked airport shuttle whose driver never looked up from his phone.

We crossed West Harrison street and walked into a park, then followed a path to a statue honoring Louis Pasteur. After checking all directions for cameras or intruding eyes, I stepped in front of Leslie and pulled out a BLASTER. I fixed the prop in place and held it up.

"Okay. Pilot safety briefing. This," I said, "is a Basic Linear Aerial System for Transport, Electric Rechargeable. BLASTER."

She choked on an abrupt laugh. I made a face.

"Oh," she said solemnly, "you're serious. Go on."

"When we disappear, we go weightless. Not affected by gravity or subject to rules for inertia."

"We've discussed all that."

"But that doesn't mean it won't hurt if we crash into something. Also, without this—device—if we lose contact with any objects or the ground, we could end up floating like an untethered astronaut."

"Can't you just reappear?"

"Not if we're a hundred and fifty feet up."

"Right. Drop like a rock."

"One more thing." I fired up the prop. "Keep your fingers away from this. It'll take 'em right off."

"Noted. How do you want to do this? Piggyback? Full hug? Platonic grip?" She spread her arms at her sides.

"Off to see The Wizard." I stepped next to her and held out my left arm. She hooked her right arm in mine and closed a grip on my hand, fingers intertwined.

"And one more time just to be sure...don't use your gun, whatever you do."

"Got it."

Fwooomp! Under Louis Pasteur's somber gaze, we vanished.

"Whoa!" she uttered. "Okay. I'm fine."

"Really? Are you ready?"

"Hit it."

I kicked the ground. We launched.

28

I took us straight up from the Pasteur statue, leveled off around one hundred feet, then followed the street layout I had memorized from my iPad. West Harrison to Damen then south to Roosevelt. Half a dozen hospitals filled the blocks between the hotel and the FBI building. I made a mental note of them for a future visit, perhaps a weekend trip to Chicago with Andy. A nice dinner. A show. And a night of prowling hospital rooms.

Leslie didn't attempt to crush the bones in my hand this time. Nor did she recite the Rosary. As I eased us forward with the BLASTER, I felt her arm tense, then she wiggled it to relax.

"My god, Will, how do you not do this all the time?" she asked. We soared above a sea of streetlights.

"Who says I don't?"

Chicago lights climbed to peaks along the shore of Lake Michigan. The sparkle and glow begged me to take a tour. I suppressed the urge and focused on navigation and on the threat of wires.

The FBI Field Office on Roosevelt blended with the hospitals and medical centers clustered around it. Something about the concrete and glass building struck me as religious as we approached it. The feeling made no sense, given its drab utilitarian look—until I realized that each cube of windows had a Christian cross within the frame. Two large rectangular windows set below two square windows gave the dividing lines the proportions of one of history's oldest religious symbols. One of those design elements which, once seen, can't be unseen.

We approached the rectangular building. I crafted a flight path around the structure, then angled down to the front entrance by flying close to the wire-free façade.

We eased to a hover near the main doors.

"Now what?" I asked.

Except for dim security lights beyond a rank of metal detectors, darkness enveloped the lobby entrance. I had expected uniformed security. A guard station, even if the doors weren't open. No one stood or moved behind the double glass entrance.

"We try the door."

I pulsed the power unit to take us to the center set of doors.

"Hold my arm. I need both hands." She freed my left hand. For leverage, I planted my right palm on the glass beside the handle. I pulled.

Nothing.

"Locked," she said.

"How do you feel about leaving evidence of a break-in?"

"I'd rather not." That eliminated the trick of breaking loose the bolt. "Let's try something else. Can you take us back up? I saw something as we came in."

I rotated and she uttered a sharp gasp. "I felt that! I felt something when you did that. Like right down my middle."

"Uh-huh." I applied power. We ascended away from the doors. I curved away until we faced the building. I saw it before she said it.

"Top floor. See the lights?"

I shifted the angle of the BLASTER and we ascended. Most of the offices in the building were unlit. Right of center on the top floor, a row of windows spilled full illumination from the building. I slowed and stopped ten feet outside the glass. We faced an open concept expanse filled with desks, tables, computer monitors and—surprisingly—a couple dozen men and women.

"So much for sneaking around after hours," I said. "That's a lot of people working an all-nighter."

"Something's up."

Men and women hunched over desks. Some worked phones. Some

hurried from one station to the next. At one table near the center of the room, half a dozen men in suits leaned over a table pointing at what I took for maps. A woman with a cell phone in her hand leaned out of a nearby office and called to the men at the table. The glass muted their exchange, but the information she imparted caused a new flurry of pointing.

Leslie said, "That's SAC Saunders. The guy in the gray suit at the end."

Saunders wore a rumpled academic look. Clean shaved with a past-due haircut, he peered over readers perched on the end of his nose. He said little while the men around him chatted and debated. A woman joined the group and bent over the tabletop with a Sharpie, drawing on the maps. She poked emphatically at what she had rendered and spoke to Saunders, who nodded.

"Should there be this many people here at this hour?" I asked.

"Only for a full fire drill."

We watched the group at the table plot and point. Information conveyed by phone to people working at desks was shouted to the map table. Additional Sharpie marks imprinted the map. Saunders checked his watch and moved away from the table. Two subordinates followed him.

I pulsed the BLASTER. We tracked a course parallel to Saunders. He crossed the length of the open space and stopped to face a bank of monitors.

"Get me closer. Over there." I felt Leslie point and smiled.

"You mean by the monitors?"

"Yes."

I maneuvered us slightly higher for an optimum angle on the LCD panels. Saunders faced screens filled with maps and data. I stopped and checked for any breeze that might carry us. The night air hung motionless around us. We remained static.

The monitors displayed lists, photos, and data we couldn't read. A set of mug shots exhibited a young man defiantly challenging the camera operated by whatever arresting officer shot the photo. A nearby photo showed a long black rifle with a substantial scope.

A screen at the far end of the monitor bank caught my eye. The graphics looked familiar. I was about to explain it to Leslie when Saunders said something decisive. The group abruptly broke up.

"Hear that?" Leslie asked.

Engines. Vehicle engines. I looked down.

A line of four black SUVs rolled sharply around the corner of the building and hurried to the front entrance. Behind the top floor windows, people broke into runs, grabbing coats, binders, bags and weapons. Roughly a dozen of the agents working in the room hurried to stand impatiently at a bank of elevators.

"Where the hell are they going?" Leslie asked.

"The airport first," I said, "then Tri-Township."

"What?"

"Look. There. See that center monitor on the far end?"

"Uh-huh."

"That's a screen shot from Foreflight. The flight planning application I use. That's a VFR sectional chart. The magenta line is from Midway to Tri-Township airport."

"How the hell can you see that from here? I can't read anything on that map."

"I'm not reading it. But I know the airport. It's right on the Mississippi, right where the river bends to the east. See it? The curve?"

"How do you know that's where they're going?"

"I don't. But their ride is here. I bet you if we followed those SUVs down there, we'd end up at Midway where there's an aircraft waiting."

She said nothing. The elevators arrived. The agents loaded up. Doors closed. Those remaining on the top floor office looked relieved, as if rushed planning had ended and an operational wait had begun.

"We can follow them to Midway and watch them fly off," I said, "or we can roll the dice and try to get to Tri-Township ahead of them. They have to drive across town to Midway. We're just a hop, skip and jump away at Chicago Executive."

"And then what?"

"Then when they arrive, we can tag along wherever they're going. My bet? They have a lead on your sniper."

Leslie didn't speak for a moment, long enough for me to realize what an idiot I would feel like sitting on the ramp at the Tri-Township Airport in the middle of the night with no squad of FBI agents arriving. Doubt inflated to fill her silence.

"Alright. Let's do it."

I hit the BLASTER before either of us could change our mind.

29

My flight bag sat on the desk in my Hyatt Center hotel room, but the aircraft keys jangled in my pocket. Having the flight bag and iPad it contained would have been nice, but it wasn't critical. I pushed the slide control on the power unit all the way forward and held out the prop to bite the air. The BLASTER pulled us up and away from the building. Leslie's grip grew marginally stronger as we gained height, which struck me as funny because we'd just been floating outside the window of a ten-story building. A fall from anything over thirty feet would probably kill us.

I've been in and out of Chicago Executive Airport, the former Palwaukee Airport, many times and knew where to find it. Like all city airports at night, it formed a black expanse in a sea of lights. Streetlights are far brighter than runway lights and more than one pilot breaking out of a low overcast has momentarily lined up on a boulevard. After locating the airport, I fixed a course for the Atlantic Aviation ramp on the northwest corner. The Navajo waited for us in a tiedown spot on the edge of the parking ramp.

I executed a nice landing beside the fuselage. Leslie learns quickly. She popped into view steady on her feet.

"Think you can untie those ropes?" I pointed. "I'll go pay the bill."

"Got it." She ducked under the tail to undo the tiedown knots.

"One under the tail, one under each wing," I called out over my shoulder. "If you miss a tiedown, we're going to look stupid trying to taxi."

Ten minutes later we rolled for takeoff on Runway 16.

"WHERE'S the rest of the team?" A county deputy met us the moment we stepped onto the dark, vacant ramp at Tri-Township Airport. "I was told to meet a whole damned team. We got three more cars coming."

Leslie flashed her badge for him.

"They're right behind us," she said. Just before shutting down the radios, I heard a King Air call on a five-mile final for Tri-Township's single hard surface runway, validating our decision. I informed Leslie that we called it correctly; it had to be Saunders and his team. The turboprop's superior speed whittled our lead down to a few minutes. Like me, they would approach over the Mississippi River, catching the silver in its surface during the descent to the runway.

"Well, they better goddamn hurry it up. We just got a call from Flatley's girlfriend. She said he took his truck and headed into town. She says he knows we were watching him."

Leslie bolted for the deputy's SUV. "You had surveillance on him? Walk and talk. Fill me in. Flatley. Location. The works."

The deputy and I followed.

"Thought you knew all this."

"Details, Deputy!" she cried out, rounding the front grille. "From the top!"

He stopped with his hand on the driver's door handle. "Are we gonna wait for the rest of your folks?"

"They'll catch up. Let's go."

We piled into the vehicle. The deputy, a man flirting with retirement age, wheeled off the ramp and onto the highway. The look on his face said he would have preferred not to deal with anything like this before signing up for Social Security. He picked up his radio mic.

"Dispatch, I got FBI with me. We're headed for Savanna."

"You got all of 'em?" A woman on dispatch duty asked.

"I'm advance," Leslie said. "The full team will be at the airport with the SAC in a matter of minutes."

"Uh, there's more coming. We still gotta pick up the rest at the airport. Donna, where's the Sheriff?"

"He's out at Flatley's talking to Sharon."

"Any idea where he's going?" Leslie asked. "Flatley?"

"Donna, any idea where Jimmy's headed?"

"Just town was all the Sheriff said."

Leslie turned to face me in the rear seat. "James Flatley. His photo was on the board." I remembered the sullen prisoner glaring at the police camera. "Okay, Deputy…uh…"

"Carlson. Al Carlson."

"Okay, Al. Please. Details."

Carlson adjusted in his seat. I noticed that he held the speed at just over sixty and didn't use the lights or siren. Empty highway flowed through the big SUV's headlights. To my left, I caught glimpses of the river through gaps in the trees.

"After we got your call, we did a drive-by like you asked. Confirmed that Jimmy's truck was at the house. We didn't approach, just like you said."

"Then why is he leaving his house in the middle of the night?"

"I'm gonna guess that he saw our drive-bys."

The radio crackled to life. A new voice joined the conversation.

"Dispatch, any word on Al and those feds?"

"I'm here, Sheriff. I got one of the feds with me." Carlson handed the mic to Leslie.

"This is Special Agent Carson-Pelham, Sheriff. I am not the full team. SAC Saunders and his team are right behind us. They should be with your people any minute now."

"Okay, Agent Pelham. You tell 'em to get a move on. Jimmy's girl-friend says she thinks he had his big rifle with him and that he might be headed for the grain elevators. The ones on the river."

"Sheriff, can you confirm what she meant by 'big rifle?'"

"Jimmy has a Barrett. Thought you knew that."

Leslie threw me a look. I mouthed a question. *Spellman?* She nodded.

"Sheriff, if he has his Barrett and he's going to high ground, you've got to keep your people back. Way back."

"Don't think I don't know that. All units, all units! Do not approach Flatley. Set the perimeter at the city limits and stay the hell out of the line of sight with those elevators. No lights. No sirens. Al, meet me at Poopy's."

Half a dozen voices checked in to confirm the sheriff's order. Carlson abruptly released the accelerator and began to slow down. A long low building appeared on the right. An unlit road sign said Poopy's Pub. Leslie leaned forward to peer through the windshield.

"Are those the grain elevators? Up there?"

A red obstacle hazard light blinked just above the black tree line half a mile away.

"Yup."

"If we can see them, he can see us. Pull around and park behind the building, Deputy. And kill the lights."

Carlson didn't question. He hustled the county SUV around the empty pub parking lot, squealing the tires and heaving me against my seatbelt. He nudged up against the back of the building in the dark.

"Al, I'm going to look. Broadcast a warning to the vehicles coming up from the airport. Tell them where you are and tell them to approach lights off."

"Roger that."

Leslie climbed out of the cab. I pulled the door latch to follow but found the rear passenger door locked. Leslie hurried around and opened the door from the outside. We trotted to the corner of the building. She carefully peeked around the edge in the direction of the town.

A row of concrete grain elevators stood against the night sky.

"A Barrett could be a match to the weapon that did the job on Spellman," she whispered.

"What's a Barrett?"

"Fifty caliber rifle, designed as an anti-material weapon, but it's also a standard sniper weapon for several branches of service."

"What does anti-material mean?"

"He can put a round through the engine block of that Chevy and stop it in its tracks. They use Barretts to set off IEDs, destroy computer and radio equipment, and pretty much turn anything it touches to junk. A shot at this distance would not be much of a challenge to someone with training."

"You think this is our guy?"

She didn't answer as a lightless vehicle slowed and pulled into the pub parking lot. Like Carlson, the driver hurried around to the back of the building. Leslie took another look at the red obstacle light blinking in the distance, then hurried back to where Carlson greeted a grim-faced man wearing a peaked cap over a nylon jacket with county sheriff's markings.

Carlson made the introductions to Sheriff John Warner. He stumbled when he got to me.

"Will," I said. "Just a civilian charter pilot who should have stayed at the airport. I'll keep out of your way."

"Good plan, son. Agent Pelham, in about two hours the sun comes up. If Jimmy Flatley is on top of those grain elevators with a Barrett M.82, he will have clear sight of a target rich environment and it's going to be damn near impossible for us to reach him." Worry lines, visible even in the dark, creased the sheriff's forehead.

"You said you spoke to his girlfriend," Leslie prompted.

"Yeah. Not good. She says he's been bad and getting worse."

"Bad how?"

"Paranoid. Not taking his meds. Not sleeping. Talking to himself. Thinking his girlfriend is somebody else. Hair trigger. He freaked when he spotted one of our cruisers doing a slow patrol out on the road by his house. My mistake. I should'a sent an unmarked."

"Probably would not have made a difference," Leslie said. "What can you tell me about Flatley?"

"Not much. He grew up around here, but I never met him. My people tell me he worked part time making deliveries for Napa Auto Parts. You folks said he was ex-military. I certainly didn't know he had a Barrett rifle for God's sake. Or that he was a head case. How in the hell did he get a rifle like that?"

Leslie didn't speculate.

"Sheriff? It's Donna." The radio in Carlson's vehicle joined the conversation. Warner reached through the open driver-side window and picked up the mic.

"Go ahead Donna."

"Sharon Pike just called in. She's pretty shook up. She went to check on her daughter and says she's missing. She thinks Jimmy took her."

Warner clenched his jaw and looked down at his feet.

"Sheriff, she says she's going after him. I told her to stay put. That we'd send somebody out. I hope I did right."

"You did. How old?"

"The little girl is three."

"Alright. Listen to me, Donna. Call Tony. Get him outta bed. Tell him to go over to Flatley's place and babysit that woman. Then I want you to call Superintendent Walsh. Get him to activate the school district snow day phone chain with a message for everybody to stay inside, doors locked, lights out. Tell him there's a dangerous armed felon on the loose. You got all that?"

"Got it."

Warner dropped the mic on the vehicle seat and spoke under his breath. "Son of a buck."

30

"Special Agent Saunders, I'm Special Agent Leslie Carson-Pelham," Leslie reached for and shook the hand of the mildly bewildered man climbing out of the front seat of a county deputy's SUV. The look on his face asked a lot of questions. Leslie hurried to explain. "I'm afraid we're on parallel investigations. I literally flew in a few minutes ahead of you hoping to track down James Flatley."

"You worked for Lindsay," Saunders said.

"I did."

"Very sorry. I knew Mitch. He was one of the best."

"He was." The exchange did not erase the questions on his face.

"Parallel investigations?"

"I'll fill your people in. Right now, I believe your man just climbed a grain elevator with his Barrett M.82."

Saunders pulled off the FBI bullet-proof vest he wore over his increasingly wrinkled suit coat. He tossed it back in the vehicle.

"Guess there's no point in wearing this."

Leslie quickly introduced the sheriff and explained the man's decision to activate the school district phone chain, and his orders to all department vehicles to establish a perimeter at the town limits. I thought she'd overstepped until I realized her take-charge air forestalled questions forming on the faces of the arriving team.

"Do we know if he's actually up there? And if he has the child?"

"We do not," Leslie replied.

Warner stepped forward. "If he is up there, he's got sightlines on every house, every yard, every road in and outta town. He spooked because he saw cops on the road outside his house. And from what his girlfriend says, he thinks the salt and pepper shakers are ninja assassins. We sure as hell can't roll a unit, even an unmarked, to find out if he's at the grain elevators. He'd have a clean shot at it."

"Hey John," Deputy Carlson approached with his cell phone at his ear. "I got an—hold on—" He spoke into his phone. "Ellie, it's Al. Christ, yes, I know what time it is. Listen to me. Just listen. I need you to go look out your front window." Carlson held up his free hand to put pause to the Sheriff's next question. "No! Don't turn any lights on. Just go to your front window and peek out. Lemme know when you get there." He lowered the phone toward his neck. "My sister Ellie lives down the tracks from the elevators. She should be—" The phone swung up. "You're there? Okay. Look over at the elevators. Can you see 'em? Good. Do you see a pickup truck? Blue Ram, I think. Blue anyway. Do you see it? Okay. Okay, good, just hold the line and I'll be right back to explain. Get away from the window and for God's sake, stay inside and don't turn any lights on!" He looked at the Sheriff and nodded solemnly, then turned away.

"Dutch," Saunders said to one of his team. "Get HRT moving. Get 'em out here now. Ten minutes ago."

The agent called Dutch shook his head. "Two hours. Minimum." He pulled his phone from his pocket and dialed.

Leslie asked, "Special Agent Saunders, your team is way ahead of me. Can I get one of your people to fill me in on your side and then I'll brief my side?"

Saunders looked at another of his agents, a woman with short-cropped blonde hair and a runner's physique that camouflaged her age. She greeted Leslie and introduced herself as Karen. They stepped away from the cluster around Saunders. I leaned against Carlson's SUV and slowly edged toward Leslie and Agent Karen.

"...worked out of New York in Director Lindsay's office," Leslie explained. "Now I'm on a special portfolio working domestic extremist groups. Flatley's name came up, but nothing suggested any of this. I just came out here today to see if I could interview him about tangent individuals. See if there were any connections. I had no idea about all…this."

"No way you would have known. We formed this unit in August. It's been held tight," Karen said. She filled in background on the unit, on the string of sniper shootings, and on the need for secrecy. Leslie gave no indication that she already knew portions of the background. Karen explained that the unit had combed thousands of service records, cross-checked them against travel records, cell data, and even extremist groups, which Karen presumed to be on Leslie's radar. "We knocked our heads against a wall until the assassination of Congressman Martin Gregg," Karen confessed. "Flatley rose to the top. His truck came up on plate readers, and then we verified it was him on highway cameras. We can put him in Green Bay and Rhinelander, Wisconsin last Friday. It wasn't perfect. He has family up that way. But it drew a line roughly in the direction of Linden and Congressman Gregg. We also verified that Flatley has a Barrett M.82 in his possession—we're working with ATF to find the source. Preliminary ballistics on Gregg strongly indicate a Barrett 12.7x99mm round."

"What's Flatley's deal?"

"Combat veteran. Trained sniper. Treated for head wounds from a fall in Afghanistan. VA records indicate he received psychiatric treatment. Mostly a clean service record but he terminated with an OTH discharge. That was ten years ago. We're tracking that down. Since then, he has a string of arrests for disorderly conduct, and a pair of assault charges that went away when the victims dropped their complaints. His sister claims he is on anti-depressants and anti-psychotics, but we haven't found any prescriptions. We haven't interviewed the girlfriend. More likely, he's self-medicating. He's been living with this Pike woman a little over a year. This might tie with what you're working, though. His online history dives deep into anti-government groups, anti-government rhetoric. Lots of chat room activity. Congress is being run by China. Vaccines are full of microchips. Mind control. Pizzagate. Chemtrails. Government overthrow. The whole sick stew."

"The girlfriend told the Sheriff he's off his meds," Leslie said.

"Or he needs a fix."

"Either way, it sounds like he's paranoid and delusional. Do we know —is the three-year-old his biological daughter?"

"No. The child is not Flatley's. I don't know if that's good or bad."

"Her being with him is bad any way you slice it. Thanks, Karen."

"What about you? Does any of this fit what you're working?"

Leslie shook her head. "Lord, no! I was just interviewing to build family trees. It sounds like I would have walked into a buzz saw. I appreciate the briefing."

Karen moved to rejoin her group. Leslie tipped her head in a gesture that suggested we stroll out of earshot. We stayed close to the back of the building. I made a point of keeping Carlson's unit between us and the cluster of federal agents and police.

"Are you thinking what I'm thinking?" she asked.

"Nope."

She issued a surprised look.

"I'm not," I reaffirmed. "You're thinking I make us both disappear and we head over to that grain elevator where you leap out and arrest this character and we rescue that child, assuming she's up there with him, which I would go fifty-fifty on. Most of those grain elevators have nothing but crappy little aluminum ladders. He'd have a tough time getting the rifle up there, let alone carrying a kid."

"So, if you're not thinking all that, what *are* you thinking?"

I heaved a sigh as dark as the shadows thrown over us by Poopy's Pub.

"I'm thinking it's time to pucker up."

Fwooomp!

I kicked the asphalt beneath my feet and left Leslie gaping at the empty darkness.

31

No matter what Leslie might argue when I returned, I harbored no heroic intentions. Leaving her behind had nothing to do with wanting to be a solo act. It had everything to do with the fact that she and I had only flown together once, and her tension level meant trouble. I would have teamed up with Andy for this in a heartbeat. Andy is a mildly reluctant passenger in *the other thing* but she knows the routine, the moves and the limitations.

From the moment Flatley took his sniper rifle to the highest point in the small Mississippi River town of Savanna, I knew it would come down to me. His vantage point and sightlines prohibited anything but a drone or helicopter from approaching his position. The rifle Leslie described had range and accuracy far beyond the typical law enforcement arsenal. His training put him head and shoulders above the local authorities. If Agent Dutch was to be believed, the elite FBI Hostage Rescue Team staged at least two hours away. By then the sun would be up and, phone chain notwithstanding, people were bound to begin moving in the small town. Sheriff Warner called Savanna a target rich environment. The phrase made me shudder.

If Flatley sprawled on top of a grain silo, he might be hard to see from below but easy to spot from above. If I could get close enough, I might catch him off guard. Grab the rifle. Toss it over the side. If he has the kid—well, grabbing kids and making them disappear is kinda my specialty.

Toss the rifle. Grab the kid.

After that, leave the clown up there to enjoy the view until the authorities pull up. With luck, I'd be in and out and back to Leslie before anyone wondered what happened to Will the civilian pilot.

LESLIE'S shocked expression fell away beneath my feet, along with Poopy's Pub, the parked SUVs and the growing cluster of law enforcement officers. I fished a BLASTER out of my flight jacket pocket and attached a prop. The group below me carried higher than average awareness of their surroundings, so I engaged the prop slowly and quietly. A lateral vector joined my silent vertical ascent. I moved toward the sparse lights of the small Illinois river town, adding power as the distance between the pub and me expanded. Night owned the sky. Dawn had not yet created contrast between the horizon and the heavens. The small town of Savanna spaced its streetlights widely, showing confidence in a low crime rate. Homes and businesses mounted exterior lights, most of which illuminated driveways, yards, and sidewalks. A thin September mist drifted in and out of lights near the river.

Poopy's Pub marked the southern edge of Savanna. A grid of homes lay to the north of the pub, separated from town by a band of undeveloped land that contained rail lines running west until they met the river. Hanging a left at the steel tracks would have taken me to where a red obstacle light throbbed on top of the grain elevators, but a more direct line crossed wetlands and an offshoot of the big river. I cut the corner and flew roughly two hundred feet above marsh and low vegetation.

The grain elevators crept into sharp relief. I found the pickup truck nosed up to the concrete at the foot of one of the five round silos. I decided to test my luck. Maybe Flatley took the child from her home, but left her sleeping in a car seat, or in the rear seat of a crew cab. Maybe he forgot why he stole his girlfriend's daughter in the first place. Or he could no longer connect the dots between the little girl and the voices in his head.

I aimed low and descended to where the pickup sat on crushed gravel. Reverse thrust slowed and then stopped me. A look through the passenger window dashed my hopes. Not only was the truck a regular cab with only two doors and a single bench seat, but no child slept on the front seat or front passenger-side floormats.

Anchored to the truck's side mirror, I studied the massive silos and the surrounding airspace. Wires stretched in and out of the darkness, making me nervous. A one-bulb light hung from a pole above a shed on the far end of the five cylinder-shaped structures. Ambient streetlight illumination painted the concrete a colorless, pale shade near the bottom, but at the top they stood black against the night sky, which hung clear overhead yet without its full complement of stars thanks to town light pollution.

I looked for a ladder. The town side of the silos gave no hint of vertical access. I knew better than to hope there wasn't any, or that access was locked up and had prevented Flatley from climbing to the top. He didn't come here to go fishing.

Like the FBI agents gathered at Poopy's Pub, I expected Flatley to be on high alert. My BLASTER can sound like a drone—volatile fuel for the man's paranoia. Maneuvering without power calls for two free hands, pushing and pulling from one grip point to the next. I stowed the BLASTER and mapped a path across the front of the silos toward the shed—then abruptly paused and held my breath.

I strained to listen.

A voice? Was someone talking?

A ventilation fan hummed somewhere nearby. I detected spoken words fading in and out of the fan's white noise.

I waited. The voice stopped.

Able to come up with no better plan, I fixed a two-handed grip on the pickup truck's mirror. I pushed and pulled twice and released on the third tug. My gentle upslope line of flight skimmed across the face of the concrete silos. I could have reached out and raked my fingers on the rough surface, if not for the fact it would have disrupted my flight path.

By the time I glided past the last silo, I had reached a height of roughly thirty feet, less than a half of the grain elevator's height but exactly the height of the pole that hung the yard light over the work shed. I arrived at the pole just below a junction of wires strung in cardinal directions. Both hands caught the rough round wood and I stopped.

I made a half turn and found what I expected to find on the river's side of the silo. Complicated steel structure housing pipes and augers rose to the top where the machinery joined a gantry with conveyors for distributing grain into the silos, and then unloading the grain into railroad cars on the tracks just below the silos, or barges moored to a dock just beyond the tracks.

A framework of steel steps angled back and forth, disappointing me. A ladder would have been tough or impossible to climb with a child. Steps, not so much.

I looked skyward. The gantry and pipes extending over the silos revealed nothing of the layout on top. It seemed unlikely to me that a sniper would nest out in the open, but also unlikely to me that good cover existed up there. The steps ascending to the top had handrails, but nothing else to shelter them. A platform at the top of the gantry looked about the same. Narrow. Open to the wind and weather. Too visible for a sniper's tastes.

I picked a path between wires and shoved off for a glide that took me to the zigzag flights of steps. I kept it slow. I didn't want to set off vibrations when I grabbed a hand hold.

There it was again. A voice. A man's voice. I could not make out the rapid-fire words. They rose and fell as if carried away by an unsteady breeze, yet the night air hung motionless. The low audio level teased my hearing.

I gripped the structure housing the steps. Hand over hand, I tugged myself higher. At the top, I grabbed the handrail. I rotated for my first good look at the pinnacle of the grain silos.

Domed concrete caps topped each of the five silos. Pipes angled from the gantry into hatches on each dome. Across the entire structure, a single narrow catwalk joined all five tops. Not for the faint of heart, it had a grid floor less than two feet wide and a single railing on just one side. The view of the town and the Mississippi River had to be spectacular, but at the price of placing faith in thin metal and old bolts. Thirty feet higher, at the top of the gantry, a single pole held the hazard obstruction light above a central bunker. The light throbbed from off to on but was shielded in a way that prevented the red glow from yielding helpful illumination.

I smelled the river and sensed it flowing south. Millions of tons of water relentlessly moving in dead silence lent weight to the moment. The gantry and supporting members reminded me of bones, luminous in a faint glow from the town lights. I looked for spotlights and found none. Who would work up here at night?

I found no control cab, no high office. More likely, crews controlled the complicated layout of pipes and augers from below, receiving and distributing grain at will.

So, where is he?

Words drifted out of the darkness.

"…know you…all lies…cancel me…"

The voice drifted across the tops of the silos from the south end. In the darkness, I couldn't see where or how the narrow walkway ended. I squinted. A shape formed and changed against the black landscape south of town. Somewhere out in that darkness the FBI mustered their forces and options at Poopy's Pub. My vantage point gave away no sign of Flatley.

How is he hiding?

Only one way to find out. I fixed a grip to shove off.

At that instant, headlights interrupted my plan to glide across empty space to the catwalk. In town, less than a quarter mile away, tires squealed. An engine revved. A pair of headlights swept drunkenly back and forth before settling in the direction of the grain elevators.

Who the hell is this?

I immediately dismissed the idea that any law enforcement officer would approach. Certainly not with such wild abandon.

Against the near silence of the town, the engine driving this vehicle roared. The car accelerated on the center line of a narrow street aimed directly at the grain elevators. The driver blew through a stop sign at the main street, ending any speculation about his or her intent. The car had one block to go before reaching a dead end at the railroad tracks running past the grain storage complex.

Crack!

The gunshot jolted me. I didn't see a flash, but there was no question of its origin. Flatley fired from a position in the dark at the far end of the catwalk on the southernmost of the five round silos.

A sharp metallic bang merged with the gunshot. The engine that had been gunning aggressively toward me uttered a harsh grinding sound before seizing. The car rolled to a stop. Smoke curled under the front bumper.

I didn't wait. I shoved myself in the direction of the dark mass at the end of the catwalk.

Flatley opening fire changed the game. All hell had to be breaking loose in the parking lot of Poopy's Pub. If the forces on the ground had not yet confirmed Flatley's location, they did now. What were the chances the FBI would feel they had no choice but to answer his gunfire?

I did not like the idea of being in the air with incoming bullets.

A car door slammed. A woman screamed out Flatley's name. I divided my attention between the catwalk handrail and movement beside the smoldering car a couple hundred yards away.

"JIMMY! DON'T YOU HURT MY BABY!"

The child's mother.

Crack!

The Barrett's harsh report echoed off nearby buildings.

The woman screamed and threw her arms up to shield her face when chips of pavement showered her.

"Next one goes in your guts, bitch!" Flatley shouted. "You betrayed me! You knew! She's the conduit!"

The woman paid no attention. She bolted forward, screaming.

So much for easy.

I took him at his word about the next shot and gave up the notion of stealth. I fired up the BLASTER and surged forward.

The dark mass at the end of the catwalk revealed itself to be a plastic tarp thrown over the last twenty feet of the catwalk frame and handrail. It formed a tent over Flatley. Lousy cover, but it served the purpose of making it impossible to distinguish Flatley from his hostage.

He still had to aim, however, and the line between him and his target was clear. I cut a path across the catwalk, then accelerated parallel to the flimsy aluminum rail. I lowered my legs. The tarp-tent swept by on my right.

The black muzzle flash suppressor on the deadly end of Flatley's rifle protruded below the skirt of the tarp. I came up on it fast and kicked it skyward. The Barrett's report slammed my eardrums. For an instant I expected complete disaster, the jolt and paralysis accompanying a terrible decision to risk another gunshot from within *the other thing*.

Instead of searing nerve pain, I felt only the jolt from catching my foot on the side of his rifle. The BLASTER pulled me through. I sailed off the end of the catwalk and over the last silo dome into empty air. I rotated quickly. Under his tarp-tent, Flatley cursed.

The woman on the street threw her hands over her head. She drew up sharply and darted sideways behind the last row of buildings facing the elevators.

I heard movement on the steel grate beneath the tarp. Flatley adjusted his aim.

I rotated and pointed the BLASTER at the end of the catwalk where the tarp hung down. I shot forward. Midway there, I stopped the prop and jammed the power unit into my back pocket. My feet hit the catwalk. I threw out both hands and gripped the rail. My fingers closed around both the railing and the plastic tarp. I threw myself backward and yanked the tarp with as much force as I could muster, planting my feet against the catwalk and using my legs for leverage. The tarp issued a fluttering whoop and flew off into empty air.

Jimmy Flatley, prone on the steel grate, looked up wild-eyed. He flailed in vain after the sailing plastic. The sheet escaped his grip and fluttered away in the darkness.

Demons infested his wild-eyed expression. Anger. Fear. Paranoia. A stew of dark emotions raged across his face—a poison made deadly by the long black rifle in his hands.

I might have fixed on his haunted eyes if not for something worse that caught my attention. The whole time approaching, I had wondered why I didn't hear the child. A three-year-old carried away in the night should have been whimpering, or crying, or screaming, or at the very least, chatty. Now I saw why.

The girl sat frozen on the exposed catwalk. She stared at nothing through glazed, panicked eyes. She cradled her left arm in her lap. My stomach turned over. An unnatural angle interrupted the line of her forearm. My momentary nausea turned to rage. Flatley had snapped the child's bones.

The pale girl shivered in shock.

An overwhelming impulse plunged me deep into a darkness I've touched before—a place in my heart where murder whispers to me at times like this, around people like this. My plan to toss Flatley's weapon over the side shifted to tossing the man holding the weapon.

Grab him. Make him vanish and go weightless. Leverage him over the side of the catwalk, over the side of the dome, over the river.

Let him go. Listen to him scream. *Bastard.*

The sequence flashed through my mind in an instant and evaporated just as quickly when Flatley adjusted his grip on the rifle. He raised the Barrett in search of whoever or whatever had just stolen his cover. If I grabbed him and he fired, the result would be tragic for both of us.

New plan. I pulled the BLASTER from my back pocket.

"Hey, Jimmy" I called out.

He jerked his head toward the sound.

"It's me, Jimmy. The Illuminati. The Deep State. I'm here for your soul. I'm here to sell you into my human trafficking pipeline. Praise Satan!"

"F-F-FUCK YOU!" he screamed.

I pulsed the power unit to get a better line on the child. Mistake. Flatley rose to his knees and heaved the weapon in the direction of the sound.

He fired.

Crack!

I have no idea how close the round came to me, but the muzzle blast and deafening gunshot drove deep into my bones. I felt a shockwave against my skin.

"Get your government mind control out of my head!" he shouted. He swung the unwieldy sniper rifle wildly from side to side. "I know! She's the conduit! She's the goddamned conduit!"

He leaped to his feet, fully exposed. How much had the string of gunshots changed the FBI's plans? How quickly were they measuring risk against loss of life? How soon would they be in range and bring their own weapons to bear?

A pulse on the power unit moved me in the right direction to set up a line of flight to the child, but in precisely the wrong direction for my own safety. I felt the target on my back as I slid into position directly between Flatley and the FBI. Even if all they had was a decent hunting rifle, if their best shooter had crept forward in darkness to within a reasonable distance it meant at any moment they might answer Flatley's fire.

A few more seconds. I needed to clear Flatley to gain a direct line to the paralyzed toddler. She sat on the catwalk with nothing but an empty fatal fall on either side of her. I prayed for her to hold her position—*just a few more seconds.*

I faced a new problem. Another blast of the power unit would bring the rifle around to bear on me. Worse, shooting forward, grabbing the child, and making her vanish before Flatley's eyes would make a target out of the empty space the girl left behind.

Flatley's tone changed. His voice fell.

"…she's the conduit…"

His pronouncement carried the tone of a revelation, and not a good kind. His affect changed. He lowered the rifle to the catwalk. He turned. Both of us now focused on the child.

"Only one way to end it," Flatley muttered.

I had a clear shot to the kid. But before I could extend my arm and fire the BLASTER, he lunged. He swept down and hooked his hands under the child's armpits and heaved her upward. I caught a glimpse of her face, locked in shock, framed in light brown curls that should have nested her head on a pillow surrounded by Care Bears or friends of Winnie the Pooh. I heard a feral growl and shout—it could have been me or Flatley.

He did the unthinkable.

He lifted the girl into the air and hurled her high over the side. My heart locked. She flew from his hands like a lifeless doll. She screamed, a high thin sound that cut open the night.

GO!

Everything that had been in focus became a blur. The core muscle I feel—the one that runs down my center at moments when *the other thing* takes command—turned to stone. Air rushed my face. Motion filled my senses. The BLASTER fell from my grip.

I slammed into Flatley's back. He flipped over the flimsy rail clawing the air. I ricocheted past him.

The child wore a night dress that rippled against the black. Despite a tsunami rush in my ears, I heard the gown flutter.

She sailed over the side of the dome.

The other thing pulled me after her.

She fell. My empty hands reached—my worst nightmare made real. Behind her, hard gravel roadbed and steel rails raced toward us.

I stretched my arms. We touched.

Fwooomp!

She vanished. I had a fraction of an instant to feel relieved that I wouldn't be forced to watch her hit, then I realized I had her.

STOP!

The world locked around us. We froze less than twenty feet from the hard earth. I pulled her into my arms, remembering too late to have a care for her broken forearm. I pressed her limp body to my shoulder and tried to grasp that we hung static, inverted, far below the top of the silo. Her baby shampoo-scented hair tickled my neck.

Quicker than my next breath, Flatley's black silhouette raced past, arms flailing. He hit the steel rail with an anticlimactic thud that abruptly silenced his scream.

I didn't look.

To hell with him.

PART III

credit card had been withdrawn. Dripping, I went to the room desk and plucked the landline handset off the receiver.

"You know that poor town stayed on lockdown until about twenty minutes ago?"

Leslie.

"Don't hang up."

"Mind reader."

"I get it, Will. I do. We have things to work out. I was pissed that you left me behind, I'll admit. But you did the right thing last night—er, this morning—or whatever. God, I'm tired."

"You woke me up to tell me how tired you are?"

"No. I need to ask a few questions. I want to make sure Saunders and his team get the right picture without getting the *full* picture."

"Are you covering your ass or mine?"

"That's harsh. But since you asked, yours. You don't know what's going on with the vacuum left by Director Lindsay. It's not good."

I said nothing. She didn't elaborate.

"Are you still going to Virginia today?"

"Flight plan is already filed," I lied. "Don't even think about—"

"Relax. Your plans are safe."

"Good. Listen, I'm dripping on the carpet because somebody woke me up and then interrupted my shower. Can we—?"

"Did you throw him off?"

I keep a hotel room cool. It helps me sleep. But the goose flesh rising on my arms had nothing to do with the room temperature.

In my head, I listened to Flatley's severed scream playing on Repeat.

"No," I said. "He came down on his own after I brought the kid down."

"The rifle was still up there. Any idea why he decided to leave it and jump?"

"Because he was nuts? He thought the kid was, I dunno, some kind of demon or conduit for evil or for the voices in his head or something. I have no idea."

"But you took the kid out of the picture. And then he jumped."

I'd given this some thought while I was alone in the Navajo during the flight back to Chicago. I debated how much to tell Leslie. And what it meant not to tell her everything. Accounting for the black mood that accompanied me back to the airport, the answer didn't come easily.

"Leslie, I need to talk to my wife. Then, like you said, you and I have some things to discuss. Can you just tell your FBI pals that Will the charter pilot hiked back to the airport when it looked like this thing was going to take all day? And stick to the story that some random stranger found that kid sitting alone in the pickup truck and then located her hysterical mother a block away. And that a completely nuts lone gunman decided to high dive off that grain elevator rather than be taken alive. Saunders ought to be able to make all those pieces fit."

Everything I said repeated a sharply clipped and decidedly one-sided phone conversation Leslie and I had in the dark after I returned to the Navajo parked on the ramp at Tri-Township Airport.

She didn't speak. I rubbed my diaphragm. I imagined the core muscle generated by *the other thing*—the muscle that powered my panicked, animal instinct to go after the child. I imagined it feeling sore. Like a little-used muscle that just got a workout.

"You're not telling me everything."

"Neither are you."

I heard her sigh into the phone. A note of truce.

"Is he the guy?" I asked, looking for a way to get us both off the conversational hook.

"Saunders' people are sold on him. Look, uh…Will…you go see your wife. I'll keep tabs on things here. After you get back, we'll talk."

"Yeah."

She ended the call before I did.

33

Chicago Executive Airport to Shannon Airport in Fredericksburg, Virginia is a flight of 532 nautical miles. A cruise speed of roughly 200 knots covers that distance in two hours and forty minutes. My troubles started on the ground at Chicago Executive, when I called for my IFR clearance. Instead of a direct flight, ATC delivered routing that took me northeast to an intersection called THORR where I was to join an airway called Victor 55 that would take me, with a few jogs along the way, to Fort Wayne, Indiana. From there, I would pick up my original route over Columbus, Ohio. Except Columbus had a VIP TFR in effect. The President of the United States felt the need to rally his faithful, which locked up the airspace around Columbus for a thirty-mile radius. My clearance diverted me south to a beacon called Yellow Bud, then east again to another beacon called Casanova. From there, it should have been a straight shot into Shannon Airport, except nothing in the vicinity of the Washington, D.C. Special Flight Restriction Area ends up being a straight shot. The clearance sent me southeast to another beacon called Brooke, then to Shannon. All of this came to my headset in a hurried reading from the Clearance Delivery frequency at Chicago Executive, prompting an adrenaline-fueled rush to get at least the first three waypoints into the navigation system—until the controller added that I could expect a release in seventeen minutes. Hurry up and wait. I told the voice on the other end that I would shut down and restart in ten minutes. Meanwhile, I plotted the full course, which added thirty miles to the total distance and another ten minutes to the flight time, on top of what turned into a twenty-three-minute ground hold. Then the weather released its gremlins. Low pressure over upstate New York dragged a fat trailing cold front across half a dozen states. Rain, low ceilings, and low visibility resulted. I penetrated the muck over western Ohio. The front carried warnings of thunderstorms which embedded themselves over the mountains of West Virginia. ATC diverted me and everyone else with east coast intentions almost as far south as Charleston, West Virginia. The trip came to over 600 miles and nearly four hours. When the wheels touched the asphalt, I congratulated myself for the wisdom of making this trip a day early.

After shutdown, I found four missed calls and a two-word text from Arun on my phone.

Call me!

34

Thanks to an extra credit question on an English Literature exam taken during my sophomore year of high school, I know one stanza of poetry. Or more precisely, two-thirds of a stanza since I cannot remember the last two lines. The four lines I know took up residence in my head for the exam, then made an indelible return a little over five years ago when I gave a nauseated woman I'd just met a ride from the airport to her apartment. As I watched her leave my car and potentially my life forever, the extra credit assignment tagged to Mrs. Bauman's second semester final jumped to mind.

> *She walks in beauty, like the night*
> *Of cloudless climes and starry skies;*
> *And all that's best of dark and bright*
> *Meet in her aspect and her eyes...*

George Gordon Byron could have known Andrea Katherine Taylor when he wrote those words.

Friday night, with the tension of the long flight unwinding, Lord Byron might as well have been sitting beside me, quill in hand, at the Bradford Inn's cozy restaurant with his eyes and attention trapped by the woman weaving her *aspect* past tables filled with chatty diners.

"Is this seat taken?" she asked, touching my shoulder. The fat burger in my hands froze in place. The ambitious bite I'd just taken silenced me. She looked around the room. "I don't want to intrude if you're on a date."

"*Mmrreees,*" I mumbled through a mouthful. I gestured at the red leather stool seat beside me and scrambled to drop the burger and find my napkin. I needed my hands.

She slid onto the seat but not before I took note of the black, form-fitting dress that ended at the tasteful upper limit of her thighs. She politely crossed her light caramel-colored legs beside me. Her auburn hair had been drawn up, showing off an elegant neck. One rebellious strand of hair hung near her eyes, accenting the mischief within. Rarely subject to applied makeup and never in need of it, tonight those eyes wore exotic shadows and accents that ignited gold flecks in her green irises.

...all that's best of dark and bright...

I fought the urge to follow the contour of her neck to where a thin chain dangled a small gold heart bearing a single diamond. The jewel nested in smooth and inviting cleavage visible at the top of her dress.

I swallowed and chased the burger bite with a slug of Corona.

"I'm not on a date," I said when I could speak, "but I'm married." I held up my left hand. She reached for the ring I wore. Although her nails were trimmed for practical purposes, she had painted them a deep, lust-inspiring red. She rotated the ring on my finger.

"I see. But you've already ordered dinner. You must not be expecting her."

"I wasn't. Not until tomorrow at noon."

"Well then, that gives us tonight." She pulled my hand against her heart and leaned until her breast pressed my upper arm. She brought her free hand up to my cheek and pulled me into a kiss. I dove in willingly, savoring the touch, the taste, the scent of her perfume.

When we came up for air, I found a devilish smile on her face.

"Hi."

"Hi, you." That's when I realized the bartender, a young woman with a smile of her own, stood facing us.

"I was going to ask the lady what she'd like, but I guess she's already decided. Would you care for a beverage to go with him?"

"I don't think so," she said not taking her eyes from me. "But I wonder…how late is the kitchen open?"

"Only until nine," the bartender replied, "however, I'm here until one. If you'd like, I can wrap this for you and put it in the 'fridge, and heat it up for you, you know…for after."

"That would be sweet of you, thank you," she said. She slid off the barstool without releasing my hand or my gaze. "Then I'll take this to go."

I LAID BREATHLESSLY AWAKE when someone knocked on the door.

"Room service!" I recognized the bartender's voice and the hint of laughter she stifled.

"They don't have room service here," Andy said. She rolled on top of me and reached for the clock radio on the nightstand. She turned the red numbers to face us.

1:23.

"Oh, dear. We never made it back down to the bar. Better answer the door." She wiggled against me and clamped my left leg with her thighs long enough to plant a kiss on my lips.

"Uh, your words say one thing, but your body is telling me something else."

She laughed in the dark.

"My body is telling me that I'm hungry. C'mon!" She rolled off and pulled the sheet from the bed, exposing all my skin to the cool air in the room. I heard her shake out the sheet and wrap herself in it. "Lights on in ten seconds, Pilot! Make yourself decent."

"Fine." I swung my legs off the bed.

She went to the door. A wedge of light painted her shadow on the wallpaper when she opened it.

"Oh, my lord!" I heard her say. A floor lamp in the room illuminated, showing me where to find my pants. I pulled up both legs.

Andy returned with a tray in her hands. She slid the tray onto the table beside a bay window. I counted two silver dish covers and two amber bottles of Corona glistening with condensation. Andy lifted the dish covers to reveal plates bearing meals identical to the one I abandoned at the bar hours ago.

"You're going to give that girl a big tip tomorrow," she told me. "I'll be right back." She hurried into the bathroom.

Ten minutes later, after I'd taken a turn, we faced each other across the small table beside dark windows. With the room softly illuminated, the windows displayed our reflections and the generous late-night dinner delivered to our door.

Andy beamed at me over a pair of hamburgers and mounds of fries. She glowed, not just with her smile but deep within the blush gracing her cheeks. Strands of unruly hair lay trapped in light sweat on her neck.

I laughed.

"What's funny?"

"I feel like I need to say, 'Hi! Nice to see you. How've you been?'"

She giggled. "Nice to see you. I guess we haven't been very chatty. But this has been good." She lifted her beer and held it out. "Really good. Us."

"Us." I clicked mine against hers and we drank.

"I was worried that Arun would not get my message to you." She dipped a french fry into a cup of ketchup.

"How exactly did you pull that off? I thought you were in communication quarantine."

"I have my laptop, but the WiFi is highly restricted. They scrub personal devices regularly. We're assigned an Academy email account— you know, to turn in papers, to get assignments, to communicate with the instructors. It's strictly for Academy use and it's monitored. I asked for special permission to send a personal message. They're not unreasonable about it."

"Why didn't you email me?"

I got *the look*. "Seriously? When did you last check your email?"

"Point taken. Much better idea to contact Arun."

"Yes," she laughed. "I emailed the one person I could trust to move heaven and earth to get a message to you, dear."

My airport call to Arun brought him on the line bubbling with a mix of excitement and panic. He had been trying to reach me. He had important instructions, he told me, from Andy. I copied the information to the same clipboard I use in the cockpit to copy IFR clearances. The instructions named the Bradford Inn and informed me that a two-night reservation in the name of William Stewart waited for me. Arun explained that

Andy planned to meet me at the inn, rather than put me through the official hassle of entering a Marine base, and that I should check in and wait for her. I assumed he meant Saturday. He didn't say otherwise.

"How did you find this place?" I asked. "And how did you know I'd fly down a day early."

"Oh, please. What does Earl say? If you're on time you're late. You are OCD about time."

"And this place?"

"Isn't it wonderful? One of my instructors recommended it. Small, quaint, on a river. There's a running trail in back—hint, hint."

"No thanks."

"I love it. More like a B&B than a hotel, but with a nice little bar and restaurant."

"It does have a certain southern charm." I waved at the room around us. The walls wore patterned paper. Deep dark wood trim glowed under layers of varnish. Stylish old carpets and posts on the bed rounded out the Antebellum feel. "Credit where due, Arun didn't give away your surprise. How is it that you're here tonight? I thought you were only allowed 24 hours."

She smiled triumphantly. "You're looking at the only cadet to ace a test on interstate law *and* turn in her completed paper on InfraGard, which earned her an additional night off campus!"

"Congratulations," I lifted my beer to acknowledge her academic prowess, which surprised me not in the least. "I have no idea what infernal guard is but keep up the good work. If you need any help studying or cheating in the future so that we can repeat...*this*...I'm all in."

"Hmmm, yes. I might find it hard to concentrate on future exams now that I know what the prize is."

"Eat," I said, picking up the burger. "And tell me everything."

ANDY TALKED. At the expense of allowing her meal to cool, she updated me on her classes, on the temperament of her instructors, and the intimidation she felt in the presence of her fellow cadets, none of whom, I pointed out, aced their interstate law exam. She talked about course content, modestly dismissing subjects that came easily and earnestly describing obscure subjects that challenged her. She expressed awe for the

37

A ndy said three miles. I told her it felt closer to thirty. I teased her with, "Are we there yet?" every few hundred feet for the last mile. The crossroads she mentioned referred to the intersection of two narrow county roads with nineteenth century buildings set on all four corners. A handful of houses nesting in rural yards surrounded this bustling center of commerce. The dominant retail store advertised *Antiques & Knicknacks*, at which point I contemplated collapsing and making my wife carry me. A café directly across the street saved the day. I made a bee line for an umbrella-topped outdoor table. Andy went inside for drinks. I checked my phone to reaffirm that the Uber app still worked.

"They're bringing out a menu, but I still haven't worked off breakfast," she said, planting her coffee and my iced latte on the metal grid tabletop. She joined me for a commanding view of the stop sign-controlled intersection. Nothing moved in any of the four directions.

I felt sweaty and tired. She looked gorgeous, fresh, and energetic.

"Are you on drugs?" I asked.

"You need more exercise."

A light breeze chilled the perspiration on the back of my neck. Sparse cotton ball cumulus floated above us, blinding white against powder blue. I gazed at the sky for a long moment. When I came back to earth, I took my wife's hand.

"That thing I told you last night, about grabbing that kid," I said. "There's something about it we need to discuss."

Andy pretended not to tense up. I took a breath.

"What is it?"

I retold the events that played out on top of the grain elevators. In the first telling, I said I had "grabbed" the child. This time I recounted every detail. How the core muscle that seems to be controlled by *the other thing* took over and pulled me directly into Flatley. How it knocked him over the railing. How I ricocheted off his back and shot over the side into a suicide dive after the screaming child.

Telling it whole, reliving it, I felt and saw goose flesh rise on my arms.

At the part where Flatley coldly heaved the child over the side, Andy pulled her hand from mine to cover her mouth, which did nothing to hide the horror on her face. With her other hand, she reached out and closed a grip on my arm.

"Oh my God, Will!"

I laid my hand over hers.

"I know. This is that nightmare I've had. The one about you falling."

"I had no idea."

"But you get what happened…right?"

"This is about *that thing*, isn't it? The thing that happened to us in the motel in Montana?"

"Uh-huh."

"Did you—I mean—was it—?"

"Did I control it? Not consciously. It launched on its own just like the other times. It executed my first, instantaneous impulse *ahead of conscious thought*. Dee, it happened so fast I felt like I wasn't in control, yet the result is exactly what I wanted. What I would have prayed for."

"Did you tell Leslie?"

My girl. Always one step ahead of me.

"That's the question. Do I—do we tell her? We're talking about *self-propulsion* here. Without a BLASTER."

"I'm not calling it that."

She squeezed my hand. Her lips parted to speak, but a teenaged boy wearing an apron stepped up to the table and laid two printed cards in front of us. He said something about a special, which I didn't catch, then told us to bring the menus to the order station when we were ready. I waited for him to go before speaking.

"Do we keep it to ourselves, or do we go full disclosure with Leslie?"

Andy frowned. "Keeping secrets never turns out well."

"Tell *her* that."

Andy ignored the cue. "What if she's with you when it happens again?"

I released a clipped laugh, more tension than mirth.

"Okay. There's that. But if I tell her, she might figure out the rest of it."

"The rest of it?"

"I told you she asked me if I threw Flatley off that elevator."

Andy shrugged. "A natural investigative question. I would have asked."

"You're not following." I pulled my arm free and held up my hands. "Here's me. Here's Flatley. He takes the girl and hurls her into the air, like so." I moved my hands and pointed. "On an angle away from me. Over the side."

She showed no sign of understanding the significance of the spatial relationships involved.

"Dee, I went from here to Flatley and hit him in the back, then plowed right over him after the child."

"So?"

"So, I could have gone direct. Straight to the child."

Realization dawned. She sat back, staring.

"Yeah," I said. "This *thing* operates on impulse. And my impulse may have been to save the child, but a stronger impulse superseded. I wanted to murder the son of a bitch."

38

Neither of us had answers. The more we talked about it, the more we struggled to separate the practical question from the darker moral question. Andy leaned toward explaining everything to Leslie. I worried that Leslie might see me as a vigilante. It would not be a leap for her.

We finished our coffee without reaching a conclusion. Lacking an answer, we elected not to beat the issue to death.

Neither of us needed lunch but we stayed at the table and enjoyed the sunshine. Andy asked about the romance between Pidge and Arun. I tattled on Arun for his sleepover. From there, we discussed the bold decision by a shy Lane Franklin to try out for the high school's fall play. I traded the latest gossip from Essex County Air Service and reaffirmed the sameness of Saturday morning gatherings at the Silver Spoon. I speculated that Chief Tom Ceeves may have something more than a professional interest in the Sheriff of Bear County. Andy scoffed at the notion the way the child of a single parent dismisses the idea of that parent dating. I scored points by telling her what I'd learned of Tom's Marine Corps service. She hadn't known, which surprised me.

We relinquished our table as the café grew crowded. I let my wife tug me into the cluttered aisles of *Antiques & Knicknacks*. She browsed. I made up absurd explanations for objects we couldn't identify. When I found a back corner of the store with three floor-to-ceiling bookshelves jammed full of used books, I lost myself in the titles. Bookstores and libraries blind me. I want to crack every cover and read every word. I eventually realized I'd lost track of both time and Andy. I forced myself to leave the book corner. I found Andy on the sidewalk outside of the store, bent over a stroller examining the tiny creature inside while chatting energetically with its mother. The two women engaged like lifelong friends. I dropped on a wooden bench in the shade and watched from a safe distance. Andy may have been in conversation with the proud mother, but her eyes never left the child. When they parted, she watched mother and child until both disappeared into the café across the street.

I thought the encounter might prompt Andy to talk about our decision to start a family, and the subsequent delay imposed by her enrollment at the FBI Academy, but she didn't broach the subject. She reverted to housekeeping items. Should we or shouldn't we buy a dishwasher? When were we, meaning me, putting the storm windows on the screened porch?

Having burned up most of the afternoon we rejoined the running trail and walked back to the Bradford Inn. Three miles passed underfoot surprisingly fast, subsumed by non-stop trivial conversation. Only after the trail rejoined and ran parallel to the river in the last half mile did I realize that I had forgotten to complain or beg Andy to let me pull out a BLASTER, take her in in my arms, vanish, and fly back to the hotel at treetop level.

The walk suited us both.

I FLOPPED on the bed for a nap when we reached the room late in the afternoon. Instead of counting sheep, I counted my sleepless nights in the last week. Andy probed something in her laptop. When she woke me for dinner, she had dressed for our Date Night, this time in a striking red velvet dress. I didn't bring my suit, but still managed to impress her with a decent pair of pants and a nice shirt.

We chatted and laughed over a slow dinner but avoided the coffee shop question. We toasted and drank a red wine while I drank in the sight of her. At one point, the jarring memory of a recent moment when I had been sure I'd lost her stabbed me in the chest. I don't think she noticed my struggle to breathe while I fought off the horrifying image of a landscape blasted and burned by a truck bomb. She powered through a critique of

Lonnie Penn's latest hair color and style, which she'd seen in *People* magazine. I snapped myself out of the dark vision by marveling that the FBI Academy had a copy of *People*, and that Andy admitted reading it.

We talked and joked and laughed until most of the restaurant emptied. The loving chatter didn't end when we returned to our room. We merely switched languages.

39

Sunday morning came bearing the inevitable bad news that Andy would be returning to the Academy and our hours together were counting down. I kept her in bed to register a wordless protest at the idea of parting. She appeared to share my desperation to make the most of our time together. Even so, eventually she hopped out of my arms and claimed the shower.

"Get up," she ordered me. "I have plans for the day."

"Plans?"

"You'll see."

An hour later we checked out of the Bradford Inn and loaded our bags into the car I had rented at Shannon Airport. We tucked our coffees into cupholders and found a safe spot for the cinnamon bun I grabbed in lieu of breakfast on the way through the lobby.

"Here." Andy held up my iPad and pointed. "Wellington Church."

"Is that a town or a building?"

"Town. An hour and six minutes."

I backed up the rented Chevy and steered out of the Bradford Inn's small gravel lot. A long driveway took us to a narrow, tree-lined two-lane blacktop.

"Left," Andy said. I followed orders. Morning sunlight angled through the trees and illuminated pillars of September mist.

"An hour and six minutes the way I drive or the way you drive?"

"The way Google drives."

I didn't really care. My only question was whether we had enough time or not. I worried that she had to clear the gates of the FBI Academy by noon on Sunday or her carriage would turn into a pumpkin.

"Five p.m. check in," she clarified.

"What?"

She grinned. "Did I mention that I aced the interstate law exam?"

I grinned back. The extra five hours lifted my spirits. I wasn't ready for this weekend to end. My only plan for the day had been to spend it with Andy. When I stepped out of the shower, and she announced that we were going on a road trip, she could have announced that we were going to the moon. I didn't care.

"I'm just a float in the parade," I happily told her, looking forward to a ride through countryside I'd never seen with a girl I couldn't take my eyes from.

Eventually curiosity caught up with me.

"Where are we going?"

"Wellington Church."

"I know that. Let me rephrase. Why are we going to Wellington Church?"

She hesitated for a beat, which told me I'd been had. That this wasn't some lark.

"Leslie sent me copies of some of the reports. From the sniper shootings."

"And?"

"And I had questions. Some of the same questions she had."

"You know they got the guy, right?"

Andy didn't answer. I approached it from another angle.

"So, who's in Wellington Church?"

"One of the guest lecturers we had. You'll see."

THE DRIVE TOOK us through Culpepper, which I envisioned as a bastion of the old south, a town of antebellum wooden homes and ladies serving secret recipe sweet tea on porches. The town had its charm, but the North's victory flag waved in the form of pavement, strip malls and a Napa Auto Parts store. A bold red KFC struck me as the Confederacy's amusing last stand.

From Culpepper, we drove the Sperryville Pike through Virginia farmland. The highway took us to its namesake and the fringe of the Shenandoah National Forest. Against the small town of Sperryville, wooded ridges lifted the horizon. We hooked right and threaded our way into a green valley so sparsely populated that the town of Wellington Church was not, in fact, a town at all. A sign marked its existence, but open fields and small single-family homes set well back from the narrow road contradicted both Google and the sign. Even the single church we found named itself the Promised Land Baptist Church, leaving Wellington out of the equation entirely.

"What kind of address is 'Rural Route 2, Wellington Church' supposed to be?" I asked after we'd driven five minutes past the dot on the iPad screen.

Andy answered by pointing. "Pull over. There."

A lean-to shack occupied space on a weedy lawn fronting a set of farm-like buildings, if a farm had been built without a barn or farmhouse. A bright flash of color popped behind a wood plank counter under the lean-to. I recognized a Boston Bruins t-shirt on a girl with pigtail hair and enormous round glasses. A hand-painted sign propped against the side wall of the shack promised Farm Fresh Vegetables.

I rolled the Chevy to a stop on the edge of pavement with no shoulder and checked the mirrors needlessly. There hadn't been another car on this road since we joined it.

Andy hopped out and greeted the proprietor of the roadside stand, who I guessed to be a few birthdays short of her teen years. The girl lit up a big smile for the pretty woman, or perhaps because Andy was her first customer of the day.

I stayed behind the wheel. Even with the window open, I was too far away to make out their conversation. Andy spoke. The girl answered and pointed. Andy looked back down the road we'd just traveled. The girl nodded and pointed again. Andy took her wallet from her satchel and gave the girl money, then returned to the car with a small, brown paper bag.

"Fresh strawberries." She showed me the treats inside. I lifted one out and bit it at the stem.

"Wow. That's sweet." I tossed the stem out my window and held out my hand for another.

"She said we missed it. It's on the right, about a quarter mile back."

"Alright, then," I said. I needlessly checked for traffic before executing a Y-turn to reverse course.

We found the driveway as advertised, but it was easy to see how it had been missed. Two tire tracks threaded their way between hay fields before disappearing into a woods. A mailbox without an address topped an old fence post.

"You sure?" I asked before turning in. I didn't care for the way the lane pointed at nothing man-made. I also wasn't comfortable driving up to a private property in rural Virginia. I pictured stumbling into a militia outpost occupied by comrades of Darryl Spellman.

"I'm sure. The little girl makes deliveries here."

I drove.

We crossed the open field, then eased through a patch of woods. The lane curved back and forth between old-growth oak trees and random mounds. Eventually it broke into the open again, revealing an unexpectedly modern home and collection of sheds. The scene reminded me of Congressman Gregg's horse farm, scaled down and without the signature wooden fences. The house had been built in a farmhouse style, but looked new, with casement windows and vinyl siding. Three metal pole barns occupied the rear of the property, two large and one small. Beyond the sheds, the land rose toward the ridges of Shenandoah National Forest. I caught a glimpse of what looked like a gravel pit cut into the rising terrain. Several old vehicles crouched against a distant wall of dirt and stone. More vehicles sat beside the sheds. Some looked new. Others looked like they'd been pulled from the deepest back corners of a salvage yard.

The tidy landscape around the house showed signs of meticulous care. The source of that care quickly came into view. A woman stood in the center of a huge garden between the house and the first shed. She wore a dress that looked like it had been ordered from the Sears and Roebuck Catalog at the turn of the previous century. White socks topped heavy laced boots. An apron spanned her middle and a broad straw sunhat shaded her face. Short and wide, she had the contours of a person who easily fit the medical classification of morbidly obese. The hem of her dress dipped below her knees, but the portion of her lower legs that remained visible had the diameter of a human thigh. Her arms were similarly full and heavy. She wore her hair tied or pulled back which accentuated the broad dimensions of her face over a full neck and bulging bosom. I couldn't begin to guess her age.

The woman watched us roll to a stop. She slipped off heavy gardening gloves and tossed them into a wheelbarrow containing assorted tools.

Andy folded the iPad cover and tucked it beside her seat. She popped her door and jumped out waving. I killed the engine and followed, catching up to Andy halfway across the lawn. The woman approached wearing a welcoming smile on a pleasant, friendly face.

I expected Andy to ask for directions again. Instead, she said, "Mrs. Palmer, I'm Andrea Stewart. I was—"

"Of course!" The woman laughed. "I remember you!"

Remember you?

Andy stopped at the edge of the garden and turned to me as the woman approached.

"Will, this is Mrs. Palmer, unquestionably the foremost ballistics expert in the U.S. and possibly in the world. Mrs. Palmer, this is my husband Will."

She extended and I shook a fleshy hand sporting a good grip. I struggled with the disconnect between Andy's words and the woman standing before me. Not much taller than Pidge, but easily heavier than me, I hated myself for thinking the warm and welcoming face belonged on a cake mix box or syrup bottle instead of at the top of her forensic science profession.

"Very pleased to meet you, young man."

"Mrs. Palmer is one of the guest lecturers I told you about. She's teaching an entire section in a few weeks."

"Pleased to meet you."

"I am impressed by your wife. Her questions at my lecture were challenging."

Andy blushed. "Oh my god, I didn't think you would remember!"

"Nonsense! Would you care for some sweet tea?"

Without waiting for an answer, she set off for the house on a waddling gait that made every step look like a struggle. I removed the dumb look from my face and fought the urge to feel sympathy for someone so short and so heavy—as well as a shameful prejudice that couldn't reconcile world-class technical expertise with her physical appearance.

Andy shot me a glance that beamed with pride for having been remembered by an A-list law enforcement celebrity.

40

Mrs. Palmer seated us on elegant postmodern furniture in a screened sunroom at the back of the house. Andy and I silently marveled at the artistic chairs while our host fetched a tray with tall glasses of iced tea and a plate covered in brownie squares.

I settled in and leaned back. "These chairs are amazing."

"Why, thank you! My own design." Mrs. Palmer handed out sweet tea.

"You made these?" I asked.

"I did." She placed the tray on a small table.

"You shouldn't go to such trouble, ma'am," Andy protested.

"Don't be silly. I get so few guests out here. I'm delighted you came." She heaved herself into a chair facing us. Her wide face fixed a smile in our direction, made warmer and more welcoming by round cheeks and sparkling eyes.

"I apologize for just showing up like this," Andy said. "I wasn't sure how to contact you, but I found your address on your website."

She has a website.

Mrs. Palmer laughed. "It's hardly an address, but letters and packages manage to find me."

"We almost didn't," Andy said. She described the stop at the roadside stand.

41

Around the time Andy pulled out her laptop to show Mrs. Palmer reports she had downloaded from Leslie, I asked for permission to explore a few of the intriguing vehicles parked outside, thinking they could just as easily ignore me outdoors as indoors.

"Please! Go wherever you like," the woman urged me. "And here." She handed me the plate with the brownies. "A person can get hungry hiking around out back. Don't go too far. The national forest starts where my property ends. People get lost in there every day. And stay in the short grass. Deer ticks."

I picked the brownies off the plate and stacked them in my hand, then left the plate. The women hunched over Andy's laptop.

I slipped out a screen door and hiked across the yard to the first of the three metal pole barns. A diverse collection of vehicles lined up against the barn. A Mercedes panel van sat beside a 1980 Corvette, which squeezed up against a Ford Explorer. Next came a Volkswagen Beetle. Then, and perhaps most intriguing of all, a pre-World War II Plymouth with sweeping fenders, running boards and a bulbous body. The long hood supported a corroding hood ornament representing the sails of a clipper ship. A mixed bag of pickup trucks, sedans and even a Mack truck followed.

Each of the vehicles settled on flat tires surrounded by a rising tide of

40

M rs. Palmer seated us on elegant postmodern furniture in a screened sunroom at the back of the house. Andy and I silently marveled at the artistic chairs while our host fetched a tray with tall glasses of iced tea and a plate covered in brownie squares.

I settled in and leaned back. "These chairs are amazing."

"Why, thank you! My own design." Mrs. Palmer handed out sweet tea.

"You made these?" I asked.

"I did." She placed the tray on a small table.

"You shouldn't go to such trouble, ma'am," Andy protested.

"Don't be silly. I get so few guests out here. I'm delighted you came." She heaved herself into a chair facing us. Her wide face fixed a smile in our direction, made warmer and more welcoming by round cheeks and sparkling eyes.

"I apologize for just showing up like this," Andy said. "I wasn't sure how to contact you, but I found your address on your website."

She has a website.

Mrs. Palmer laughed. "It's hardly an address, but letters and packages manage to find me."

"We almost didn't," Andy said. She described the stop at the roadside stand.

"You met little Laurel! She's a sweetie. I make the best pies from those strawberries," she said. Mention of pies caused me to note the absence of a Southern accent. I guessed Midwestern.

"I know!" Andy said. "They're so good."

"You've gone to some trouble. Let me guess—you're going to write a paper on measurable metallurgic deformation as a key to determining impact force—that was part of your question at the lecture, I believe."

Andy blushed again. "I just can't believe you remember me, ma'am."

"You don't give me enough credit, Detective Stewart," Mrs. Palmer said, one-upping her with glitter in her eye. "I never give a lecture at the Academy without obtaining a full class list. The genuine law enforcement professionals in the room stand out among all those lawyers, some of whom think that ballistic science is just a report that will be delivered like room service by a lab that never seems to work fast enough."

"There may be some entitlement in the ranks, that's true," Andy said politely.

"I prefer young people like you, dear. People who ask the questions, seek the knowledge, *investigate*. People who drill down to a full under-standing, not just a lab result they can use to justify a warrant."

Oh, you have no idea, I thought. I had a feeling that the woman with the brownies and sweet tea would be doing a deeper dive into Andy's biography before the dust settled behind us when we left.

"I don't have much experience with gun crimes," Andy said. "Thank-fully, that hasn't been an issue in my job to date. But I don't believe that any investigating officer, at any level, can operate without a foundation in the sciences that support accurate analysis of the evidence." Andy stopped abruptly and pressed her fingers to her lips. "Oh my god. I sound like a complete suck up, don't I?"

The woman laughed, a deep and genuine expression of humor that made me chuckle. Mrs. Palmer's whole body jiggled. She put down her tea before it spilled.

"Of the worst kind," Mrs. Palmer said catching her breath, "and I mean that as a compliment, dear. Oh, lord."

"I'm so sorry—I—!"

"Detective, if the stuffed shirts at Quantico could fill their graduating classes with men and women like you, the Bureau wouldn't still be trying to kill off the ghost of J. Edgar. Now please, try these brownies. You may rest assured that cannabis is *not* one of the ingredients…"

I reached for and took one of the cubes.

"…because I keep those for myself," Mrs. Palmer winked at me.

The brownies might not have been laced, but the bite I took revealed the best brownie treat I ever tasted.

"Oh, hell, that's good!" I exclaimed. "Um…sorry…"

"Hell yes, they are good." She leaned forward in her chair. "My secret is agave nectar."

I had no idea what that was, but it sounded exotic and capable of producing the heavenly taste in my mouth. Andy took one, tasted it, and lifted her eyebrows.

"Wow."

"Excellent! My brownies are a success. Now tell me who or what I have to thank for the pleasure of meeting you."

Andy quickly swallowed the bite of brownie.

"Ma'am, are you familiar with a string of sniper shootings dating back to last summer? The most recent of which was Congressman Martin Gregg?"

Like a popup thunderstorm that blackens a summer sky, the look on the woman's face transformed from light to dark in an instant.

"Tell me more."

41

Around the time Andy pulled out her laptop to show Mrs. Palmer reports she had downloaded from Leslie, I asked for permission to explore a few of the intriguing vehicles parked outside, thinking they could just as easily ignore me outdoors as indoors.

"Please! Go wherever you like," the woman urged me. "And here." She handed me the plate with the brownies. "A person can get hungry hiking around out back. Don't go too far. The national forest starts where my property ends. People get lost in there every day. And stay in the short grass. Deer ticks."

I picked the brownies off the plate and stacked them in my hand, then left the plate. The women hunched over Andy's laptop.

I slipped out a screen door and hiked across the yard to the first of the three metal pole barns. A diverse collection of vehicles lined up against the barn. A Mercedes panel van sat beside a 1980 Corvette, which squeezed up against a Ford Explorer. Next came a Volkswagen Beetle. Then, and perhaps most intriguing of all, a pre-World War II Plymouth with sweeping fenders, running boards and a bulbous body. The long hood supported a corroding hood ornament representing the sails of a clipper ship. A mixed bag of pickup trucks, sedans and even a Mack truck followed.

Each of the vehicles settled on flat tires surrounded by a rising tide of weeds and grass. Each also had been peppered with bullet holes. Some of the holes were marked with fluorescent orange paint. The old Plymouth looked particularly devastated.

"Christ, who was driving this?" I asked aloud. "Bonnie and Clyde?"

I touched places where the holes marred the steel body. Some of the holes were the size of a pencil eraser. Some were large enough to fit my thumb.

I strolled past the line of cars and trucks to the back of the property where someone long ago carved a bowl-shaped bite out of a low hillside. Judging by the content of the naked slope left behind, I guessed the objective to be gravel. The pit made a perfect shooting range. In addition to a rusting Cadillac and riddled black Jeep, Mrs. Palmer propped up a variety of materials and objects downrange—wood, plastic barrels, steel panels, a refrigerator. Scores of bullet holes punctured the items. A series of old tables at measured intervals provided shooting stations. I strolled out to the first table, two hundred yards from the back wall of her private range. The table rested on neatly cut grass. Not so much a lawn, but what might be called a mowed meadow. The reason for the manicure was easily apparent. The ground around the table was perfectly clean; not a single shell casing glinted. For the hundreds of rounds fired, the scientist collected every piece of brass, no doubt to study.

I tried to picture Mrs. Palmer with a rifle at her shoulder, or a handgun clasped in her chubby grip. The idea of her smiling sweetly at a target before blasting it made me chuckle.

Returning from the gravel pit, I overstepped my welcome. I wondered what she harbored inside the buildings. A big sliding door at the back of the largest shed refused to move, thanks to a lock inside. I pulled the door half an inch away from the frame. Through a sliver of space, I spotted more vehicles. Skylight panels at the top of the shed illuminated curved rooftops, fenders, and glints of chrome. Cars, vans, SUVs, and large trucks. I wondered if those vehicles were also pockmarked with bullet holes.

The small shed built between the two large sheds had windows and the look of a workshop. A side door was locked and deadbolted. The windows wore covers mounted on the inside. It made sense to me. She must have a cache of weapons and ammunition. Storing them safely had to be a priority. I wondered if there was a Mr. Palmer, then scolded myself for thinking a woman needed a man around to protect her and her property. In fact, I made a guess that this woman could shoot the pants off an intruder without scratching his skin.

The idea of someone underestimating this sweet lady only to be met with a hail of gunfire amused me. I wore the smile most of the way back to the house.

Andy and Mrs. Palmer remained deep in conversation, poring over the laptop, pointing at the screen, chatting and scrolling. I found a chair on the lawn under the natural umbrella of a mature maple tree and settled in to finish the last of the brownies.

Bits of conversation reached my ears, but not enough to justify an effort to listen. Instead, I let the rustle of maple leaves in the rising midday breeze lull me into a mild waking coma. The air felt good. The intimacy with Andy over the last thirty-some hours felt fresh on my skin. The childlike wonder on Andy's face in the presence of someone she clearly admired had an infectious quality. I might have been jealous of anything that took Andy away from me during our limited time together but seeing her excited not only to meet this woman but to be welcomed by her—I couldn't resent that.

A good thing because they kept me waiting the better part of an hour.

42

The screen door opened. Andy stepped onto the lawn followed by Mrs. Palmer.

"I have to ask...is that old Plymouth the car Sonny Corleone was driving when he got whacked?"

Mrs. Palmer laughed. "Sonny got whacked in a 1941 Lincoln Continental Coupe. That's a '37 Plymouth. Furthermore, Mr. Corleone would have died behind the wheel, not standing next to his car."

I must have looked bewildered.

She explained. "The gangsters were firing Thompson machine guns which throw a .45 caliber bullet. The first half dozen shots Sonny took would have killed him. Yet somehow Mister Ford Coppola has him crawl out and stand by the car while he is shot another hundred times. Hollywood, right?"

"I guess. That's quite a collection of vehicles."

"I wrote a book. *Projectile Impact Metrics Applied to Motor Vehicles*. My editor wanted to call it *The Impact of Ballistics on Motor Vehicles*, but that would have been redundant."

"After your lecture, I wanted to order your last book, but we don't have that kind of online access," Andy said.

"Suck up," I joked, which Mrs. Palmer found funny. Andy didn't.

"Wait right here!" Mrs. Palmer hurried inside.

"Please, no! I didn't mean—"

Too late. A moment later, Mrs. Palmer returned and handed Andy a hardcover book with a plain blue jacket and white title type. *Trajectory Studies: Theory, Fact and Fallacy in Forensic Ballistics.* No dramatic photo of a gun. No image of a bullet or cartridge. The author's name at the bottom simply listed as Palmer.

"Ma'am, I didn't mean to ask. Please," Andy swung open her satchel, "let me pay you for this."

"Baloney! I have a closet full of them. DOJ paid for the printing. Take it!" She pressed the thin volume into Andy's hands. "You're probably one of the only students in that class who will understand half of this. Don't bother with the math but do read the section on atmospheric conditions. I guarantee you, if you ever have a gun-related case, you will want to secure copies of the weather reports at the hour of the crime."

Andy quickly reached in her bag and pulled out a pen.

"Is there any chance...?" She held out the pen and book. This brought new laughter and a refreshed smile.

"Me and Stephen King, right?" She opened the cover, wrote a brief message, then signed with a flourish. "There you go!"

Andy accepted the book as if it contained precious metal.

43

"Omigod! I can't believe that just happened!"

I glanced at Andy after turning onto the narrow road. She bubbled with the energy of a middle-school girl who just sat beside the cute boy on the bus. She clutched the book with both hands.

"That's a very smart woman," I said.

"Oh! You have no idea. Will, she has a professional grade cappuccino machine *that she built herself!* I saw it in her kitchen—which, by the way, is the most high-tech kitchen I've ever seen. I didn't recognize half the appliances."

"You were sneaking around her kitchen?"

"No! God, no. I asked to use the restroom. Also a marvel, I might add."

"Good with guns and grout, huh."

"Don't make fun. This woman is the Werner von Braun of forensic ballistics. Her books are required reading for anyone entering the field. She does her own experimental work, field testing, compilation, analysis. Here, look." Andy flipped open the cover of her book. "This is—um, six, eight, nine—this is her tenth book. She lectures at the Academy. She's trained Interpol. She's amazing!"

"I get that. Don't read this wrong, but is there a Mr. Palmer?"

Andy shook her head. "She never married."

RAGING fatigue caught up with me at ten thousand feet over Ohio. Few things are as deadly to a solo pilot, even more so when the air is clear, smooth, and boring, and the Sunday evening air traffic control chatter is minimal. I cancelled my IFR flight plan and asked for vectors into Columbus. I landed and taxied to where Air Force One had graced the ramp two days ago.

Parked.

Took a taxi to a hotel and crashed on a bed instead of in an airplane.

I woke up a little after three a.m. recharged and refreshed.

My wheels touched Runway 31 at Essex County Airport as the sun broke the horizon behind me.

45

Two text messages greeted me after shutdown on the ramp in front of the Foundation hangar.

Arun: *Please check your email. I sent the itinerary for the week.*

Chief Ceeves: *Silver Spoon 8 a.m.*

I replied to the chief in the affirmative. I answered Arun's message in person when I found him standing in the center of the empty hangar as I raised the big door.

"How is the lovely and charming Mrs. Stewart?" he asked.

"Smarter than all the other cadets."

"That goes without saying. Is she enjoying the experience?"

"Goes without saying," I replied.

Arun seemed to take genuine pleasure in the news. "Good! Good! This is a perfect step for her. The American FBI is the topflight. I knew she would do well."

I told him about the exam she aced, and the extra time it afforded us over the weekend.

"That's what I mean. Splendid! You're going to win your bet."

"I got your message. What's special about the itinerary?" Arun followed me as I fetched the electric tow bar.

"Nothing. Other than I need you to read it so that I'm not standing out here tomorrow morning wondering how to fly this airplane myself."

"Where are we going?"

"Back to St. Louis. I have a second set of meetings to conclude the grant process. It's our largest grant to date. Seven million dollars."

I lined up the tow bar on the nose of the airplane and clamped the connection onto the nosewheel pins.

"What time are we departing?"

"No later than nine-forty-five."

"Out and back, or overnight?"

"We will be returning tomorrow afternoon at three-thirty."

"Good," I said. "Now I don't have to read the itinerary."

I glanced up at Arun in time to watch his blood pressure rise.

"You should make yourself familiar, Will. The schedule I prepare is important." He stopped short of scolding me. I enjoyed watching him bottle it in.

"Why would I do that when I have you, buddy?"

"Not funny."

THE SILVER SPOON is a three-minute drive from the airport, which gave me an hour. I used the time to refuel the Navajo, check weather for the flight to St. Louis and file a flight plan based on Arun's wheels-up time. I added half a quart of oil to the left engine and made a note of it on a clipboard I keep for tracking oil consumption. I checked the hours to the next oil change and mentioned to Arun that I'd be taking the airplane off the flight schedule for a day next week for maintenance. Arun's comment about the size of the grant for St. Louis public schools wasn't lost on me. The desktop tide of paperwork and binders surrounding his laptop attested to the work required to give away money.

I wondered how he would feel if the hundred million in the Foundation's account turned into a billion.

A few minutes before eight I hopped into my old Toyota Corolla and drove to the Silver Spoon. Chief Ceeves sat at a table for two near the back, ruling out room for any joiners. This was business, then.

Seconds after I sat down, the regular weekday waitress, a veteran of the Spoon with several decades of seniority over the high school girls hired for weekends, filled my coffee mug and waved a menu at me. I declined it, which she expected. She tucked the menu under one arm and topped off Tom's mug. He waited for her to circulate to other tables before skipping a greeting.

"Gregg's allies are spinning the business of you finding Casey Gregg into a 'man on the grassy knoll' story."

"Doesn't mean he didn't try to kill his wife," I said. I sipped the coffee. Too hot, but excellent brew. "I have to ask. Why do they care? He's still dead, isn't he?"

"Doornail dead. But remember. Gregg had his head pretty far up the executive ass. The Tweeter in Chief wants to know what's being done to find the unknown individual who had Mrs. Gregg and probably murdered the Congressman."

"*Had Mrs. Gregg?* What happened to rescued? What happened to an investigation?"

"That's the price of not sticking around to tell your story. Or at least making up a story."

I felt the urge to get angry, then wondered why. "Ask me if I care. How is the Congressman's widow?"

"Recovering."

"Does she remember anything?"

"That's between her and the FBI. The docs finally let them interview her yesterday."

"Yesterday? Wow. It took that long?"

"She was in bad shape. Point is, Will, there's political pressure. Gregg sang the praises of the President, which means The White House doesn't want this splashing back on him or the party. Gregg is guilty as hell, which means they need to find someone else to blame. You make a good bogeyman."

"You mean the guy no one can identify or find, right?"

"Makes it worse. You know how conspiracy theories work." Tom folded his huge hands around his mug. The staff at the Silver Spoon kept a soup mug specifically for the Chief. Orange letters on a green field spelled out Big Cheese on the side. A Packer logo graced the other side. "Thought you should know. Your FBI pal poked around a bit."

"She told me."

Tom didn't ask, and I didn't tell. The coffee cooled enough for consumption. I took a few sips and welcomed the effect.

The waitress took our orders. I asked for the full bacon and eggs breakfast, feeling a buildup of hunger. On my clock it was practically noon.

"Does anyone care that Gregg's murder has been pinned on a guy in Illinois?"

Tom looked at me sharply.

"I saw that on the news," I lied. It felt like he knew it.

"The Republicans don't care. They're spinning the fact that he got assassinated into proof that he didn't kidnap his wife—don't ask me how. They want to pin the kidnapping on the unknown stranger so they can bury their asshole with flags flying."

"So much for the truth."

"They're not in the truth business, Will. All they care about is how they're trending for the next election. How's my detective doing?"

"Kicking ass and taking names," I replied, grateful for the change in topic.

I told Tom how Andy's exam performance gave us extra time together. The news twisted up one corner of his mouth. From her earliest days at the Waukesha County Technical College, Tom had noticed and followed Andy's progress, ultimately hiring her. His pride in her ran deep. I mentioned how thrilled Andy had been to meet Mrs. Palmer, a name Tom recognized. I expected him to be impressed, but his expression darkened when I described Andy's interest in Leslie's reports.

"You tell your FBI pal to leave her alone. She doesn't need any distractions."

"Really? Have you meet my wife?"

Tom muttered or growled, I could not tell which.

"How's Sheriff Kresky? Did you stay on to give her a hand?" I suppressed a schoolboy grin at the crude double-entendre, knowing that Tom was more than capable of slapping me across the room and calling it an arrest.

"Fine. And no." If he thought that would end it, he was mistaken.

"Nice woman. I like her style."

"Uh-huh."

"You're not going to tell me, are you?"

"Nope."

Our breakfast came. They're fast at the Silver Spoon.

46

The problem with seeing Andy for forty-eight hours, with locking our attention on each other to the exclusion of the rest of the world, with becoming deeply, deeply intimate, is that the interlude satisfied nothing. Our time together only made me miss her more. Monday dragged.

I went home, trudged through running a load of laundry and performing household chores, watched a bad cop movie (in Andy's eyes they're all bad) and turned in early for a fitful sleep. I found comfort in the knowledge that the morning alarm put me one day closer to Friday when Andy planned to call at her usual hour. In my head I rehearsed versions of pestering her about our next visit.

Leslie called Monday evening. I suspected the call was more to keep contact with me than to report anything new. I asked her about the information she shared with Andy, and how she felt about Andy sharing with Mrs. Palmer. Leslie gave me the same awestruck response to Mrs. Palmer as Andy. I asked if Saunders and his team knew that Leslie shared details from their investigation with the great Mrs. Palmer. I got a firm hell no. Even over the phone, I detected Leslie's crooked smile through the call connection and sensed she was not above one-upping Saunders.

"Saunders is fixated on Flatley," Leslie said.

"And you're not?"

She didn't answer at once. When she did, I heard her arguing with herself.

"I don't have good reason not to be, but…I need a few more bricks in that wall. You know what I mean?"

"Did you know Andy would ask Mrs. Palmer to look things over?"

"Of course. Brilliant idea. I was surprised the woman would see Andy. Or any cadet. Look, Will, if you're reading me as having doubts, you're right. But I'm not looking to prove Saunders wrong, I'm looking to prove him right. He needs to be right. Because if he's not—*if we're not*—that's a whole new shit show. If Mrs. Palmer helps nail the coffin lid on Flatley, praise the Lord. Did you see Saunders' press conference?"

"No. When?"

"Oh, that's right. You were at the homecoming dance with your wife. Saturday. The cat's out of the bag on the sniper killings. He went ahead and tied them all to Flatley. The country now knows that it missed a chance to become irrationally terrified."

"Bit of a risk in that if it turns out Flatley wasn't the guy."

"He *is* the guy. There. I said it. He *is* the fucking guy."

"Uh-huh. You sound like you're trying to convince yourself."

"I know. I need to work on that."

THE NIGHTMARE VISITED ON MONDAY, or perhaps early Tuesday. I didn't check the clock. This time Flatley heaved the child high in the air and when I went after her the extra trick performed by *the other thing* didn't kick in. I floated, helpless, struggling to pull a BLASTER out of my pants pocket while the girl kept falling and falling. I woke up before she hit the steel rail below the grain elevator.

"Okay. That sucked." I said it aloud to the dark bedroom. I stretched out my left arm, but it fell flat on the empty mattress where Andy sleeps. "That, too."

Sometime later, sleep found me again.

47

I maneuvered to a halt on the Spirit of St. Louis Airport ramp and killed the left engine. I watched the suction gauge. The left-engine red indicator light flashed on, reflecting the loss of the left vacuum pump, precisely as it should. I pulled the mixture on the right engine, which rumbled to a stop. The right-engine vacuum failure indicator lit up, again as it should. All good. I moved my thumb down the shutdown checklist.

Arun tapped my shoulder.

"They're taking me to lunch. Do you want to join us?"

"Thanks. I'm okay. I might run an errand, so text me if there's any change to the itinerary."

He squinted at me, trying to determine if I was making fun of him. I tightened my poker face. He shook his head and headed to the rear of the cabin to let himself out.

After supervising the lineman during refueling, I visited the FBO desk. The kid remembered me.

"Pizza, right?"

"Yup. Nice to see you again." I handed over the Foundation credit card. "For the fuel and ramp fee."

"Staying overnight?"

"Not this time. We're leaving around three-thirty."

The kid made quick work of the fuel charge, ran the card, and handed it back. "Anything else we can do for you?"

"Not today. Thanks!"

I slipped the card in my wallet, and my wallet in my back pocket. For a moment, I stood trying to decide between the exit and the pilot's lounge. I could easily mope all day in a fat leather chair in the pilot's lounge. Or...

An idea tickled the back of my mind. I wasn't sure when it germinated. Possibly in that last instant of consciousness before I fell back asleep in the aftermath of the nightmare. I might have been looking for comfort and this idea blossomed in answer.

"Screw it," I said to myself. I headed for the exit.

St. Louis lists four children's hospitals. A week ago I had picked the one near Forest Park. A vague notion that the park offered an open expanse for escape accounted for the selection, although I couldn't imagine a scenario requiring that kind of evasion. For me, there's always *up*.

On my last visit I drove a rented car. This time, I took a cab. The cab deposited me at the front door behind a van disembarking an elderly woman in a wheelchair. The momentary bustle of activity at the entrance meant I didn't have to enter alone. I tucked my logo-less ball cap down against my sunglasses and said a friendly hello to the attendant pushing the wheelchair, pausing with him for the sliding doors, strolling and exchanging comments about the weather. Looking like I belonged.

Inside, I veered off and headed for the gift shop. I purchased a trio of mylar balloons. From that point on, wherever I detected a camera, I maneuvered the balloons into a blocking position.

The elevator took me to the fourth floor. I followed the familiar corridor to past a Y junction of hallways, past a nurses' station, toward a door that grew more foreboding as it drew closer.

No panicked nurse hovering outside this time. No trotting deputy. No alerted and alarmed staff.

I sucked in a deep breath at the door, then swung inside. My plan was to pretend embarrassment for entering the wrong room. To look lost. To answer questions with a joke or a laugh. Maybe leave a balloon as a friendly gesture.

"Can I help you?"

Caught. I stopped short. The woman beside the bed stared directly at me. Her hands clutched a bundle of linens. She wore a uniform, but not nurses' or doctors' scrubs. A badge on a lanyard dangled over her bosom.

I glanced down at the bed.

Empty.

"Uh…I was…" I looked around the room. All signs of a personal touch were gone. I didn't recall if Amber had decorated her room, but I vaguely recalled clothing tossed on the occasional chair, shoes lined up on the floor. The IV stand that towered over her bed was gone. No medicines. No IV or treatment pouches. No litter of medical supplies. The room was clean. The woman facing me paused in the middle of changing the bed linens. "Do you know…did the girl in this room move to another room? Her name was—"

"Amber," she smiled. "Are you a relative?"

"Friend of her uncle." I tugged on the balloons. "I'm a little behind on the family news. I meant to come last week, but you know how it is."

The words came surprisingly hard. An empty room offered two possibilities, and in that instant the worst of the two floated to the top. Was it over? Had the inevitable happened? It chilled me to think I'd just handed this poor woman the terrible task of explaining tragedy to an idiot with a handful of balloons.

"You don't know?" she asked.

This is a mistake. This is why you never go back.

I took an involuntary step backward.

The woman broke out a huge grin.

"She went home yesterday," she said, following with a choked laugh and sob. Her eyes became wet. "My lord, I'm still emotional about it."

"Home?" *Via low swinging chariot?* The old spiritual lyric, imprinted on me by a fourth-grade music teacher, intruded on my mind.

The woman pulled a tissue from her tunic and dabbed her eyes, still grinning. "A miracle. The girl is a miracle. She went home with her family. She just woke up one night and went down to the cafeteria and filled up on junk food and—I'm sorry—I just—you didn't know?"

I didn't answer. I had stopped hearing. The woman's words reached my ears but didn't register on my brain. She spoke, smiled and gestured. I nodded a couple times. The thin ribbons holding the balloons slipped through my fingers. I heard a light drum sound when they hit the ceiling.

I think I muttered a *Thank you* before I slipped out.

"Do you want your balloons?" she called after me.

I planted one foot in front of the other on the burnt orange carpet. Weight shed with each step. A grin took charge of my face. I waved to the nurse at the nurses' station as I marched past.

She went home. One for the win column.

This put things in balance. Amber's outcome had everything and nothing to do with how much I missed Andy. Amber made it; she went home. Credit her doctors. Credit her meds. Credit her new diet of junk food. She left this place alive. The gloom clouding the prospect of a long week alone disappeared so fast that it left a cartoon sparkle in its wake. I felt as if air entered my lungs for the first time since Sunday.

Andy was crushing it at the Academy. Fulfilling her dream. I supported that dream, but damn, it had grown exhausting. Adding Amber to the win column put fuel in my tanks. Even Leslie popping out of the woodwork with some new scheme didn't dent my blooming good mood.

I stopped caring about cameras. I smiled and paid out a cheerful Hello to staff passing me in the hall. I felt weirdly hungry despite a solid breakfast. Maybe a trip to the cafeteria for some good healthy junk food would do the trick. The notion made me laugh.

I glanced into a visitor lounge to look for vending machines. A KitKat or Reese's Peanut Butter Cup in Amber's honor felt appropriate. The lounge contained a random arrangement of comfortable furniture, a kitchenette, a gas fireplace, and a widescreen television mounted high on one wall broadcasting constant cable news, but no vending machines.

A blazing headline on the widescreen caught my eye, block white letters on a red banner.

BREAKING NEWS.

Police vehicles, flashing lights, and uniformed officers filled the frame. From the hallway I could not hear the television audio, which played at a low level to an empty room. The subheading stopped me.

Serial sniper kills Presidential Advisor.

Washington, D.C.

The on-screen image used a long lens, which jiggled slightly. Mixed among the police vehicles were military vehicles. In one corner of the frame, compressed by distance, a portion of the U.S. Capitol dome hung over the scene.

Son of a bitch.

48

M y phone rang as the cab pulled up to the curb.

"Hang on a second," I told Leslie. I fumbled with my wallet and cash, overtipped the driver, and hopped out. "You there?"

"Did you see?"

"Yeah. Saunders is screwed."

"Will, the whole country is screwed. It's what I was afraid of. This is the D.C. case all over again."

I paced the sidewalk in front of the FBO, holding the phone to my ear. "I only caught a glimpse of a TV. It said he was a presidential advisor. Did this happen at the White House?"

"Oh, God no. He was on a golf course in Virginia."

"I don't get it. The TV showed emergency vehicles near the Capitol."

"D.C. is on lockdown. Practically martial law. And no, the guy—his name was Renner Stemple—wasn't technically a 'presidential advisor.' He was a crony of the President. Frankly, he was a slimeball one step ahead of a grand jury. Now, of course, he's a saint. The White House is talking about having him lie in state at the Capitol, which is insane."

"I never heard of him, but I'm no authority on current events."

"Stemple was a lowlife. The guy practically wore out the sidewalks in D.C. pimping his connections to the Oval Office. He was a fly on—never mind. Forget the politics, Will. This thing just blew up. Christ, they're talking about closing schools. Where are you?"

"St. Louis again. Why?"

She didn't answer.

"Leslie, are you now part of this sniper thing? Officially?"

"Everybody's part of it, Will. FBI. State. Local. Every cop in America is on this. The cat's out of the bag, and since that thing in Triple County—"

"Tri-Township."

"Whatever. Since then, I don't need an invitation from Saunders. So yes, I am in. Which means I may need you."

"Right now?"

The line hung silent. It lasted long enough for me to imagine Arun's response if I took the airplane and left him a note suggesting he rent a car and drive seven hours back to Essex.

"I'll call you. But one more thing…" I waited. It wasn't like Leslie to look for words, yet I sensed hesitation.

"Yes?"

"Has anyone called you? Anyone reached out to you?"

"About what?"

"Lindsay?"

"Uh…" I had no idea what to say.

"Never mind. Forget it."

"Whoa! No, no, no. You don't get to do that. Who are you talking about?"

"I told you. They're digging into Lindsay."

"Who's digging into Lindsay? And how does this matter to me?"

"It doesn't. Forget it. Lindsay didn't keep any notes or files on you."

I let the line hang silent for a moment, then said, "You really need to work on being more convincing, Leslie."

One thing I hate about cell phones. There's no dial tone. I had to look at the screen to realize Leslie had hung up.

49

A run occupied the entire return flight with nervous chatter about the news. Every few minutes, he received an update on his phone. CNN. *Washington Post. New York Times. Chicago Tribune.* None of his up-to-the-minute reports offered anything of substance. His sources sounded reputable, but to my ear the "Breaking News" sounded like a lot of rehash and speculation. The headlines carried an undercurrent of blame hunting. To the media, SAC Saunders had called "Mission Accomplished" in the worst way. I didn't comment. Nor did I mention my way-too-personal encounters with the sniper case.

Arun seemed anxious to access his laptop when we landed, so I brushed off his usual kind offer to help secure the airplane and close the hangar. He hurried to his office.

I called the fuel truck from Essex County Air. One of the young flight instructors, doing double-duty, drove up and topped off the Navajo. We traded pilot talk in the descending twilight. It felt cleansing. I remembered being in his position with a wallet full of ratings and an empty logbook. At his age and stage in aviation, I would have given just about anything to get some flight time in a big twin like the Navajo. Before he left, I told him to tell Rosemary II that she should watch the flight schedule for a day I have an out-and-back trip that he could co-pilot. He beamed at the idea and assured me several times before driving away that he'd be in touch.

I realized as I rolled the airplane backward into the hangar, that I had used the brief discussion with a fellow aviator to stall facing an evening alone. After placing the Navajo's nosewheel on a tape mark I established on the pristine hangar floor, I parked the electric hand tug and collected my flight bag. I took a few minutes to record the day's flights in my logbook and in a database Arun had created. I leaned into Arun's office to find him hypnotized by his laptop screen. He didn't notice me. I slipped out to my car.

The Foundation hangar sits in a line of private hangars lining both sides of a short airport road, which connects to State Highway 34. I pulled up to the highway and began a long wait for perfectly spaced traffic going in both directions to give me an opening.

A right turn would take me home to an empty house.

I turned left.

"JESUS, the people you meet when you haven't got a gun." Dave Peterson grinned at me from his seat at the bar in the "other" Mexican restaurant in Essex, the one with the attached bowling alley. "Pull up a stool, partner. I haven't seen you for a while."

I had planned on grabbing a taco plate and a beer alone, but the company of a fellow Essex County Air Service pilot who wasn't Pidge carried a refreshing appeal. Dave and I had been regular bar flies before Andy entered my life. He saw in her many of the same things I saw and forgave me for choosing her over our brotherhood bond. Not too long after Andy and I married, Dave took a corporate jet job, which ended abruptly when Andy put Dave's boss in jail, an event that indirectly launched the Christine and Paulette Paulesky Education Foundation using a now-dead billionaire's money. Circumstances landed me a new job and gave Earl a chance to rehire Dave. It's funny how circles open and close.

"Corona with lime," I told the alert bartender. I hopped on the stool beside Dave. "What's new with you?"

"Well…" he said, making an exaggerated gesture at the seat opposite me. "I got a girlfriend."

I made a show of looking at the empty bar stool.

"Uh-huh," I said. "And she seems nice. Much nicer than your last imaginary girlfriend."

He laughed. "Bite me. She'll be back in a minute. I'll introduce you."

I was happy for Dave. He'd gone through a downturn in life by losing his jet job and then falling hard for Sandy Stone, who had no interest whatsoever in romance after a near death experience from a marriage of eyeblink duration. I was glad that Dave had moved on.

"Where's your better half?"

"Studying to become an accredited member of the Federal Bureau of Investigation."

Dave stared at me as if I'd spoken Albanian.

"She's at the FBI Academy in Quantico, Virginia."

"No shit?"

"No shit of any kind."

Dave leaned back. "Wow! Oh my god, when did this happen?"

"Really? I can't believe you didn't know. Rosemary II is off her game."

I skipped the part about a Mexican drug lord who tried to kill the entire United States Supreme Court and simply told Dave it had been Andy's dream, and the opportunity came out of nowhere, and she took it in a heartbeat, good for her. I told him how proud of her I was, and how this meant the world to her.

"So, she dumped you for the FBI. I knew that girl was smart, dude. And way too good for you."

"Hell, I knew she was too good for me, but she hasn't wised up yet. We just spent the weekend together. She's doing great and loving it."

"Fantastic. Give her my best."

The bartender dropped my beer onto a coaster just as an attractive blonde woman walked the length of the bar and slid onto the stool next to Dave with a not-too-trusting glance at the stranger that had just become a third wheel on her date night. It did not escape my notice that this woman bore a passing resemblance to Sandy Stone.

"Marissa, this is Will Stewart. Will, Marissa Copley."

I lifted my beer to her rather than reach across Dave for a handshake.

"Very nice to meet you, even if you have shown exceptionally poor judgment in dating this scoundrel." I got a cold look and immediately noted that my usual Dave-humor could not have landed wider of the mark.

"Nice to meet you," she said, even though it clearly wasn't. "How do you two know each other?"

"Will's a pilot. He used to work for Earl."

"Want to see my scars?" I asked. Another direct miss.

Dave squirmed in his seat. Marissa Copley made a face that suggested she didn't quite understand the question, but which translated to *who is this idiot and why is he interrupting my date?*

"Listen, man," I said, clapping Dave on the back, "I'd love to hang with you two, but I've got laundry in the dryer and my wife will kill me if I overcook her delicates again. And she carries a gun." I hopped off the stool. "It really was nice to meet you, Marissa. I hope you can meet my wife someday."

Yes. I'm married. Dave has a married friend. The clarification seemed to score a few points, but not as many as me leaving.

"Very nice to meet you, too, Will."

"Later, bro."

I grabbed my beer and headed for the end of the bar. Glancing back, I watched Marissa laugh and nudge Dave's shoulder, reestablishing sole possession. Making certain that neither of them saw me, I placed the unfinished beer on the bar, slid a five under the bottle, and headed for the exit and my empty home.

50

Somebody's in there.

Movement caused me to see it. Like looking for air traffic in the sky or against cluttered terrain. You don't look for an airplane, you look for something moving. A shadow. Barely a shadow. It rippled within the frame of the upstairs hallway window just as I eased off the gas pedal of my car. Nothing else about the house and yard hinted at trouble, which on its own felt like cause for warning.

My foot lingered above the accelerator but did not touch the brake. I rolled past the driveway. Between the trees, I studied the window frame. I didn't recall leaving a light on, but for a shadow to have registered at all, there would have to be a source of light inside.

Lewko! The son of a bitch had decided to make good on his threat.

I'd been down this road before. My home had been invaded by someone looking for more of the accident debris that Lewko ultimately acquired, more evidence of *the other thing*. It wouldn't be Lewko himself. It would be professionals. The best that unlimited money could buy.

They'll know your car. I slowly accelerated back up to the 45 mph limit, bypassing the property. In a moment, walls of drying corn stalks formed on either side of the car. Perfect cover for a team waiting to spike strip the tires, swarm down and grab me before I could escape the vehicle.

I hit the button for the car's sunroof. Not much works on my old

Corolla, but the power sunroof has remained faithful. I glanced up to check something I never thought I'd ask myself. Can I get out through the roof? It would be tight but doable.

What if they throw a net over the car? Lewko was rapidly turning into a Bond villain in my head, full of nefarious gadgets. Spike strips to take out the tires. Rocket-powered netting to cover the vehicle. Dart guns to drug me. My gaze flicked from side to side, checking the rows of corn for movement the way I watch for deer at dusk and dawn.

Nothing attacked me. The intersection of my county road and the next road on the mile-square road grid came up. I ran the stop sign and heaved the car into a left turn that tested the grip of my old tires. I downshifted and accelerated quickly, heading north.

The last time this happened, Arun had been driving. I practically dove out of the car after we descended into a dip in the road, out of sight of a team of men who were watching my house. This time I had no one to drop me off and keep the car moving.

Why go home? Why not go back to the hangar? Or Earl's office? Or the police station?

Lewko may be arrogant and entitled and even above the law in his own eyes, but he wasn't dumb. Any team he sent for me would have all the bases covered. Including the possibility that I might drive right by the house. I felt more vulnerable by the minute.

The western horizon held onto faint blue sky. I killed the car's headlights. After a few seconds, my eyes adjusted. More than enough twilight remained for safe navigation of the narrow country road. James Rankin's countless cornfields surrounded my home. Soon his giant harvesting equipment would come to cash in the crop. His equipment used wide lanes between the fields for access. Midway up the one-mile stretch of road, I downshifted sharply, avoiding brake lights. I turned onto one such utility lane. Now pointed west, I drove the reasonably smooth dirt lane deeper into the fields. I kept the car in second gear to avoid kicking up dust.

The lane ended almost directly behind the house Andy and I rent. At its terminus, the utility lane butted against a much narrower, older cow lane. A right turn went north into a woods bordering a meadow bisected by a creek. A left turn went south to the barn and farmhouse. I turned north and rolled into the stand of old trees, bumping harshly on the much rougher cow lane until I felt certain the car could not be seen. I killed the engine but left the car in gear to bring the vehicle to a stop, avoiding brake lights.

Getting out of the car felt important. I quickly pulled two power units from my flight bag. I stuffed one in my pocket and assembled the prop on the other.

51

F *wooomp!* I vanished where I sat behind the wheel. I reached up and grabbed the roof. I pulled.

And jerked against my seatbelt.

Old pain in my once broken pelvis throbbed lightly, apparently insulted by the reminder of how it had been broken in the first place.

Shit!

"Calm down, idiot." I took a breath to settle my heart rate. I unsnapped the belt and tried again. Escape proved awkward. My shins bumped against the steering wheel. My feet knocked the stick shift out of gear. I slithered out the car roof, giving the car seat a kick to launch into the thick limbs of an old oak tree. I tapped off the first limb and ascended to grab the next in line, figuring that rocket powered netting wouldn't work in a tree.

My fear wasn't entirely unfounded. The kid who found debris in the wreckage of Six Nine Tango claimed that he and his nerd companions developed a sonic detection technology. Lewko stole the debris. I had to assume that he stole the technology as well. Imagining that Lewko's people might be able to see and track me threw gasoline on my burning paranoia. I felt sinister eyes on me. This was not a safe place to be.

I eased power to the BLASTER and shoved off sideways to get out of the tree. Once clear, I aimed the power unit straight up and let it pull me skyward. Trees dropped away around me. Cornfields and meadows sprawled and expanded in every direction. I searched in vain for the black clad ninja types who were no doubt crouching in every corn row, in every ditch, behind every tree. Half a mile away, the barn behind my house promised to be infested with Lewko's mercenaries.

It pissed me off—the idea that he could violate my home, treat me like property, and think that his wealth gave him lawless leave to do whatever he wanted.

"Screw you," I told him and the empty sky.

I gained height, but instead of turning in the direction of Essex to find sanctuary in Tom Ceeve's office or heading up to Andy's sister's home on Leander Lake, I aimed for my home.

My flight plan took me directly above the house where I reversed power and stopped. I aimed the BLASTER straight down. In the dark, I misjudged my descent rate. The farmhouse roof peak came at me fast. I held the BLASTER straight down and applied reverse power.

Just before an abrupt touchdown, I stuffed the BLASTER in my pocket and rotated. I reached out. My palms met the coarse shingles on the roof and arrested the descent. I clawed a grip under the edge of shingles on both sides of the peak and rotated my body parallel to the roof. I crawled to the edge and examined the yard.

No cars. No vans. No sign of intruders. I expected nothing less from Lewko's team. But they had to be watching, waiting.

Andy keeps a gun safe in the downstairs dining room closet. I know the combination and know the weapons inside. Her Baretta M.92 can be modified with a suppressor. I've used it before. I had no interest in lethal force, but that didn't diminish an angry urge to put a couple of 9mm rounds into the ass cheeks of the people violating my home.

Let 'em try and shoot back.

The house has a front door and a back door, but it also has a set of Bilco doors leading into the storm cellar, protected by a padlock. The key hangs in our kitchen.

The edge of the peaked roof placed me directly above the angled dual doors. I pulled myself clear of the roof and heaved myself downward. I grabbed the old iron door handle, then closed one fist around the padlock. The body of the lock vanished, leaving the shank visible. On the line between the hidden body and visible shank, the steel frayed and blurred. I twisted and the steel snapped. I tossed the body aside, then carefully pulled the shank out of the latch loop. Using one hand to brace against the left door, I lifted the right door.

I didn't need much. Just enough to squeeze through. I extended myself parallel to the door opening, wiggled my shoulder and hips through, then let the door settle.

Inside, I descended the old stone steps. Close to a hundred and fifty years old, the cellar had dirt floors and stone walls. Andy and I vowed on arrival that we would store nothing in this cellar except an emergency radio and a flashlight. I could have used the flashlight, but it and the radio sit on a shelf beside steep steps that rise to a door in our kitchen. As I approached the steps, light seeping under the door showed me the way.

I pulled myself up the handrail. Before opening the door to the kitchen, I peered through the gap at the floor, looking for boot-clad feet.

All clear.

I let myself out and carefully closed the door behind me.

The house did not feel empty. I can't explain it. The shadow in the window imprinted a tactile presence on my senses.

They're here.

I maneuvered through the kitchen to the dining room. A steady glide took me to the closet with the gun safe. Twisting the closet doorknob slowly, I gained silent access. I tapped the gun safe combination on the finger pad. The latch released with a loud *Thunk!* I froze and waited for a reaction. When none came, I pulled open the gun safe door.

Andy's M.92 lay on its designated shelf, loaded and ready. The licensed suppressor lay beside it. I picked up the weapon and attached the suppressor. I didn't need to confirm that a round lay in the chamber. Andy stores the weapon loaded and ready, reasoning that in time of need, the split second required to rack the slide could be fatal.

Armed and dangerous, I didn't bother closing the safe door or the closet door. I folded the weapon into my shirt until it too vanished, then slid around the corner to the living room.

Empty.

I held the gun in my right hand and hooked the living room entrance with my left, then pulled myself above the furniture to meet the stairway railing at the midpoint. Up and over, I ascended, grateful that I did not need to plant my feet on the creaking old steps—the Will and Andy farm-house alarm system.

I stopped at the top of the stairs and glanced in both directions. Illumination spilled under the upstairs bathroom door, casting a painted trapezoid of light across the wooden floor. A faint scraping sound came from behind the door.

I looked for and failed to find men in shadow waiting for me in the hallway. The doors to the master and guest bedrooms stood open, dark, and threatening.

This is not right.

I felt my chest tighten. A powerful urge to turn and get out of the house tugged at me, but a counterforce of anger narrowed my focus and drove me forward.

I pulled myself around the corner and ascended to glide past the open bedroom doors above the doorframe top. My heart hammered as I passed each black space laden with crouching intruders. Clear of the doorways, I lowered myself and listened outside the upstairs bathroom. The faint scraping sound had stopped. My breathing ceased.

I repositioned my feet near the floor, ready to accept my weight.

Do it and do it fast.

I lifted the weapon and slid my finger into the trigger guard. I closed my left hand on the doorknob.

I silently twisted the knob to the stop.

FWOOOMP!

Gravity dropped me to the floor.

I jerked the door open and heaved the weapon up.

My finger touched the trigger.

Six pounds of pressure nearly caused the worst mistake I would ever make.

Over the sights of the gun, I saw—

Andy.

Kneeling in front of the toilet, her hands covered in bright yellow gloves, her right fist closed on the handle of a scrub brush.

Andy. Her hair tied back. Startled by the door smacking its stop.

Eyes ringed in red, smeared and damp.

Crying.

I heaved the weapon skyward and jerked my finger from the trigger guard.

"*Dee! What the hell?!*" My pulse thundered in my ears. Tremors wracked my arms. The gun took on the weight of an anchor. *"What the hell are you doing here?"*

"Cleaning." Her voice sounded tight, strained. "Cleaning the bathroom."

The words were nonsense to my ears.

The horrifying image of Andy centered on the gunsight flashed in my mind. I lowered the weapon to the countertop, careful to point the muzzle away from both of us.

She wore old jeans and a faded Mickey Mouse t-shirt. She had secured her hair the way she fashions it for gardening or housework, lifted free of her neck and bobbed for cooling. Loose strands framed her face. She wore yellow rubber gloves. The bucket containing our household cleaning supplies sat on the floor beside her.

"I'm—I'm cleaning the toilet."

"I see that," I said, "but *what are you doing here?*"

She stared at me for a moment, then at the brush in her hand. A quiver attacked her lower lip and her chin. The glitter in her eye became dewdrops. They fell, streaking her cheeks.

The brush clattered into the bowl. She folded.

I rushed forward and fell to my knees. I caught her and pulled her into my arms. Her body trembled and jerked with deep, consuming sobs.

I pulled her close. Her head fell against my shoulder.

"*Oh, Will!*" she cried. "*They—they suspended me!*"

52

I 've been told by men who have decades invested, that I have a better chance of finding Amelia Earhart than solving the mystery that is marriage. However, one of the few elements I have mastered in my union with Andy is knowing when she wants my touch, and when she doesn't. After a desperate initial embrace and a cloudburst of tears on the tile floor of our bathroom—during which I had the good sense not to interrogate her—she pressed herself free and asked to wash her face and clean herself up. She told me to get her a glass of water and to wait for her explanation downstairs.

I retreated to the kitchen and poured the water, but also poured Bailey's Irish Cream over ice in two tumblers and set up the beverages on our coffee table coasters.

Ten minutes later Andy descended the stairs without making eye contact. She stepped around the end of our old sofa and folded her legs under her on her favorite spot, signaling that my embrace, my touch, was not needed.

She reached for the table. I expected her to reject the alcohol, but she surprised me. She ignored the water and lifted the Bailey's. She downed half of the glass in one hit.

I ventured to the edge of the middle cushion.

For a silent moment, she stared at her hands. I waited. When her eyes found mine again, they glittered. Her lip quivered again. She fought it, found control, and spoke slowly, deliberately.

"They suspended me. Yesterday."

I had no words. The pain in her voice and on her face stabbed me in the heart.

"What happened?"

"They said I cheated on the Interstate Law exam."

"That's insane!"

She shook her head. "I told you they scrub our personal devices. They picked up my laptop on Monday. An hour later the deputy administrator called me in. I was informed that the device was impounded, pending a full investigation, and that I was—" she bit her lip and I stopped breathing "—that I was suspended."

"That makes *no sense*. It's impossible."

"They said restricted academic materials were found on my laptop. Materials specific to Friday's exam as well other materials pertaining to other courses."

"This is some kind of setup."

"I don't know how," she said. "I've been over it and over it and over it. I can't imagine how someone got their hands on it."

"Was it out of your possession?"

"Maybe when I was in the shower, but my room was locked."

"Is it password protected?"

"Of course."

"Was it tampered with?"

"How would I know? The laptop is impounded. It's in an evidence locker."

"Did someone—Jesus—I don't know—did they show you whatever it was they claimed you had?"

"No. Only that I had breached their server and removed certain files. Which is ridiculous. I'm not a programmer. I'm not on a cyber security track."

"Are there students on such a track?"

"Of course. The FBI plays a huge role in cyber security."

"So, these students, these classmates, they're hackers? Programmers?"

"A few," Andy said. She read where I was headed. "No, Will. Not possible."

I wasn't so sure, but I set the idea aside.

"Is this about those files?"

"Which files?"

"The ones Leslie sent you. The sniper case."

She shook her head.

"Is there any chance Leslie's files had a virus or a trojan horse or whatever the kids are calling it?"

"And what? You think Leslie sabotaged me?"

"I don't know. Maybe she doesn't like to share her toys and she thinks I'm one of her toys."

Andy shook her head. "It wasn't Leslie, and it wasn't her files. I never had them on my computer. She sent them to me through Dropbox, and I copied them directly to the flash drive."

"Are you sure that's how it works?"

"Pretty sure."

I pressed the heels of my hands to my eyes for a moment, then said, "Dee, they have to let you defend yourself."

"No. They don't. There will be a formal review by a faculty committee, but they said the evidence was damning. The committee's only purpose is to convert suspension to expulsion. I can appeal, but it would be pointless. Even if I won, even if they let me back in, I'd be marked. After which the committee will determine whether to bring charges or not."

"*Charges?*" I could not believe my ears, or how calmly she said it. "Charges for what?"

She didn't explain.

I pulled out my phone. "We need to call Leslie."

"Will—"

"Dee, whoever she leveraged to get you in—"

"Will, stop."

I froze, phone in hand, poised to dial.

"Stop, please," she said. "Just...stop. I know you. I know you want to fix this. But please stop."

"Dee, there's no way you did any of this. Somebody did this to you!"

"You think I don't know that? I am well aware, believe me." Anger edged into her tone. She heard it, closed her eyes, and held a hand up between us. "Can you just…just not be you for a second. Can you just try not to rescue me for a second?"

The fight building in me wanted to argue, a mistake I recognized. I clenched my jaw against a flood of outrage.

Andy's chest rose and fell.

"They gave me an hour to pack my things and evacuate the campus. I was escorted to the Visitor Center. Half the class saw them walk me out."

Now I wanted to murder someone.

"This was yesterday? Dee, I…why didn't you call? Why didn't you call me? I would have come."

"I know. I know you would have. I—I couldn't face you. I couldn't face anybody. Do you understand? I needed time."

"How did you get home?"

"After they walked me out, I, uh, I guess I just sat there for a while. I guess for a couple hours. The center closes at eight. They asked me to go, so I called an Uber."

"You took an Uber to Wisconsin?"

"No. To Dulles. I rented a car." I didn't see a car in the yard, but before I asked, she explained. "I drove to Mitchell in Milwaukee and turned it in, then took a bus to the stop on 41. Then an Uber from the bus stop home."

I shoved my hand into my hair, trying to comprehend. "Jesus! That's like, what? Thirty hours of driving?"

"Fifteen. I didn't start until late last night. And I had to wait for the one o'clock bus."

"Have you slept?"

She shook her head.

I laid my hand on her knee. She slowly reached out and covered my hand with hers.

"I'm okay," she lied. She spoke softly. "Will, just…please…just give me a little time. Okay? I know what you want to do for me. And I love you for it. You'll get your chance. Just promise me, promise you'll give me some time. I need to sort this out."

I barely heard her. A voice thundered in my head.

Somebody will pay for this.

53

Tom Ceeves rolled his big SUV to a stop on my gravel driveway. I tiptoed out of the living room where Andy lay sleeping on the sofa and where I sat awake most of the night watching her. I hurried through the screened porch and met him halfway across the lawn. The look on his face told me either he had heard the news, or the earth was about to take an extinction event hit from an asteroid.

"Is she here?"

"Sleeping," I said.

Tom stopped in his tracks.

"News travels fast," I said. "How did you hear?"

He made a disgusted face. "City manager."

"How on earth did the city manager hear about this?"

Tom gave me a look that questioned my IQ.

"Jake Summers?"

"I know who the city manager is, Chief."

"Did you know he's Armand Collingworth's cousin?"

I flashed back to a very public meeting involving the school board. *Sandy Stone's dismissal.*

"Summers is Collingsworth's cousin? Oh, crap."

Collingsworth had been on the school board led a fight to dismiss Sandy Stone based on bogus accusations launched by the man who tried

243

to murder her. Andy's role in exposing the truth led indirectly to embarrassing Collingsworth. The episode cost him his school board seat.

I didn't know that the city manager was Collingsworth's cousin. I rarely thought about the city manager, except that his name showed up on Andy's paychecks. Paychecks that continued landing in our checking account since Andy had applied for and received Temporary Duty status during her studies at the FBI Academy. Summers objected to her application at the time, but Tom backed her.

The dots connected.

"I got a call this morning," Tom said. "Summers wants me to meet with the city attorney to discuss severing Andy's employment."

"Oh, for chrissakes."

"What happened?" Tom asked.

I told him what I could.

He shook his head. "No. No. Not possible. No."

I agreed. Andy and I had gone over the details several times. We dissected the logistics of someone accessing her laptop. She described the protocols permitting academy cadets use of an electronic device. She ran down her practice of keeping it padlocked in a footlocker in her room, which made it sound impossible for someone to gain access. The suggestion that she hacked the academy's sophisticated servers and acquired materials restricted to the teaching staff carried no credibility. Aside from being repellent to her, Andy wouldn't have had a clue where to start.

"What about your FBI pal?" Tom asked. "What does she have to say about all this?"

"I kinda told her to go to hell last night."

"What?"

"She called. Late. I didn't pick up. I sent her a text."

"Were you drunk?"

"No. Pissed. I told her I never wanted to speak to her again."

Tom rolled his eyes.

"Really? You're going to judge me for that? Leslie got Andy invited in and then they gutted her."

"Not sure it went like that."

"Probably not," I admitted. "Truth is, I blame me."

Tom squinted.

I had given the matter a lot of thought, sitting in the dark.

"Andy got a shot at the FBI because of me. They want me to work for them because of *the other thing*, so they threw her a bone in the name of harmony. But you know as well as I do that she deserved a shot more than any ten people in that class. If this travesty stands—I swear, Tom, all bets are off. I'm done with them. They get nothing from them." I waited a moment for my blood to cool. It didn't. "So…what? Summers is going to have her tossed off the department?"

Tom said nothing, but his expression spoke volumes.

"Are you shitting me?" My voice rose. I glanced at the house.

Tom followed my glanced and lowered his voice. "Summers wants to void her TDY status. He's arguing that she was leaving anyway."

"Dammit."

"Will," he said, "you might want to unburn that bridge with your FBI pal."

"She's not my pal."

"She's a direct line to whoever got Andy the slot. That opening came from higher up."

"And there's a whole fucking can of worms. I have no idea who 'higher up' is these days, and my FBI pal isn't making it sound like it's someone with our best interests at heart. So?"

"So, suck it up. That's a pay grade that might be able to deal with this. I'm just saying. Meanwhile, I'll go to bat for her at the city level. If Summers wants her gone, he'll have to go through me. She might not be able to keep her detective rank, but I think I can keep her on patrol."

"Well, that's big of you Chief!"

The color in his face and the tendons on his neck told me I'd just stepped on a land mine. He lifted a finger and pointed it at me but said nothing.

Thank God.

"Sorry," I muttered. "Really. I'm sorry, Chief. I know you'll fight for her. This whole thing is just…"

"Fucked up."

"Yeah."

He glanced at the house. "Don't tell her I was here. And don't say nothing about Summers. Got it?"

"Got it."

"And fix things with the FBI."

54

I waited for Tom to back out of the driveway. After he accelerated in the direction of Essex, I walked around the house to the storm cellar doors and picked up the broken padlock. Waste of a good lock. I stuffed the pieces in my pocket and crept quietly in the back door, through the mudroom to the kitchen. I needed coffee and set about making some, avoiding known creaks in the floor and operating the coffee maker as quietly as possible. Andy needed sleep and I intended to see that she got it.

Until I heard the distinct sound of the shower upstairs.

I finished making the coffee and set up to scramble some eggs.

THE WHISKED eggs ended up in the refrigerator. Andy took an hour for herself. At one point, I heard her descend the stairs and I expected her to appear in the kitchen. When she didn't, I looked for her. She was nowhere to be seen. Neither was her bag, which she had left in the dining room. Familiar floor creaks in our bedroom told me she had set about unpacking, a process that involved more than just removing clothing from a suitcase.

Andy eventually joined me in the kitchen. Strands of damp hair touched her shoulders. She'd taken the time for a full wash; air drying her hair restores natural waves and curls. Despite comfortable jeans and a casual untucked t-shirt, she carried the wear and weight of the last two days—and something else.

"Really?" She lifted her M.92 and pointed it at the ceiling, careful to hold her finger outside the trigger guard.

I completely forgot about the weapon. I had left it on the bathroom countertop like a lethal hair dryer.

"I thought you were Lewko's goons."

"And did you ask yourself the next question?"

"Which is?"

"You shoot one of them. Or three. Or whatever. *And then what?*" Andy repeated Leslie's 'next question.' I wondered if that was coincidence or conspiracy.

"And then I call the police—and maybe a paramedic."

"*And then* you're looking at possible criminal charges."

"I was only going to shoot them in the ass," I protested.

"Oh. I see. And because you're such a crack shot, you'd be sure to miss any vertebrae, because that would cause lifelong paralysis—and you'd never hit a femoral artery, of course, causing death in around thirty seconds."

Her sarcasm surprised me. Here I was, doing my best to help her, and she came at me with the worst of all weapons—being right.

"And assuming you're not serving time for manslaughter, do you mind telling me where we would get the money to defend civil suits for the next ten years?"

"Alright. Alright."

She reversed herself and took the gun back to its safe while I simmered in the kitchen. She called out to me. "What makes you think Lewko has goons? And why on earth did you think they were in our bathroom?"

"You want coffee?"

She didn't answer. I heard the gun safe door snap shut and the closet door close in succession. I poured her a mug, refreshed my own and carried both to the kitchen table. She joined me and wrapped her hands around the warm mug.

"Will, what aren't you telling me?"

I felt my cheeks go to Auto Red.

"Fine. I didn't have a chance to tell you. Lewko was here."

"*Here?*"

"Showed up last week pretending to be Peter Fonda." I explained the billionaire's visit.

"You didn't have a chance to tell me?"

"I didn't think it was important...?" It landed as a question.

"Oh. A billion dollars in our checking account, and you didn't think it was worth mentioning."

"He didn't mean it. He was just throwing his weight around."

The coffee had cooled sufficiently. She sipped and studied me.

"You asked me about our checking account balance. In Virginia. My god, you took him seriously."

"No, I didn't."

"You did...at least, a little."

"Dee, I also fantasize about what I'd do if I won the lottery, assuming I ever buy a ticket. He didn't mean it."

"That's not the question. The question is, would you accept it?"

"You mean, can Lewko buy me? Buy us?"

"The offer is on the table, isn't it?"

I leaned back and took a fresh measure of my wife. I had anticipated navigating a range of emotions. Anger. Grief. Despair. Loss. Her initial anger over the weapon dissipated. Calm detachment—far scarier—took its place. I sensed a screen between us, like a scrim in a stage play that reveals lurking characters when the backstage lights are turned on.

"Where are you going with this?"

She shrugged. "Are you telling me you didn't think about it?"

"Are you telling me I should?"

"Who wouldn't?"

"Oh. I see. A billion dollars in our checking account solves everything."

"You could buy an airplane."

"I don't need an airplane."

"You could get one of those jets, what are they called? The kind Lonnie Penn flies around in?"

"Gulfstream. I don't want a Gulfstream."

"You wouldn't have to work."

"Uh-huh. And *you* wouldn't have to work. Right? You could finally give up this monotonous, boring law enforcement thing, right? Become that happy homemaker all those 'fifties TV shows worshipped?"

"Maybe. Maybe I…"

"What?"

"Maybe I'm done with law enforcement. Okay? Maybe it wasn't meant to be."

There it was.

I know when my wife does not want my touch and I respect that. But I also know when she wants me to fight through a hastily erected barrier. I put down my coffee and lifted her mug from her hands. I took her right hand and turned it palm up, then gently placed my fingers on the veins lining her wrist.

I stared up at the ceiling for a moment.

"What are you doing?"

"*Shhhh*," I replied. I waited. "Got it."

"What?"

"Your pulse. It's still there."

She tried to pull away. I held on. "Well, of course it's still there."

I shook my head. "No. It's there because you're a cop. That's what makes it beat. It's still there so you're still a cop, Dee. Doesn't matter what happened or how—and believe me when I tell you, we will learn both—but the fact that blood continues pumping through your veins means that whether you give up, or you fight, or you take up drinking and wallow, you're still a cop and nothing—not this frame-up at the Academy or Lewko's billion—changes that."

"What if I have no choice, Will? Do you understand the stigma that will stick to me? This will follow me for the rest of my life."

"Maybe. But it's not who you are. And tons of people know that. Chief Don Schultz from Milwaukee emails you every other month, reminding you that he has an opening for you. His brother in Chicago would take your call in a heartbeat."

"You have no concept of the political firestorm they would face if they tried to hire me after *this*."

I felt firm ground underfoot. She had just admitted to being and remaining a cop. The rest would be easy.

"You hungry?"

She turned over her hand and used it to squeeze mine.

"I could eat."

I squeezed back, then went to the refrigerator and pulled out the bowl of ready-to-scramble eggs. I placed pans on the burners and grabbed sausages from the freezer.

Andy sat with her back to me. She sipped her coffee and gazed out the kitchen windows. Early October carried crystal in the air. A light breeze stirred the trees in the yard, nudging the leaves to turn. A few of the trees had already been touched with autumnal color.

Encouraged by a degree of success, I contemplated our next move. Tom had been right. My harsh treatment of Leslie had no merit. I decided to call her after breakfast if she didn't call me first.

"Will?"

"Yes?"

"What did the Chief want?"

Dammit.

55

I didn't hold back any details about the Chief's visit.

I got stony silence. Andy said nothing about the city manager. She gave no hint of concern over losing her job with the City of Essex Police Department or suffering a demotion. She did not rage or cry. I almost wished she would.

"I need a computer," she said when she broke her contemplative silence. "They have my laptop. I need a computer with internet access."

I offered my iPad, but she didn't think it would do. We settled on borrowing Arun's laptop. I sent him a text to ask if he was at the hangar. He immediately responded in the affirmative. Without mentioning Andy, I wrote back that I planned to stop by and asked if he could spare his computer for a while—the equivalent of asking for his first-born child. He surprised me with cheerful thumbs-up emoji reply.

Andy and I finished a light breakfast. Her lack of appetite was not lost on me. She let me grab a shower and shave before we gathered ourselves to leave. We stepped out of the house and faced an empty yard.

"Where's your car?"

"Crap."

I admitted to Andy where I left my car. The confession pulled the corners of her mouth into a faint smile. The light in her eyes returned, if only for an instant. It warmed me.

"Hey," I said. "This won't stand. I mean it."

She hooked my arm and planted a kiss on my cheek.

"I know."

I pressed her arm against my ribs. "Wanna fly?"

Her brow furrowed. "Can we just walk? It's a pretty day."

"Sure."

WE BUMPED and bounced down the old cow lane in second gear after using most of the box of Kleenex to wipe the dew off the seats. I shouldn't have left the sunroof open but excused myself for doing so in the heat of the moment, although the notion of "Lewko's goons" edged toward comical in retrospect.

We drove toward the barn between walls of tall corn. The fields ended and the lane curved left behind the barn. Coming around the barn hill, I dropped the clutch and stepped on the brake.

"And who the hell is this?" I asked Andy and the windshield.

A gaudy gold van sat beside the house. Not a minivan, but a conversion van, the kind that had once been the popular choice for modifications that included picture windows, bubble domes, shag carpets and airbrushed murals on the slab sides. The chrome bumpers on this van showed pitting and the wheel arches suffered from corrosion. Heavily tinted windows obscured the interior.

"Virginia plates," Andy noted. She automatically reached for her shoulder bag.

I let the clutch out and rolled the Corolla to a stop in front of our garage. Andy hopped out, leaving her door open. I caught myself just in time to avoid slamming mine, a violation of police practice when arriving on a scene. Treating this as a crime scene told me Andy's senses ratcheted higher. I took solace in not being the only paranoid in the family.

We approached the van and found no one behind the wheel or inside after pressing the glass to see through the heavy tinting. The back door of the house, which we had left unlocked, remained closed. I hopped up the concrete steps and looked inside.

"Nothing."

Andy moved toward the front of the house. I hurried to catch up and we rounded the corner together.

"Hello there!" A cheerful voice greeted us.

The woman standing on our worn porch steps wore a faded one-piece mechanic's jumpsuit and a big smile. She held out a foil-covered pan.

"Mrs. Palmer?"

"I brought you a pie!"

PART IV

56

"How did you hear about it?"

"Dear, I'm on the faculty. It's like any other faculty. Full of gossips. I heard the news Monday night."

We congregated around the kitchen table. I served out the last of the coffee and started another pot. Andy produced dessert plates and a pie knife. Mrs. Palmer surgically sliced into a golden-brown pie crust and dished out wedges of the American classic.

"Oh! I nearly forgot!" she climbed off the high kitchen chair and hurried toward the mudroom. "Be right back!"

She moved with remarkable speed. Andy and I traded wide-eyed bewilderment. Aside from telling us she had an apple pie we absolute *must* try and that she knew all about Andy's suspension, Mrs. Palmer had offered no explanation for her arrival.

She returned bearing a blue bowl sealed with more aluminum foil.

"Homemade whipped cream," she announced breathlessly. She brushed a curl of hair from her forehead and lifted the foil cover from the bowl. Andy fetched a serving spoon.

"Ma'am, I'm honored that you came, so please don't take offense, but...why are you here?"

"Taste first," she insisted. She took the spoon from Andy, dug into the mound of cream in the bowl, and dropped a dollop on top of my waiting slice of pie. She then served Andy. "Go on. Go on."

I did as ordered.

"Oh, holy hell!" I said after savoring my new favorite dessert. Mrs. Palmer beamed at me, then at Andy.

"It's my secret ingredient. I'll give you one guess."

"Something nectar," I said.

"Agave. Agave nectar. I swear, I'd put it on hamburgers if I could. Young lady, what are you waiting for?"

Andy took the cue and a bite. I relished the flash of involuntary delight the taste prodded through the stony seriousness on Andy's face.

Mrs. Palmer took her seat and served herself a slice with a double dollop of cream. "I shouldn't, but then what difference would it make, right?"

I felt a tinge of embarrassment at her reference to her body shape and size. Our kitchen chair seat disappeared beneath her. Her feet dangled childlike above the floor. She closed her eyes as she enjoyed a bite of her creation. She swallowed and followed it with a sip of coffee. Then she abruptly turned to Andy.

"Did you do it?"

"What? No!"

"Did you speak up about something, something one of the instructors said or did. Something that you may have interpreted as harassment of a sexual nature?"

"Nothing. There was nothing like that!"

Mrs. Palmer searched Andy's face. "Because you know there's been talk…women feeling unfairly treated. Rumors of a lawsuit."

"I'm not aware of any of that."

"Were there…unwanted advances? Did you reject—?"

"If I reject an unwanted advance, believe me, they'd be scraping the remains off the floor. What's this all about?"

Mrs. Palmer double-checked me, then Andy. She cleared her throat.

"If what you tell me is true—and I do believe you—then you're being railroaded, young lady. And I believe it has to do with this sniper situation."

Andy blinked.

"Have you been following the latest news?" Mrs. Palmer asked.

"I…uh…I heard about Renner Stemple, if that's what you mean."

"It's panic. Government offices are closed. Politicians in hiding. Congress is asking the military for armored transportation. The President has ordered the Secret Service to establish a three-block perimeter around the White House—which is nonsense. Apparently, no one briefed him on the effective range of a Barrett M.82."

"How is this connected to Andy?"

Mrs. Palmer leveled a quizzical look at me.

"Andrea. My wife. How is it connected to her?"

"Oh," she said. She flashed a smile at Andy. "With an 'i-e'?"

"With a 'y.'"

"I sometimes call her Dee—"

"Mrs. Palmer doesn't need to hear that story. Go on, Mrs. Palmer. Please."

"Let me answer the question with a question. Who else knew that you were bringing those files to me?"

Andy shrugged. "Only the FBI agent who gave them to me. Special Agent Leslie Carson-Pelham."

"Ah! The one with the pretentious name. Yes. But I checked. She's not formally assigned to the sniper investigation."

"Not formally, no," Andy said. She shot a glance at me. I did my best to shake my head without moving.

Mrs. Palmer asked, "How do you know Special Agent Carson-Pelham? And how does she have access to case files from what is *the* priority investigation in this country?"

I stuffed another piece of pie in my mouth, not wanting any part of answering the question.

"I met Leslie, if you please, in the aftermath of the Siddley Plantation bombing. She worked for Director Mitchell Lindsay. I'm afraid I can't give you much more than that, Ma'am."

"Of course, of course. Special Agent Carson-Whatzit shared the sniper files with you because…?"

"I asked. May I ask why you're asking?"

"I don't mean to question the woman, but someone—and I'm not suggesting it's—oh, let's just call her Leslie, it's much easier—someone learned that you had access to those files and that you shared them with me."

"Why would that matter? Within the investigation they're accessible to dozens, maybe scores of law enforcement and intelligence officers. I was also told that my suspension concerned academic materials. If it was about the case files, then I can easily ex—"

"No, you're quite right. Quite right."

"Because those files are nothing special," Andy said. "Ballistics reports. Scene surveys. A lot of data with no conclusions. You've seen them, Mrs. Palmer. They're S.O.P."

"Wait," I said. "Back up the truck. Are you suggesting the sniper is someone in law enforcement?"

Mrs. Palmer tucked her chin and lifted her eyebrows at me.

"The investigation *has* focused on people with skill and training," Andy said. "Primarily military training, however a lot of people go from the military to law enforcement. But I still don't get how setting me up as an academic cheat has any bearing on the sniper investigation."

"That's easy, dear. The steps taken to destroy your credibility were preemptive. Meant to remove you from the board, so to speak. Unless, of course, you actually *did* hack the Academy server and steal restricted instructional materials. You didn't, did you?"

"Ma'am, I would never—"

"I didn't think so!" Mrs. Palmer patted Andy on the arm.

"Hold on," I lifted a stop sign hand. "She's a cadet at the Academy. She has far less knowledge of the sniper investigation than...I dunno...the average agent assigned to the investigation."

"But you asked Agent Leslie for the files, isn't that true, dear?"

"Yes," Andy said. "I asked Leslie to send me anything she would be willing to share."

"But why?"

"It was you, Mrs. Palmer. Your talk to the class got me wondering about the ballistics. That's why I brought the files to you."

"And so you did. And therein lies the cause of your troubles. I studied the data and the reports you shared with me. I found something. Something significant. I want to know if you found the same thing."

"Me?" Andy shook her head. "I don't know what you mean."

"Are you quite sure?"

"Ma'am, believe me, if I had anything to contribute to the case, I would."

"As I expected," she replied. "When I heard what happened to you, I concluded that someone assumed you found the same thread I found."

"What thread?" Andy and I asked in unison.

"I'll get to that. Right now, my point is…what was done to you was deliberate. You need to know that. I came as quickly as I could. I don't fly, of course."

I don't understand people who make that declaration, but I didn't ask why.

"Terrified," she explained anyway. "I know, I know, the statistics say otherwise, but I find flight so utterly terrifying that fear alone would probably kill me before the plane ever left the ground. Besides, I like driving. I've driven everywhere in the U.S., practically."

I wondered if she knew what I did for a living. I said, "Andy mentioned that you've consulted with Interpol and European agencies. How did you get there?"

"Boat. A more civilized way to cross the ocean if you want my opinion."

"Excuse me," Andy interrupted. "Can we get back to this 'thread'— this information someone thinks I have?"

"Oh, I doubt it matters," Mrs. Palmer said, "whether you have the information or not. The simple fact that someone *thinks* you have enough pieces of the puzzle in your possession to develop the information makes you a threat. I suppose me, too, now that you've brought me in." Mrs. Palmer patted her arm again. "I don't blame you, of course. I'm glad you did. I'm not worried in the least about me, but in your case, what better way to terminate the threat than to utterly discredit and disgrace you?"

"Why not assassinate me?" Andy asked. I hated the question.

"And point directly at the very thing they're trying to hide? No, no. That would not do."

"So, what is it? What's in those files?"

"It isn't necessarily *just* something in the files."

"But you said you found something," I said.

"I did. And I'll get to that. But as to discrediting your wife, I believe it's a combination. Like a chemical reaction. Multiple ingredients. Starting with the files which were on your laptop—"

"They were never on my laptop."

Mrs. Palmer twisted in her seat. "They were never on your laptop? I'm confused. We looked at them together."

"We looked at the files on the drive I left with you."

"Which came from your laptop, no?"

"I copied them directly to the flash drive from a cloud source."

Mrs. Palmer clicked her tongue. "Of course! Of course, you did." She frowned for a moment, then blinked away whatever complication this presented. "I'm a complete idiot when it comes to computers."

"So, what's in the files?" I repeated. "The 'thread' you mentioned."

"Ah! Yes. I looked at them in deep detail and I found something. Mind you, I'm not the detective you are, dear, but still, it's something I am quite proud of noticing."

She spread a Cheshire Cat grin across her face, then waited to be prompted.

"Which is?" I asked.

"First, let me ask you both: What is the one advantage the sniper has over all of us? Over all the king's horses and all the king's men?"

"That's easy," Andy said. "He or she knows the target. We don't. He or she—"

"Let's just call him a 'he' and be done with it," Mrs. Palmer interrupted. "But go on."

Andy continued. "He knows the target, the when, and the where. We only know someone has been hit after the fact."

"Precisely!" Mrs. Palmer turned to me. "Young man, this wife of yours stood out from the very first lecture I had with her."

"She knocks my socks off every day."

Andy ignored us. She leaned into the conversation. "So, you were saying…he knows the target…"

"He does. And I think I may as well!"

57

"Follow me!" Mrs. Palmer hopped off the kitchen chair. She darted halfway through the mudroom before Andy and I realized she was leaving. I reluctantly dropped my fork, which had been poised to claim another delicious bite of apple pie. I followed Andy out the back door.

Mrs. Palmer hurried to the rear of her van. She pulled a key ring from a zippered pocket, selected a key, and inserted it in a lock mounted in the bumper, something I'd never seen on a vehicle. The lock clicked and the bumper moved a fraction of an inch. Mrs. Palmer pocketed her keys and grasped the bumper and pulled. It slid smoothy away from the van, revealing a large drawer built into the back of the vehicle. A clever piece of storage engineering.

The drawer reminded me of Andy's gun safe. Lined with a dark felt, it had divided compartments filled with ammunition boxes, tools, compact zipped pouches, and several large rifle cases.

Mrs. Palmer leaned over and pointed at a box of ammunition within one of the compartments.

"Hmmm...yes, that one." She gestured at Andy, who picked up the ammunition box. Mrs. Palmer then pulled the largest rifle case free and turned it parallel to the drawer's bumper handle. She unzipped the case and flipped the top half back to reveal a twin to Jimmy Flatley's ugly black sniper rifle.

Andy leaned over. "Is that a Barrett M.82?"

"Long Range Sniper Rifle, Caliber .50, M.82 according to Barrett, but designated M.107 by the U.S. Army, which is to say yes. Go ahead, Detective. Pick it up. Meet your adversary." Mrs. Palmer stepped aside.

Andy is comfortable with weapons, but she didn't immediately lift the rifle from its case. She absently handed the ammunition box to me and looked over the rifle.

"I understand it's a short-recoil design," Andy said.

"About an inch," Mrs. Palmer said, warming to the topic. "After the short travel, the lower part of the accelerator arm is hinged in the bolt carrier, and the middle portion strikes it back to the barrel by a rod in the bolt carrier." She pointed. "Part of the recoil energy of the barrel transfers to the bolt for cycling and to unlock it from the barrel. Here," she pointed again, "the bolt is unlocked when it turns in the curved cam track, and the barrel is stopped by the combined effect of the accelerator, buffer spring and the muzzle brake while the bolt continues back to extract and eject the spent case. Voila! The bolt strips a fresh cartridge from the magazine and you're good to go again."

The woman smiled at us as if she'd just introduced her grandchild.

"Picatinny accessory rails," Andy added, "and Leupold sight. What's the range?"

"The manual claims forty-four hundred yards."

"Holy crap," I said. "That's two…"

"Two and a half miles."

"No wonder—" I stopped. I almost said *No wonder we didn't see Spellman's shooter.* I bit my tongue.

"Yes!" Mrs. Palmer finished the thought. "No wonder the shooter hasn't been seen in any of the killings. Go ahead, Detective. Pick it up. Do you have someplace we can shoot?"

"Uh…" I looked at the yard. "If that thing sends a round two and a half miles, we're going to want something backstopping the target. Is the barn hill okay? We can set up on the far side of the lawn. That should give you a decent hundred and fifty yards."

Mrs. Palmer looked in both directions. "That will do. What I have in mind doesn't require distance. Do you have a board or a piece of plywood?"

"On it!" I trotted toward the garage. Behind me, Mrs. Palmer encouraged Andy.

"Go ahead. It won't bite."

I glanced back to watch Andy lift the rifle from the case. She cradled it carefully, putting her hands where they belonged.

"Not as heavy as I expected."

I opened the garage and grabbed a partial sheet of scrap plywood leaning against one wall. I carried it to the man-made hill that rose to the back of the barn and the loft I call Area 51, the place where I first experimented with flight within *the other thing*. I leaned the plywood against the weedy side slope of the hill and hurried back to follow Andy and Mrs. Palmer across the lawn. They walked to the eastern edge of our mowed grass, then turned.

Mrs. Palmer directed Andy to lay the rifle on the grass and explained how to extend the bipod supports. Andy settled into a prone position behind the weapon.

"Will, please give your wife the ammunition."

I handed the box back to Andy. She lifted the cover.

"This one," Mrs. Palmer said, pointing at the cartridges. "And this."

Andy plucked two from the cardboard dividers. Without hesitation, she ejected the rifle's magazine and inserted the cartridges.

"Oh, goodness! I almost forgot."

Mrs. Palmer scurried in the direction of her van. I crouched beside Andy.

"Is she for real?"

"I told you she knows her stuff."

"Do you get the impression she doesn't trust Leslie?"

Andy didn't answer.

Neither of us spoke while Mrs. Palmer hurried back to us carrying a roll of black cloth and three pairs of safety glasses. She handed out the glasses, then laid the cloth on the ground beside Andy and pulled to unroll it, uncovering a long, black cylinder.

"Suppressor?" Andy asked.

"Titanium," Mrs. Palmer replied. "None of the reports I read indicated that anyone heard the shot fired. Obviously, the shooter used a suppressor. This is the standard issue developed for the M.107. Go ahead."

"Doesn't a suppressor affect the aim? The bullet...uh...trajectory?" I asked.

"A myth," Mrs. Palmer replied. "A correctly designed suppressor has no effect on ballistic path."

Andy picked up the tube, examined it, then crawled forward and attached it to the business end of the weapon, extending the rifle length by another eight or ten inches.

"I take it we don't need ear protection," I said.

"Quiet as a baby's naptime. When you're ready, Detective, place a round in the center of that piece of plywood."

Andy slid back into the shooter's position, spent a minute or two adjusting the telescopic sight, then wiggled to find a comfortable fit for the rifle's stock against her shoulder. Mrs. Palmer and I stepped behind my wife and the rifle and waited.

Andy adjusted herself, stared into the scope, then slowly eased her finger onto the trigger. She worked her breathing into a shallow, measured count.

The shot, when she fired, scarcely registered. I was astonished. Flatley's shots slammed my hearing. Andy's suppressed discharge could be felt more than heard, a throb in the air pressure.

Downrange, a black dot appeared in the center of the plywood.

"Now put the second one in the same hole," Mrs. Palmer instructed.

Andy took her time, controlled her breathing, and fired again.

A fresh black dot appeared below and to the right of the first, less than two inches away.

"There! Do you see?" Mrs. Palmer exclaimed and pointed. "We're less than two hundred yards away. Multiply that times twenty-two and you have the full range, but that difference you see, that tiny difference, at full range is a miss."

"Looks really close to me," I said, feeling a need to defend my wife.

"Wildly off to someone shooting at the level of our sniper. Wildly off. I do not mean to criticize, Andy. This is not your profession, nor your training. But my point is this. Despite this close range, despite her best efforts, despite a respectable level of skill, it is still a miss. But what's to account for it?" Mrs. Palmer, energized, leaned over, put a palm to the grass, and took a knee beside the rifle. "I contend that every shot should be perfect. It's simple math. The alignment of the barrel. The trajectory of the bullet. The application of gravity and the movement of the air through which the bullet travels. All fixed values. *Know each factor and every shot should be perfect.* But there is still one more variable."

She treated it as a quiz question. I had no clue.

"The bullet," Andy said.

Mrs. Palmer beamed. She looked at me, the class dunce. "Are all cartridges the same?"

"Trick question," I said. "To the eye, yes. But…"

"You are correct, Will. In appearance, but to the closest possible measurement, accounting for tiny differences in manufacturing, no they are not at all the same. Even match grade ammunition has imperfections. And by virtue of those differences, the entire equation is disrupted. Difference of even the smallest degree guarantees no two shots can be perfect."

"How can any two shots be perfect?" Andy asked. "The human factor alone disrupts the equation."

"Indeed. Remove the human factor and perfection is achieved. Since the human factor cannot be removed, it can be trained and controlled. After that, all other elements must be perfected. And that's what I found in the reports."

Andy and I waited, granting Mrs. Palmer a dramatic pause.

"I haven't seen the recovered bullets, but the weight of the recovered bullets was non-standard. Also, deformities in the recovered bullets displayed anomalies."

"Anomalies?" Andy asked.

Mrs. Palmer pointed at the box of ammunition Andy had drawn from. "The two that you fired: standard issue, match grade, straight off the shelf." She touched her toe to the ammunition box and tipped it over. Brass spilled onto the grass.

"But look at these. Look closely."

Andy picked up one after the other and examined them.

"These are different."

"You see it," Mrs. Palmer said.

"They're…sculpted."

"And?"

"They appear identical."

"They are mathematically identical. Down to the hundredth of a grain. The bullet. The load. Within a handful of molecules in perfect shape, including a slight aerodynamic twist that amplifies the rifling to obtain true flight. You're looking at perfection, Detective."

"How?"

"I did what our shooter has been doing. I took the bullet variable out of the equation. Those rounds are 3D printed to a tolerance that eliminates randomness. Perfect duplicates. Entirely mathematical. With the ability to know or control every variable, the path of a bullet can be planned with the same perfection that calculated the path of the moon shot or the Mars explorers."

"Okay," I said, "but you still have a human being pulling the trigger. No disrespect for your achievement here, but all you're really telling me is that the shooter exercises superior quality control. That's nothing new. A hundred years ago, the most successful flying aces in World War One used calipers to measure each round they loaded into their ammunition belts. They did it to avoid jams. The same principle. So, the shooter is careful. We kinda knew that."

Mrs. Palmer bobbed her head in agreement and gave me a tolerant smile. "You are correct, Will, but perhaps your wife can tell you what's happening here. Now that she knows the shooter is crafting his own ammunition."

"You mean perfect, identical ammunition," I said.

"These are," Mrs. Palmer said, "*but the bullets used by the sniper were not entirely identical.*"

Andy sat back on her haunches. She let her gaze drift into the middle distance, rereading the files and reports in her mind, looking for the clue that Mrs. Palmer prompted her to find, a student led to revelation by the master. After a moment, Andy reigned in her gaze and fixed it on our strange guest.

"He's sending a message."

58

"We need to look at the files again," Mrs. Palmer said. She produced the flash drive from one of the many pockets in her jumper.

"I don't have a laptop here, but we can use a laptop at Will's work office," Andy told our guest.

"Good. Do you have a gun safe? Do you mind?"

"The rifle is too big, I'm afraid." Andy plucked the spilled cartridges from the grass and slotted them in the cardboard grid within the ammunition box. She handed me the box and picked up the rifle.

"The rifle, I can store in the van. I'm more concerned about the ammunition," Mrs. Palmer said. "You have no idea what I had to do to create them."

"I'll see that they're locked up."

I followed the women back to the house. Andy secured the ammunition in her gun safe while Mrs. Palmer visited our bathroom. I took the opportunity to pull Andy aside.

"Are you buying all this?"

"Will, if there's anyone in the world who can find significance in one extra layer of molecules on special ammunition, I believe she's that person. What it all means...?" She shrugged. "I'm not sure where she's going with this business of a message from the shooter, but if the thread she's tugging helps undo my mess with the Academy I'm on board. Am I being selfish?"

"Hell, no. Makes sense to me."

Andy closed her hand on my arm. "I'm counting on you to keep me clearheaded. If you say I'm going off the rails, I promise, I will listen."

"I'd ask you to do the same, but I spend most of my time off the rails. Here she comes."

Andy squeezed my arm and dusted my cheek with a kiss. Her affect seemed lighter. The crushing weight of her suspension felt temporarily lifted, and for that I was grateful to Mrs. Palmer. But I also knew that false hope leads to deeper falls.

"I'll drive," Mrs. Palmer announced. She pulled a pair of leather driving gloves from one of the many pockets in her jumpsuit and flexed her fingers into them. "I'd never fit in your little clown car."

59

A run withdrew slowly from his office, reluctant to lift his gaze from his laptop as Andy and Mrs. Palmer slid behind his desk. I thought I saw him wince when Andy adjusted the angle of the screen and inserted Mrs. Palmer's flash drive.

"Police business," I reassured him, gently pressing his shoulder to help him through the office door. He appeared in pain as I closed the door behind him.

"Will, is there coffee?" Andy glanced up at me and flicked her eyes at the door.

"Uh...I'll go make some." I took the hint and exited the office. "Yeah." I told Arun. "They threw me out, too."

"Who is that woman?" he asked.

"She is a world-renowned expert in ballistic sciences and their application to law enforcement. One of Andy's instructors at the Academy." I regretted the word the instant it cleared my lips.

"The Academy? What's Andy doing here in Essex?"

"Working on a special project," I lied, wishing I had kept my big mouth shut. On the other hand, Arun would have inevitably raised the question.

"And they need my laptop?"

"Andy left hers at Quantico."

"Ah." Arun checked his watch. "Do you think this will take long?"

"Yup." Another wave of pain crossed Arun's face. "Hey, it's close to lunch. You should wander over to Essex County Air. See if Pi—Cassidy is free. Go grab a sandwich."

He glanced in the direction of the offices across the tarmac. "I shouldn't bother her…"

"Nonsense! Save her from eating lunch out of the vending machine. Go. This could take all afternoon."

"*All afternoon?*"

"Easily. Can you work at home for the rest of the day?"

He mulled it over. "I suppose I could use my old laptop…"

"Go."

Arun struggled with the decision but mention of Pidge tugged his attention in her general direction.

"Fine," he said abruptly. He delivered a rapid-fire verbal rundown of the schedule for the remainder of the week, an entirely unnecessary exercise since there were no flights planned, which relieved me of listening. Then he patted his pocket to assure himself he had his phone and bolted for the door.

I KILLED the next forty-five minutes in the hangar. Cleaning bugs off the Plexiglas windshield and engine nacelles on the Navajo kept my hands busy while my mind wandered to Arun's office. I toyed with the image of Andy as apprentice and Mrs. Palmer as sorceress, the two of them conjuring over Arun's laptop. I understood Andy's impulse to exclude me. She wanted to isolate Mrs. Palmer's attention, to focus. Mrs. Palmer seemed to have developed a connection to Andy, something I dared hope my wife would take advantage of, if not outright exploit. Andy puts people at ease. Men, because they're attracted. Women, sometimes for the same reason and sometimes because they don't expect someone with Andy's looks to be approachable. Mrs. Palmer's motive may have been more complex. Being a world-class expert didn't necessarily engender friendships or guarantee fair treatment. Andy was less than forty-eight hours into what might be the worst crisis of her professional life, which is to say her life. I wasn't sure this was the best time to have to deal with a clingy new best friend.

This jumble of middle-school soap opera thinking told me one thing for certain. I had too much time on my hands. The prolonged secret conference behind closed doors was messing with my head.

Arun's office door opened just as I crawled under the wing to wipe a film of oil off the skin behind the left engine. Laying on the hangar floor, I heard voices on the other side of the glass wall that separated the hangar from the lounge. I craned my neck to see Andy hurry to follow Mrs. Palmer though the lounge to the door. For a moment, I feared they were leaving without me. Both disappeared through the door to the parking lot. I heard Mrs. Palmer's van start.

"Don't pay any attention to me," I muttered.

A moment later Andy returned. She spotted me under the wing and set a course into the hangar.

"We have to go," she announced.

"Anywhere in particular?"

"Detroit."

60

"It's an eight-hour drive. That will put Mrs. Palmer at the Renaissance Center just before seven p.m. I told her we would meet her there. I offered to have her go with us, but she said just walking past the airplane in the hangar gave her shortness of breath."

"Me, too, but for different reasons." I crawled out from under the wing and stood up. "Are you going to tell me?"

Andy slipped into a blank stare which told me her mind raced ahead on whatever mission had been concocted. I waited patiently until she returned and saw me standing in front of her.

She shook off the daze.

"It's probably crazy. It's definitely out there. But there's a chance that she's decoded the shooter's intentions. C'mon. We have time. I'll show you."

"Here." Andy clicked open a spreadsheet. "We put this together from the ballistics reports, from the victim files and from public internet sources. She did most of this, but she walked me through it." Andy pointed at the left column, a list of names. "These are the known victims. Remember, until the pattern emerged, some of these were off the radar. The task force assembled this list from open case files all over the country. The common denominators are the sniper-style shooting, the weapon, and the bullet used."

I studied the list. Renner Stemple's name, the President's friend and advisor, held the top position. Next on the list, Martin Gregg. And below that, Darryl Spellman.

"This column contains the date of each shooting." She pointed. "Time of day. Location. This is just a note about surroundings. Golf course for Stemple. County courthouse for Gregg, etc. Then she breaks down bullet recovery status—you can see here that a couple of the bullets fragmented and not all the fragments were recovered. Most were. Which gets us to this column." She pointed.

"Bullet weight?"

Andy nodded. "This is where Mrs. Palmer went full armory nerd. She gave me a ton of background on the fifty-caliber round. There's a wide variety of uses, so there's a wide variety of, I guess you'd say, versions. The military has ball, tracer, sabot—"

"English?"

"Lots of stuff for lots of jobs. Setting all that aside, the rounds used in all the sniper cases are nearly identical...except in weight. And that's the key to her thesis. Still with me?"

"Always."

She glanced at me. A shy dimple emerged at the corner of her mouth before she let serious intensity chase it away.

"Like I said, there's a variety of ammunition, hence a variety of weights. But on average, a fifty-caliber round runs around 660 grams. Some are higher. Some lower. But for our purposes, and this shooter's purposes, the weights should be identical. The materials used are the same metal compounds Mrs. Palmer used in a 3D printer to make her perfect rounds."

"She was serious about that? She actually printed the bullets?"

"The woman is a perfectionist. After she assessed that the shooter was printing his own bullets, she experimented and became convinced. That led her to studying anomalies in deformity patterns in the spent rounds. Anomalies that she backward-interpreted to come up with the conclusion that the shooter is making bullets that are nearly aerodynamically perfect, complete with subtle twisting to match the purpose of the rifling of the barrel, which is what gives the bullet its spin."

"Right. That much I knew."

"Ah, but did you know physics diminishes a bullet's spin during flight?"

"Okay, but that can't be much of a factor. We're talking about a flight that is just seconds, if that."

"In Mrs. Palmer's world, that's a lifetime. She deals in nanoseconds. Perfection. Her take on the bullet deformities led her to that sculpted bullet, which enhances the effect of muzzle rifling and makes the flight even more accurate. This shooter can't miss."

I pointed at the screen. "So, where's the hidden message?"

"Look at the bullet weights."

I examined the column. "Um, for a guy who's obsessed with perfection, these seem a bit random. I mean, if he's really 3D printing his bullets for perfection, wouldn't they be exactly the same?"

"Yes!" Andy clapped her hands together. "Yes, and that's where the message lies."

"In the bullet weight."

"Precisely. And I mean that literally. Look again at the weights."

I looked.

606.18

606.27

607.03

The list went on. None of the numbers were duplicates.

"And now look at this column."

"Those are dates."

"Give the man a cupie doll! Yes, those are dates. Taking the last two digits of the whole number and the first two decimal points of each weighed bullet—whole bullet, because we can't account for the ones that fragmented—and you get a date."

"The date of the shooting? Because that's not correct for Spellman or Gregg."

Andy shook her head.

"Will, do you know who Harry Shannon is?"

I had heard the name, but beyond the names of fighter pilots and aviation pioneers, I gray out, particularly with names in popular culture. Still, it sounded familiar. "I want to say...Fox News?"

"*Was* with Fox News. Until about a year ago, he was one of their prime-time news personalities. What the network insists is entertainment, not news. A top ratings guy until allegations of sexual misconduct surfaced and led to his 'wholly unrelated decision to resign and pursue other opportunities.' Since then, he's been one of the biggest names lured to a start-up streaming network called America First News."

"No bias there."

"America First News might have been a forgotten footnote to the internet if it hadn't become a favorite of the current President. He's given them dozens of telephone interviews. I know you don't follow these things, but there's a lot of speculation that he's fallen out of favor with Fox or the other way around. Anyway, he's been a shot of adrenaline for this start-up network. In a matter of months, they went from streaming on a set in some guy's basement to claiming millions of viewers. I think this AFN network is the direction General Winslow Pemmick wanted to take Josiah James before he decided James was a liability and murdered him. Full tilt political bias to the party in power, no real standards of journalism, and certainly no obligation to truth. A straight-up propaganda vehicle. Pemmick thought he could court the President the way AFN is courting him."

Politics isn't my thing, but it had been hard to avoid over the last few years. Still, most of this was new to me.

"What does an unconvicted sex offender switching from one right-wing media outlet to a more-righter-wing media outlet have to do with bullet weights that should be perfect but aren't?"

Andy gave me a coy look that made me want to take her, right then, right there on Arun's desk, for which he would never forgive me, and which was probably the farthest thing from my wife's mind at that moment.

"I don't think Mrs. Palmer is right when she says that I could have seen all this. I think only she can look at these numbers and recognize them for what they are, the way an autistic person has trouble with the words but can brilliantly process images. Look at the bullet weight for Sheila Lynn Anders, the Texas legislator."

606.19

"So?" I asked.

"Oh six nineteen. That's the date that Harry Shannon did a live streaming interview with Dan Boulton—the next victim after Sheila Anders. Now look at the bullet weight for Boulton."

604.17

I cheated. I looked at the next column, which had the heading "Shannon."

Andy beat me to the punch. "Oh four seventeen. That's the month and day that Shannon did a live streaming interview with Darryl Spellman."

I squinted at the screen. The weight and date numbers matched all the way down the column, excluding the bullets listed as Fragment.

She turned and grasped my forearm, transmitting electric tension. "Do you see it?"

I saw the pattern. And I chose my next words carefully.

"The weight of each bullet identifies the next victim by the date they were interviewed on some bogus news network? Is that what you're saying?"

"To a tee. Every one of them. At least, the bullets that remained whole."

"Did you come up with any part of this?"

Andy shook her head. "I never would have come close. Whoever sabotaged me because they thought I might connect these dots has a way too high opinion of me. This was all Mrs. Palmer, because this is her world, this is how she sees things."

"Okay," I said. "I just wanted to be sure. Because this is the dumbest thing I've ever seen."

61

"Come on, Dee," I pleaded. "This is the kind of thing you'd tear apart in some bad cop movie. The impossible conclusion arrived at only because the protagonist read the screenplay."

I hadn't chosen my words carefully enough. Calling it the dumbest thing I'd ever seen might have been one of the dumber things I ever said. I forget sometimes that my wife, who can show a spine of steel in her job, lends undeserved weight to my ill-chosen words.

"How are you not seeing this?" she asked. I felt a barrier rising, one that would morph into sullen withdrawal if I failed to redeem this.

"Okay, I may have worded that a bit strongly. I'm sorry," I said. "I see the numbers. I get the theory. But...seriously?"

Andy folded her arms across her chest.

"Fine," she said. "Show me where this is wrong."

"What? Prove a negative?"

"This isn't a negative. The numbers are there in black and white. Show me where this is wrong."

Fwooomp! I vanished.

"Not funny. You dug this hole for yourself. Come back here and show me how this pattern isn't a pattern."

Fwooomp!

She glared at me, but she did it while suppressing a smile over my childish attempt at escape.

"Okay," I said. I leaned closer to Arun's laptop screen putting on a show of carefully examining the columns and numbers and notes, none of which helped me in any way.

"You can't," she said after I wasted the better part of a minute.

"Just…hang on…" I wasn't ready to surrender. Despite not having any evidence to support it, I felt certain this was idiotic.

"Will, you're not going to—"

"Ha! I have it!" I wound up a smug grin. "Nailed it." I pointed at the screen. "Look at the weight for the bullet that killed Renner Stemple. See it? Ha! When the shooter made that bullet, the weight represented a date in the future. All of the other dates represent appearances on that network *in the past.* So there."

Andy smiled at me the way an art teacher smiles at the worst, least talented of her students. She closed the file, ejected the flash drive, selected system shutdown from the menu and closed Arun's laptop. She stood up.

"I'm going home to pack. You need to preflight. We're flying to Detroit," she said.

"Why?"

"Because that date in the future is today."

"So? Who's the guest on Shannon's show today?"

Andy headed for the door, determined. "Shannon isn't hosting a show today. He's traveling with the President to a rally at the Renaissance Center in Detroit. Shannon is the MC for the rally."

The *Holy Shit* look on my face did double-duty as a surrender flag.

62

"I can get us into Coleman Young Airport on an IFR flight plan. It's closest to downtown. Otherwise, there's a TFR scheduled for the President's arrival. He'll be tying up Detroit Metro with a no-fly zone right around rush hour. That's got to make the airlines happy."

I reached for Andy's roller bag and lifted it into the cabin. Having hitched a ride to the hangar with Mrs. Palmer, Andy's whirlwind trip home required first walking over to the Essex County Air offices and borrowing the crew car from Rosemary II. I gave her credit. She packed quickly and light. I told her not to bother with anything for me. I keep a ready bag at the hangar, which I now tossed into the cabin beside hers.

In Andy's absence, I checked the weather and filed a flight plan.

"Dee," I said, pausing at the airstair just as she stepped up to board, "you know this is a wasted trip, right? There's no way this rally is taking place with this sniper on the loose."

"I checked. It's already been announced. He's going ahead with it. Call it ego, call it whatever you want, nothing gets between this President and his loyal followers. He's telling everyone he's a hero for not giving in to 'terrorists' while the Secret Service practically checks for head lice for two miles in all four directions."

A whisp of breeze crossed the airport ramp and pulled a lock of

Andy's hair across one eye. She let it hang, a signal of her own determination. Her war flag.

"Then you've got to call someone. The Secret Service. The FBI. Hell, call Leslie."

"Not me."

The answer surprised me.

"What do you mean? This is a—"

"No, Will. Not *me*. I can't call the FBI, or anyone. Look who I am right now. The cheat who just got kicked out of the FBI Academy. A textbook candidate for the disgruntled, angry former cadet profile. I *can't* call anyone and be taken seriously."

"But somebody has to—"

"Yes. Mrs. Palmer. The woman has connections we can't even imagine. She's got eight hours of driving with her cell phone autodialing every agency director she can reach. We discussed it. I told her this is way bigger than us and she agreed. Trust me, Will. She's on it."

I should have guessed.

"Then they'll call off the rally. They'll have to."

"Maybe. But I don't think so. I don't think the President will allow it. I hope he doesn't. I think this is a chance, possibly our only chance, certainly our best chance, of drawing out the sniper. And we have a secret weapon. Mrs. Palmer. She's the best person to survey the terrain, determine the site lines and figure out where and how the sniper might operate. We have a real chance, Will. And if there's any danger at all, there's no way the Secret Service will let him appear in public. She's going to text me her location once she gets in position. I want to join up with her."

I let the unspoken "Why?" paint itself on my face.

"Because I think she genuinely wants to help me clear my name," Andy said. "And I'm all for that."

"Okay." I stepped aside and gestured for Andy to board the plane. "Me, too. But I still think you should call Leslie."

Andy paused.

"What?" I asked. "Are you buying Mrs. Palmer's doubts about Leslie? Really?"

"Do we know where Leslie was during each shooting?" Andy asked.

"I'm about to say something stupid about that being the second dumbest thing I ever heard."

"And I agree. Really. I do. You know how I feel about the 'cop turns out to be the bad guy' idiocy. I get it. But she wasn't with you when Spellman got shot. Or Gregg. Yet she's insinuated herself into the investigation. That's why Mrs. Palmer has doubts." I started to speak but Andy lifted gentle fingers to my lips. "And yes, I know what you're going to say. Mrs. Palmer doesn't know the real reason for our—your—relationship with Leslie."

"Which is why her suspicions about Leslie are absurd."

"Agreed. But let's turn this the other way around. Mrs. Palmer knows people. For all I know, she is in touch with the Director of the FBI, the head of the Secret Service, maybe even the White House. With full authority. With impeccable credentials. What more could Leslie contribute to that? If we leave Leslie off the call list for now—where's the harm? What could she do that isn't already being done?"

I said nothing.

"On top of that, we're not entirely sure who she answers to. If she keeps inserting herself into things, people will start asking questions. Which could lead back to you."

Andy's gold-flecked green eyes fixed on me. I sometimes wonder if she understands the power they hold over me.

"Fine. Mrs. Palmer calls in the cavalry. We nail this sniper. *What could possibly go wrong?*"

63

Mrs. Palmer's eight-hour drive from Essex County, Wisconsin to Wayne County, Michigan represented a precise segment of time in my mind. Andy and I spent the first stretch of that segment in Arun's office with Andy preaching Mrs. Palmer's bullet weight theory to a reluctant congregation. The second segment went to Andy rushing home and packing a bag for a trip to Detroit while I downloaded weather information and filed a flight plan which I hoped would steer us clear of the busy Detroit Class B airspace that was about to be complicated by an aircraft with the call sign of Air Force One. The third piece of the time ribbon measured out the minutes I allow for loading, start-up, run-up and taxi of an airplane—the part of every trip that spans from climbing in the airplane to holding short of a runway for takeoff. The fourth segment fit the hour and forty-six minutes needed to get from Essex County Airport across Lake Michigan to Detroit's Coleman A. Young Airport. I chose a route that deliberately included Flint Michigan and took us north of Detroit's Class B airspace for a right hook into Canadian airspace to intercept the ILS 33 approach, thereby avoiding the hornet's nest around Detroit Metro airport.

This fourth segment of time felt the most comfortable to me. My speed was fixed. My altitude was assigned. My route was clear and a glance at the Garmin GTN 750 on the panel told me the precise moment we would touch down. Air traffic control threw a couple curve balls, but nothing to disrupt the calm certainty of flight. I remained comfortably in command right up to the moment the wheels squeaked onto the concrete at Coleman Young.

"One Tango Whiskey, right turn on Charlie, contact ground one two one point eight five."

I repeated the clearance, allowed the Navajo to slow without pounding on the brakes, and looked for the Taxiway Charlie sign, which steered me on an angle clear of Runway 33. I tapped the ground control frequency into the touchscreen comm and reported in.

"One Tango Whiskey, right turn on Alfa, cross Runway 25, taxi to Special Parking One."

Special Parking One?

I read back the clearance and checked the taxi chart on the navigation system screen. Easy and direct to the ramp but the parking designation set me on alert.

I cleaned up the airplane, adjusted the fuel mixtures for taxi idle and opened the cowl flaps for engine cooling. I turned on the taxiway and immediately saw something out of place.

"I see it," Andy said.

Flashing blue and white lights sparkled on the distant parking ramp. As we rolled closer, we spotted the SUVs that mounted the light bars. Still too far away to make out the door emblems, the vehicles were nevertheless clearly law enforcement.

"An incident?" I asked my detective wife.

"More likely a reception committee. This airport is the closest to downtown. Now that I think about it, I'm surprised they let us in, being this close to the rally."

"Maybe it's the cavalry. Do you think Mrs. Palmer sent them to meet us?"

"She doesn't know where we're landing."

Andy remained silent as we rolled toward the ramp. A police officer in full SWAT gear waved us in from the taxiway. He used an orange wand to point at another officer who waved at us to park near the chain link fence between the airport and the city street on its border. One other aircraft, an executive jet, occupied the ramp. It sat much closer to the terminal building. They clearly wanted us as far away from the terminal as possible.

Two more officers stepped out of the parked SUV. All four officers carried semi-automatic weapons.

"Well, this looks friendly," I commented.

"Let me go first."

Andy unsnapped her seatbelt and twisted herself out of the copilot's seat. She brushed past me to the cabin. I glanced back to see her lift her satchel off the passenger's seat, then securing the airplane tugged my attention back up front. Using differential power on the engines, I swung the Navajo around in a tight turn, putting it on the dime indicated by the cop on the ramp. I did a quick shutdown. The left engine rumbled to a stop. Then the right.

Almost immediately, Andy released the door latch and lowered the airstair. That's as far as she got.

"Ma'am, please remain in the aircraft," a voice commanded her from outside.

She held up her badge.

"Detective Andrea Stewart, Essex Police Department. I am carrying."

"Roger that. Again, please remain in the aircraft."

"What's going on?" By the way Andy lowered her voice and dropped to a knee on the cabin carpet, I guessed that the officer outside had approached. He spoke for a moment or two in a voice too low for me to hear from the cockpit. Andy responded with clipped acknowledgements, then asked him to stand by.

She retreated up the aisle to the cockpit.

"The airport is on lockdown. Everything between here and the Renaissance Center is locked down as well. All the streets are closed. They gave us a choice. We can stay in the aircraft, or we can ask for clearance to depart."

"Do you think they mean for us to stay here until Air Force One is wheels up after the rally?"

"I don't know."

"What about asking if they'll escort us to the terminal so we can get a car to our hotel?"

"We don't have a hotel, which they can easily check. And the streets are all closed anyway. It's the same either way."

"No escort to the terminal?"

She shook her head. "He said the terminal is closed."

"Okay. Looks like we go with Plan B."

"Did we ever have a Plan A?" She returned to the airstair and said, "We'll hold up here for a while, sergeant. Work on our options."

I heard him ask if we needed anything. Water? Andy laughed.

"If you bring us water, then we'll definitely need to exit the aircraft. I think we'll be fine. Thank you."

He said something that ended in "Ma'am" and I watched him stroll back to the duo standing beside the Detroit Metropolitan Police Department SUV.

"Leave the door open," I said, removing the headset and detaching my seatbelt. I twisted out of my seat and joined her. She moved the shoulder strap for her satchel over her head so that the strap crossed her chest on a diagonal.

"I guess we do this the *other* way," she said. I was struck by the contrast between Andy and Leslie. Andy sat on the left aft seat by the door, at the ready. I had no concerns about her reaction to what was about to happen.

I grabbed my flight bag and extracted three small flashlight-like BLASTER tubes. Each had a small carbon-fiber propeller attached by rubber band. I pushed two in my cargo pants pocket, then assembled the third. A quick test of the slide control set the prop spinning and blowing cool air over my wrist.

"Um...won't Mrs. Palmer wonder how we got to the rally?" I asked.

"Why would she ask? And if she does, I'll tell her I badged a ride from local PD. Professional courtesy."

"I guess."

"Got your earpiece?" she asked. She slipped her Bluetooth earpiece in place beneath her hair.

"Why? You're going to be right there with me."

"Humor me."

I pulled a small jewelry box from the flight bag and extracted my earpiece. I hooked it over my ear, fixed the bud in place, then adjusted the mic along my cheek.

"Testing one, two, three. Can you hear me?"

"Um. I'm right here, darling. And we're not connected."

"Roger that. You're loud and clear."

I stowed the flight bag and moved down the aisle, careful to avoid Andy's perturbed stare.

"Hang on," Andy said. She lifted her phone and touched a speed dial button. She tapped speaker phone and waited. It rang four times.

"This is Rolling Thunder," Mrs. Palmer answered.

"Uh…"

"Sorry!" she said cheerfully. "That's my CB handle. Where are you?"

I suppressed a chuckle.

"Detroit," Andy replied. "We're at the airport. Were you able to get through to anyone?"

"Absolutely! Excellent response. I reached out to Homeland and detailed everything. They're meeting me."

"And the rally? Is it cancelled? Or at least postponed?"

"The President insists on holding the rally, but Homeland assures me that they will hold the President back if we cannot resolve this. I'm certain that once I'm in position we can isolate the potential sightlines and have a real shot at this sniper, no pun intended. Gotta go! Call coming in!"

"Text me a rendezvous location."

"Roger! Wilco! Over and out!"

Andy and I stared at each other.

"Does that woman sound…giddy?" I asked.

"It happens. People get involved with cops, they think they're helping, it can be heady. Remember, she's been behind a microscope all her life." Andy glanced out the open door. "Two back in the vehicle. One on the ramp, and I can't see number four, but the one by the taxiway must be keeping station there."

I flicked the prop on the BLASTER. The insect buzz it generated reassured me.

"Alright. Let's do this."

She held out her hand. I took it.

Fwooomp! We both vanished.

I felt her slide back on the seat to let me go first. The exit was awkward. My feet wanted to use the airstair, which is a delicate operation under normal circumstances. But without weight, trying to align with the steps proved difficult. Instead, I grabbed the edge of the door and swung myself out over the ramp. The move allowed me to pull Andy out and position her behind me.

"Hang on," I said. I pushed downward until the soles of my boots touched the asphalt. Then I reached for and grabbed the door. "Anybody watching us?"

I felt Andy move.

"Can't say for sure about the two in the SUV. Otherwise, we're clear."

I lifted the door and pressed it shut using contact with the ramp for counterpressure.

"Better if they think we're just holed up in there fooling around."

She said nothing but managed to find and slap my shoulder.

"Ready?" I asked.

"Never."

I flexed my ankles and pushed off the asphalt. We rose. Andy snuggled in and closed a grip on my arm. I waited a moment, letting us gain height, then reached out with the BLASTER. Slowly at first, to avoid drawing the attention of the officers below, I converted simple floating to forward flight. Thirty feet above the ramp, we surged toward the street. I flexed my wrist and aimed for the cylindrical Renaissance Center towers on the cityscape horizon.

64

"Man, they weren't kidding," I said.

The street grid below us lay empty. The sun hovering above the western horizon told me it was after six p.m., and although rush hour might have been waning, only something apocalyptic could account for the absence of traffic in the Motor City. Squad cars and what looked like military armored cars occupied major intersections. From above, the display of flashing emergency lights gave the cityscape the look of a lawn infested with mating fireflies.

We moved at a steady fifteen to twenty knots through the air. Any more than that, and it became hard to see without protective goggles.

"I don't understand the location for this rally," I said.

"Detroit? Blue collar. Working class. Don't forget he's up for reelection next year. Michigan is a swing state."

"So, these are his people? His base?" The blocks flowing below us looked rough. Poor.

Andy chuckled. "Not *these* people. I doubt many of the residents of these neighborhoods have passes to this rally. The President's political appeal rests with the rural parts of Michigan."

"That's my point."

"It's optics, Will. This is the motor city, even if they don't build all the cars here anymore."

The Renaissance Center towers loomed ahead. A central cylinder dominated four shorter, roughly square towers. For all the times I'd flown into Detroit airports, I'd never been inside the city or near the headquarters of General Motors.

"There," Andy said. "Dead ahead. See them?"

"What?"

"Busses. That's his base. They're bussing people in from outside the city. That's where he gets his enthusiastic studio audience." Andy may be apolitical, but she's also much better informed than me.

A centipede line of busses stretched for blocks away from the Renaissance Center towers. City busses mingled with school busses. As we approached, we began to make out a second line, this one amorphous, making its way from the parked busses toward the plaza overlooking the Detroit River. A vague funnel formed, dominated by red. Red hats, red shirts, red and blue flags. The funnel fed into a zigzag line that ultimately passed through security checks and entered the site of the rally. Bleachers had been set up in an arc facing the waterfront, interrupted at the center by a fountain with a sculpture of what looked to my eye like a UFO or an aluminum donut. Rows of American flags topped the bleachers. A stage faced the seating, using the Detroit River and Canada as a backdrop. Twin cranes behind the stage dangled huge American flags. I'd seen images of this President's rallies. Someone learned early on to put cheering supporters behind him for his speeches, usually in precisely messaged t-shirts. The animation of pumping fists and waving flags lent visual emphasis to his populist pronouncements. This time, the waterfront and the big flags served as backdrop, although small bleachers already filled with select supporters flanked the big flags on either side.

"What do you want to see?" I asked.

"Circle the rally site."

I veered right, putting Andy in the best position to look down and survey the scene as I flew a circuit around the carnival-like event. The half ring of erected bleachers facing the stage had rows of tents on the back sides. People milled about at the tents. I saw why. The tents contained tables full of colorful political merchandise. Hats. Shirts. Flags. Things I could not identify from one hundred feet up, but which were flying into the hands of eager buyers. People below us pulled on freshly purchased t-shirts and sweatshirts or landed bright red caps on their heads.

There had to be costs to a rally of this kind. From the brisk sales taking place, I estimated that the profit more than covered the overhead.

Andy served up a running commentary, which I realized I had only half listened to. I tuned in.

"...I'm sure the towers are all locked down. And you can see police and Secret Service presence up on top. The sightlines on the flanks are blocked. And the bleachers create a wall on this side. There's a Detroit Police station beneath the plaza. That's his point of entry. See there? The road goes under the plaza. If he hasn't already arrived, his motorcade will enter there."

Police vehicles lined the road that stretched away to the southwest and northeast along the waterfront. Nothing moved in either direction.

"He'll come from the police station," Andy narrated. "They have a cordon set up. And look. See it?"

"What?" I had no idea.

"Bullet-proof glass. They set up a channel of bullet-proof glass. Wow. The logistics of doing this in the middle of a sniper scare must be mind boggling."

"He wants to be seen making an entrance. That must have been a crazy transport and setup issue. I wonder why he didn't just come in by helicopter?"

"Real estate," Andy replied. "A landing pad would have taken up valuable real estate. The rotor wash would have blown away all those money-making tents, too. Will, take me down to the stage."

"Seriously?"

"I want to see the sightlines."

I tightened our arc and curved us inward. A path over the rapidly filling bleachers took us down toward the small stage. Of all the pieces of this extravaganza, the stage appeared to be the simplest. A raised rectangle containing a single podium adorned with the Seal of the President of the United States. The stage rose roughly four feet above the surface of the plaza and extended just twenty feet on either side of the podium. The news footage I'd seen of the President at one of these rallies always showed him stationary behind the podium.

In a direct line with the podium, also raised, a walkway extended toward the waterfront, passing between the giant American flags and the twin bleachers. The flags formed a stage curtain through which the President would make his dramatic entrance. Behind the curtain, the walkway ended with a set of steps that rose out of the ballistically protected channel.

No one stood on the stage as we approached, but a row of widely spaced Secret Service agents, men and women in dark suits, took up station all around the platform, facing outward in all four directions. Police in heavy vests lined fences that separated the speaker from his audience.

We sank into the bowl created by the arc of grandstands. Loud rock music rose to meet us. Springsteen's signature chorus proclaimed birth in the U.S.A. I wondered if the crowd, some of them bobbing and rocking to the music, genuinely understood the lyrics.

I reduced speed with bursts of reverse thrust from the handheld propeller, the sound of which easily succumbed to the music. We passed over the heads of the security line. Although fully aware that we could not be seen, I still worried that one of them would lift their stone-faced gaze skyward and spot us. I imagined panicked pointing and weapons raised. Flying over cornfields and meadows induced pure joy. Flying over people made me nervous.

Andy must have had similar thoughts. Her grip tightened.

We glided to a stop beside the podium. I pocketed the BLASTER and reached out for a grip on the podium lip. Firmly anchored, I swung us around to face the crowd from the position the President would occupy for up to two hours. Twin teleprompters stood at forty-five-degree positions facing the presidential lectern.

The bleachers filled quickly. People jostled together, urged to squeeze tighter by ushers wearing armbands conferring them with authority. Few people sat. Most craned for a better view, lifted cameras for photos of the empty stage, or posed for selfies proving their attendance in the presence of their Leader. I felt power gathering. I could easily imagine how exponentially that power would be amplified when "Hail to The Chief" replaced Springsteen and the object of all this adoration strutted onto the stage.

I remembered a similar devotion to the crusading conservative talk show host and conspiracy virtuoso Josiah James.

Andy leaned close to me. Her lips tickled my ear.

"He's protected on all four sides. The bleachers. The glass. And the waterfront. I thought the rally was a terrible idea, but they seem to know what they're doing. Will, I don't think this is going to draw out the sniper. Not here, at least. Not during the speech. There are no high points that can't be cleared and covered by security. No vehicle hides he can use. If there are, I'm not seeing it."

A bank of video cameras dominated a platform directly facing the stage. Technicians stood behind the cameras, swinging them back and forth, looking for images of interest. One or two of the cameras held their lifeless glass eyes on me, inducing an involuntary shiver. Bold placards announced the camera owners. Network names and news organizations I did not know. The America First Network had hung a banner spanning the platform. I looked for signs of major news networks but found none.

"This thing is going to start soon," I said. "They always have warmup speakers before the big man comes out. What do you want to do?"

Andy said nothing for a moment. I felt her turning, looking in every direction. Then she spoke. "Turn us around. I want to go out the way he comes in."

I used the podium for leverage and rotated us to face the empty waterfront. We eased out between the flanking bleachers. The flag curtain contained just enough gap to allow us to slip through sideways. The size of the big flags became fully apparent up close; they had to be forty feet tall. The walkway ended in a set of steps which joined the protected channel. A small army of police, people in suits, people with clipboards and headsets, and people trying to look official occupied the backstage portion of the plaza. A cluster of people milled near the bottom of the step joining the runway to the stage. A makeup artist hurried to pat last-minute powder on a man who kept touching his hair.

"That's him," Andy said. "That's Shannon."

I searched my memory for a reason to find him familiar but could find nothing specific. He fit the casting stereotype for a news anchor, although the dye job on his hair seemed a touch dark, as did a tan that looked sprayed on. Maybe it's a lighting issue. Maybe stage lights subdue color that looks gaudy backstage.

He stroked the makeup artist's hand aside abruptly, a gesture I found rude but which the young man took in stride. The hand slap signaled an end to the makeup session. I caught sight of a smirk twisting up the makeup man's lip as he walked away.

As Andy and I passed over the group another attendant hurried to adjust Shannon's shirt, tie, collar and even an errant hair behind one ear. I let us drift a dozen yards beyond the small crowd before pulsing the power unit to stop, turn and hover.

A Jackson Browne song followed Springsteen, then ended. Racks of lights on portable poles illuminated, painting the makeshift arena with light and color, and igniting a cheer through the crowd.

A new urgency propelled the last of the crowd to fill the grandstands.

"Is this the best place to be?" I asked Andy.

"As good as any."

Fifteen feet above the heads of scurrying aides, officials, and security officers, we waited for the President of the United States.

65

"Hang on," Andy said abruptly. "Call coming in."

I felt her lift one hand from my arm to touch her earpiece.

"This is Andrea." She spoke softly.

I aimed the BLASTER upward and gave it power to put some space between us and the clusters of officials below. Without the ability to see my watch, I couldn't be sure how much time had passed. The show began with Harry Shannon pumping up the already energized crowd. Two minor politicians seeking reelection followed. They shouted breathless praise of the President.

I listened to one side of Andy's conversation.

"Yes."

"Yes, at the rally site."

"Where?"

Andy remained silent during what I assumed to be a detailed description.

"No, that's no problem."

"About ten minutes to get across the bridge."

"Right. No lights. No sirens. No problem."

"I'll meet you there."

She touched her ear again to end the call.

"That was Mrs. Palmer. She's coordinating with a team from Homeland. They think they might have identified a possible sniper sightline. She wants me to join her."

"Where?"

"Canada."

"Canada? Are you sure? And are you sure you want to go now?"

"Why?"

"Look to your left."

A parade of vehicle emergency lights snaked down the street that followed the contours of the Detroit waterfront. Motorcycle police led, followed by state patrol cars, city police SUVs and what looked like armored personnel carriers. At the center of the snake, a black limousine cruised with fluttering flags on the fenders.

"He's here."

66

I rotated us and held the BLASTER out. Slowly at first, to avoid being heard, I navigated toward the waterfront. A rocky river wall passed beneath us. We soared over the black waters of the Detroit River. The sparkling lighted shoreline of Windsor lay a half mile ahead. For the first time I noticed a pair of police patrol boats cruising the middle of the channel. Nothing else moved on the water.

I accelerated. Wind flapped our clothes. We cruised thirty feet above dark water highlighted by glittering reflections from the city lights on either side. A little over a mile away the Ambassador Bridge carried international traffic high above the river. In the opposite direction, an island shaped like the prow of a ship split the channel into two equal parts. A bridge joined the island to the American side.

Andy spoke in full voice. "Straight ahead. There's a park on the shore. To the left of that hotel and casino. She said to meet there."

"Did she find something?"

"She seems to think so."

Painted in light, twin hotel towers flanking a curved centerpiece mounted the word *Caesars* in fiery red lettering. I aimed us at a dark band beside the bright complex. I gauged the breadth of the river. Half a mile didn't seem like much when looking through a sight mounted on a Barrett rifle.

Life on the Detroit side of the river had come to a standstill for the President's visit. On the Windsor side traffic moved without interruption.

We passed the halfway point over the river.

"Go left."

I adjusted course.

"More left. Good. That's it."

Andy's navigation pointed us at a dark strip lining the busy, lighted waterfront on the Canadian side of the river. As we drew closer the darkness rendered an expanse of park. A bike path curved through the park, dipped toward the inland side, then swung back to follow the shore. It skirted a small playground, then a low pavilion. To the right of that, a sparsely filled parking lot separated the park from a broad concrete plaza not unlike the one hosting the rally on the other side of the river.

"I need to get into that parking lot, but we can't just appear."

"Got it."

I aimed high and we soared.

"Where are you going?"

"Up. Wires. I want to be sure."

I put us on an arc that lifted us several hundred feet as the shoreline passed under us. Leveling off, I maneuvered over the pavilion building. I pulsed the BLASTER to come to a stop, then held it over my head and reversed the thrust. We performed a slow elevator ride to the sidewalk beside the building.

"Hang on," Andy said. I felt her look in all directions. "Okay, we're good."

Fwooomp!

We reappeared and settled into gravity's grip. Andy stepped back and glanced down at her clothing, a white and blue striped top over jeans.

"It's colder out than I thought," she said. "I should have brought a sweater."

"I can go steal a sweatshirt with the President's reelection slogan."

"No stealing." I took that as a coy way of saying she wouldn't be caught dead wearing a political statement. "Mrs. Palmer said to meet her in the parking lot."

Andy stepped to the corner of the building. She kept cover while leaning out to survey the parking lot. I followed her lead and stole a glance.

"Do you see her?"

"I don't see anyone."

"Shouldn't we be seeing...I dunno, a lot of cops? U.S. Homeland Security and Canadian Mounted Police? Or City of Windsor cops?"

Andy studied the parking lot several hundred feet away.

"Um...not if we're trying to avoid spooking the sniper."

"I should think you'd want to spook him. To prevent him from setting up a shot. It sure seems to me that shooting across the river wouldn't be that difficult for that big rifle. At least, in the hands of a pro."

Andy didn't answer. I knew better than to interrupt her thinking. I watched the spectacle on the other side of the river. The cranes with the American flags dominated the scene. The ring of stadium-like lights erected all the way around the rally site sent glittering reflections across the water's surface. Faint music crossed the international border bisecting the river.

"Will, I don't like this." Andy let her hand slip to the flap on her satchel. "This doesn't feel right."

"Call her."

Andy weighed the merits of the idea, then pulled out her phone. She touched the screen, then waited as the Bluetooth earpiece transmitted the call to her ear.

"She's not answering," Andy said after a moment.

"What do you want to do?" I asked. "It sounds like the main event is about to start over there."

Andy touched her screen again. This time my earpiece signaled an incoming call. I tapped the earpiece to open the connection. Andy pocketed her phone, then spoke. The words slipped from her lips, into her cheek microphone, then directly into my ear with startling intimacy.

"I don't like this. I want you to go back over to the other side."

"What? Why?"

"I'll see if I can find Mrs. Palmer here. But Will, if I don't find her and if all else fails, I think you should stop that rally."

I pulled her away from the corner and put my hands on her shoulders.

"Are you insane? Then you should come with me. You're the cop."

"No. You can do it. Just cause trouble. Make a loud noise. Yell, 'Gun!' and the Secret Service will have him in his limo before anyone can ask why. Keep this line open. Maybe it won't happen. Mrs. Palmer has to be here somewhere. She said she's working with a team from Homeland. As soon as I find her, I'll give you the word. You probably won't have to do anything."

"Now I don't like this."

Andy shook her head. "I'll be fine. You'll be fine. We're just covering all the bases. Go."

She locked her eyes on me, then flicked them in the direction of the rally.

I lifted a hand to the back of her neck and pulled her home for a kiss.

"Be careful," I said.

"You, too."

67

The flight back to the rally generated tension I hadn't felt on the crossing to Canada. After vanishing, I pushed off and deployed the BLASTER. Andy briefly lifted her face in the direction of the sound, then went back to what suddenly felt like police business, planning a move on the sparsely filled parking lot.

I knew she wanted me to hurry back to the rally, but I carved an arc through the air over the paved lot. A mix of cars and SUVs filled widely separated spaces. I looked for and easily found Mrs. Palmer's bulky van.

"She's here, Dee."

"Where?"

"In the row at the edge of the water. She's in the last space on the end near the hotel. Backed in."

Andy took a moment, then said, "I see her."

"Want me to scope it out?"

"No. I got it. You need to get back to the other side.

"I'm on my way."

I curved right and accelerated over the water feeling the uncomfortable tug of leaving Andy behind grow stronger. I aimed for the bright lights of the rally. The two patrol boats in the river stepped up their pace, cutting paths through the water ahead of potent wakes. I timed my crossing to catch them as far from my line of flight as possible. Men on the decks, some of them cradling long rifles, remained focused on the river, the shore, and the rally site.

"That's her van," Andy said in my ear. "I don't see her." Her report told me she had crossed into the parking lot.

"She probably hooked up with that Homeland team. If she has a line on the sniper, she'd be the best person to guide them."

Andy didn't comment. I prayed she would quickly find Mrs. Palmer and forty grim-faced SWAT team types armed for bear.

I didn't give voice to my doubts, but rather focused on the task ahead. The Detroit side of the river approached. Fifty yards from shore I backed off the power and gave a few short bursts of reverse thrust. The effect slowed me. On the last burst, I added an up angle to my grip on the power unit so that the reverse thrust not only slowed me but changed my trajectory to a descent.

Backstage officials lined the ballistic glass channel. I took that to mean that the President had not yet entered the channel or taken the stage. Harry Shannon's voice boomed in the makeshift arena. To my ear the words were garbled, but his breathless banter carried his feelings loud and clear. Admiration. Adulation. He shouted something about a great man, about game-changing, about things only one man could do.

Energizing all of this, a throbbing bass and drumbeat rose from the plaza. Build-up music spurred on the cheering crowd. The big flags obscured most of the arena as I approached. I descended toward the narrow runway connecting the stairs to the podium.

The President's followers cheered. They waved their arms. They hoisted flags with the President's name. Half of the crowd wore red hats with his signature slogan. The other half waved professionally printed signs bearing his name or his slogan or a call for *Four More Years*. The faces beneath those hats and behind the signs glowed with wide-eyed excitement. This felt more like a revival tent show than a political rally.

Steady cheering eliminated all worry about noise from the BLASTER. Over the runway to the podium, I gave it several quick shots to halt my descent and forward progress. I eased off to the side of the walkway. A gap between the runway and the flanking bleachers gave me room to hover.

Andy spoke in my ear.

"Are you there yet?"

"Affirmative. Where are you?"

"I'm at her van. It looks empty. I want a look inside."

"Are you breaking into her van?"

"Don't have to...open..."

"Dee, I can barely hear you. It's crazy here."

"Stand by."

Harry Shannon lifted his voice to a climactic finish.

"LADIES AND GENTLEMEN, PEOPLE OF THE TRUE AMER-ICA, I GIVE YOU THE MAN, THE MACHINE, THE PEOPLE'S CHOICE, THE PRIDE OF OUR NATION, YOUR PRESIDENT OF THE UNITED STATES!"

Shannon's full-tilt introduction blew feedback through the sound system. The crowd went wild. The audio technician instantly blasted "Hail to The Chief."

Staff and supporters standing on the plaza at the back of the rally uniformly turned and clapped their hands. Some waved. Women blew kisses.

"Will, she's not here. I'm inside the van. And we have a problem."

"What?"

"I said we have a problem."

"Dee, I can barely hear you!" I cupped my hand over the earpiece. "Say again!"

Andy said nothing. At the bottom of the back stairs, the President's light-colored hair appeared. He climbed the steps slowly, waving left and right at staff. He wore the same blue suit and red tie I'd seen in his photos, reminding me of the now-deceased Congressman Martin Gregg.

"Will, the rifle is here. She has it set up with the scope. There's a portal through the taillight. I'm taking a look."

"Andy, speak up!"

"...my god..."

The President finished climbing the steps then paused, lifting his chin, letting the adulation wash down on him while he withheld his presence from his adoring supporters. He remained at the end of the runway. His head bobbed slightly to the music.

"...looking through the gun sight. She must have used this to find a line of sight for the sniper...Will, I can see the rally. I see—good lord—I see the President!"

"What?"

"…Palmer was right…can see him…sniper has a shot!"

The music drudged on. The leader of the free world remained rooted in his spot at the end of the runway, waiting for the crescendo's peak before making his entrance through the red, white and blue flags. The crowd found a new level of frenzy. He absorbed the outpouring with his chin held high.

"…him!"

"Andy, if you can hear me, I can't hear you!"

He stepped off, strutting forward. Up close, his suit looked oversized and rumpled. His belly tested the strength of his belt.

"—op him! Will, get him out of there!"

"Are you kidding? How am I supposed to—?"

"Will, just do it!"

The President strutted forward. A chant grew out of the shouting.

"*Four more years! Four more years!*"

Blood hammering in my temples joined the words jumbled in my ears. *Stop him, how?*

I had no idea. Seize him? Make him vanish? The idea flashed through my head, followed by images of frenzy among the dozens of protectors watching him.

He approached. Three steps away. Two.

"DO IT!" Andy cried in my ear.

He approached the curtain.

I pointed the BLASTER straight up and hit full reverse. The shot drove me down until my feet planted on the concrete below the runway. Now, with the runway at my chest height, the President marched past me. I reached out and grabbed one foot and jerked.

The foot I grabbed had been about to swing forward for a step. Locking it in place robbed him of his balance. His arms shot out, pinwheeling. He wobbled and tipped. He fell forward. He kicked his foot out of my grip and staggered into the flag gap. For an instant I sensed failure. He appeared to regain his balance. Then, his center of gravity betrayed him. His feet stomped the wooden surface of the runway but failed to catch up to his lunging torso. He accelerated through the curtain out of control.

His hair flipped upward. He tumbled.

He hit hard. One hand found the runway, but he had veered off center. His torso bounced. His left hand skidded off the edge of the runway. Nothing stopped a slow roll sideways. On the downstroke of his bodily bounce, he careened sideways off the edge and dropped four feet to the concrete below.

"Oh crap," I said aloud.

The crowd issued a collective gasp, more than audible over the thundering official anthem of the President. Someone at the soundboard acted swiftly and killed the music, which only made matters worse. Sudden silence underscored the President's pratfall.

I heard a snap and glanced up to see a hole burst open in the lectern. Following a line of sight down the runway to the hole in the lectern, I looked across the rally floor at the facing grandstand. My eye went directly to a man clutching his chest. He wore red but white lettering on his t-shirt betrayed a bloom of blood. Blood seeped into the fist he pressed to his diaphragm. He tipped forward and crashed down on the row directly in front of him.

A woman beside the man screamed. Heads turned, but he was a sideshow. The crowd remained focused on the empty runway where the President had tripped and fallen.

The Secret Service burst into action. Men leaped to the stage. Agents surged forward from backstage. They raced down the channels on either side of the runway.

Directly at me.

I kicked the pavement and shot up just as the first agents reached my position. On the concrete below the runway, I saw the blue backside of the President's suit. He landed face down. The first agents swarmed him. Some rendered assistance, others formed a protective cordon around him.

He cursed the hands trying to lift him.

On the opposite side of the arena, confusion surrounded the fan who had fallen onto the people in the row below him. One or two pushed him as if he'd attacked from above. They drew back hands coated in blood. The offender lay limp, motionless. People on either side of the body scrambled away.

I shot higher. The scene fell away beneath me. Tremors jiggled my limbs. How close? How close had this bullet come? Because it had surely been another bullet passing through the lectern and into the chest of an unsuspecting supporter of the President.

"Will! Was he hit?"

Andy's voice was both immediate and distant. In the scene beneath me, Secret Service agents tried to lift the President to his feet. He fought them. They struggled.

"Will! Are you there?"

"I'm here."

"What's happening?"

"He's okay. But I think the sniper fired a shot."

"Is the President hit?"

"No. I said he's okay. Jesus, Dee, I think it just missed him. It hit a guy in the grandstands."

"Hang on," she said.

Really? I was pretty sure all the action was on my side of the river, and she was telling me to hang on? I lifted my eyes from the chaos below and glanced across the river.

Blue flashing lights lined the riverbank in front of the heavily illuminated casino towers. Emergency lights flashed and raced together from both directions.

She'd done it. Mrs. Palmer located the sniper and called in the cavalry.

Better late...

Below me a general rumble rippled through the grandstands, pulling my attention back to the rally. I heard shouts. The crowd burst apart in the section where the man had gone down. People shoved and jumped away from him. Accelerating panic cleared the seats. Men and women tumbled and fell. Police rushed forward. Some were caught up in the surge. Others pushed and fought. An officer jumped from row to row until he reached the downed man. He probed and searched the limp body.

"Will, are you there?" Andy's voice carried a calm that contrasted with the panic below me. "I think I have a problem here."

That was all I needed to hear. The President and all his men would have to work this out without me.

I held out the BLASTER and thumbed the power until it pulled me toward the Canadian side of the river.

"What problem? Talk to me, Dee."

"The police are here."

"Good."

The cluster of flashing blue and white emergency lights in Canada grew larger and clearer. I recognized their location. They surrounded Mrs. Palmer's van.

"No," Andy said. "I don't think it's good."

Below me, the twin patrol boats carved hooks in the river and shot toward the rally shoreline, igniting their own emergency lights as they surged ahead of expanding wakes. I sailed over them.

"Is Mrs. Palmer with them?"

"I don't think so," Andy said.

The line fell silent again. I held my breath.

"Will, someone just shot at the President. And I'm in a van with a Barrett rifle pointed at the President."

"Well, yeah. She used it to—*oh, crap*." I saw it.

"Yes. It's the same rifle I fired at our place. There's a shell casing on the floor here, too. And I bet it has my fingerprints on it. I know the rifle does. You're right."

"About what?"

"What you said. Oh crap."

68

I pushed the slide control on the power unit to the maximum. The blade howled. Wind rushed my face. My eyes watered. My vision blurred. The emergency lights lining the river ahead blended into a slash of flashing blue and white. My depth perception over the black water, already minimal, became nil. I used the expanse of Canadian riverfront as a perspective guide and hoped for the best.

"Will, I'm going to surrender to the police."

"Hold up! I can get you out."

I heard commands shouted through a police PA system.

"There isn't time. Not if they think I might fire again."

"You didn't fire!"

"They don't know that. But by now, I bet they know somebody did. If it were me, I'd take this down right now."

"Dee, wait!"

"I'll be fine."

I willed myself to go faster. Instead, the scream of the BLASTER's prop changed its note slightly, slowing.

Batteries!

The power unit lost strength. I faced a choice. Take the time to change units or accept the gradually reduced speed. I chose the latter and powered forward.

"Dee!"

She spoke, but not to me. Her voice slammed into my earpiece. "I'm an American police officer! I am unarmed! Don't shoot! I'm coming out."

I wiped wind tears from my eyes and blinked rapidly. The blurred scene on the Canadian waterfront shifted in and out of focus.

Mrs. Palmer's van held the corner parking space of a broad, rectangular lot. The van had been backed into the space. Andy's mention of a portal through the taillight made sense. A perfect sniper hideaway with a line of sight on the rally across the river. A half-circle of police white vehicles trapped the boxy vehicle in blazing headlights and spotlights.

Fifty yards. Forty. Thirty.

I arrived just as Andy stepped from the side door of the van with her arms extended above her head. Silhouetted officers in black swarmed from the spaces between the parked police cars and SUVs. Most shouldered rifles. Some held up handguns. All wore helmets. All of them pointed their weapons at my wife. In one hand, Andy showed her Essex Police Department badge. Her shoulder satchel was missing, no doubt left behind with the Glock 17 she carried inside. She looked small and helpless against the men in heavy body armor.

Andy took two steps forward, then carefully knelt on the pavement.

I had a chance. A mad full-power dive would take me across the van roof to her. If I hooked one hand on the van's cargo rack, I could swing down and drop right behind her. Grab her. Vanish her. A kick of the pavement and we would soar out of reach.

Too late. Powerful men in black converged on her. One tore the badge from her hand. Two others grabbed her arms and twisted them behind her back. They forced her forward, face down, onto the pavement. She hit and winced. The jolt stabbed me in the chest. My breathing seized.

I shot across the roof of the van while four men held my wife against the pavement. Officers carefully probed the open van.

I fired full reverse to stop. To hell with the noise. Heads lifted.

Get off of her!

The men holding Andy down gave no quarter. I told myself it wasn't their fault. That it was their job. Their protocol.

I told myself that Andy would convince them. A fellow officer. Doing her job.

I stifled a scream.

Radios crackled. Voices issued commands. Below me, an officer wearing command insignia plucked a microphone from a shoulder mount.

"We have the shooter. Repeat. We have the shooter."

The hell you do!

I swung around over the cordon of police cars. The flashing lights and intense spotlights mutated the shadows painted on the pavement, the van, and the stone lining the waterfront.

I rotated sharply and searched for an opening.

Strong arms lifted Andy from the pavement, not gently. Two men gripped her upper arms and carried her toward a gap in the cars. She stumbled trying to keep pace.

"I'm a police officer!" she shouted.

"We know," someone said. His cold tone chilled me.

A boxy black vehicle marked with Windsor Police insignia rolled to a harsh stop behind the vehicle cordon. Diesel fumes touched my nostrils. Doors at the rear of the big van split open and more men jumped to the pavement. The officers restraining Andy marched to the rear of the vehicle.

I looked for a chance. I could take them all. Andy. The two cops. I could grab them all and make them vanish. Kick off and take them for a ride. The cops would lose their cool and let her go. I would happily watch them fall. Serve them right.

Doors at the back of the big vehicle split open and two men leaned out. Before I had a chance, they heaved Andy into the transport and slammed the doors. Several officers raced to their cars. Engines started. Under flashing emergency lights, the patrol cars pulled out to lead the way.

"Dee! Can you hear me? Are you there?"

Nothing.

Someone must have pulled her earpiece. Or else they found her phone in her satchel and killed the open connection.

The caravan rolled. I considered my dying battery pack and made a rapid decision. I rotated and aimed at the roof of the big transport. Cargo racks and equipment mounts on the black vehicle offered ample grip points. I dove to intercept it. As it accelerated, I slapped a handhold on a bar running along the side of the roof above a short ladder.

I killed the power on the dying BLASTER and tossed it over the side.

I searched for a hatch, thinking I could break it open, startle the occupants, and lift Andy out. No such hatch existed. A new plan formed.

Lower myself to the rear door, pull it open and grab Andy. Except that pulling the door open would only swing me out over the receding pavement.

So what? The door pops open. One of the cops reaches out to close it. Grab him. Toss him out on the street.

Will, stop. Andy's voice in my head interrupted my scheming. *Someone will get hurt.*

Plans to break Andy free of the moving vehicle abruptly dissolved.

The ride lasted less than two minutes. The van and its escorts passed Caesars hotel and casino complex, drove one block and turned a sharp left into a forest of tall buildings. One more block, and the motorcade turned left again. Almost immediately the lead vehicle pulled away. The van slowed and peeled off to the right, into a sally port on the side of a tall building constructed of tan stone and greenish glass. I failed to notice signage. Too big to be a substation, I guessed this to be the Windsor Police Service headquarters. If the Windsor police believed they had arrested the sniper who had been terrorizing America—a murderer who had just taken a shot at the American President—they would sequester Andy in their most secure location. She would sink into the deepest recesses of high security and even higher bureaucracy.

I ducked. The van plunged into the building. A rapid open/close door dropped behind the vehicle the instant it cleared. Pale fluorescent lights swept over me. The driver kept the speed up and made hard turns. Tires squealed on the concrete until he braked to an abrupt stop beside a set of glass doors. Word traveled fast. Half a dozen officers waited, including several laden with significant rank on shoulder epaulets. Peaked caps with bright red bands reminded me that Andy and I were in a foreign country.

Following Andy inside the building—the challenges would grow exponentially. Doing anything meant doing it here.

I knew, or thought I knew, what she would want. Let her handle this. Let her communicate with her fellow officers in a professional, reasonable manner. This was all a misunderstanding. Andy would feel confident in her ability to sort this out.

And she would be wrong.

I saw this situation in a single headline.

Disgraced FBI Trainee Seeks Revenge.

Andy had no capacity for seeing herself framed as a reject from the FBI Academy. She would seek respect from people who might otherwise have granted both, if not for prejudices outpacing reason. She would fail to see herself through the eyes of her captors. Kicked out of the academy. Found in the van with the weapon. A weapon she had fired. With her fingerprints everywhere. And how, I wondered, would she explain entering Canada?

If professional courtesy hadn't already evaporated, it would the instant the Canadian authorities spoke to their American counterparts.

Whether she wanted it or not, I needed to get her out of this.

I pulled myself to the rear of the van. Two officers hurried to open the dual doors. The phalanx of senior police spread out to watch the prize captive emerge. I swung my legs over the back of the van and used the top of the open right-hand door to shimmy outward.

Andy kneeled in the center of the van, which appeared designed to transport a special weapons team to a crime scene. Twin benches lined the sides and spanned the bulkhead behind the driver's position.

Two officers bracketed Andy. Strands of her hair hung across her eyes. She did not look from side to side, but instead studied the audience anticipating her arrival. She looked from face to face, from insignia to insignia.

"Who's the senior officer?" she asked. "I need to speak to the senior officer."

"Let's go." The men beside her ignored her request. They took her by the upper arms and lifted her to her feet.

She didn't argue or resist. If it had been me, I would have panicked twice over. She remained calm and compliant. The officers, however, did not reciprocate. They fixed firm grips on her and pushed her forward. Rather than give her the chance to step down from the interior of the van, they lifted her and lowered her to the pavement. The maneuver meant transferring control of her to the two men holding the doors open.

My chance.

Hands still bound behind her, Andy found her feet and faced the men watching her. She came erect and spoke as the two in the van let go of her arms.

"I am a police officer. I need to speak to your senior officer."

I grabbed the door midway down, near the latch, and rotated until my legs pointed at the ceiling. Now within easy reach, I raced her nearest guard for a grip on Andy. He had the advantage, so I diverted. Instead of grabbing Andy by the arm, I swung my hand into his face and backhanded his nose. Fair game. His heavy aftershave assaulted mine.

He startled. Instinct propelled his own hand to swipe away whatever it was that had just touched his face. I jerked my hand clear and grabbed Andy by the upper arm.

"Dee!" I whispered loudly.

Fwooomp!

"No!" she called out. Too late. She vanished.

The officer on the other side of her had been inches from closing a grip on her upper arm. Now he froze, blinking.

Andy went rigid. I feared she would fight me. I tightened my grip on the door and heaved her upward. The second officer flinched and then flailed at an unseen attacker when her legs swung sideways and kicked him. I felt the impact but followed through until I could be sure she swung over the open door to a position above the roof of the van. I pushed off the door. We rose to the ceiling. We bumped against raw concrete. I threw both arms around her and pulled her close.

Her breath heaved. I prayed she would force herself to remain silent.

Startled curses rang out from the cops below us.

"Where'd she go?"

"What the fuck?"

"Hey!"

"Where is she?!"

Astonished guards searched in vain. Command officers stood in wide-eyed shock. There was no denying it. Half a dozen police officers just watched a suspect in custody vanish before their eyes. Chances were good that the whole thing had been caught on video.

I didn't care. I had bigger concerns.

By the rigid posture I felt in my embrace, I knew my wife was more than a little pissed off at what I'd just done.

69

For what felt like half an hour we floated just inside the closed sally port. Andy's silence matched mine, but hers radiated anger. Windsor officers searched the area around the transport van, then fanned out. Commanders gathered in a lengthy and heated consultation. We hovered too far away to hear them, which I regretted. There were shouts. Gestures. The conversation would have been interesting. Eight or ten trained law enforcement professionals all bore witness to the impossible. All dealt with the burning question. *What the hell just happened?* And the question after that. *Now what?*

A more interesting conversation would be the one Canadian officials held with American officials, because I had no doubt that word had already been passed across the border announcing the successful apprehension of the sniper.

As if to distance themselves from an embarrassing error, the senior officers retreated into the building. The remaining men spread out inside the garage, searching. They did not swing their arms probing for someone who had vanished, but I heard one of them say, "She's got to be here. That's some kind of stealth shit."

Staying clear of the search party proved no problem. Pipes and conduit lined the garage roof. Andy was of little use in maneuvering with her arms bound behind her back. I wasn't sure she would have helped in any case. Neither of us spoke.

I pulled us across the ceiling and up the ramp to a position near the exit. The sally port door eventually opened to release the boxy transport van from the scene. We slipped out with the big van. I heaved us toward the street and upward. Squad cars with lights flashing quartered the block. Officers patrolled the sidewalks, at the ready. Others clustered near their cars and talked.

Gliding over their heads, I extracted a fresh BLASTER. After hooking my arm in Andy's to free up both hands, I fixed the propeller in place and gently advanced the power unit slide control, keeping the prop whine to a minimum.

Thrust carried us higher. A residential building faced Windsor Police Services. Ranks of stacked balconies lined the structure's face.

As we ascended, I surveyed the glass behind each railing. With the sun long gone, building residents turned on lights and gathered around televisions or over dinners. Second from the top, I found a balcony with black windows. Someone was not only not home but had neglected to leave on a light.

I closed in on the railing, slowed and fixed a grip. Twisting my wrist, I lifted us both over the railing and swung our legs into position for landing.

Fwooomp! We appeared.

Andy stared bullets at me.

"They know who I am," she snapped. "What were you thinking!"

"Exactly that. That they know who you are."

"Yes. A police officer. Now I look like a guilty police officer. You should have given me a chance to talk to them."

"Dee—"

"*You don't think.* You just act. You don't care what effect this has on me. The damage it does."

"I do think."

She did not move. Storm clouds boiled behind her withering gaze.

"Disgruntled cheat. Disgraced FBI cadet. Dismissed from the academy."

She opened her mouth to argue, but I dove all in.

"*Assassin seeking revenge. That's who they think you are. I know it's*

not you, but that's who they think they arrested. The moment they estab-
lished your identity they saw you only one way."

Her mouth hung open.

"Dee, there's no question that you were set up for this. No question.
The bullshit at the academy. That business with the van. My god. How did
we not see this coming? You handled the rifle, the bullets."

Andy pursed her lips. The gentle underbite that sometimes arouses me
to intimacy now gave her lower lip dangerous prominence. I felt myself
making headway, but only marginal and under threat.

"Argue with me if you have a better idea, but I bet by the time the
ten o'clock news airs you'll be at the top of the FBI's Most Wanted
List."

She held harsh eyes on me for moment, then lowered her gaze to the
police headquarters across the street. She watched the police organize a
cordon around the building.

"They're in the gun safe," she said distantly.

"What?"

"Those special bullets. Mrs. Palmer got me to put them in our gun
safe."

"Jesus." I pulled out my phone. "We need to call Tom and tell
him to—"

Andy closed her hand over the phone in my hand.

"No. Will, stop. We can't ask the Chief to tamper with evidence."

"Planted evidence!"

She shook her head. "That's not how we do this."

She eased my phone out of my hand and pried it from its case. With a
deft and practiced touch, she snapped the back from the phone and pulled
out the sim card, then the battery. She handed me the pieces. I pocketed
them.

"Just how do we do this? Because it sure looks to me like Mrs. Palmer
played us from the start."

"Or she's dead."

Something I hadn't considered.

"Dead?"

"Mrs. Palmer found the sniper's sightline. What if the sniper found
her?"

"How?"

"She may have led him straight to her. She said she reached out to Homeland. Maybe she reached out to the wrong person."

"Oh, now it's someone with Homeland? The good guy is the bad guy? Come on, Dee. Have you considered that maybe she maneuvered you into putting your prints on the gun and the bullets, then set them up for the cops to find?"

"Maybe. Maybe she just needed those bullets in the safest place possible…for now."

Andy heaved a long sigh and her eyes found mine, and in them I detected the faintest spark of forgiveness. It might not reach her lips anytime soon, but it gave me hope.

"I had to do it."

"You didn't give me a chance."

"They weren't going to give you a chance." She didn't respond. "What do you want to do now?"

She turned and presented me with her hands, still bound in silver cuffs behind her back.

"For starters, get me out of these things."

Fwooomp! I vanished and closed both hands on the metal, then pushed until *the other thing* spread over the chain and the bindings. With some gentle twisting, the border between seen and unseen frayed, then snapped. Broken metal dropped to the balcony floor.

Fwooomp! I rejoined her.

"We need to go," she said.

"Where?"

"I need a bathroom. We need food. And then…Virginia."

70

"I got this," I told Andy. I closed a grip on the sliding glass door handle to the condo that owned the balcony under our feet.

Fwooomp! I set myself to push *the other thing* over the lock and snap it. Andy touched my arm and then put her hand over mine and slid the door sideways.

"It's not locked, love." She pushed the door open and me with it. She stepped inside.

"Why would it be?" I muttered to myself. "This is Canada."

Fwooomp! I reappeared and followed Andy into a broad sitting room.

"Don't touch anything," Andy warned me. "Including the lights."

She set off across a white carpet in search of the nearest bathroom. I headed for what looked like a dining room, which led to a kitchen. Faint city light from the expanse of windows lining the balcony reached the kitchen.

I opened the stainless-steel door to a refrigerator.

"Jesus, who lives here? Supermodels?"

A few jars of strange looking vegetables, a dish with something that looked like seaweed, and some wrapped salad greens shared space with a carafe of water. No real food. No beer. A drawer contained two apples. I lifted out both.

I heard a toilet flush. Andy appeared a minute later with her hair knotted at the back of her head. I noted a scrape on her cheek. They may have been colleagues in law enforcement, but I now wished I had broken the nose of the cop at the van door.

Andy saw me staring.

"It's nothing. We should go." I handed her an apple. I thought she might refuse it. Stolen property. When she closed her hand around it, she included my fingers in her grip. She held on for a moment. Her touch melted a fraction of the anger still riding her brow. "Do you think we can get to the airplane and take off?"

"Depends," I said. "They know who you are. The question is, do they connect you to me. And me to the airplane. And even if we can get to the airport and get in the air, I'm not sure they won't shoot us down. The TFR for Detroit lasts for another few hours."

"By now they've got the President back on his airplane. I would think."

"Probably."

"So…once he's gone, don't they lift the flight restrictions?"

"The TFR duration is based on the President's schedule. That's been blown to Hell, so who knows?"

She took a few steps toward the balcony door, then turned.

"You know this is all your fault. You're the one who asked the question."

"What question?"

"What could possibly go wrong?"

71

F *wooomp!*
   We tensed. I gently tapped my toes and we rose beside the railing that separated people in a luxury condo from a fall to their deaths. She increased her grip on my hand when I gave the BLASTER a shot of power and it pulled us over the railing.

I accelerated quickly. We turned sharply right and swung in a tight arc around the corner of the building.

The police cordon around the central headquarters had expanded. White Windsor Police Service vehicles guarded major intersections surrounding the scene of Andy's disappearance. Flashing lights painted streets and sidewalks blue and white. Officers on foot patrolled the sidewalks.

We left the search behind and soared over the riverfront. Several blocks away, a frenzy of activity continued around Mrs. Palmer's parked van.

I aimed us over the black river at the still blazing lights of the President's rally. The Coleman A. Young International Airport lay northeast of the Renaissance Center. I could have steered a direct course, which would have taken us closer to Grosse Point than to the site of the rally. But I wanted to make the side trip and assumed the same for Andy.

We sailed high over the cranes that suspended the giant flags. The carnival atmosphere built to a frenzied crescendo with the President's big entrance was gone. Except for men in black combat gear, the plaza had been deserted. Police vehicles added sparkling emergency lights to the scene. The grandstands stood barren. A cluster of emergency workers surrounded the place where one of the President's ardent followers gave his life in place of his Leader. The fallen fan had been removed, but heavily armed security officers guarded the spot and the evidence with rifles slung across their chests.

A colorful line of people, many carrying flags that drooped and dragged, extended from the rally site to the long line of busses. They trudged away in stunned silence.

I saw no sign of a Presidential motorcade. The area behind the grand-stand was vacant. None of the officials remained at the site of what had become a crime scene. No one cared to stand around in the path of another bullet.

We did not linger. We swept over the plaza, then curved to the right. I set a course of roughly 060-degrees, leaving behind what I hoped was the first and last time I'd ever attend a political rally. A dark patch on the cityscape guided us. The alternating white and green of an airport beacon confirmed my navigation.

72

"They haven't been released. The cops."

Andy spoke for the first time since leaving Canada. We angled downward toward Special Parking One at the Coleman A. Young International Airport. I saw what she saw.

"Same tactical deployment," Andy said. "Two men in the SUV. One man at the taxiway. They haven't been released, but they haven't been put on high alert either. And they're not blocking the plane. I think we might be okay."

"I think you're right. If someone set off alarm bells about us, they'd be all over the airplane." The Navajo sat alone at the north end of the ramp, opposite the SUV near the jet and terminal.

"Or there would be reinforcements."

"Hold up," I said. I abruptly reversed power. The relative wind against our faces stopped.

"What?"

"Dee, what if we pop that door open and just step out?"

"And surrender?"

"Think about it. We have four police witnesses that have no choice but to swear we were here the whole time. What are they going to say? 'Uh, we took a coffee break so they must have slipped past us'? They could be our—your alibi."

Andy said nothing for a moment.

"It might provide a way to get you in the clear."

"No."

"No? Why?"

"They have my badge, my bag."

"Say they were stolen."

"And how do I explain having had my badge here when I arrived, and now not having it?"

"Dee—"

"That's not all. Will, if I turn myself in now, even with a claim that I never left the airplane, they will detain me for who knows how long while they sort it out. You can't break me out a second time. That will only make things worse. You shouldn't have done it the first time. No. We have to go."

I drew and released a long, slow breath. I lifted my arm and aimed the power unit at the Navajo parked on the airport ramp.

Andy squeezed my arm.

"Thank you," she said. "For the idea."

I squeezed back.

"You're still not forgiven," she added.

WE TOUCHED down beside the fuselage.

"I kinda wish we hadn't closed the door," I said.

"Agreed. Okay, so how about this? Open the door and lift me in. Then let me appear. We'll make it look like we opened the door to tell them that we're leaving. You slip in and we go." She asked as an after-thought, "Would that work? Can we just go?"

"I don't know. I might have to throw together a quick IFR flight plan and file it, but then, yes. I think we can fly out. Unless they've completely freaked out and locked down the whole world."

"It's worth a try."

"I need both hands."

Andy repositioned her grip on my arm. I pulsed the power unit and drifted to the fuselage door. I used my left hand to wedge myself between the fuselage body and the pavement under my feet. With the other hand, I snapped open the door latch and pulled the airstair open. The instant it deployed, I shifted to the right and lifted Andy into the cabin. I felt her rotate, then let go of my arm.

Fwooomp! She reappeared. She misjudged slightly and dropped to her knees on the cabin carpet. She recovered quickly.

"I'm coming out."

She scrambled down the airstair and stepped onto the ramp. She smiled and waved at the police SUV sitting on the ramp forty yards away.

I reached into the cabin and grabbed the back of the left rear seat. I snaked my way in, bumping and pulling myself forward. Andy kept up the smiling and waving act. Through the cabin window, I saw the passenger door of the SUV open. One of the officers stepped out.

"Good-bye!" Andy called across the ramp. "We're just going to go."

She waved one more time. The officer turned back to confer with his partner. Andy didn't wait. She climbed back in and pulled the airstair door closed.

Fwooomp! I reappeared in the cabin aisle. I heaved myself into the cockpit. A glance at the police vehicle brought bad news.

"Dee! I don't think they're on board with us leaving."

Both cops trotted toward us. The first one waved at us, and not in a friendly way. He shook his head back and forth.

"Are you sure you don't want to try and talk to them?"

" I think we better go." Andy's urgent tone left no doubt.

I shoved the mixture controls full forward, flipped on the battery, and hit the primers for both engines. Fuel flow needles swung over and peaked. I hit the starters simultaneously, straining the battery. The props swung over.

Both engines fired. Sweet thunder rumbled from all twelve cylinders.

I worked the throttles to a steady idle and stole a glance at the two cops. Their next move would make the difference. If they simply stopped, I'd call Ground Control for taxi clearance and take my chances with standard procedures. If not—

The cops made the decision for me. Both officers stopped in their tracks, then reversed and bolted for their vehicle.

Shit!

I flipped switches. Primary Flight Display. Instrument lights. Cabin lights. I touched the toggles for the navigation lights and beacon, then pressed both to ensure they were off.

Andy slipped into the copilot's seat. She craned her neck to see past me.

"They're going to block us," she said. "It's what I would do."

I grabbed the throttles and goosed them. The Navajo broke free. In my peripheral vision, emergency lights flashed and began to move. A taxiway ahead and to my left, halfway between us and the police vehicle, offered immediate access to the runway. No sooner had I pressed left rudder to steer for it when the police SUV shot toward the same taxiway. They had the advantage. Getting there first and blocking access to the runway was never in doubt.

Despite a losing race, I pressed left rudder and swung the nose for the taxiway.

"Will! They're cutting us off!"

"I know," I said.

The police SUV raced ahead. In a second, they would sever my access to the runway. I watched their path carefully to see if they planned to block the taxiway or if they would swerve right and try to block me.

They opted for the taxiway.

I pulled the right throttle and pushed the left. The left engine surged. Full right rudder pedal and the asymmetrical thrust jerked the nose to the right. Instead of the runway, I now aligned with the taxiway that ran parallel to the runway.

"Here goes my license," I said.

I shoved both throttles forward. My wings spread the full breadth of the taxiway. I glanced back at the police. Not to be denied, the SUV tore onto the runway and turned hard right. They accelerated. Using the runway, the SUV raced in the same direction as me. Ahead, an angled turnoff would take them off the runway and plant them directly in front of me.

I pressed both throttles forward to full takeoff power. Balls to the wall.

Andy gripped the armrests and said nothing. The engines roared.

I checked the manifold pressure and RPM needles for full power. The airspeed indicator danced to life. We gained speed rapidly.

The SUV accelerated off my left wing, surging ahead. Their zero to sixty beat mine but by the time they reached the runway turnoff, I paced them. They made the turnoff. Only a catastrophic collision with an airplane swinging two deadly propellers at maximum power would prevent us from leaving. Their choice.

They braked sharply and stopped.

I shot past them at the taxiway intersection and immediately dropped them from my short list of worries.

Using a taxiway for takeoff had two disadvantages. First, I had joined it a third of the way down the runway, dramatically reducing my available takeoff room. Second, the taxiway jogged to the right at precisely the wrong point. It wasn't a sharp jog, but it came at me just as the nose grew light and the wings gained lift. Turning wasn't an option. Nor was flight. I needed a few more knots to break ground.

I dropped the flaps to the first notch, the approach setting. The sudden change in wing shape ballooned the airplane off the ground just as the taxiway veered right under my wheels. Taxiway lights shot under the wing, threatening a prop strike. The nose wanted to heave upward. I shoved the yoke forward and fought the airplane back into ground effect, the cushion of air that airplanes experience within one wingspan's distance of the ground.

By feel, I found the landing gear switch and lifted the gear.

Lowering the flaps reduced my stall speed. Ground effect added a touch of lift. I leveled off six feet above the airport and accelerated.

We cleared the airport perimeter and shot over the cemetery next door. I reached to raise the flaps, then changed my mind. I abruptly pulled the throttles back and pushed the nose down.

Andy's hand shot to the instrument panel as city rooftops filled the windscreen.

"What are you doing?"

"Staying down in the clutter," I replied.

I focused on the path ahead.

"Grab my iPad. It's in the bag behind the seat. Hold it up for me." I commanded. We skimmed rooftops. The airspeed hovered around one hundred knots. I reduced power and eased the airplane into a shallow right bank. Violating common sense and good piloting, I kicked right rudder and skidded the tail, creating a condition of uncoordinated flight at a dangerously slow speed. An inadvertent stall would be violent. At least the end would come quickly.

Andy held up the iPad. I removed my hands from the throttles just long enough to give the device my fingerprint and tap the Foreflight app icon.

Back on the throttles, I wiggled the power even lower still. The airspeed dropped to ninety. Eighty-five.

"Okay. Touch the Map function. Down at the bottom."

Andy's finger found the right spot. The screen switched to a moving map.

"Zoom in. Double tap the map. Good. You see us at the center."

"Got it."

"Look for a freeway. It'll be a highway line, but double."

"Right under us!" Too late. I missed it. Streaks of headlights and tail-lights passed directly under the Navajo. I turned farther right.

"Good," Andy said. "Good, keep turning. Okay...stop! There's a double line just ahead!"

"I see it!"

A highway crossed our path, coming up fast. I rolled in left bank and cheated a second time on the rudder. The Navajo's nose swung left. A six-lane highway flashed under us. It angled northeast. I kept up the turn until we tracked parallel, then intercepted.

The interstate highway cut through the city. We raced the traffic barely sixty feet above cars and trucks.

"Keep an eye out for wires and cell towers and other shit that will knock us down."

Andy raised herself in her seat and peered over the high instrument panel. The sight of the city shooting under the wings at a hundred miles an hour made her eyes grow wide.

Too fast.

I pulled more power from the throttles and added nose-up trim to take the pressure off the yoke. The airspeed trembled between eighty and eighty-five knots.

"Why are you doing this?"

"We may still be under the President's TFR. If we are, and if those cops called in a rogue aircraft taking off, and if there are F-22s in the air, we just became the number one reason for the existence of Homeland Security. I need to keep us down in the clutter and make us look like a goddamned truck on a freeway. And pray that we don't get picked up on radar."

"Maybe next time mention all this before takeoff." She resumed her search ahead.

"Yeah…in retrospect, this might not have been a good idea."

Somewhere to our right the Lake St. Clair shoreline lay in darkness. We were too low to see it. I thought about diverting. Over water, I could sink to just a few feet above the surface and hug the shore.

The airspeed dipped below eighty. I felt a pre-stall shudder. I added power to wallow on what pilots call the "back side of the power curve," a location in the flight envelope I studiously avoided.

"Lights!" Andy cried.

Tall light poles streaked under our left wing. I jerked the nose up, then fought the overreaction. The line of light poles ran down the center of the six-lane freeway beneath us. Cars raced in the opposite direction on my left. I rolled out to follow the right-hand lanes. The light poles off the tip of the left wing shot past like strobe lights, illuminating the cockpit, and taking a toll on my night vision. On the upside, they provided peripheral navigation guidance. I let them stream past while I studied the highway ahead.

Traffic was light. Long gaps stretched between vehicles. I let the Navajo dip lower. We maintained greater speed than all but a few vehicles who raced us in the left lane.

"Bridge!" Andy called out.

I lifted the nose. A concrete overpass flashed beneath us. I let us settle again. We overtook a pair of tractor-trailer trucks. The props cleared their tall exhaust stacks by mere feet. Andy glanced out her side window at the cabs.

A mercifully straight stretch of highway lay ahead. Sensing I had cleared the two trucks, I allowed the Navajo to settle toward the pavement.

"Please don't do this to impress me," Andy said.

"Trust me…" My grip on the yoke and throttles would have crushed a tennis ball. I stopped talking. I wasn't sure I was still breathing. I wasn't sure the props wouldn't strike pavement if we hiccupped.

The highway shifted left. Then right. I used rudder to follow the center lane through the turns. A flick of my eyes to the airspeed indicator suggested we were somewhere around 80 knots. Practically falling out of the sky, yet still too fast for the traffic. We overtook a cluster of cars, which forced us higher.

"Will, what's this dashed blue line?"

"Where?"

"On the iPad. We're coming up on a dashed blue line."

"Somebody's airspace." I could not pull my eyes off the road ahead. We briefly tucked in behind a pack of cars, but slowly overtook them, forcing me to rise again. We skimmed their rooftops. The noise had to be shocking for the drivers below.

"What's Selfridge ANGB?"

"What? Shit!" I glanced at the iPad, then pulled up, added power and broke left. Andy grabbed the panel again.

"What's wrong?"

"That's a military base. Busting through that is a really bad idea."

Andy braced against my sudden left turn. "And this isn't?"

She watched me dive toward the rooftops again. With no highway to follow, our path crossed a span of congested city dwellings with occasional high-rise buildings for good measure. We passed between what looked like a pair of apartment buildings. I heaved us over an office building.

"I don't know if Air Force One used Detroit Metro or that air base. If it's there, and we plow through—that would be bad. Are we clear of that airspace?"

"Clear."

An itch at the back of my neck reminded me that we were violating the second most secure airspace in the country. At any moment, we might either be detected or simply reported by someone with a cell phone and a quick touch. The Presidential TFR reached out for thirty miles. My only hope was to get clear of the TFR without going high enough to be seen by anyone who cared.

I had no idea whether fighter jets routinely patrolled when the President went on tour. If they did, this could easily be the worst idea in the history of bad ideas.

Amazingly, I found myself settling. I flexed my fingers to allow blood back into the tips and adjusted my sweaty grip on the yoke and twin throttles. I had yet to move my hands from the throttles to the prop controls, but we were operating at a power setting so low that the RPM was controlled by the throttles. I adjusted power to synchronize the throbbing engines.

I found another highway, a city boulevard. It brandished light poles and transmission lines, but I reasoned that no one builds condos and office towers in the middle of a street. I followed a string of automobile tail-lights west.

"Tell me when I can turn north."

"You're good now."

I watched for the next major road. A broad boulevard approached. I turned to follow it. Light poles rose from a grass median. I skimmed just above them.

Traffic flowed in both directions beneath us. I could only imagine what they thought. The noise from the airplane had to be terrifying. I had no way to look back and see if anyone freaked out enough to cause an accident.

"Dee, do you see the radio stack? And the transponder at the bottom?"

"Yes."

"Turn the knob on the left all the way to Off."

"The radios are already off."

"I know that. Turn the knob."

Andy reached for the panel and turned her wrist. I took it on faith she had done it right. By feel, I reached for and flipped on the avionics master switch. The entire radio stack came alive except for the transponder.

"Hand me my headset, please."

She did better. She found the headset on its hook behind my seat and lifted it over my head, wiggling the cups comfortably onto my ears. The noise reduced dramatically. She gently moved the boom mic into position.

"Top of the panel," I said. "Press the button that says Comm 2."

She touched the audio panel control, then found and put on her own headset. Her voice reached me through the intercom.

"What's on Comm 2?"

"Guard," I replied. "Emergency frequency. If anyone finds us, that's how they'll try to call us. Pray no one finds us."

The highway angled to my right, but suddenly offered a new option. A swath of darkness shot under us. I glanced down just long enough to register a glitter at the center of the irregular darkness. A river.

I heaved us left. We wallowed through a turn. Too much bank, and we would stall. I let the aircraft swing a wide arc until the river parkway fell in front of the nose. Then a right turn put us on a northwesterly track to follow this new path.

I had no idea how far this would take us, but every minute put another mile and a half between us and the apex of the President's protected airspace.

Up to this point, I had flown without lights. Over the winding black void, I needed forward light. I flipped on the powerful landing lights. Black treetops became gray mounds. The landing lights made us more than visible to anyone ahead and below, but they also increased my chances of spotting and reacting to transmission lines or cell towers.

We jogged left and right as the river parkway cut a swath through Detroit's northern suburbs. A set of wires forced me to jerk the aircraft higher, and for a split second the stall warning horn chirped. I added power. The wires sliced under us. I pushed the nose back down again. The airspeed quickly shot up to one hundred knots. I pulled the throttles back again until we wallowed between eighty and ninety knots.

The parkway that provided sanctuary for our escape suddenly split. The dark swath narrowed and took a sharp turn to the left, heading south-west. Back into the city. A much smaller swath angled north between carefully planned suburban housing. I took the turn to the right. It paid off when, a moment later, a small lake appeared. I dove for the water and leveled off less than ten feet above the surface.

The lake didn't last long, but as we shot out the north end and I rose to clear unseen obstacles, a much darker countryside presented above the nose. The dense city fell behind us. I felt a measure of relief.

"Aircraft at low altitude over Stoney Creek Lake, this is Raptor Two One, identify yourself."

Electric panic shot through me.

The radio voice shattered my calm and my hopes.

"Aircraft exiting Stoney Creek Lake northbound, this is Raptor Two One, you are being intercepted. Identify immediately."

Andy sent me a look that reflected my own stark fear.

73

"Who is that?"

I glanced at Andy. "Air Force, probably. F-16 or F-22. Either way..." I shook my head.

Game over.

I eased the throttles forward and lifted the flaps. After briefly settling, the Navajo responded with a shallow climb. I let the speed increase to one hundred knots but did not go to full power. Something told me not to make any sudden moves.

"Raptor Two One, we copy. We are an unarmed civilian aircraft. We will comply. Repeat, we will comply."

I scanned the black sky above us but saw nothing. A serious tingle down my spine said they were behind me, although they had to be flying a weave or circling because there was no way a military fighter jet could stay in the air at my speed.

"Unidentified aircraft, squawk two six two niner, climb and maintain three thousand. Fly heading three six zero. Do it now."

"Transponder is inoperative," I lied. I wasn't entirely sure why. "Out of niner hundred for three thousand. Three-sixty on the heading."

"Identify and say type."

Cold fingers gripped my guts. We were caught. The black spiral that began with Andy's Academy ejection and had spun out of control through this horrific night reached its full and deadly climax. They had to know we were the aircraft that broke a dozen Federal Aviation Regulations at Coleman A. Young Airport. They must have been tracking us all along. I'd been a complete idiot to think we could evade and escape.

My arms felt weak and shaky. Tunnel vision threatened to close in. The full measure of my blunder pressed in from all sides. The pilot of the fighter jet tracking us had weapons that would reduce us to flaming debris in a matter of seconds. Our only hope lay in giving no cause.

I looked for and found agreement in Andy's eyes.

"Raptor Two One, this is Piper Navajo One Tango Whiskey. I am accelerating to one three zero knots, climbing to three thousand, heading three six zero."

I slowly pushed the throttles forward to the stops. As if relieved, the engines sang out their normal potent note. The airspeed needle quickly settled on one hundred and thirty knots. I fixed a five-degree up angle on the nose. We climbed rapidly. Free of terrain dangers and able to tear my eyes from the path ahead, I searched the sky above and around us. Still nothing. It didn't surprise me. It would have been impractical for high-speed jets to fall into formation with us. They could easily see me on radar and by now with their own eyes.

I realized the landing lights were still on. Rather than switch them off, an action potentially interpreted as an attempt at evasion, I added the red, green, and white position lights, the rotating beacon and the aircraft strobe lights.

Any moment, I expected the intercepting aircraft to instruct us to divert to Selfridge Air National Guard Base somewhere behind us on the shore of Lake St. Clair. This time the security vehicles meeting us would ensure that we were blocked.

"When we get on the ground, we'll disappear," I told Andy. "If we can get the door open before they get to it—"

"No. Stop."

I looked at her. She shook her head. "We're done with all that. This needs to be made right."

I didn't share her faith, but I had no argument for her. She settled in her seat.

The altimeter touched three thousand feet. I shifted focus to the one and only thing that could keep this disaster from overwhelming my senses.

Flying.

I set the power for economy cruise, closed the cowl flaps and adjusted trim.

"Level at three thousand, three sixty on the heading," I reported to my unseen escort.

"One Tango Whiskey, stand by."

I rolled the autopilot heading bug to match my course. With the power set and the aircraft trimmed, I punched on the autopilot heading and altitude hold. I could have hand-flown the numbers, but the fighter interception unnerved me. Extra help from the autopilot might prevent an unintended wrong move.

Silence on the radio felt like weight on my ears. We cruised the night sky above a sea of lights. I could not keep myself from searching the windshield and side windows in vain for the fighter jet and his inevitable wingman.

A minute passed. Then two.

Andy threw me a glance full of unasked questions. She seemed reluctant to speak, even though her intercom did not broadcast over the radio.

I returned her unasked questions with a shrug lacking answers.

"One Tango Whiskey, stand by to copy."

Here it comes.

I grabbed my mini clipboard from the side pocket and pulled the attached pen free of its Velcro mount.

"Tango Whiskey ready."

"One Tango Whiskey, proceed on course. Squawk VFR. Frequency change approved. After landing, call this number." He read off a phone number, which I jotted down, scarcely recognizing my own writing as the ramification of his words sank in.

Proceed on course?

I read it back to him, then waited. There had to be more. We were the object of his training, a genuine full-fledged violator of the sacred airspace that follows the President everywhere he goes. On the heels of an attempted assassination, we were Target Number One. Low flying. Off radar. Evading. Intercepted. Caught and locked on.

What the hell?

Silence followed us through the night sky. Seconds became a minute. Then two. Then the radio spoke once more.

"Buddy, you need to buy a lottery ticket. This is your lucky night. We're outta here."

I had no idea how to answer. The frequency fell silent. We cruised on the steady hum of the Navajo's engines. I was afraid to touch anything.

Andy turned to me.

"What just happened?"

"I have no idea."

74

The wheels touched pavement after what felt like the longest flight I'd ever made. We rolled out on the narrow blacktop of Runway 27 at Putnam County Airport in Ottawa, Ohio. I had to peel my left hand from the control yoke. My arms and legs felt like rigid cable. We taxied back and turned onto the small airport ramp at the mid-field point. A single light illuminated the self-serve gas pump. I maneuvered to park and killed the engines, lights, switches, battery and magnetos.

Andy and I pulled off our headsets and sat without moving.

The decision to fly to Ohio came slowly. Left to our own navigation without explanation by never-seen Air Force fighters that scared the hell out of us, we slowly returned to Plan A—return to Virginia. Getting there meant getting to the other side of a Presidential TFR that I wanted no part of. I assumed that the phone number I had been given would be the angry air traffic control tower at Coleman A. Young International Airport in Detroit, if not the furious head of the FAA himself. The specter of another revocation of my pilot's license loomed in my head, but it paled beside the fact that my wife more than likely occupied the top of the FBI's most wanted list.

When the shock of being released by the fighters cleared, I rolled the heading bug to a westerly course. I remained at three thousand feet. I switched on the transponder and set the VFR code of 1200 as instructed. I monitored the Guard frequency in case someone had a change of heart and ordered to land.

No one spoke to us.

Just short of Lansing's airspace, I turned the autopilot heading bug due south and crawled out of my stupor. We needed fuel. I wanted gas at an airport that didn't require contact with air traffic control. An airport that, at this hour of the evening, would be unattended. I wanted to put my feet on the ground, fuel in the tanks and my arms around Andy without someone asking if they could get us a car, help with a tiedown or be of any other service. I wanted no one to take note of our N-number.

Several candidates popped up on the iPad. Putnam County Airport rose to the top of the list.

Pilot-controlled medium intensity runway lighting guided us to a landing. In fifteen minutes, the runway lights would shut off until the next pilot clicked the mic five times the way Dorothy clicks her magic shoes. The Airport Facility Directory warned of agricultural activity, but I failed to find the signs of crop dusting such as a row of chemical tanks or parked trucks. A large hangar housed the fixed base operation office near the east end of the rectangular ramp. A row of tiedowns sat empty. Scattered hangars were closed and secured for the night.

"Give me your phone," Andy said. She held out her hand.

I pulled the pieces from a Velcro-flapped pocket and turned them over to her. She handed back the protective cover. She snapped the sim card and battery in place, then pressed the power button to bring the phone to life.

"What's that number?" she asked.

I read ten digits to her from my notepad. She tapped it into the screen. I started to point out that she was about to speak to some aviation authority when she touched the speaker icon and I heard a phone ring. Once. Twice.

"This is Leslie. I know where you're going. I'll meet you there."

"Leslie?" I asked the phone Andy held between us. Andy touched the red button to end the call.

"That was a recording," she said. She dismantled my phone again.

My mouth hung open. Andy handed back my phone parts, along with a questioning look.

"Dee, are we on the same page here? Did a pair of Air Force fighter jocks about to blow us out of the sky just pass us Leslie's cell number and then peel off like we were lost tourists? Do you have any idea what kind of wheels need to turn to make that happen?"

"I have a pretty good idea. And I think I'm starting to see some pieces of all this fit."

I waited. Andy unbuckled her seatbelt.

"And?"

She simply asked, "Do you want coffee?"

75

I gassed up the airplane. Andy walked across the ramp to the entrance to the fixed base operation. A moment later she returned and dangled a key from her fingers. She told me the key fit a Buick Roadmaster parked on the other side of the building, an airport crew car. She swiped my wallet from my back pocket and lifted out two twenties.

"I'm going for coffee and food."

"And I will love you forever if you succeed. Don't be gone long. I just used the Foundation credit card for the gas." I didn't need to explain what that might mean to someone trying to locate us.

She returned fifteen minutes later with two tall coffees and a bag from Wendy's. We loaded everything into the airplane and took off.

I climbed with the lights on but returned the transponder knob to the Off position.

"I think I know but tell me again. What difference does that make?" Andy asked after I pointed it out.

"My good buddy Arun knows everything under the sun, including when the new ADS-B requirements for aircraft go into effect. That's the next generation of air traffic control, where aircraft talk to ground stations and to each other using transponder signals carrying GPS data. He had the airplane outfitted just after we bought it."

"Are you telling me that controllers and other airplanes can't see us?"

"We won't show up on the box in the cockpit, but ATC can still pick up a primary radar return."

"How safe is that?"

"It's a big sky. We'll operate VFR at a legal altitude. It's safe. The problem with turning it on is that it not only sends our altitude, position, and speed data, it sends the aircraft ID, the color of the pilot's eyes and the hotness of the copilot, which in this case is off the charts. Next thing you know, we'll have every Lothario with a pilot's license after us."

Andy creased the corner of her lip and gave up a dimple, if not a full smile.

"What do you make of Leslie's message?"

Andy didn't answer immediately. She gazed at the sky ahead. Stars filled the windshield above a horizon splashed with clusters of smalltown lights.

"We haven't talked since I spoke to her at the Bradford Inn. I sent her a text about seeing Mrs. Palmer, but she didn't comment. She said she was in D.C. and I assumed she was busy. And then the Academy blew up in my face."

"Yeah…and I kinda told her to go to hell."

Andy looked at me. "Are you thinking we can't trust her?"

"Your Mrs. Palmer didn't seem to think much of her."

"*My* Mrs. Palmer?"

"Just sayin'…"

Andy squinted at me. I avoided her displeasure by leveling off the airplane and setting up for cruise.

"What *are* you thinking about Mrs. Palmer?" I asked after making fine adjustments to the power and props.

"That she's either dead at the hands of the sniper, or she set me up to look like the sniper. Neither case is good."

"So, you don't think she reached out to Homeland Security? You think she lied about all that?"

Andy shrugged. "No. She must have called. How else would RCMP have tipped to the van by the river? Beyond that, I don't know anything for certain."

"Here's what I know for certain," I said. "I'm starving. The captain has turned off the seatbelt sign. The cabin crew is now free to serve dinner."

76

I drank too much coffee too fast. Despite promising myself I would sip it sparingly, I finished it off apace with the burger and fries Andy picked up in Ottawa.

By the time we touched down on Runway 22 at Culpepper Regional Airport two hours and forty minutes later, my bladder sang an aria for every bump we hit. I made the second mid-field turnoff and quickly spotted exactly what I wanted. Using more power than usual, I taxied at high speed to the first turn and hurried to the far end of the ramp. A row of tiedown spots welcomed transient airplanes. I turned into the last spot, adjacent to a small grove of trees.

I set a record getting out of the airplane. I dashed off the end of the asphalt and picked my way into the trees for blessed relief. Halfway through the endeavor, headlights swung onto the ramp and lit me up. A car cruised across the empty ramp and pulled up beside the Navajo just as I wrapped things up and double-checked to ensure I had zipped.

I jogged back to the airplane and found Andy facing Special Agent Leslie Carson-Pelham. Tension hung between them. Leslie's hands were empty. Her weapon remained holstered. Keeping things casual, I moved to within reach of Andy.

"Did you just pee in the bushes?" Leslie asked. Not the question I expected, but in the dark, her expression was difficult to read.

"Better than in my pants," I said. "Dee? You want to go? At this time of night, I doubt the FBO is open."

"Before I answer that, let me ask Leslie a question. Are you here to arrest me for shooting at the President of the United States?"

"Did you shoot at the President?"

"No."

Leslie shrugged. "Then I'm not here to arrest you."

"Then yes, I need to go." Andy hurried around the tail of the airplane. "If he turns around, shoot him."

"No problem," Leslie said.

I smiled at Leslie, who smiled back. "That's how we keep the romance alive."

77

Leslie drove. Andy claimed shotgun. I rode in the back. The small Jeep resembled the one Leslie rented in Coeur d'Alene, except this one was black. The rear seat geometry challenged my knees.

Leslie pushed past the speed limit while she talked. The combination made me slide to the center of the rear seat and stare intently at the winding road illuminated by the Jeep's headlights.

"About an hour before the shot was fired, Mrs. Palmer called a contact at Homeland Security. I only know this because she set off alarms that rippled all the way to the sniper task force."

"What did she say?" Andy asked.

"I was only told she alerted her contact to a flaw in the security plan for the President's rally."

"How did she gain access to the security plan for the rally?"

"I'm not sure she did. Could have been her own analysis. Far too many details of these rally plans leak from the President's campaign staff. Or it could have been through channels using her security clearance."

"Security clearance?" Andy asked. "How high?"

"High."

"The nice lady that makes the pies has a security clearance?" I asked.

"I wouldn't underestimate her. Anyway, she also gave Homeland a rough outline of some theory about bullet weight. I don't know what that's—"

"We do," Andy said. She explained the theory to Leslie.

"Wow. Talk about minutia. Did you review her data?"

"I did," Andy said. "It appears to hold up."

"Appears?" Leslie looked sideways at my wife.

"If the numbers are all correct. If she's not just reading tea leaves. What happened after she alerted Homeland?"

"Protocol dictates taking it straight to the President's Secret Service detail. I heard it bypassed the detail and went to The White House Chief of Staff. Either way, somebody determined that the show must go on."

"You're telling me they ignored a credible threat? That's insane."

"Again. I'm not part of the White House inner circle. That's the scuttlebutt. This administration doesn't welcome advice from the experts when it conflicts with their intentions. All I know for sure is that someone alerted the RCMP, who tipped off the Windsor Police Service, who followed the tip to a van parked on their riverfront which contained a Barrett rifle with a clean shot at the backside of the President. Oh—and you, Detective."

"Not my finest moment," Andy admitted.

"Yes, we'll get to that. What I found more interesting was the video which is now playing non-stop on just about every news channel except the stinkers on the far right." Dark eyes in the rearview mirror flashed a mischievous sparkle. "The video shows the Commander-in-Chief stumbling through a pair of oversized American flags and doing a Chevy Chase impression on the stage at his rally. If it weren't for the fact that it saved his life, it would be comical. Well...it is comical. But there's no question that it saved his life."

"And cost the life of someone else," Andy said.

"That too. The thing is, I watched that video closely. He's just walking, and it sure looks like one foot gets caught...except there's nothing there. And his foot is raised like it's caught on something, so he's not tripping on a stage seam. Any idea how that happened?"

The eyes in the mirror found me again.

"The hand of fate?" I offered.

She laughed. "Right. The White House has already issued a statement —I presume it came from Air Force One while it was still in the air—that the President heard a shot fired and dove for cover. He also gave an audio interview to Fox describing his split-second decision and athletic prowess in detail."

"Um...there's a bit of impossibility in that. Speed of sound. Speed of the bullet," I said.

"And the fact that the sniper fired from half a mile away using a suppressor," Andy added.

"How do you know he used a suppressor?"

"Because I was on the other side of the river. I did not hear a shot."

"Well," Leslie smiled, "let's not muddy the spin cycle with facts or science. The media that favors the President credit his unerring sixth sense. He told Fox that people are now calling him superhuman."

"People cannot possibly believe any of this, can they?" Andy asked.

"My goodness, girl. What time capsule did you just fall out of? Of course, they believe it, although largely dependent on party affiliation. By the weekend, the incident will be a sketch on SNL. And on the other side of the aisle, the NRA will probably give him an award." Leslie tossed a glance to the mirror again. "I think I have a solid idea of what really happened. And what happened shortly afterward at the headquarters of the Windsor Police Service. Word got out that they had the shooter, and then they didn't. It seems there's some confusion on that point."

"Which is unlikely to be cleared up any time soon," Andy said. "How did you hear about all that?"

"I'm still part of the sniper investigation team, remember? Although... maybe not for long..."

"How did you know those fighters would pick us up?" I asked.

"I put two and two together when a report came in that a certain two engine airplane departed Coleman A. Young International without clearance and may have violated the protected airspace around the President. Figured it had to be you."

"That incident will prove justified if we can find out what happened to Mrs. Palmer," Andy said, again coming to my defense.

"Yes. Mrs. Palmer. When did you talk to her?"

Andy explained, then asked, "How did you know we were coming here?"

"I've been in D.C. the last few days. Because of the Renner Stemple shooting and...other downslope shit. I was at the office tonight following the play-by-play. When I figured out that you two were involved—and were more than likely on that plane belonging to the Foundation you work for, Will—"

"What? How did they know—?"

"The F-22 pilots took a lovely photo of you."

"Jesus. I never saw them."

"In any event, there's only one place you would go for answers, Detective. Mrs. Palmer's. More so, now that you're saying she has gone missing. Can I assume you don't think her vanishing act was voluntary?"

Andy answered with a question. "Do you think she reached out to the wrong person at Homeland? Someone who may have been involved in this sniper case from the start?"

"That's one possibility. If that is the case," Leslie said, "and that's a big 'if,' then this situation just got a whole lot uglier and a whole lot more dangerous. For all of us."

"I don't think Mrs. Palmer told me—us—everything."

"Is that why you came here? You think maybe she left something behind—something that will point us at the shooter?"

Andy didn't answer.

"That would suit me," I said. "I don't like people thinking Andy took that shot."

"Yeah...about that..." Leslie hesitated.

"What?" Andy and I asked simultaneously.

"You're not going to want to watch the news tonight," Leslie said to Andy. "Or for the rest of your life, if we don't figure this out."

Andy leaned back against the headrest and uttered a word I've heard from Pidge a thousand times.

"I'm not sure how it got out, but Reuters got their hands on an image of the badge that the Windsor Police confiscated. And the AP tied it to a leaked story out of the FBI Academy about your...um...*issues* there. There's a lot of speculation."

"So much for due process," I muttered.

"Speculation in the media? Or in the task force?" Andy asked.

"Both."

"I have a question," I said. "What is Mrs. Palmer's security clearance? And why does she even have one?"

"It's high," Leslie said.

"That's what you said, but why? For a consultant? A part-time instructor at the FBI Academy? She's not a full professor. She may be a walking ballistics encyclopedia, but how does that translate to a top-level clearance?"

"Rumor is that it anchors with DOD."

"Department of Defense?"

"That's the rumor."

"What the hell does she do for the Department of Defense?" I asked.

"I would assume it has to do with bullets. They use a lot of them, you know."

"If she has such a high clearance," Andy said, "and did top secret work for DOD, then I would think that someone might be a little concerned that a government asset who just saved the President has gone missing."

"Or," Leslie said, "someone high up became concerned that this government asset took too much interest in the sniper case, and that's why she is now missing."

None of us spoke. Leslie eased off the accelerator and rolled to a stop. In the dark, I didn't recognize the location. Then I saw the narrow lane that struck out through a field and into black woods.

"Well, we know she's not home," Leslie said, "Let's check this out."

She eased off the brake and turned onto the twin tire tracks leading to Mrs. Palmer's home.

"Wait," I said. Leslie stopped. "One more question. What kind of mountain did you move to get an F-22 jockey to pass me your phone number?"

Leslie turned in her seat and looked at me.

"That's classified."

"You had to go through someone higher up, right? Leslie, who do you answer to?"

"Classified."

"And what do they know about me?"

"Classified. And right now, highly unsettled." I started to speak. Leslie correctly read my rising anger and lifted her hand to calm me. "Will, you better than anyone understand the position I'm in. It's the position Director Lindsay adopted to protect you. That hasn't gotten easier with him gone. Just the opposite."

"I'm getting a vibe here, Leslie. Government assets don't really get treated as assets."

"You came to the government. Not the other way around. No one forced you. I have done my level best to meet your wishes. I pulled strings you cannot imagine. I got Andrea into the Academy. I kept you hidden. You want to have this discussion. Fine. Yes. Let's have this discussion. But not now, okay? I'll buy you a beer after we convince the world that your wife didn't shoot at the President."

"I think you should stay here, Leslie," Andy said. She unbuckled her seatbelt and opened her door.

"What? No. I'm going in with you."

"Yes. But Will and I should go first. We'll scope it out, make sure it's clear, and then you can drive in. Wait here. Give us a chance to look things over without tipping our hand."

Leslie looked at Andy, then at me. "Five minutes."

"Fifteen," I said. "I want a look in her shed and her workshop before we do anything."

Andy shot me a glance that asked if I had something on my mind, but I said nothing.

"Ten." Leslie countered.

"Twenty," I said, "now that I think about it. What's the rush? She's not home. There's no way she beat us here, assuming she's even alive."

"Give us twenty, Leslie," Andy said, "please."

"Fine."

I followed Andy out of the Jeep. Leslie killed the lights and the Jeep engine. Andy slipped her arm around my left arm.

Fwooomp! We vanished.

"Twenty and counting," Leslie admonished us.

I gently pushed the ground. Andy and I floated upward. Leslie's upturned face disappeared into the Jeep's interior.

Andy shifted her position beside me. She wrapped her arms around my left arm. I felt her come close to the side of my head. She whispered.

"Did you just declare a vote of no confidence in the only real friend we have?"

I gave it a beat to create the impression that I had a clue.

"Probably."

78

We ascended in what passes for silence on the fringes of the Shenandoah National Forest, which is anything but silent. The steady whistling chirp of crickets broadcast natural tinnitus into my ears. An owl declared territorial claims, which made me wonder if the night hunter sensed an intruder in its airspace. Distant yelps betrayed a coyote family at play or celebrating a kill.

Languid air hung all around us. Detroit, while cool, had been warm for October. The President had lucked out with the weather for his rally, if not with anything else. Virginia felt like summer, warm and humid, right up until *the other thing* wrapped up Andy and me with its signature cool sensation. The scent of fall and open fields teased my nostrils.

I fumbled with a BLASTER, then aimed it in the direction dictated by the path worn between the road and Mrs. Palmer's property. We left Leslie and her Jeep behind. For the moment, at least, she did not follow.

"Keep us low," Andy whispered. I didn't know if she had a tactical reason for the request or if she simply preferred not to deal with height. I dropped my arm and brought us down until we skimmed forward between the tire tracks. Tall grass and an occasional thistle brushed our feet.

We crossed the hayfield bordering the road and entered the wooded portion of the property. My eyes adjusted. A bright sliver of moon splashed light between the shadows.

The trail wove back and forth between trees and around mounds of earth until it opened on Mrs. Palmer's expansive yard. A bright security light on a pole between two sheds created stark shadows. A pair of incandescent lights on either side of her front door established a warm and welcoming glow on her sidewalk. Behind the house, a yard light painted the trees under which I had dozed while Mrs. Palmer and Andy conferred.

If not for the row of sheds or the black surrounding forest, the property would have looked domestic and suburban.

"House," Andy whispered.

I took her to mean that we should orbit the house and check the windows for signs of life.

"Do you think she's alive?"

"I don't know."

We crossed the lawn and approached the front of the house. A large window overlooking the lawn showed us the interior sitting room and a portion of a dining room. Light inside the house emanated from the kitchen.

Nothing moved inside.

I cruised the perimeter. We passed dark windows with drawn shades.

"We need to get inside," Andy said after we finished a full orbit of the house.

"Hang on. There's something I want to see first. In the big shed. And then her workshop. You okay with that?"

Andy twisted beside me.

"As good as any place to start."

AT THE BACK of the big shed, I returned to where I found the sliding door latched from the inside. I squeezed my fingers through the gap in the door and pressed them on a rusted hasp.

I pushed. I felt *the other thing* flow outward. The gap was too narrow to allow me to see inside. I gave it a minute, then planted my foot against the ground at the base of the big door. I pulled.

The door resisted for a second, then jerked loose. I heard something fall to packed dirt inside the shed door. On rusty rollers, the big door slid sideways.

Fwooomp! I reappeared and completely forgot that Andy hung on my arm. She dropped awkwardly and stumbled backward. I grabbed her before she fell.

"Give me a little warning next time," she said. "What's in here?"

I pushed the big sliding door open far enough for the two of us to slip inside.

Moonlight filtered by translucent plastic panels in the metal roof revealed a fleet of vehicles.

"You name it," I said. "We got a minivan. A station wagon. That looks like a UPS truck. That's an old Postal Service Jeep. A gravel truck. Damn. She's got a Kenworth tractor in here. What the hell does she do with all this stuff?"

"She does a lot of ballistic testing," Andy said.

"Right. But I'm not seeing bullet holes."

Andy and I squeezed between vehicles crowded bumper to bumper inside the shed. We worked our way inward. I started counting but gave up at the eleven I could see, knowing more were parked farther ahead and at the fringes.

The shed had the signature smell of machinery. Oil and dirt and grease. The scents told me that these vehicles functioned. I dropped to a knee and scanned in all directions.

"What are you doing?" Andy asked.

"The tires. None of them are flat. This isn't junk. Look at that limo. That's practically new." A stretched Lincoln Town Car wedged itself between the UPS truck and the shed wall. Sheen in the paint attested to recent cleaning.

Andy climbed in the open side door of the UPS delivery truck. I followed, expecting to see nothing in the dark interior. A roof made of translucent Fiberglas produced a twilight effect.

The interior offered nothing significant to my eye. A rack of shelves on either side provided space for packages. A center aisle ended at the big rear door. Andy knelt and examined a pair of brackets bolted to the floor.

"What are those for?" I asked.

She shook her head. I thought she was finished, but she stepped to the rear door and began running her hand across the door panels.

"What are you looking for?"

"Not sure…"

Whatever it was, she didn't find it. She led me back out to the shed floor, past the UPS truck to a parked Winnebago. She tapped the motor home on its side and sent me a questioning look.

"She did say she drives everywhere," I offered. "Maybe she likes to vacation on the road."

We moved forward. The back of a gravel truck loomed on my right. Andy stopped.

"What?" I asked.

She examined the truck. Painted blue, with a decal bearing the name Hagel Trucking LTD on the driver's door, the truck looked ordinary enough. Andy turned around and pressed past me to examine the rear.

"Spellman. That was Idaho, right?"

"Uh-huh."

Andy curled a finger and beckoned me to join her.

"Look," she said. "Idaho plates."

Andy moved to the rear quarter of the truck, looked up, then dropped to a crouch.

"Will...what's wrong with this picture?"

I tried to see what she saw. The light in the shed ranged from poor to miserable.

"I give up. What?"

"Look at the springs."

I dropped to a crouch beside her.

"Ah-ha!" I exclaimed as if I had a clue what I was looking at. "What?"

"This truck has a full load of gravel. Did you notice?"

"Sure." I hadn't seen any such thing.

"Well, with a full load like that, why aren't the springs compressed?"

"You notice shit like that?"

"All the time. It's how we pull over trucks that are overloaded. This truck is completely unsprung. Like it's empty."

I stood up and backed away. She was right about the load.

"Looks like a full load to me."

"Can you get me up there?" Andy asked. She joined me and wrapped her arms around mine.

Fwooomp!

I tapped my toes and sent us into an ascent, then grabbed the top of the tailgate. I felt Andy move beside me.

Thump! Thump!

"It's fake!" she said. "Feel it."

I reached for and rubbed my hand on the load of gravel in the bed of the truck. *Damn.*

"That's—what is that? Fiberglas?"

"Okay. Then what's under a fake load of gravel?"

I heaved us over the tailgate. We rose until I was able to reach for a wooden crossbeam beneath the roof. The false mound of cream-colored stone below us betrayed no entrance or hatch. I pushed back down again until our feet touched the dirt floor.

Fwooomp! Andy didn't wait for me. She hurried down the side of the vehicle to the driver's door. She pulled the door open and climbed in. I caught up to her kneeling on the seat, examining the back of the seat and the back of the cab.

"I don't see access. There's got to be something."

She spent a few minutes tugging on the seat, studying the cab, looking for anything amiss. I climbed up on the running board and leaned behind the cab. The dump box fit snug against the back of the cab, but I could not see anything suggesting an access panel.

Andy dropped down to the floor again and regarded the cab, the box and the vehicle as a whole.

"There has to be a way in," she said.

If there was, we weren't finding it. Not in the darkness of that shed. For lack of a better idea, I moved around to the front of the vehicle. The big grille loomed high over me. Trucks like this, up close, can be intimidating.

"Dee..." I said slowly. "I feel like I've seen this thing before."

"You think this was in Idaho when Spellman was shot?"

"Maybe. Or else I'm superimposing it on my memory. You know who would know? Leslie. She has that video I shot out there."

"Okay. Now I'm with you. I really want a look in the workshop."

WE MADE the trip between sheds hidden in *the other thing.* The workshop lock gave away easily. I hesitated before opening the door.

"Alarms?"

"Maybe. Might be motion sensors. We should...you know..."

I grabbed the door jamb to anchor us and then pushed the shop door open.

"I want the lights on," Andy said. "It shouldn't matter with nobody home." She twisted at my side. I heard her hand pat the wall until she found a panel of switches.

Flourescent lights flickered to life above a long, low workshop.

"Holy crap," I said. "Earl would kill to have a shop like this."

Having grown up on and around farms, I expected the usual country workshop. Dirt floor saturated with oil and grease. Rust and spider webs on old tools hanging on the walls. The smell of gasoline and engine oil.

Mrs. Palmer's workshop might have been a clean room at the Rolls Royce jet engine manufacturing plant. The acrylic floor wore a gloss like spilled water, doubling the effect of the overhead lights. Pristine white tables spread out tools I recognized and devices I didn't. One wall mounted an array of widescreen displays stacked by twos. I counted eight. In a corner to my right, what looked like a dental x-ray machine hung from the ceiling on a sturdy articulated arm. A lead smock hanging on a wall hook confirmed my assessment. Several tool chests on rollers lined up on another wall.

The room ended at a glass wall. On the other side of the wall heavy machine tools lined up in two rows. I'm no machinist, but I recognized an industrial-sized lathe, a CNC machine, a drill press that looked like it could bore out an engine block, and a series a saws and grinders. Overhead, a track-mounted block and tackle rig promised to handle heavy lifting.

The woman could build anything she wanted with this kind of equipment.

"Do you see any cameras? Motion detectors?"

"Above the door. Looks like a camera. If it is, there's no one here to watch it. If she's alive, she's still on the road. It would take her hours to get here. I don't know about motion detectors."

"Let me down." Andy unwrapped her grip and released. I felt an electric snap run up my arm, a mild version of the funny-bone tingle generated by an inadvertent bump on the ulnar nerve. She reappeared and dropped lightly onto the balls of her feet. We both listened for an alarm. Nothing happened.

We resumed exploring. Andy, fully visible, strolled an aisle between two rows of workbenches. I remained vanished and used the edge of a countertop to push for height, then propelled myself on an angle across the room using light fixtures to adjust my path.

"I don't see weapons. Do you? Or bullets?"

Andy shook her head but pointed at a bookshelf. "She has manuals. A lot of them." Andy picked up a complex piece of something full of shine and edges and holes. "Will, I think she made this. Whatever it is. Over there. See it? That's a 3D printer."

"Looks like a valve for a cooling system. Or something fluid. Hydraulics, maybe. Look at this. She has a water tank. I presume for ballistic testing. I don't see any tropical fish." I spent a minute admiring the tank, the way it was built. Clever touches allowed for a weapon to be discharged under protective cover, and the spent round to be retrieved from the far end of the tank using an articulated strainer. "Dee, did you tell me she built her own cappuccino machine?"

"Designed and built it. I'll show you when we go inside. Here. Check this out." Andy pointed at an array of compact equipment joined to bulbous lenses.

"What is that?"

"I'm not sure, but my best guess is these are high-resolution cameras. Very high resolution. Like maybe military grade surveillance and recon cameras." She held up a boxy device with a large fish-like eye on one side. "It has mounting points and digital outputs."

I pushed myself in the direction of the glass wall. Tables with scanners and microscopes and digital devices stood a slim chance of attracting my attention over an industrial lathe or powerful drill press. The next room looked far more interesting.

Just as I pushed myself away from the ceiling and planted my feet with the intention of reappearing so that I could explore the machine side of the shop on my own feet, Andy called me.

"Will, what is this?" She held something up. "One of your flying magazines has been on the bathroom counter at home for about six months. I swear this is in an ad on the back cover. It looks just like it. Lord knows, I've seen that ad enough times."

She had my attention. I pushed the wall to glide back to the center of the room and face her across a tabletop.

"It's a servo," I said. "Specifically, a Garmin autopilot servo."

"You sure?"

"Absolutely. We have them in the Navajo. They're incredibly precise." In addition to the servos, the bench contained wires, soldering equipment, and precision tools for electronics. "What the hell is she doing with…" The look on Andy's face stole the words from my mouth.

Andy wore an expression of bursting enlightenment. She stared simultaneously at me, at a point a thousand yards past the back of my head.

"*Good lord,*" she whispered. "She told us." Her focus reeled in sharply and fixed on me. "She told us, Will."

"Told us what?"

"*Remove the human factor and perfection is achieved.*"

"What are you talking about?"

"Servos. Cameras. Those vehicles. Bullets that fly a perfect flight path without human error. She removed the human factor, Will. That's why a sniper will never be found at the scene."

Derrick Spellman's head exploded again in my mind, and with the absolute certainty painted on my wife's face, I knew how and why. I knew what lay under the false load of gravel in a truck that had been parked not far from Spellman's suburban home.

Neither of us had the opportunity to speak. A high-pitched voice dripping with sweetness and charm called through the open shop door.

"Andrea Stewart, come out here!"

79

A ndy turned for the door.

"You're not going out there!"

"I am," Andy said. "She knows I'm here, which means she saw me poking around but not you." Andy pointed at the camera.

"How the hell did she get here so fast?"

"Probably the same as us."

My head rushed the logistics. Mrs. Palmer had to drive out of Windsor and back to the American side. Then to an airport not affected by the TFR. Custer, perhaps, near Monroe. Or Toledo. Then what? A charter? Too easy to document. A discrete friend with a plane? What did Andy say?

Mrs. Palmer knows people.

Andy derailed my dot-connecting. "Leslie will be here any second. Stay close to me."

She walked back to where we'd broken into the workshop.

"Wait!" I heaved myself down the aisle, hooked the end of the table and pulled up behind Andy. I grabbed the waist of her jeans and gave a double tug. Ready for a tow.

"You don't have to be *that* close."

"Yes. I do."

She held out her hand.

"Give me your phone." I pulled the device pieces from my pocket and released them over her palm. They snapped into view. She reassembled the phone, powered it up and swiped the screen. She poked the voice memo app and pressed Record, then handed back the phone. "Put this in your pocket."

I wrapped my hands around the device to make it disappear, then tucked it away, careful not to touch the screen.

She glanced in my direction. I instantly regretted that she could not find my eyes. That we could not telegraph something wordless, deep and true. I rubbed the small of her back. She nodded, drew a breath, and stepped stiffly through the door. I floated after her like a balloon tied to a toddler's belt.

Mrs. Palmer waited for Andy in the center of the flat, empty yard. She resembled a human boulder, largely for her rigid, hunched posture. The blue-white security light above the sheds did no cosmetic favors. Shadows chiseled the rolls and folds on the woman's face. Her eyes floated in pools of black. The tilt of her head, slightly forward, signaled malice. Her stare and stance chilled me.

I checked her hands. Empty.

The sweet pie-serving charmer spoke to my wife in a dainty voice that could have just as easily offered seconds with ice cream and sprinkles.

"Are you armed, Detective?"

Andy walked to within ten yards of the woman and held out her hands.

"Turn around, please, dear. All the way around."

I released my grip. Andy performed a slow three-sixty. When she completed the turn, I hooked her jeans again.

"And now your phone, please. Don't bring it. Toss it."

"My phone is in Windsor. See?" Andy patted and smoothed her shirt. Her snug jeans demonstrated the absence of an embossed phone outline.

Mrs. Palmer said, "No matter. If you have one, I'll find it."

"I thought you didn't fly."

"Yes, well, self-absorbed bimbos like you will believe anything if it's served up with a smile and a dash of inferiority." The tone remained sweet despite the assertion. I felt as if lightning had flashed, a cheap special effect in an old black and white movie, a trick that revealed a skull's rictus grin beneath a mask of skin. She leaned to look past Andy. "Where's that husband of yours? I assume he flew you here."

"He did. But with the whole country looking for me, he was afraid to let the airplane be found on the ramp. He's staying in the air until I finish with you."

"That's unfortunate. He'll run out of fuel."

Andy ignored the implication.

"It was you."

"Oh, my." Mrs. Palmer chuckled. "Are we doing this? Closure? A confession before I kill you?"

"Is that the plan? Kill me and play the Jack Ruby role?"

"No. That would be a bit on the nose, a little too much attention for my tastes. No, you will die alone and disappear. The D.B. Cooper role."

"I don't need your confession. I've seen your workshop. Those are high resolution reconnaissance cameras on your workbench. And aircraft autopilot servos. Congratulations. You removed the human factor. You created a sniper weapon that cannot miss. A sniper weapon without a shooter. Without a spotter. Add facial recognition software, a measure of artificial intelligence, and the system is fully automated. Am I right?"

"Still looking for teacher to give you a gold star?"

"The vehicles in your shed. Extraordinarily ordinary. You mounted your weapons inside benign vehicles the way the D.C. Sniper used the trunk of his car. Figuring out that part was easy. But that's not what I meant when I said it was you."

Mrs. Palmer waited, then lifted her palms. "Are you planning on telling me or do we stay tuned until after the commercial break?"

"The Academy. *It was you.*"

Mrs. Palmer laughed. Shadows on her face and neck jiggled.

"Dearie, I picked you out the moment I saw you in my first lecture. The hottie with a free ticket into the FBI. Too easy to guess how you pulled that off. I might have simply ignored you, but you handed yourself to me on a silver platter by coming here to play teacher's pet with your files and your questions. I couldn't resist."

"You loaded restricted files on my laptop when I used your bathroom." Andy spoke softly, slowly—the exact opposite of my hammering pulse.

"How many blondes does it take to screw a light bulb into their own eye socket and see the obvious? One—hair color aside—you. You with stolen files on your laptop. You with your fingerprints on the rifle that shot the President of the United States."

"In *your* van."

Mrs. Palmer laughed again. The sound echoed off her sheds and carried the quality of a shriek.

"My van? My van? Your DNA is all over that van. Your hair. Along with a few personal items I borrowed from your home. There's nothing of me in a distinctive van seen on countless highway cameras between your little farm and Detroit. God only knows where you stole it from. Now it's your turn to confess, Detective. How are you here and not in custody? I *handed you* to Homeland."

"They let me go."

"BULLSHIT!"

The rage in her outcry jolted me. I tensed, ready to throw my arm around Andy and make her vanish.

Contrary to all common sense, Andy took a step toward the woman.

"STOP!" Mrs. Palmer threw up a hand. She swallowed her fury. The saccharine tone resurfaced. "There are three separate weapons tracking you, Andrea. The trusty Barrett, of course. A Steyr SSG 69. And Finland's little-appreciated but worthy SAKO TRG 42. This entire zone has been digitally mapped and modeled. You have been identified as a potential threat. Come within ten feet of me and all three are programmed to turn that empty head of yours to shrapnel. Oh, and don't make any sudden moves, dearie. Or try to run. Or pull a gun out of your panties. Same deal. Poof." She smacked her fingers together, then made them bloom.

I tugged twice on Andy's jeans. Time to get her out of the line of fire.

Andy shook her head sharply. A message for me that I did not like.

"Empty head? Bimbo? Is that what this is about? Mrs. Palmer, are you fixated on me?"

"Don't flatter yourself, honey. I got over your type a long time ago. You're nothing more than an opportunity to create chaos. Misdirection."

"A patsy?"

"Please. No one worth their investigative salt will credit all the sniper shootings to you. Just the one that counts. You're meat for the media feeding frenzy. Since you brought it up, look at how fast and clumsily they dealt with Oswald—and that was back when journalism pretended to rely on facts. In an age when any asshole with a phone and a thumb is a journalist, the media won't get past your bust size, let alone within shouting distance of the truth. Don't feel bad. The sound bites will be delicious. '*Bombshell assassin. She screwed her way into the FBI Academy. Cheated. Got kicked out. Assassinated the Commander in Chief.*' I'll cook up a few memes myself. You'll be dragged through the meat grinder while I sit back and dish out seasoning. Seeing people swallow such unfiltered nonsense would be funny if it weren't so tragic."

"The killings—"

"YES! Can I get an AMEN?" The shout stole her breath. She bent forward to regain it. I tugged on Andy's waist, but she shook her head again.

Mrs. Palmer huffed air into and from her lungs.

"I fixed what could not be fixed. No amount of truth, no amount of debunking, no amount of exposing the con budges the needle. My God, a sitting congressman thought he could murder his wife! And do you know why? *Because he believes his own bullshit.* These people, Detective, have no shame, no moral compass, no concept of hypocrisy. Never mind objective self-assessment. They have *nothing* up here." She stabbed a finger at her temple, digging the nail into her flesh. "When utterly insane crap drools out of their mouths and gets lapped up by their echo chambers, *they fucking believe.*"

Andy took a step.

Mrs. Palmer tipped her head and spoke calmly. "Detective, I am absolutely sincere when I tell you that if you come any closer, you will never know what hit you. Do take me at my word."

Headlights bobbed in the trees. Beams defined by humidity saturating the night air swung across the lawn.

"And who would this be?" Mrs. Palmer asked politely, as if the Ladies Christian League had come to call with a cargo of bakery and unfinished knitting.

"That would be the FBI, ma'am."

"Ah. Special Agent What's-her-face." Mrs. Palmer shifted to an exaggerated whisper. "*You can't trust her, you know. There's a dark conspiracy afoot in the FBI. Deep state. Goes to the highest levels. Trust no one. All will be revealed!*" Mrs. Palmer laughed. "It's astonishing how easily people abandon logic and eat that shit up. Your own senator from

Wisconsin went on national television and proclaimed that he did not trust the CIA or the FBI. In one stroke, he severed the public from truth. He demolished faith in established institutions while he steered the pathetically stupid to oceans of internet baloney. I would add him to the target list if he hadn't just tripped over his own inflated dick and got himself arrested for treason."

Misty headlights broke into view. Fifty yards away, Leslie drove the black Jeep into the yard. Projector beam illumination painted Andy and Mrs. Palmer. The woman's utter lack of concern chilled me. A heartbeat later I knew why.

A sharp *Clang!* followed by metallic grinding stopped the vehicle in its tracks. I recognized the sound and instantly saw the result. Smoke curled from under the Jeep's front bumper.

Mrs. Palmer clapped her hands.

"Right through the engine block. I told you. This entire zone is mapped and modeled. Fully automated targeting. Didn't hear the shot, did you? I build my own suppressors, you know. Now watch this. I don't have to lift a fin—"

"LESLIE, STAY IN THE CAR! OVERWATCH!" Andy shouted.

Except for the whisp of smoke, nothing moved. The Jeep's doors remained closed. Darkness and slivers of reflection obscured the windshield. I could not see Leslie behind the wheel.

"Cute," Mrs. Palmer said. "Fine. I don't care. Let her rot in there. The vehicle and its occupant have been tagged as a threat. The moment she pokes her head up or steps out..." She mimed another explosion with her hands and fingers. "Head shot. You...you're tagged as a mobile *potential* threat. Your actions dictate your fate."

"My actions?"

"Don't approach. Don't make any sudden moves."

"What happens if you lose optics?"

"Still trying to be the class know-it-all?"

"Indulge me."

"You mean if you disable my cameras? You'd have to find them first. Good luck with that. And even then, blinding my optics won't help you. Once you've been acquired, the software builds a three-dimensional predictive model of you. If optics fail, the system calculates and projects the likely move you would make in the next one hundredth of a second and delivers a round downrange. Poof. Targets in Afghanistan used smoke and sometimes dust to foil our sniper teams. My weapon drops them through the smoke. The target along with any ancillaries that go non-optical."

"If I simply vanish, the bullet goes where it thinks I will be by the time it reaches me. Clever."

My guts went cold. If what Mrs. Palmer said was true and I made Andy disappear, she would be dead before either of us flinched.

I searched the perimeter of the yard, testing the idea of finding the hidden weapons. The only vehicles in sight were the shot-up cars and trucks parked weed-deep in a line beside the largest storage shed. Any one of them could provide concealment for a weapon, a compact space vastly reduced by eliminating the need for a shooter. Black forest surrounded the lighted yard. A dozen weapons could be hidden in darkness, in vegetation, in mounds of dirt, or nesting in fake Fiberglas rocks akin to the false load of gravel in the shed. Fifty feet away. Or a mile away.

We never should have walked into this.

Panic clawed up my spine. Andy maintained the cool and calm that slipped my grasp. She said, "Smart. Which is what I don't get about you, ma'am."

"That I'm smart?"

"Insulting me. Calling me a bimbo. Treating me like a blonde joke. You can't possibly have suckered yourself into this insanity on the back of pedestrian self-esteem issues."

Mrs. Palmer chuckled. "That is the worst attempt at reverse psychology I've ever witnessed. Proves my point about you. What? I'm just some sad Lifetime movie character? I'm a serial killer because I've been the butt of every fat joke in the book? Is that it? You think I suffer a tragic lack of self-esteem because I have the body of a troll who got fucked by the Pillsbury Doughboy? Want to know a secret? Want to know what I see when I look in the mirror?" She took a step closer to Andy and leaned into her words. "I see you, Detective. In the mirror. I see you. The whole package. The never-ending legs. That ass. The skinny little waist. Those tits—my god, woman, do you even wear a bra? Please. Spare me the kindergarten psychology. If God's joke on my body motivated me, I'd shoot people like you instead of conspiracy theory dimwits."

"To what end?"

"Seriously? Tell me the collective IQ of the nation didn't rise after I offed that moronic bitch in Texas. Tell me democracy wasn't preserved by killing that loudmouth, Boulton. Tell me I didn't spare us another Oklahoma City bombing by ending Spellman."

"I get it. Cleansing the fringe. Some of the feds probably root for you, secretly. Up to the point of shooting at the President, of course."

"Can you see a bigger threat than—?" She froze. She tipped her head slightly. "Did you say '*at* the President?'"

"You don't know?"

"Know what?"

"You missed."

"My weapons don't miss."

"This one did."

Mrs. Palmer shook her head. "See? This is what I mean. That's the best you have to offer? That's sad. This needs to end." She took a step toward Andy.

Too damned close!

Andy sensed it, too. She matched Mrs. Palmer's step in reverse.

"Oh, that's right. You would have been in the air. You flew here. Not a charter. Too easily traced. And there isn't an airline connection on the planet that could get you here that fast. Something private and light— except you had no WiFi on the plane—most don't. No…that's not it. You ditched your phone. The one we spoke on had to have been a burner—and you ditched it. Even a burner would ping a line pointing here. Your personal phone, I'm sure, never left this property for the same reason."

"This is like watching a child learn to use the potty, Detective."

"No phone on the plane. No news. A bit overconfident, don't you think? Did you plan to get a good night's sleep and savor the assassination aftermath on the *Today Show* over coffee and pie? Too bad. You missed the President's call-in to Fox News."

"You're embarrassing yourself."

"He called from Air Force One. He claims he heard the shot and dove for cover. There's video. He dives out of the bullet's path. The miss killed a civilian attending his rally."

"Ridiculous. Even an imbecile knows that hearing the shot is impossible. Again, Detective, you make my point about women like you. I suppose it hardly matters." She heaved an exaggerated sigh. "I have had a long day and I'm tired of you. I'll clean you up in the morning. You and the FBI hiding in that car. By then, I have no doubt she will grow impatient and think she's faster than a bullet. She will be wrong."

"She already called for backup."

"No. She hasn't. Cell disruptors. My lord, you *are* dim."

"Your system failed in Detroit. It killed the wrong person." Andy turned slightly. Her elbow nudged me.

"You have no idea what you're talking about. But let me show you. I will walk toward you. When I get within ten feet, your head will simply… burst. If you run, you will be shot. If you attack me, you will be shot. Any sudden move, you will be shot. Your body will never be found. Your guilt will be posthumous and permanent. Good-bye, Detective."

Mrs. Palmer stepped off. Andy tensed.

"Her feet, Will. *Her feet. Stay low!*"

Mrs. Palmer hesitated.

"Excuse me?"

It dawned on me what Andy meant.

Someone needs to be removed from this equation.

Someone needs to vanish.

But not Andy.

Caught without a power unit in hand, I used my grip on Andy to shift to her right for a clear shot. The lateral move was awkward and too damned slow. Still, I saw what I had to do. Mrs. Palmer's ankles filled my mind and—

GO!

The core muscle controlling *the other thing* tightened like wound wire. My lungs compressed. My vision blurred. My body swung into a prone position. A jolt propelled me past Andy, downward. The same jolt that drove me into Jimmy Flatley. I covered the distance in an instant, faster than my mind could form words to express it.

My outstretched hands collided with the woman's ankle flesh. Soft and fluid, hard to grip. My fingers nearly slid off. The impact might have knocked a lighter woman off her feet. Mrs. Palmer gasped.

"*What in heaven's—?*"

I glanced up to see Mrs. Palmer's face, a pale moon riding the night sky. Shock ignited white-eyed flares deep in her shadow pool eyes. She glared down and tried to kick free of the unseen entanglement.

I tightened my grip. I pushed the levers in my mind hard against the stops.

FWOOOMP!

Her flesh in front of my face vanished.

The sound that followed startled me. Three impacts in close succession—a clipped wet raspberry.

Something splashed and spattered the gravel. Something damp dropped on my back, my neck. Behind Mrs. Palmer, glistening matter fell like oversized drops of slow summer rain. Some of the goo resembled the sweet strawberries little Laurel sold. Some of it was larger. A quarter rind of cantaloupe. With hair.

What the hell?

The fight I anticipated from Mrs. Palmer did not materialize. I expected her to kick and struggle. I expected curses. I made ready to heave us both skyward—as far from Andy as possible.

"Will!" Andy cried out. "Are you okay?"

Me? I'm not the one in trouble here.

"Will!"

"I'm fine, I'm fine. I got her."

The composition of Mrs. Palmer's ankles changed. Tight muscles beneath her flesh relaxed. Hard tendons softened.

"Will. Let her go. Just…let her go."

My arms remained outstretched, my grip rigid.

"Are you crazy?"

"Let her go."

I glanced back to see if Andy had expanded the distance between her and Mrs. Palmer. She hadn't.

"Move back."

Andy took two careful steps.

I coiled my arms, then pushed and released. An electric snap coursed my fingers. The woman reappeared. Most of her.

Mrs. Palmer's headless body dropped in a heap.

80

I may have shrieked. I slapped and clawed the ground to get away. A mistake. Panic sent me sailing upward, backward over Andy.

"What the hell?"

Andy remained frozen. She did not lift her head to look for the sound of my voice.

Debris surrounding the body glittered in the stark light. Blood the color of deep red wine fanned out from Mrs. Palmer in three directions and coated what I can only describe as *chunks*. The concave piece with hair lay several yards away. There were teeth, still set in a jawbone. In the center of it all, released to the embrace of gravity, Mrs. Palmer's body had collapsed on itself. Her legs bent awkwardly under a torso that landed largely on its back.

I slapped my pockets for a BLASTER, found one, and pulled it free. My hands trembled. I attached a propeller and gripped the unit. A shot of power stopped my ascent. A second shot returned me to Andy.

"I'm here, Dee." I spoke softly, but she jittered regardless. "I'm here. Jesus. What just happened?"

"You made her disappear."

"That was the idea, but—"

"...and all the ancillaries..."

Andy stared at the motionless corpse.

"What?"

"She didn't account for it, Will. She never imagined the possibility that *she* would vanish. Who would? It's an impossible variable."

"You mean—?"

"Yes. Her weapons interpreted her disappearance as a loss of optics."

"What the hell? What if one of her damned cameras shorted out?" We talked like two people who had diffused a bomb after guessing which wire to cut. Nervous. Breathless.

"I bet they were networked…"

"…so losing one camera doesn't cause a misfire."

"That's how I would have done it."

"Jesus…"

"Disappearing translated to a threat."

"I never meant—"

The words ran out. My mouth went dry. I fought paralysis and listened for the next heartbeat.

Cricket calls filled the abrupt silence. Had they been there all this time, rubbing their leathery wings together while Mrs. Palmer taunted Andy? I had no idea, but they owned the night now.

"Her weapons are still live." A mildly hysterical chuckle slipped from Andy's lips. "I guess there's good news."

"What?"

"I'm not dead, too."

I wanted to scream. I dug deep for calm that my wife had over me in spades.

"I can't make you disappear, Dee."

"No. For heaven's sake, no. We've seen what happens."

"Can you move?"

"I guess." Andy pried her gaze from the bloody heap. She glanced from side to side. "I made it from the workshop to this point. I think the system—her programming—allowed that. Not her. Not manually. I didn't see Mrs. Palmer operate any kind of remote. Did you?"

I reluctantly studied the body on the ground. "Her hands are empty."

"My actions determine my fate. That's what she said anyway."

"So?"

"So, I guess it all depends on how I move."

"*Guess?*"

"Do you have a better idea?"

"Hold on. Just—just wait a minute. Let me try and find the damned things."

"That could take a week."

"*Wait! Just*—" I struggled. "This can't be—there has to be—Dee, there has to be *something*—"

Andy waited patiently. I think if she could have seen me—my frustration, my desperation—she would have patted me on the hand or touched my cheek.

She knew I had nothing.

"I'll be fine." She sighed. "I love you. Do me a favor and go up high. Please. I don't want you hit if…you know. There's no telling which direction the bullets will come from."

This can't be happening!

I froze an *I love you* on my lips, terrified that uttering the words would call cruel fate down upon us and give me a lifetime to remember the declaration as my last.

Andy turned around.

I stopped breathing. My pulse pounded.

She took a step.

Another.

I felt the weight of inhuman eyes on my wife. Eyes capable of measuring the thickness of an eyelash. Attached to those camera eyes, sophisticated servos micro-adjusted the aim of three—or maybe more—deadly sniper rifles. Target crosshairs rode Andy's face, her temple, her hair, moving as she moved. Rifles that would not, could not miss.

Andy took the longest walk of our lives.

Three steps back inside the workshop I collided with her. I swept her into my arms.

FWOOOMP!

The cool sensation never felt so good.

81

A ndy thumped the driver's side window of the Jeep.

"Don't move!" she warned Leslie who sprawled awkwardly across the front seats.

"Andrea? Will?"

"We're here," Andy said. "Whatever you do, don't lift your head. This whole property is a kill zone. Stay where you are. See if you can roll down the window. We'll get you out."

Leslie's pale hand emerged from spilled-ink darkness inside the Jeep. She patted her way across the dash until she found the start/stop button. One push and the dash lights flashed to life. She reached for the driver's power window control and failed. Too far.

"Do the passenger side. We'll come around," I said.

I pushed away from the stalled Jeep. Thin smoke, smelling of burnt oil and ground metal, rose from beneath the chassis. A pulse of the BLASTER moved Andy and me to the rear of the vehicle. I flew a tight radius around the liftgate and glided until I stopped myself by grabbing the passenger-side mirror.

"We're here," Andy said.

Leslie looked up through the open window as if expecting to see us.

"Is she still out there?"

I glanced at the heap in the center of the yard. Even in death, the woman did not possess recognizable human dimensions. Her claim to Andy that she dismissed issues about her size and shape rang hollow to me. I felt a flicker of sadness, or maybe pity, for Mrs. Palmer. The fleeting emotion conflicted with simmering hate and boiled away quickly, a drop of water on a white-hot burner.

"Yes, she's still out there."

"She's not a threat, but the threat is still very real. Will, can you get Leslie out?"

I reached through the window. "Raise your hand."

Leslie lifted her arm. I clasped her wrist. At my touch, she reciprocated with a tight grip on my arm.

Fwooomp!

Leslie vanished and uttered a groan. "Thank the Mother of Christ! I have had a cramp in my thigh for the last ten minutes."

I lifted. Leslie thumped her way through the open window. Her final kick propelled us away from the Jeep. We drifted through the thick air. I rotated her into position beside me. She faced the opposite direction, thanks to the hand-to-wrist grip joining us. On the other side, Andy squeezed my left arm, to which I had transferred the BLASTER.

"What the hell just happened?" Leslie asked.

"Let's get away from here," Andy said.

"Jesus, is that her?"

"Yup."

MINUTES later we reached the roadside. I expanded the safety margin by cruising half a mile down the moonlit two-lane before easing to a stop beside little Laurel's fruit and veggie stand. The girl wouldn't be making any more deliveries to the pie-making lady.

There it was again. That pang of pity. A flash, and then gone. Bioluminescence from the lightning bugs cruising tall grass on the side of the road lasted longer.

Fwooomp!

Andy settled. Leslie staggered, massaging her thigh.

"Are you okay?" Andy asked.

"Are you?"

"Uh-huh."

Andy turned her back to Leslie, reached in my pocket and pulled out my phone. She satisfied herself that the recording had not stopped, then touched the screen, closed the app and pocketed the phone. She turned back to Leslie.

"It was her. All of it. The sniper. The Academy."

Andy gave an abbreviated version of the events in Mrs. Palmer's yard. I watched for traffic. Leslie listened without interrupting.

When Andy described my role in making Mrs. Palmer vanish, Leslie fixed an appraising gaze on me. Something about it launched me back to the hangar. To the moment when she rested her hand on her thigh and said, *I have to ask.* The way she looked at me now suggested that she no longer needed to ask.

"We should go," I said. "We have enough battery to reach the airport. Maybe you can call the cavalry and we can get my wife off the evening news. Gather round."

Andy moved in close. I extended my hand to Leslie.

She remained rooted to the pavement.

"What's wrong?" Andy asked.

Leslie shook her head. She planted her hands on her hips and dropped her gaze to the pavement.

"Ugh!" she cried out. She spun around and walked five paces away, then spun again to face us. "Don't go back to the airport."

"What?"

She shook her head.

"Don't go back to the airport. Go anywhere else. Not there. They're waiting for you."

"Who's waiting for us?" I asked. Spiro Lewko's smirk materialized in my mind. "Leslie, exactly who's been pulling the strings here?"

"Look, Will, Andrea, I like you. And that's about to royally fuck me over. I tried to tell you. Since Director Lindsay was killed, I've been out here on my own. I've been hiding things—hiding you—from people who really, *really* should never know about you."

"Your new boss?" Andy asked.

"Worse. So much worse."

A billion dollars. What percentage of that would it take to buy an FBI agent?

Leslie remained immobile in the dark. Moonlight revealed her face, but not her thoughts. I eased my hand toward Andy and closed a grip on hers, thinking this might go bad very quickly.

"You never should have come to the FBI. Director Lindsay might have pulled this off, but you cannot imagine the stress he was under. The stress the whole Bureau has been under with this administration. The Bureau has been a target, with Director Lindsay in the ten ring. When you showed up, we had long discussions about what it meant to bring you into the picture. He thought he could do it. We both knew how it might go so very wrong. When he was—when—" She put a fist to her lips for a moment. "When he died, the rug went out from under everything. I thought I could salvage the program, but with him gone they tore into his work. They tore into everything he did."

"Who?" Andy asked.

Leslie huffed a disgusted sigh. "Sebastian Manor."

"Who?" I asked.

"He's with the White House. One of the 'in the room' people around the President."

"Wait...what?" I asked, thrown completely off my train of thought. "That little guy? The one who looks like Himmler?"

"Looks and thinks," Leslie said. "He has a particular hard-on for the FBI."

"Damn," I said, "that's not who I was expecting you to say."

"Who did you think it was?"

I waved off the question.

"What authority does some White House twit have over the FBI?" Andy asked.

"Manor got himself named Special Counsel to the Acting Director of Homeland Security. He got top security clearance and full access."

"I remember," Andy said. "It made the news. He didn't qualify, but they gave it to him anyway."

"He's been digging. A lot. He's been hurting people. Ending careers. Will, you asked what mountain got moved to call off those F-22's? It wasn't me. It was Manor. He found something. I thought I scrubbed Director Lindsay's files, but Manor found something. And he came to me. That's why I've been in Washington. He called me in."

"What are you saying?" Andy asked.

"Manor knows. I'm not sure how or how much, but he knows

enough."

"You lied to us," I said. "All that crap about how you deduced it was us in the plane out of Detroit. About how you figured everything out. You lied about the whole thing!"

"I didn't—" Leslie stopped herself. She lifted both hands as if to sculpt something in the air between us. "Will, I didn't lie about what counted. About what I knew. I lied about *how* I knew. That's all."

"Dammit, Leslie! There's a huge difference between having our backs and doing the bidding of some White House power player!"

"Use your head, Will. Am I doing Manor's bidding by tipping you off?"

"She's right, love." Andy squeezed my hand.

Leslie took an urgent step toward us.

"*Manor wants personal control.* My God! In his fascist dreams someone who can do what you can do, Will, would be an autocrat's perfect weapon. He wants you. That's why you can't go back to the airport."

"They're waiting for me?"

"No. They're waiting for her. As of tonight, Manor zeroed in on your wife. I'm sorry, but Mrs. Palmer landed you in his pocket, Andrea. I'm sure she never intended it. But she gave Manor the leverage he needs."

"To do what?"

"I can't be sure, but my guess is that he plans to take you into custody for shooting at the President. He can hold that over you to force Will's full cooperation. I'm sorry—"

"You came here to trap us."

Leslie leveled a flat look at me.

"Those were my orders, yes. Manor sent me to hold you at the airport. But I called an audible by coming here with you because I saw a chance to get you out from under him."

"But we know the sniper was Mrs. Palmer," Andy said, "or at least her machines."

"Yeah," I said. "Frankly, we don't need your help. We've got—"

"All that evidence in her workshop," Andy interrupted.

I forced myself not to look at Andy or the phone in her hip pocket.

"And I will do my best to get the truth out. But don't kid yourself. Until then, the story will be whatever story Manor tells—a story that is currently a media wildfire. But if you're in custody and he has a chance to quietly clean up all of this…" She waved her arm in Mrs. Palmer's direction. "You won't have any control over that story."

"What the fuck, Leslie!"

Andy released my hand and stroked my arm.

"It's not her fault, Will."

"I'm sorry. I'm telling you this now so you can run. Manor needs Andrea under his thumb. It's how they operate. Everything is transactional. Manor has his eye on becoming Secretary of DHS for the 'new order.' He thinks you're his ticket."

I felt it again. The spiral. Just when I thought we were pulling out.

Andy took my hand and squeezed. One step ahead of me as always, because the next float in this shitty parade announced the collapse of life as we knew it, the very thing that crazy Lillian had predicted on a street in Des Moines and again in a motel in Florida. A catastrophe that was one hundred percent my fault.

"I saved that son of a bitch's life tonight," I muttered.

"I don't think the President is in on it."

"Seriously? How could he not be?"

"You don't understand Washington, Will. Manor is a shark swimming in the President's tank. He's threatened by everyone else in the tank. He'll secure his own position before he risks giving an advantage to anyone else, including the President." Leslie walked back to us in the dark. "His self-interest may be the only thing going for you. But it won't last. Manor won't stop."

Andy and I traded glances. I found weary resignation in her expression.

Leslie said, "You need to go. I'll do what I can to hold him off. You can't go back to the plane. Or home. I'm sorry. Don't call me. Get rid of your phone."

Moonlight ignited moisture diamonds in her dark eyes. The pain I saw on her face robbed me of anger straining its leash.

Andy walked to Leslie and pulled her into an embrace.

I gave them a moment, then eased my wife away, bit the curses on the tip of my tongue, and—

FWOOOMP!

—vanished.

EPILOGUE I

82

The blonde crossing the gilded lobby of the Pennsylvania Avenue hotel topped the list of women I'd seen in a venue where power attracts the attractive. She moved with lithe grace in a green silk dress. I wasn't alone watching her. Men coming, going, or just hanging around this junction of money and influence stole and stored quick portraits. Women spied on her, too, assessing. The dress label. The shoes. The skill with which makeup had been applied, or in this case, largely not.

She found a wide, low chair and sat down, placing an expensive-looking bag beside the chair arm. She leaned back and crossed her legs, then rested her arms in parallel on the chair, gazing ahead through round, tinted glasses.

"That's my second favorite hair color on you." I floated into the narrow space behind her chair.

"I think it's gaudy," Andy said. "Like this hotel. Seriously? Painted gold beams? They're steel beams, people. That's all."

"I like that dress. It might be my new favorite."

"We're not keeping it." I wondered if the fact that we'd stolen it from a high-line boutique enhanced my appreciation. "Or the shoes. Or the bag. It all goes back."

The petty larceny of our life in hiding—stealing supplies for our move against Sebastian Manor, living in the clothes we wore until the need for something more elegant prompted the theft of a beautiful dress—these crimes were nails on a chalkboard to Detective Andrea Katherine Taylor Stewart. One of the first things she stole was a pen and pad of paper from a convenience store. From that point on she kept a meticulous log of each stolen item and its owner, including the pen and pad of paper.

"Right," I said. I crouched and spread the top of her handbag. I checked for traffic and wandering eyes. All clear. I lifted out a black capped cylinder and stuffed it into my shirt where it vanished.

One can Krylon spray paint, black, Ace Hardware, Alexandria, VA

I pulled the second item from the bag and added it under my shirt.

One plastic squirt gun (painted black), *Ace Hardware, Alexandria, VA*

"I followed him up to six."

"Room number?"

"613. He went in alone. His date's not here yet."

"Do you think his boss comped the room?"

Andy laughed. "I doubt it. But on the bright side, I don't think he told his boss about you. If he did, he'd either be in trouble for losing control, or he'd be in the penthouse as a reward." Andy thought these things through more in depth than me.

"Alright. I'm off. I'd kiss you, but…lipstick. I do like the color."

"Ugh. Too red. Not my shade. Please don't drop him." Everything about the plan ran against her grain. She worried with good reason. I intended to implement a few ideas I had not discussed with her. Ideas she would have vetoed out of hand.

"Promise."

"Will, I mean it."

ANDY and I had operated on a shoestring for two days. We spent the first twelve hours getting our bearings and staying away from people. Random televisions in poorly lit bars and near-empty diners reported that the nation's law enforcement agencies had identified Detective Andrea Stewart as the prime suspect in the attempted assassination of the President. On the first day, Andy obtained the blonde hair dye job at a tiny salon in a low-income section of the District of Columbia. I sweated out the hours-long process by floating outside the storefront window, ready to make her vanish at the first sign of police, but the stylists inside were too busy admiring Andy's lush locks to connect her with the photo of the assassin flashed in the media. The salon had a television, but the owners and patrons preferred daytime courtroom comedy to Fox News, who covered the story as if Rupert Murdoch had a stake in the manhunt.

We spent the first night preparing and planning. Andy used cop magic and a public library to locate Sebastian Manor's apartment in George-town. Upon arrival, we performed a neighborhood reconnaissance, worked out an entry and an exit to his building, and assessed the traffic patterns of his neighbors. A little after nine p.m., Manor let himself in, but we agreed that we weren't ready to make a move. We broke into a garage across the street and curled up in the back of a Land Rover parked inside. The next morning, we followed Manor to the White House and enjoyed the thrill of sailing past the Secret Service's extensive security. A young woman waited for him outside the West Wing entrance. Things grew interesting when she led him away from the officers at the security check-point. We dropped down in time to overhear him confirm an evening liaison with the woman, a tryst at the hotel on Pennsylvania Avenue. Dumb luck, but dumb luck happens, just like the shit at the other end of the spectrum. We adjusted the plan, picked up the spray paint, squirt gun, extra batteries, and an outfit for Andy to wear inside the hotel. In an elegant dress and stolen shoes, Andy followed Manor into the hotel and up to the sixth floor where she smiled at him as she walked by Room 613. I bristled at her proximity to him, but she insisted.

"He wasn't looking at my face," she commented on her return.

Elevators are problematic for me. Armed with the squirt gun and paint, I found and used an open stairwell to ascend to the sixth floor.

Fwooomp!

I reappeared outside the door to his room. I pulled a cap we had stolen—

One Washington Nationals ball cap, 7-Eleven, Alexandria, VA

—down as far as possible and adjusted a pair of cheap sunglasses.

Sunglasses, 7-Eleven, Alexandria, VA

The original plan had been to invade his apartment in the middle of the night. The technique had worked on the billionaire, Bargo Litton. Waking someone from a deep sleep by putting a gun to their head carried the advantages of surprise and disorientation. Breaking into Manor's hotel room offered an unexpected opportunity, but also presented a problem. I can use *the other thing* to sever a deadbolt, but key card locks are magnetic. Doesn't work the same.

"So just knock," Andy had suggested.

I did.

Footsteps hurried to the door.

The door swung open. Sebastian Manor, Special Counsel for the Secretary of Homeland Security, grinned for the would-be sexual partner he expected. He held two loaded champagne flutes.

I shouldered the door open and pushed the black plastic gun against his forehead.

"Close your eyes if you want to live. Do it. Now!"

The words, the scene, the unreality paralyzed him. He blinked. Then he snapped his eyes closed. The door slammed behind me. I flipped the internal locks.

"Keep 'em shut, or I'll blow a hole in that wormy head. Turn around."

Manor complied. I clamped a grip on his bony shoulder and shoved him into the room.

"Stop. Toss the champagne."

"What?"

"Toss it!"

He flinched. The flutes sailed across the room, distributing a fan of golden liquid. One shattered.

"Now listen to me as if your life depends on my every word. I don't need to leave you alive tonight, but I don't need to kill you, either. Do you understand?"

His head bobbed emphatically.

"Eyes stay shut. If you see me, your life is over. Got it?"

"Got it."

"Take off all your clothes," I commanded, veering off script.

He hesitated. "What?"

I pushed the gun against the base of his skull. "If I have to repeat myself, I will shoot you and get it over with. Clothes. Off."

His shirt came off, revealing a wife-beater t-shirt. The t-shirt went over his head. He kicked off his shoes, then tugged off his socks.

Sebastian Manor owned a boyish, skinny body with a decent case of acne on his back. A dome of male pattern baldness glistened with sweat by the time he dropped his trousers to reveal tight sports briefs. He stopped there.

The woman planning on spending the night with Manor wasn't in it for his body. Skinny arms and legs, narrow, weak shoulders and a little too much leg hair told me she was in it for his position power, or because of it. Andy's assignment to intercept Manor's date and explain that she'd been replaced for the night was a mission of mercy.

"Don't make me tell you," I pressed the flat black water pistol against the back of Manor's head.

"What do you want?" He found his voice as he slid the briefs to the floor.

"I want you on the floor, face down, hands clasped behind your head. Go!"

Manor dropped to his knobby knees and sprawled beside a coffee table. He intertwined his fingers behind his head and pressed his nose to the carpet. He kept his legs tightly together. I contemplated telling him to have no fear in that department but amplifying his worries suited me just fine.

I took a moment to survey the room and found what I wanted. I grabbed the television remote. Kneeling beside Manor, I groped inside my shirt for a small roll of duct tape.

One roll duct tape, silver, Ace Hardware, Alexandria, VA

"Disconnect your hands. Good. Now take this." I placed the remote in his right hand. "Hold it."

This part made me nervous because I had to lay down the gun. For insurance, I planted a knee on the center of his back. He released a startled grunt.

I picked up the tape, pulled out a length of it, and wound it around the hand holding the remote. Over and over. To excess. When his hand looked like a silver ball, I tore off the tape end and rubbed it down flush. The end would be hard to find and harder to peel off. I stuffed the tape back in my shirt and pulled out the spray paint.

"Listen to me, you're not—"

I grabbed the gun and shoved it hard against his temple. "Go ahead! Tell me I'm not going to get away with this! Say it! Give me a reason to stop screwing around and just shoot you!"

He said nothing.

"I thought so. One more word and it's your last. Turn over. Eyes closed."

He rolled, grunting. With my free hand, I pulled out the spray paint. I shook it until the ball inside released and chattered. I popped the top off with my thumb.

"Hold still."

I aimed the spray can at his chest and let loose. He winced and shivered. I worked hard to ignore the man's full-frontal aspect.

I applied a few strokes of paint. Not my best artwork, but the obscene symbol I rendered left no doubt.

"Keep your eyes closed, shut your mouth and hold your breath."

He pinched his lips tightly together. I leaned down and sprayed his face in a steady circular motion. Not too much. I couldn't have him gagging and choking. As it was, he gasped and coughed when I finished.

"Roll over again. Hands behind your head."

He obeyed. I set aside the spray paint.

"Face down. Eyes closed. Do not move. Got it?"

He coughed and could not answer.

I stood up and hurried to the double-hung windows. I had feared they would be locked or restricted. Surprisingly, the old-style window opened. I leaned out and examined the ledge running beneath the window. The narrow concrete span, roughly fourteen inches wide, circumnavigated the building. Perfect. A man could stand on that...if he kept his cool.

I pushed the lower pane as high as it would go and stepped back. The opening would be tight for two, but I could make it work. Plan B had been to smash the whole works out. Manor's room overlooked the 12th Street side of the building, not Pennsylvania Avenue. Either way, smashing out the window and frame would have drawn attention.

One more thing.

I picked up the spray can, stepped to the nearest wall, and went to work.

He watches me
I'm the only one who can see him
He commands me to kill them all
Blow up the White House
Bomb
This one was Andy's: *No one believes me*

I filled most of two walls, added copies of the nasty symbol I had painted on Manor's chest, then wiped down the can and cap with my shirt and dropped both on the carpet.

Manor lay rigid. I stepped over him again.

"Stay as stiff as possible. Got it? Don't bend your knees. Don't bend at the waist. Stiff."

"What are you—?"

"Shut up!" I poked his head with the gun. "Stiff! At attention! Now!"

He strained to obey. His butt cheeks flexed weirdly. I clamped my hand on the back of his neck.

FWOOOMP! We both vanished. Not a moment too soon.

"Oh god oh god oh GOD! *What is this?*"

I lifted him with my left hand, pocketed the gun and pulled out a BLASTER. I pressed the butt end of the BLASTER against his head in lieu of the gun.

"Eyes closed. Stiff! Or you'll die. Only a few more minutes, then I'm gone."

"*Please don't kill me please don't kill me!*"

"Quick reminder, Seb. Shut the hell up!"

He whimpered.

I rotated parallel to his floating body and held out my arm with the power unit, aiming for the window.

Stark doubt hit me.

No way no way no way...this is not going to work.

The window suddenly looked small. I gave the BLASTER a shot of power and we accelerated. The skin on Manor's neck grew slippery under his clammy sweat. I tightened my grip and closed the space between us.

We went through the window headfirst. Trying too hard to make sure Manor fit, I banged my shoulder into the frame. The collision stopped us. I adjusted and gave the BLASTER another shot.

We sailed over 12th Street, six stories up.

"Open your eyes."

He screamed. Manor erupted into a flailing, writhing mass.

"HOLD STILL! If you break my grip, you fall. Got it?"

He froze. His entire body trembled. His breathing became a rasping, wheezing motor.

"Calm down. You'll hyperventilate."

"It's you! This is real!"

"Sorry. No. This is all a figment of your sick imagination, Seb. You've lost your mind. You think you're floating sixty feet in the air, but you're not."

"Please, please, I'll do anything. I won't say a word about you. I'll let your wife off the hook. We can cover it up. Detroit. We can cover the whole thing up. *You've got to believe me!*" I made a note to ask Leslie what, precisely, Manor had found in Director Lindsay's files. "I'm sorry! This was all just a way to—"

"To what?"

"I want to work with you! I do! This is all a misunderstanding!"

I applied power to the BLASTER. We flew around the corner of the ornate old building, level with the concrete ledge. Traffic pressed bumper to bumper in both directions on the streets below. Not far away, Washington, D.C.'s prominent monuments and buildings wore bright decorative light under a clear night sky.

"A misunderstanding? Tell you what, Seb," I said. "I'm going to put you down, and then we can discuss this."

"Yes! Yes! Anything you want! I can make it happen!"

"Don't move. This isn't easy."

I powered us to the Pennsylvania Avenue side of the building. A clock tower loomed above us. I aimed for where the ledge ringed at one of the turrets near the center of the former U.S. Post Office's signature façade.

"Lower your hands to your side."

He shifted.

We approached the curved stone turret. I eased off the power. At the last second, I stuffed the power unit into my pocket and extended my right hand to meet the gray wall. We stopped. I rotated Manor until he hung, unseen, upright in my grasp. The maneuver took some wiggling and twisting. I swung him around to face away from the building. I used shots of BLASTER to gently push him backward until he bumped the turret. He flinched. Gripping a seam in the stone, I used fingertip leverage to lower him until he stopped.

"Feel that? Under your feet?"

"Uh-huh!"

"Okay. Get ready. If you panic, you fall. Nothing I can do about it. Ready?"

"What? *What are you doing?*"

I released my grip on him. An electric snap bit into my hand.

Manor reappeared. He issued a girlish shriek. He slapped his hands against the stone and clawed for a grip. He glanced down at his toes curled over the lip of the concrete and shrieked again.

"Hold still." I hovered at the ready in case he freaked out and lost control. I wouldn't mind seeing him take the dive, but Andy would not forgive me.

Six stories below, beneath a row of American flags, the entrance of the hotel met the broad sidewalk. Cars pulled up at the curb, stopped, unloaded, then pulled away. People strolled in and out, animated by their intentions and plans. Ben Franklin stood on his pedestal near the corner, stoic in stone and apparently unconcerned about what had become of his post office.

Through clenched teeth, Manor begged. *"Don't do this! Please! You can't do this!"*

"Deep breaths, Seb. Stay calm. You don't want to lock your knees, either. Try not to faint."

White rims in his eyes projected abject terror.

"Please! Anything! I'll do anything! I have influence at the highest levels!"

"Yeah…that's the problem. Besides, you'll say anything. I wouldn't trust you, well, as far as I could throw you. And right now, my guess is that even with a good jerk you wouldn't make it to the curb. So, I'm going to spell this out for you. Are you listening?"

I tapped him on the shoulder. He flinched, wobbled, and almost lost it. He whimpered loudly and plastered himself against the turret. He clamped his eyes shut.

"Are. You. Listening?"

"Yes," he whispered. *"Yes. I'm listening."*

"I don't exist. You don't come near me or my wife. After tonight, you'll be lucky if you can influence sewer policy, but I want it clear that if I so much as wake up from a bad dream thinking you're interested in me or my wife, I will come for you, and next time I won't bother with the ledge. Clear?"

His head bobbed minutely. Tiny, desperate acknowledgement.

"Say it."

"C-c-clear!"

"Good." I pushed lightly off the wall and drifted backward. "One more thing…"

I rotated and looked down at the people below.

I shouted at the top of my lungs.

"KILL THE PRESIDENT! KILL THE PRESIDENT!"

Heads turned. It took less than a second for the first pedestrians to find Manor's pale form.

"I HAVE A BOMB!"

"What are you doing?"

"BLACK LIVES DON'T MATTER!"

A woman screamed. Figures darted from the building and looked up. Arms lifted and fingers pointed. A police officer appeared, spotted Manor, and pulled his radio to his lips.

I drew a deep breath.

"I HAVE A BOMB!"

"You son of a bitch! Motherf—"

"I'M GOING TO BLOW UP THE WHITE HOUSE!"

I reached out and tapped Manor on the chest. He jolted, wobbled, then flattened himself against the stone. Whimpering sobs broke from his lips.

"Remember what I said."

FROM OVERHEAD, I watched Andy leave the hotel. She threaded her way through the gathering crowd. She stopped briefly and glanced up at Manor on the turret ledge. The first police vehicles arrived. Traffic came to a halt.

Andy shook her head and resumed walking. She crossed 12th Street.

I maneuvered to a dark doorway ahead of her. The engraving on the pediment above the door said Post Office Department. With nearly every eye on the street upturned and locked on Manor, reappearing carried minimal risk. I caromed off the door, rotated and—

Fwooomp!

—reappeared in stride on the sidewalk and intercepted my wife.

"Naked? Really?" Andy tried to frown but couldn't conceal the smile tugging at the corners of her mouth.

"It was his idea. Nature lover."

"The poor man has it all hanging out."

"It's not that cold up there," I said. "He's just not very…you know…"

Andy slapped my shoulder. "You're having too much fun with this. And the blackface is a mean-spirited accent to the swastika on his chest."

"I thought so."

She released a serious sigh. "Do you think this will work?"

"If he doesn't fall, he's finished in D.C. Beyond that…I guess we'll find out."

I slipped my hand around Andy's waist and pulled her close. Her skin felt mysteriously soft and at the same time firm beneath the silk. My mind wandered as it always does when we touch. We stopped. I turned to face her. The blonde hair disoriented me, but in an intriguing way. I wondered if she might leave it like that. Just for a few nights.

She looked up at me and warmed my soul with a smile.

"And all that's best of dark and bright meet in her aspect and her eyes," I said.

"What the heck is that?"

EPILOGUE II

83

Andy brought me a cold Corona with a wedge of lime decorating the lip of the bottle.

"You're not having one?" I asked.

"It's a little early." She slipped onto the edge of my old lounge chair and tugged at her heavy sweater. The air on our screened porch barely reached sixty degrees in the sun on this late October afternoon. With the angle of the sun sinking lower each day, I knew we wouldn't see many more days like this.

Maple leaves in the yard amplified brilliant light from the blue sky. Few of the leaves had fallen. The mature trees blazed, giant benign torches.

It felt good to be home. Five days away, first in hiding, then in an FBI safe house, seemed a lifetime. I could never forgive the murderous Mrs. Palmer for the lives, however flawed, she had taken, or for singling out Andy in her scheme, but I admitted to Andy that another piece of her apple pie would have been heavenly. I hinted that we might include agave nectar on the shopping list, to which Andy replied that I was welcome to learn how to bake apple pies.

At least she brought me beer, even if the clock barely cleared three p.m.

My day had been spent retrieving the Navajo, which nested at

Culpepper Regional Airport longer than either of us could have imagined when we landed there a lifetime ago. The flight home cleansed me. It helped that the fuel being sucked from the tanks had been paid for by the FBI.

Mainstream media outlets made a significant story out of Sebastian Manor's meltdown and mental break. Rumors surfaced that Manor battled an imaginary magical foe who he claimed stole his clothing, painted him with Nazi swastikas, made him disappear and then flew him to the hotel ledge. He accused the husband of the police officer who allegedly took a shot at his boss. His claims were ignored by authorities who reminded the press that Manor's hotel room was locked from the inside. The story fueled a week's worth of cable news while late night comics had a field day and political leaders condemned the man's overt racism. The White House announced that Manor resigned prior to his breakdown and produced a backdated letter to prove it. The President stated that he barely knew the man while three women came forward accusing Manor of using his power over their careers to force sexual favors. I had no idea what became of Manor after the D.C. Bomb Squad evacuated the hotel and the White House, then vetted him for two hours before the fire department used their longest ladder to extract him from the building ledge.

We ambushed Leslie outside FBI headquarters in D.C. the morning after discrediting Manor. Andy remained at the top of the Most Wanted List, a situation that demanded fixing. I expected resistance from Leslie, but she welcomed the reunion. The bright smile on her face told us she had closely followed the breaking news on Pennsylvania Avenue. Manor's removal from her orbit cleared the way for Leslie and the FBI to verify and announce that a woman named Palmer was the sniper. Three days in, law enforcement had yet to determine a non-fatal way onto the woman's property, a situation complicated by sudden interest from the Department of Defense who, according to Leslie, had an embarrassing stake in Mrs. Palmer's high-tech sniper system.

Leslie secured us in a safe house while the FBI labored over an official acknowledgement of Andy's innocence. Andy's status improved when the Windsor Police Service found an automated sniper rifle mounted in a parked vehicle painted to resemble a Spectrum Cable service van. The vehicle might have gone unnoticed except for an angry cable customer who grew impatient waiting for a service call from a van sitting idle outside her building near the Detroit River. I figured it would have been found eventually, since Mrs. Palmer wasn't returning to retrieve it. Inside, another Barrett rifle's sightline remained fixed on the rally venue across the river, lined up behind a clever hatch behind the license plate. High-resolution cameras maintained a soulless overwatch through heavily tinted glass, perhaps hoping for a second chance at the assigned target.

Leslie told us the Windsor Police Service wanted an interview with Detective Stewart. Andy grew concerned.

"What did you say?"

"I said I'd forward the request to the State Department. There are protocols. Lots of red tape. It could take a while." Leslie's crooked smile signaled delight.

I had no patience for the safe house and chaffed at sitting idle while Leslie and the FBI established Andy's innocence. In the end, Leslie's efforts fell short. After multiple interviews that carefully avoided mention of my involvement, and after finally securing the machinery and vehicles Mrs. Palmer used in her killings, Andy quietly ceased to be a "person of interest." The FBI issued a press release. News networks uniformly covered the announcement, but only briefly. The scandal of a government consultant to both the FBI and the Department of Defense being identified as the sniper nudged the story of Andy's innocence aside.

On the day we gained release from what increasingly felt less like a safe house and more like custody, Leslie appeared for a final time at the bland suburban home in Alexandria. The woman does nothing to hide her affect. At the door I instantly assessed that her news was not good, even if her first words contradicted the defeated look on her face.

"The Academy board withdrew all of the charges against you, Andrea."

"There's a 'but' coming," Andy said.

Leslie nodded. "They're not willing to reinstate you."

I jumped in. "*What the—?*" Andy closed a grip on my arm.

"I tried," Leslie said. "I went to the mat. I took it to the Acting Director. To the top."

"And?" I asked.

Leslie shook her head. "He didn't put it in so many words, but it's bad optics. There's been too much media coverage. Too many questions about how you were added to the class in the first place."

"For Christ's sake, Leslie. Short memory. She got in because she almost single-handedly saved the United States Supreme Court. *And now the President!* What does it take to—?"

"Will, please. It's okay."

"It's not okay. It sucks. Maybe it's time for the damned director of the FBI to get a midnight visit."

"He doesn't mean that," Andy informed Leslie.

"Too bad," Leslie said. "I'd drive you."

Andy didn't have anywhere near the meltdown I did on the issue. I eventually reigned in my anger to give her room to express hers, but she buried her feelings, which made it worse. I hurt for her. For her law enforcement dream dashed.

I wanted someone to pay.

On the second day after our return to Essex, Tom Ceeves dropped by for a visit. He and Andy talked for nearly an hour over coffee while I conjured ways to stay busy in my garage. After I heard his big SUV start and roll down the gravel driveway, I wandered back into the house. She teased me by not saying a word until I finally blurted out the single question burning a hole in my tongue.

"Well?"

She turned to face me, lowered her chin slightly and lit me up with her green eyes. "You're still married to a detective."

Dimples dancing at the corners of her delicious lips told me there was more.

"And…?"

"And the Chief is thinking about naming an Assistant Chief. Looking ahead, he says."

"Or poking a sharp stick in the city manager's eyes."

"Maybe. I think he is having thoughts of retirement that have to do with a certain Sheriff in Bear County."

"Damn," I said. I pulled her close. "From America's Most Wanted to Assistant Chief. Not bad."

She gave me her best imitation of cheerful, but pain and loss lingered beneath the surface. She could frame the news any way she wanted, but this was still a sad consolation prize after the Academy's decision. The wound might eventually heal, but that wouldn't mean the injury never happened.

"Not yet," she said, tapping a finger on my lips. "And not a word to anyone." Her kiss came on strong and sweet.

Retrieving the Navajo helped put a period to the Mrs. Palmer chapter. Leslie promised to try and repair some of the damage done and to advocate for us, but she could not swear that every shred of our interchange with Deputy Director Mitchell Lindsay had been redacted. Nor could she deliver anything resembling a retraction or apology from The White House. After days of condemning Andy on social media and to the press, the President ignored the truth when it emerged. I grumped about it, reminding my wife that I saved his substantial ass. Failing to acknowledge the truth had the effect of leaving his ardent followers convinced that my wife attempted to assassinate the anointed leader of their world. True believers.

I found myself contemplating Mrs. Palmer's fix for that affliction. Leslie took me aside and told me the fringe media was clinging to Andy's guilt, claiming a government coverup, claiming a conspiracy. I asked pointedly if we should worry. Leslie lied and said no. She meant well.

Although the Corona Andy served lacked a twin, I lifted the bottle anyway.

"Us."

Andy rapped a knuckle against the bottle. "Us."

Looking for reassurance where we always found it.

Just as I touched the lime-tinged bottle to my lips, I spotted a silver car decelerating on our quiet country road. Andy turned her no-longer blonde head.

"Who do we know that drives a Prius?"

Oh, crap.

DIVISIBLE MAN: EIGHT BALL
October 16, 2020 to July, 5 2021

ABOUT THE AUTHOR

HOWARD SEABORNE is the author of the DIVISIBLE MAN™ series of novels as well as a collection of short stories featuring the same cast of characters. He began writing novels in spiral notebooks at age ten. He began flying airplanes at age sixteen. He is a former flight instructor and commercial charter pilot licensed in single- and multi-engine airplanes as we as helicopters. Today he flies a twin-engine Beechcraft Baron, a single-engine Beechcraft Bonanza, and a Rotorway A-600 Talon experimental helicopter he built from a kit in his garage. He lives with his wife and writes and flies during all four seasons in Wisconsin, never far from Essex County Airport.

Visit www.HowardSeaborne.com to join the Email List
and get a FREE DOWNLOAD.

PREVIEW THE NEXT DIVISIBLE MAN ADVENTURE

Please enjoy the beginning of
DIVISIBLE MAN: NINE LIVES LOST

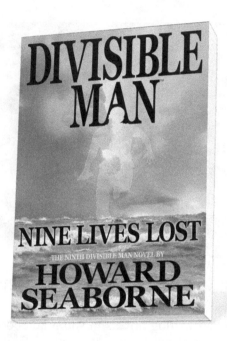

AVAILABLE JUNE 2022

A simple request from Earl Jackson sends Will on a desperate cross-country chase ultimately looking for answers to a mystery that literally landed at Will and Andy's mailbox. At the same time, a threat to Andy's career takes a deadly turn. Before it all ends, Will confronts answers in a deep, dark place he never imagined.

Available in print, digital and audio.
Visit us at **HowardSeaborne.com**

DIVISIBLE MAN - NINE LIVES LOST

TWO WEEKS AGO

Although the Corona Andy served lacked a twin, I lifted the bottle anyway.

"Us."

Andy rapped a knuckle against the bottle. "Us."

Looking for reassurance where we always found it.

Just as I touched the lime-tinged bottle to my lips, I spotted a silver car decelerating on our quiet country road. Andy turned her no-longer blonde head.

"Who do we know that drives a Prius?"

Oh, crap.

NOW

"Earl's looking for you."

"Pidge did it."

"What?"

"Whatever has him on the warpath." I checked the coffee station for Styrofoam cups, figuring I could pour the fresh contents of the mug I held into something portable and make a run for it. Plan B: make my getaway with the ECAS mug in hand and return it later.

"Don't fucking throw me under the bus, Stewart!" Pidge's voice hunted me from the flight instructor's office down the hall.

"Sorry! Didn't know you were back there!" I turned to Rosemary II and silently mouthed, *She did it.*

"You two are worse than children." Seated behind the front counter, Rosemary II turned her attention to her computer and the shop orders stacked for billing. She issued commands with her mouse. The computer beeped obedience. I have offered to turn off the audio that annunciates her every action, but the Goddess of the Sacred Schedule insinuated that touching her computer would result in amputation without anesthetic.

I reconnoitered the hallway that runs down the center of the one-story fixed base operation building attached to the Essex County Air Service hangar. The stretch outside Earl's office radiated the aura of Mordor. I edged toward the front door.

Without looking up Rosemary II said, "Do not test me."

Earl Jackson may be the owner of Essex County Air Service, but Rosemary II is the commander-in-chief.

"I don't even work here anymore," I muttered.

"Then why are you here every morning drinking the coffee?" She pulled a fresh invoice from the printer and stapled it to the work order.

"It's your fault for making it so good."

"Go. *After* you wash out that mug."

This was not the way I planned to start my day.

Earl Jackson was not in his office. I found him reclining on a creeper on the concrete floor of the maintenance shop. He probed an open inspection cover in the aft empennage of a Beechcraft V-tail Bonanza. Doc, the company's licensed mechanic, bent over him, glasses perched on the tip of his nose.

"This one?" Earl asked.

"Which one?"

"This one, dammit. Wiggle it!"

Doc manipulated the airplane's ruddervator.

"Nope."

"How 'bout this one?"

Doc repeated the wiggle.

"That's the one."

Earl pulled his hand out of the tail cone. "Tell 'im he's got to replace it or he's gonna find himself flying with no pitch control."

"That's what I said."

I'd seen this comedy routine before. In a moment, the two of them would vigorously argue the same point. Instead, Earl spotted me. He rolled off the creeper, heaved himself upright and launched his bowlegged stride in my direction.

"You lookin' for me, Boss?"

A head gesture told me to follow him to his office.

"Close the door," he commanded. "Siddown."

In my early days of working as a flight instructor and air charter pilot for Essex County Air Service, Earl's Attila the Hun management style petrified me. I've since determined that true danger only exists when he stops speaking. I took the only other seat in his tiny office. He dropped onto his Army surplus office chair and fixed a searing squint in my direction.

Ever since Earl watched me leap out of a Piper Navajo without a parachute one thousand feet above the Chowan River and then saw me vanish, his piercing stare carries something extra. Like he expects me to disappear at any moment.

I can count on my fingers the number of people who know about me and my ability to vanish, which I unimaginatively call *the other thing*. One of those fingers represents a deceased FBI agent named Lee Donaldson. Another represents a Washington lobbyist facing multiple life sentences for murder. A third represents a former White House advisor and Special Counsel to the Director of Homeland Security who was apprehended naked on a hotel ledge after threatening to kill the President. He can talk about me all he wants. It only makes him sound crazier.

Closer to home, Earl Jackson and Essex Police Chief Tom Ceeves both know I can disappear at will. They fall in the "boss" category. Andy works for Tom Ceeves. My paycheck comes from the Christine and Paulette Paulesky Education Foundation, but Earl will be my boss for as long as he draws a breath. Maybe even after that.

Pidge told me that after Earl witnessed my airborne departure from the Foundation's Piper Navajo, he slid back into the copilot's seat, snapped his seatbelt, slipped on his headset, and turned his Inquisition Squint on her. She claimed that she seriously considered following me.

Earl asked her one question.

"You knew about this?"

I don't recall Pidge telling me how she answered, but she did tell me that after my leap, even after the explosion at Siddley Plantation nearly tossed Pidge and Earl into Albemarie Sound, Earl initiated no further discussion on the matter. Since then, opportunities for Earl to interrogate me have come and gone. He asked nothing. I said nothing. Now, bathed in his searing squinty-eye, I surmised that the moment had arrived.

I was wrong.

"'Member me telling you about Tommy Day? My backseater?"

"I do." Lieutenant Thomas Day had been Captain Earl Jackson's Weapon Systems Officer in the back seat of a McDonnell Douglas F-4 Phantom II flying out of Udorn Air Force base in Thailand. A lucky shot from the ground hit the jet's ejection seat and blew Earl out of the plane. Day didn't make it and was never found. Earl has no memory of the shoot-down. An itch he told me he cannot scratch. He shared the story after my own aviation accident left a hole in my memory.

So…connect the dots.

My mind jumped to a woman in Minnesota with five married names trailing her maiden name. Last winter, I met Tommy Day's widow, who later married Earl, albeit briefly. Earl and I helped her dispose of some unwanted property.

I now wondered if the caper had come back to haunt her.

"Tommy had a kid sister," Earl said.

"I didn't know."

"'Course you didn't. I never told you. She must'a been twelve years younger than Tommy. I only saw her twice. Once when we were still training at Luke when she was just a little squirt. Then once more when I got out in 'seventy-six. I went up to see her and her parents. They lived in Portland."

The squint shifted from me to somewhere on the Pacific Coast.

"She was older then, a handful of angry hippy teenager who hated the government, hated the Air Force and most vehemently hated me. I had it in my thick skull that I oughta look out for her, or something equally stupid. When she got done laughing at me, she called me names her mommy and daddy never taught her. She kicked my ass off that property right smart."

"Sorry to hear that."

"Yeah, you hear that shit about people calling soldiers baby killers, and some of it is true, but some of it is just fat old farts down at the VFW trying to belong to something that's grown larger with time. I can tell you for dead sure, however, that hippy chick sister of Tommy's had me down as an A-Number-One Murderer of Innocents—starting with her brother. I don't remember leaving anyplace on this earth with my tail between my legs except for that little vegetable patch in Portland."

"Doesn't seem fair."

"Nothing about that shit show was fair. I know they would'a hung me for treason but emptying a couple hardpoints on McNamara's head crossed my mind more than once. That foul-mouthed little sister of Tommy's wasn't entirely wrong."

I glanced up at the portrait of Franklin Roosevelt above Earl's desk. A sworn Democrat, Earl did not let party affiliation put rose-tinted lenses on his view of history or the Kennedy/Johnson policies that strapped his ass to an F-4 Phantom II over Vietnam.

"I need you to look in on her."

"What? Who?"

"Tammy. Tammy Day. The kid sister."

"Uh…" my mouth hung open. "Isn't she…? Wouldn't she be like *old*? I mean…grown up?"

"Well, you ain't gonna find her in bell bottoms shimmying to Janice Joplin. Of course, she's grown up—although she might still wear bell bottoms. She dove into the deep end of the whole anti-war movement, and the feminist thing after that, and then Greenpeace and what-all."

"Sounds like you did look out for her." Earl shrugged off the notion, which told me it was true. "And Joplin had a set of pipes."

"That, she did."

"You want me to go to Portland?" Excuses formed ranks in my head. Arun Dewar, the *de facto* boss of the Christine and Paulette Paulesky Education Foundation that writes my paychecks, had been patient with me over the last few weeks, during which time I'd been AWOL from my pilot duties. Not that he hadn't, on a few occasions, benefitted by my absence when Pidge filled in on one or two overnights. One of the worst kept secrets at Essex County Air Service was that Pidge and Arun were dating.

"Why would you go to Portland?"

"Because you said..."

"She lived in Portland fifty years ago. Nah. She's up in that little hole in the wall Sandy Stone's been pumping money into. What-cha-call-it...Ekalaska?"

"Ekalaka. Montana."

"Ekalaka."

"No, it's Eee-kalaka. Eee. Not Eh."

"Whatever the hell. Tammy Day has a ranch up there, if you can call it that. It ain't exactly the Ponderosa."

I had no idea what a chain steak joint had to do with this but chose to conceal my ignorance.

"She claims twenty or thirty thousand acres, but last I checked, she just had a couple double-wide trailers in the weeds, and she spends her time raising vegetables."

"She's not a rancher?"

"Hell no. She raised and sold homeopathic veggies or some shit, and before that she ran some new age crystal therapy scam. She might'a farmed some weed, but I don't think it grows well there."

"So, you want me to fly to Montana...and what?"

"Look in on her. I told you."

"You mean...?"

The squint tightened.

"Do what you do. Christ, Will, do I gotta spell it out?"

"No. I just want to confirm that you're not telling me to drive up to her double-wide, introduce myself and tell her that Earl Jackson says hello."

"Use my name around that woman and you're like as not to get your ass full of buckshot. Hell no." Earl scratched behind his ear. "Look. I got a couple friends up that way."

"I remember. You told me." Earl's tale of hauling a load of marijuana from Tijuana and sliding off Ekalaka's single runway in a snowstorm still tickles me.

"After I heard that Tammy bought that ranch, I checked up on her from time to time through those friends of mine. Everybody in that part of nowhere knows everybody else. There ain't enough population to leave anybody a stranger."

"And?"

"And lately they said she stopped coming into town. Nobody's seen her doing her shopping up in Baker. She had a couple horses, but the vet says they're gone. There's a guide service that used to lease her land for hunting. I hear she cut them off, too. Nobody's seen her for a while. On top of that, there's rumors that she took up with some new folks. Outsiders."

"What outsiders?"

"I dunno. It's all rumors. Could be anything. Animal rights. Eco terrorists. Save the Montana Whales for all I know. Maybe it's nothing. Maybe she's running a nudist camp."

"You think something serious is going on?"

Earl didn't answer. His gaze shifted back to the west, this time not as far as Portland. "I tried calling. Got her number from those friends of mine. She didn't pick up, so I told her if I didn't hear something from her, I'd be at her door. And if she didn't want to see my ugly mug, she should get a message to me to stay away. I didn't hear nothing." He reeled in his distant gaze and focused on me. "So? Are you up for this or what?"

Earl knew I couldn't say no, but it was decent of him to ask.

"Just one question. They named their son Tommy and their daughter Tammy?"

"It was the fifties."

I stood. My Earl Sense told me the meeting was over. "Andy made dinner plans with her sister and her parents for tomorrow night."

"That mean you'll go on Saturday?"

"Hell no. It means I'll leave in the morning."

Earl gave me the company's other Beechcraft Baron, a 1971 E-55. I like flying the Education Foundation's Navajo, but I love flying that Baron. The E-model arrived near the end of the 55 series production run and uses the larger engines and larger tail intended for the follow-on 58 series. It's a hotrod, stable and solid, easily trimmed, light on the controls and comfortable to fly. Earl's model has up-to-date avionics, including a lovely digital autopilot. I rolled for takeoff just after dawn, tearing up to cruise altitude at 130 knots with a nineteen hundred foot per minute climb rate. I popped out of a layer of lightly iced clouds at sixty-five hundred feet with nothing but blue above. At my cruise altitude of 8,000 feet, I found smooth air and a negligible headwind. Since Earl was picking up the fuel tab, I set the power for speed instead of economy. Even with the headwind, the GPS groundspeed pegged at 189 knots on the Aspen primary flight display.

Full fuel tanks could have taken me all the way to Ekalaka, but only barely and with no reserve. I stopped in Aberdeen, South Dakota to top off the tanks and empty my own. The Hangar 9 FBO offered good coffee, quick service, and a quiet lounge space for the most challenging portion of the trip.

Andy picked up the call after the third ring.

"You're where?"

"Aberdeen. It's in South Dakota."

"I know where Aberdeen is." I grimaced. Andy's tone told me she also knew where this conversation was headed.

"Earl asked me to do this. It's a personal thing. It has to do with Tommy Day. You remember me telling you about him."

"You're going to blame this on Earl?"

"Blame what?"

"You know perfectly well what. Dinner tonight. Unless you're going to tell me that it's a quick turnaround and you'll be home in time to change and have cocktails with Lydia, Mom and Dad."

"Yeah...that's the thing. Aberdeen is the halfway point. I'm on my way to Ekalaka, Montana."

Silence.

After years of family warfare, peace broke out between Andy and her parents for two salient reasons. First, after three years of marriage, she finally introduced me and explained that I may have saved their daughter and her unborn granddaughter. And second, because Andy's father finally saw the passion in Andy's love of law enforcement, a passion she never could have nurtured in the legal career he had crafted for her. It helped that Andy's sister Lydia moved the grandchildren—all four of them, counting the stepchild carried and delivered by Lydia's teenaged nanny— to Leander Lake in Essex County. Lydia's miserable excuse of a dead ex-husband managed to impregnate the nanny within days of doing the same for Lydia. Lydia delivered a beautiful baby girl named Grace. The nanny brought The Infant King Alex into the world—the only male in a household full of women. I admit to a little jealousy of that smiling kid. Giving my nieces a baby brother dislodged me from God-like status in the eyes of Grace's two older sisters, Elise and Harriet, whom I adore. Those little girls cannot get enough of their baby stepbrother.

Each time the family gathers Andy reminds me that her parents, Louis and Eleanor Taylor, have embraced me. I don't argue, but a gremlin voice whispers in my ear that her society-conscious mother and father wish their daughter had done better. As much as I love spending time with my atomic-powered nieces, dinner with Mom and Dad rates on par with getting an FAA Flight Physical.

"Sweetheart, you know I was looking forward to dinner."

"No, you weren't." I detected a hint of a smile at Andy's end of the digital connection, which gave me hope.

I bit my tongue. Half the battle is not overselling.

"When do you think you'll be back?"

"Earl wants me to look in on Tommy Day's sister at some ranch. Discretely. I think I can get that done tonight, rest overnight and be outta there in the morning. I'd say I'll be home for dinner tomorrow night."

"Okay. That works. Because Mom and Dad are staying through the weekend."

Now I knew she was smiling.

The Ekalaka Airport ramp was deserted when I taxied in. An agricultural operation hangar dominated the ramp, but it appeared closed for the day, if not the season.

I took my time shutting down the myriad switches on the Baron's panel, double-checking that I didn't neglect something that would drain the battery. I spent a minute with the iPad reviewing the flight path to the Day Ranch, which lay ten nautical miles to the south adjacent the highway I had seen. Ten miles fell within the limits of my battery-powered BLASTER—Basic Linear Aerial System for Transport, Electric Rechargeable—a device that looks like a flashlight with an electric motor driving a model airplane propeller on one end. I carried four on this trip, with extra batteries for each. A charged BLASTER yields roughly forty minutes of use at maximum power, which I rarely use. Half power gives me a speed of nearly thirty knots. Reaching the Day ranch required a flight time of twenty minutes each way. That left power in reserve. I brought along a pair of ski goggles to keep the wind out of my eyes at higher speeds.

Cracking the cabin door open introduced a sharp chill to the heated cabin. I grabbed my flight jacket and gloves from the back seat and shoved them out on the wing. I laid the row of BLASTERS and their companion propellers next to my phone on the seat, then scooted over them and performed the gymnastic move that is climbing out of the Baron's front seat onto the wing.

"Hi! You must be Will."

A woman wearing a goose down vest over a flannel shirt and jeans leaned against a well-worn Ford Explorer that she had parked behind the tail of the Baron. She had short brown hair, an attractive face with a confident smile built in. Her chipper presence and friendly recognition of me caught me by surprise. I stood upright on the wing and pulled on my jacket, leaving the power units on the front seat out of sight.

"I'm Sue," she said. "I heard you fly over. I live right over there." She pointed across the runway at several buildings on the other side of the highway, the last structures counted in the town census before empty ranchland took over.

The confused look on my face changed her smile from one of greeting to amusement.

"Deb called me. She would have come, but she doesn't have a car right now. Terry has the rear end taken apart. She had to use a neighbor's car this week to deliver meals to seniors."

"Okay," I said cautiously. "I have no idea who Deb is. Or Terry."

"Oh." Sue laughed. "Deb and Terry are your boss's friends. Your boss is Earl Jackson, right?"

"That's the boss."

"Mr. Jackson called Deb to let her know you were coming. He thought she might be able to give you a car and a place to stay. Unless you planned on staying up at the Midway or the Guest House, but this time of year, during hunting season, they're booked up." I guess I still had a lost look on my face, because she repeated, slowly, "Earl called Deb. Deb called me."

"And you are...?"

"Sue. I'm still Sue." She laughed. "My husband and I own J&J Guide Service. And since Deb doesn't have a car or a place for you to stay, here I am. You can have this SUV, and we have one empty bunk—if you don't mind snoring hunters. We're fully booked, but one fella dropped out sick."

"I don't know what to say. Thank you."

"Well, hop in."

"Uh…okay. Lemme get my bag."

I leaned into the cockpit and stuffed the four power units back into my flight bag.

Sue drove out of the airport gate and followed a narrow road toward the cluster of buildings that constituted metropolitan Ekalaka. For the next five minutes she identified town landmarks with pride in her voice. The post office. A church. The new hospital. She explained that the hospital joined the senior living facility, and that she worked at both when she wasn't cooking meals for hunting parties. And sometimes when she was if staffing fell short.

"Downtown" appeared to be a triangle of gravel roads. She identified the fire department, the storefront public library, and the Dawg House Pub. A message board at the Dawg House advertised an all-male dancer review appearing for one night only, about which Sue made no mention.

"That's the new Mexican restaurant." She pointed. Neon signs decorated the windows of a brick building that had the look of a bank. "It's really good. Everything is authentic—although I wouldn't try to get in much after five. It gets pretty busy." She turned from one gravel road onto another. "That's the Carter County Museum." A stone building topped with a cavalry fort blockhouse hugged the sidewalk. An Indian lance crossed with a cavalry sword shared signage with silhouettes of dinosaurs. "It's a great museum, if you have extra time."

"Probably not on this trip."

"Hey, my brother is a pilot."

"I like him already. What does he fly?"

"I think he flies something with two engines, like what you came in. And he flies a helicopter. He built it himself. In his garage."

I thought that was crazy but didn't say so.

"You're here about Tammy Day."

I glanced at her to determine if this friendly reception masqueraded as a warning against poking around where I didn't belong. Her friendly aura remained undimmed.

"My boss, Earl, knew her brother."

"Didn't he die in Vietnam? The brother, I mean."

"Do you know Ms. Day?"

"Oh, yes. We buy vegetables from her. Or we did. Not so much this past year. We used to buy her fresh raspberries, and lots and lots of zucchini."

"People who grow zucchini always have lots and lots of it."

The smile faded a little, replaced by a cooler assessment aimed at me. "I trust Deb. Deb trusts Earl. That means you should be trustworthy. Are you trustworthy?"

"My wife tells me that I blush automatically if I stray from the truth. I guess that means you'll be able to tell."

"And you're not here from ParaTransit? Or Energy Stone?"

"I don't know who either of those are. Is that something you might want to tell me?"

"I wish I could. We've been worried about..." She let the sentence trail off. She assessed the nonexistent traffic and turned onto the widest paved road I'd seen so far. The highway marked Montana 323 headed out of town.

"Worried about?"

"Well...like I told you. My husband and I run a guide service."

"I'm not sure what that is."

"We lease land, government land and private ranch land, and we guide hunters. My husband Rich and our hired guides. All the seasons. Gun and bow. We have three camps in Montana. We're the second-largest service in the state with access to over a million and a half acres."

"Impressive. Is that a good business?"

"We're booked for the next three years. In fact, I'd go with you, but I start cooking for fourteen hungry hunters in about an hour. I know it sounds like I'm bragging, but my point is that we depend on leases and Tammy's land was one of them. Until this year. She didn't renew. And she stopped providing produce for us. She never was much for visiting town, but she wasn't unfriendly either. Something changed. I haven't seen her since summer."

"Does she live alone out there?"

"Mostly. I heard that recently she had outsiders with her. People said it was kind of a religious thing. Other people said it was oil speculators. We have no shortage of rumors in our small town. Honestly...I'm not sure."

"So, who is Para...Transfer? Or that other thing?"

"ParaTransit and Energy Stone. We don't know. That was another rumor. People said a real estate agent from Baker went out to the ranch, representing those two names. That's the rumor. I have a feeling Tammy would have run somebody like that off the property."

"Do you think it's about oil or mineral rights?"

"Not much of that around here. You'll see a few wells down by Alzada."

"Anybody been out to the ranch to check on her?"

"I went last month. She had a locked gate on the road up to her place. I called a few times, but she didn't answer."

"Did you report any of this to the local authorities?"

She chuckled and pointed to the left side of the road. A black and white Sheriff's SUV sat nosed up to a small ranch house on a cluttered property.

"That's our deputy. Not a bad guy, but not exactly an investigator. Most of the time, that's where you'll find him. But a locked gate could mean she isn't home, or it could mean she just doesn't want to be bothered."

Just as the highway entered open country, she pulled off the road onto a broad gravel shoulder. To my right, on the other side of a grassy field, I could see the airport and the Baron tied to the ramp. Sue pointed left.

"This is me." A tidy house spread itself beneath shade trees at the end of a mid-length driveway. A small cabin shared the property on one side of the house. A Quonset-style shed hid behind trees on the other side. I had expected a hunting lodge made of logs and adorned with antlers. This residence had the pleasant look of suburbia. Small gardens, now brown for winter, accented the home. "The mail came, so I'll get out here. The truck has gas. When you're done, just drive it in and knock. Don't worry if it's late. I'll set you up in the new cabin. Oh. Do you need a map?"

"I have my iPad." I patted the flight bag between my knees.

Sue's smile and the sparkle in her eyes remained undiminished, but she hesitated for a moment before climbing out.

"If you see Tammy, ask her to call me. I'd be careful about trespassing, though. That's a thing around here."

"Noted. And thanks for the wheels. Much appreciated. It was nice meeting you."

"You, too!"

We both hopped out. She crossed the road. I trotted around the front grille and took the driver's seat. She tossed me a cheerful wave as I pulled away.

This hadn't been my plan. Earl's interference twice removed had derailed my intention to simply fly up to the ranch property for a look around. Now I saw the benefits. Connecting me with this pleasant woman provided information. The owner of the guide service also revealed another vital detail.

The location of a good Mexican restaurant.

I performed a U-turn and drove back into Ekalaka.

ALSO BY HOWARD SEABORNE

DIVISIBLE MAN

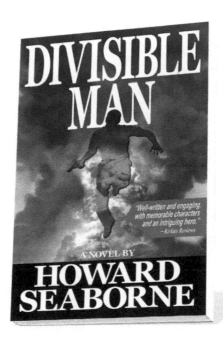

The media calls it a "miracle" when air charter pilot Will Stewart survives an aircraft in-flight breakup, but Will's miracle pales beside the stunning after-effect of the crash. Barely on his feet again, Will and his police sergeant wife Andy race to rescue an innocent child from a heinous abduction—*if Will's new ability doesn't kill him first.*

Available in print, digital and audio.

Learn more at **HowardSeaborne.com**

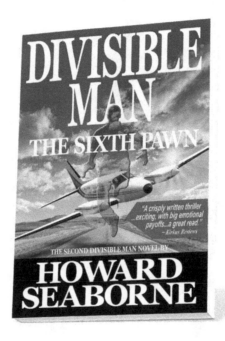

ALSO BY HOWARD SEABORNE

DIVISIBLE MAN: THE SECOND GHOST

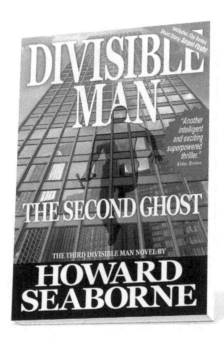

Tormented by a cyber stalker, Lane Franklin's best friend turns to suicide. Lane's frantic call to Will and Andy Stewart launches them on a desperate rescue. When it all goes bad, Will must adapt his extraordinary ability to survive the dangerous high steel and glass of Chicago as Andy and Pidge encounter the edge of disaster. **Includes the short story, "Angel Flight,"a bridge to the fourth DIVISIBLE MAN novel that follows.**

Available in print, digital and audio.

Learn more at **HowardSeaborne.com**

ALSO BY HOWARD SEABORNE

DIVISIBLE MAN: THE SEVENTH STAR

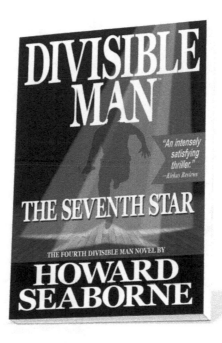

A horrifying message turns a holiday gathering tragic. An unsolved murder hangs a death threat over Detective Andy Stewart's head. And internet-fueled hatred targets Will and Andy's friend Lane. Will and Andy struggle to keep the ones they love safe, while hunting a dead murderer before he can kill again. As the tension tightens, Will confronts a troubling revelation about the extraordinary after-effect of his midair collision.

Available in print, digital and audio.

Learn more at **HowardSeaborne.com**

ALSO BY HOWARD SEABORNE

DIVISIBLE MAN: TEN MAN CREW

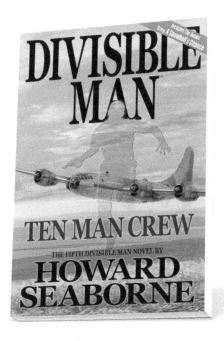

An unexpected visit from the FBI threatens Will Stewart's secret and sends Detective Andy Stewart on a collision course with her darkest impulses. A twisted road reveals how a long-buried Cold War secret has been weaponized. And Pidge shows a daring side of herself that could cost her dearly.

Available in print, digital and audio.

Learn more at **HowardSeaborne.com**

ALSO BY HOWARD SEABORNE

DIVISIBLE MAN: THE THIRD LIE

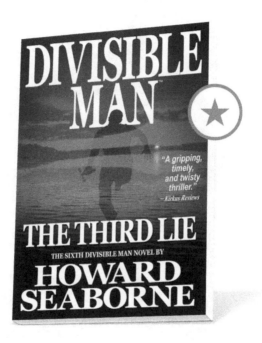

Caught up in a series of hideous crimes that generate national headlines, Will faces the critical question of whether to reveal himself or allow innocent lives to be lost. The stakes go higher than ever when Andy uncovers the real reason behind a celebrity athlete's assault on an underaged girl. And Will discovers that the limits of his ability can lead to disaster.

A Kirkus Starred Review.

A Kirkus Star is awarded to "books of exceptional merit."

Available in print, digital and audio.

Learn more at **HowardSeaborne.com**

ALSO BY HOWARD SEABORNE

DIVISIBLE MAN: THREE NINES FINE

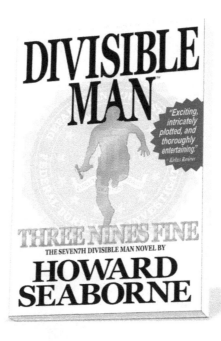

A mysterious mission request from Earl Jackson sends Will into the sphere of a troubled celebrity. A meeting with the Deputy Director of the FBI that goes terribly wrong. Will and Andy find themselves on the run from Federal authorities, infiltrating a notorious cartel, and racing to prevent what might prove to be the crime of the century.

Available in print, digital and audio.

Learn more at **HowardSeaborne.com**

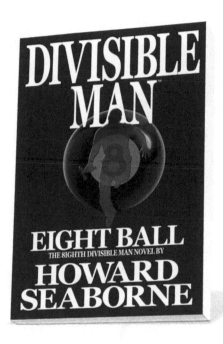

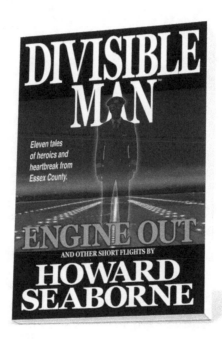

ALSO BY HOWARD SEABORNE

DIVISIBLE MAN: NINE LIVES LOST

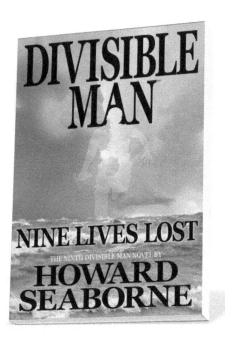

AVAILABLE: JUNE 2022

A simple request from Earl Jackson sends Will on a desperate cross-country chase ultimately looking for answers to a mystery that literally landed at Will and Andy's mailbox. At the same time, a threat to Andy's career takes a deadly turn. Before it all ends, Will confronts answers in a deep, dark place he never imagined.

Available in print, digital and audio.

Learn more at **HowardSeaborne.com**

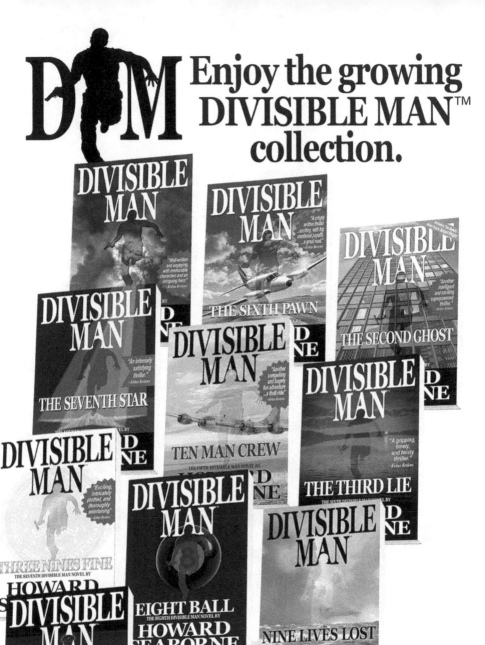